The Dead Don't Get Out Much

A Camilla MacPhee Mystery

The Dead Don't Get Out Much

A Camilla MacPhee Mystery

Mary Jane Maffini

RENDEZVOUS PRESS

Cover art: Giulio Maffini

LE CONSEIL DES ARTS | THE CANADA COUNCIL
DU CANADA | FOR THE ARTS
DEPUIS 1957 | SINCE 1957

We acknowledge the support of the Canada Council for the Arts
for our publishing program.

Napoleon Publishing/RendezVous Press
Toronto, Ontario, Canada

Printed in Canada

09 08 07 06 05 5 4 3 2 1

Library and Archives Canada Cataloguing in Publication

Maffini, Mary Jane, date-
The dead don't get out much / Mary Jane Maffini.

(A Camilla MacPhee mystery)
ISBN 1-894917-30-8

I. Title. II. Series: Maffini, Mary Jane Camilla
MacPhee mystery.

PS8576.A3385D42 2005   C813'.54   C2005-903468-8

ACKNOWLEDGEMENTS

Many people have been generous with their time, sharing information and memories that helped in the writing of this book. Special thanks to Ora Ryan Abraham, Dr. Peter Duffy, Alfonso Maffini, Sgt. Sheila Maloney, Sandra Ryan, Wayne Tupper, Leslie Weir and Brad White. Nano McConnell's wonderful book *We Never Stopped Dancing* was a revelation, as were the military histories of Mark Zuehlke. Any errors are my own, which should come as no surprise to anyone.

My father-in-law, Vittorio Maffini, left a legacy of stories of the Italian partisans, and my father, John Merchant, left a view of the times in one hundred and twenty-five love letters to my mother, Isobel Ryan Merchant.

Victoria Maffini and Linda Wiken offered very useful comments, and Giulio Maffini, as usual, offered more insight and support than I could ever hope for. My good friend Lyn Hamilton always made time for me.

The RendezVous Gang, Sylvia McConnell, Allister Thompson and Adria Iwasutiak, were splendidly resolute throughout the whole long process.

Here's the thing: this is a work of fiction. That means you make it up. This can involve inventing streets, restaurants and people as well as playing fast and loose with times and weather. I have taken liberties with historic Florence—so don't waste your time in that wonderful city retracing Camilla's steps. Alcielo, Montechiaro, Pieve San Simone and Stagno Toscano are not real, although I wish they were. But you can find many other places just as intriguing throughout Italy as well as many fine meals.

21 Frank Street
Chesterton, Ontario
September 12, 1941

Dear Vi,

Well, aren't you the one! The whole town is still talking about how you up and joined the army. I think it's just grand! You'd better hope the Canadian Women's Army Corps doesn't find out what a daredevil you are and send you packing home again. It would be a shame to miss a chance to see the world. Like me! Mum will hardly let me out of her sight in case I try to follow in your footsteps. That's not likely to happen. I'll never sign up, even with those smart uniforms. I am comfort-loving at heart, and I can't really leave Mum alone when her health is so poor. Anyway, you wouldn't catch me living in a tent with a bunch of other women. Now, I'll be lucky I don't break a leg climbing out my bedroom window after Mum's asleep. Make sure you keep that a secret!

I imagine you are enjoying your great adventure. People are saying that the gals who sign up are mostly stuck working as cooks and laundresses in the most dreary army towns in Canada. They don't know what they're talking about. How could anything be drearier than Chesterton? Especially now that we have rationing of gasoline and everything is getting pretty scarce, especially metal. Even if you have the money, you still can't find appliances. People have taken up stealing bicycles to get around. Last week, someone stole Mrs. Benton's sewing machine. They won't get far on that! Thank heavens we still have the movies, or I don't know how we'd keep smiling. I saw "Rebecca" last week at the Vogue. It gave me goose bumps, and the ending was such a surprise. You would have loved it. The other good news is that I got a lovely new hat for the Fall. Soft brown with a little feather and a brim.

All three of the Delaney brothers signed up last week. Mrs. Delaney hasn't stopped crying since, although people have been very good about bringing her peach and apple pies. We're all knitting socks at the Carry-on-Club. And if things get much worse, we'll be knitting them in the dark. Oh well, mine will probably turn out better that way.

Betty Cannot (Oops, I meant Connaught) left for Normal School last week. I just bet her mother is getting her spies ready in Toronto. There won't be much to find out about Betty. She's always been such a boring goody-two shoes. Not like her scamp of a brother, Perce. I can't say I mind Perce leaving, but I do miss you and Harry something awful. The town's not the same without you. I sure hope you are back here before Betty gets her teaching diploma and comes home to lord it over everyone.

Love from your best friend in the world,

Hazel

P. S. Will you really be teaching the boys to drive trucks? You are the limit!

One

Close your eyes. Imagine this. You're stretched out on a cushioned lounge chair at the edge of an endless sandy beach. The sun warms your body. You smile as the gentle breeze ruffles your hair, and you wink at the passing waiter, which is all it takes to get another margarita. You sip the tangy drink, savour the salt and close your eyes in pleasure as the perfect turquoise sea laps at your toes. You feel very relaxed and maybe just a wee bit amorous. At that moment, you are the only person in the world who matters, except me, of course. And hey, there I am, lying beside you with the coconut-scented suntan lotion in my hand, awaiting your instructions."

I shook my head and stared at the telephone receiver. "Who is this?"

Silence.

I said, "Hello?"

"It's Ray, Camilla." Oops, chilly tone there.

"Ray, that's great. Uh, what was that all about? I mean the sand and the sun and the amorous part?"

"What do you mean, who is this? Who else would be applying your suntan lotion?"

"No one. Especially in November. And, no offence, but what time is it?"

3

"About six thirty. I'm getting ready to go on shift."

"Ah. You mean it's six thirty Atlantic Standard Time. Hmmm. Well, that would make it five thirty here in Ottawa Snoozing Time."

"Not so fast, my friend, aren't you the queen of the three a.m. calls?"

"Oh, come on, Ray. Why would you say that?"

"Because I've gotten quite a few myself, and I'm not the only one. People talk, you know."

"True, but most people don't talk to me at five thirty in the morning. However, I take your point. Goodbye now, Ray."

"I can't believe you didn't know it was me. How many guys call you up and whisper sweet nothings about warm beaches and feeling amorous?"

"Don't forget the margaritas and the sea lapping at my toes. No guys call me to whisper sweet nothings. Nor are any guys whispering anything else, now that you mention it. Especially at five thirty a.m."

"So what do you think?"

"I think this is probably just a dream."

"It's real. And?"

"And what?" I tried to keep my voice pleasant, because Ray Deveau is the best damn thing to have happened to me in many, many years. He is worth working hard to be nice to.

"And you are stretched out on a warm beach, blah blah blah."

"Actually, I am stretched out under a tumbled mass of duvet, which I seem to be sharing with a large, stinky dog. There's a calico cat licking my toes, and that actually seems a bit creepy. No one is filling my margarita, although now that I'm *wide* awake at five thirty in the morning, I wish someone would bring me a cup of coffee before I head out into the cold, damp, miserable November morning to walk the smelly dog

4

that has been awakened by the sound of the phone ringing."

"So you're saying the beach does sound like an improvement."

"Yes. Too bad it's not happening."

"It should happen. We could take a holiday together. Wouldn't that be good after everything we've been through in the past couple of months? You never did have a proper recovery time following those concussions."

"Me? What about you? You almost died."

"That too. So, a holiday, well-deserved by both."

"Are you the same Ray Deveau with the two teenage daughters you can't leave in the house alone?"

"Yup."

"Not to be picky, but are they part of the beach dream too?"

"Nope. That would be insufficiently romantic. Anyway, the girls will be in school."

"How can you just…?"

"All taken care of. My sister, Sharon, the one who lives in Dartmouth, has a few weeks after she moves out of her old house and before she moves into her new one. She's going to spend it here. As the resident guard."

"Don't you want to spend time with her?" I said.

"Let's put it this way. Are there circumstances where you would opt to spend two weeks in a confined space with one of your sisters and a couple of teenage hormone factories?"

"Point taken."

"I've got some holiday time coming, and it's use it or lose it. So I've been looking through travel brochures. I keep seeing your face in all the photos. How about Mexico?"

"I don't know, Ray."

"Okay, Dominican Republic?"

"I'm not sure I can do it. I got so far behind in my work

when I was recovering. I couldn't concentrate on anything. You know I haven't even reopened Justice for Victims since we got evicted. There are so many people who desperately need a service like ours when they're dealing with horrible situations and jackasses in the justice system. If I'm not there, who's going to ensure they're not revictimized by vindictive criminals and their bulldog lawyers?" I didn't mention cops, since Ray's a Sergeant in the Cape Breton Regional Police, and he might not want to be on a list with jackasses.

"Thanks for the lecture, but I already know what you do," he said.

"And you also know people are counting on me."

"Yeah. I think I might be one of them."

"You know what I mean. How can I go away after I did nothing useful all fall?"

"When was the last time you had a break that didn't end in an emergency room? Leave everything with Alvin."

"Alvin? You must be joking. How's he supposed to cope?"

"He'd be thrilled if you were out of the office. I mean, that's just a guess."

"We don't have an office. We're going to set up in my new house, remember? Which is also not set up. There is junk piled up to the ceiling."

"Camilla?"

"Yes?"

"I am up to speed on what's been happening to you. We do talk every day, although I'll save you the trouble of saying 'not usually at five thirty in the morning'."

"Then you know I'm not unpacked. And you should know I don't feel right about inheriting this house, or about anything else that happened. It's just a really bad time for me."

"Do something pleasant for yourself for once. Think about

swimming in the crystal blue water."

"Small problem. Other people packed my stuff when I was in the hospital. I don't know where anything is, like, for instance, my bathing suit."

"I'd be willing to spring for a bathing suit. At least, a small one."

"And the idea of leaving Alvin in charge, that's just plain scary." That would account for the way my heart was racing.

"Tell you what, I've got to hit the road. Think about where you'd like to go and call me," Ray said.

"Okay."

"New plan, I'll call you."

"Wait! Today's Remembrance Day. I'll be at the ceremonies."

"No problem. I'll give you a ring tonight."

"That'll be good," I said.

I listened to the dial tone for a long time and reminded myself that Ray was the best. Why was I such a jerk sometimes?

* * *

As we reached the eleventh hour of the eleventh day of the eleventh month, "O Canada" was followed by "The Last Post". The goosebumps lasted after the notes faded. The cannon boomed, marking the beginning of the moment of silence. My personal silence was accompanied by a stream of icy water wending its slow way past my collar and down my back.

Entirely appropriate.

I was squeezed on the mezzanine terrace of the National Arts Centre, too many feet above the sidewalk, along with hundreds of strangers jostling to observe the Remembrance Day ceremonies. Below, thousands clustered in the rain to mark the moment. Somewhere on the far side of the throng, the Prime Minister, the Governor General, the military brass, the Silver Cross mother, representatives of every diplomatic mission and a busload of big shots were assembled.

I jockeyed for position with college kids, moms and toddlers plus one beagle busy nosing crotches. I was too close to a spiny shrub for comfort, and the crowd was so dense I couldn't raise my umbrella without knocking someone's eye out. At least I was close enough to the edge to have a decent view of the street below. I looked down at a sea of faces, young and old, white, aboriginal, black, Asian and combinations. Overcoats, jean jackets and rain slickers brushed shoulders with a wide variety of military uniforms: Canadian, British, American and lots I didn't recognize.

Somewhere on the parade route, my father, Donald Angus MacPhee, would be lined up to march with his fellow vets. I would watch him with pride as I have every Remembrance Day since I was old enough to toddle. I'm pushing forty, but I have trouble feeling like an adult when I see how stooped and frail he's become.

The last few years, I've been at the ceremonies to honour my friend, former neighbour and personal hero, Mrs. Violet Parnell. Mrs. P. would never miss a chance to squeeze into her Canadian Women's Army Corps uniform and march with her head high.

The crowd stretched as far as I could see, jamming the sidewalks on Elgin Street, around and past the War Memorial, spilling onto Wellington Street and up the grassy hill by the East Block of the Parliament Buildings. Every inch of the property surrounding the NAC had someone standing on it. People clung to the small ledges on the flag standards. Over their heads, Canadian flags fluttered, and the provincial and territorial flags cracked and flapped in the wind and rain. Thousands of poppies provided splashes of red.

I scanned the crowd for signs of my three sisters. They'd be wearing their designer sunglasses, like so many others, even though the sun never shines on Remembrance Day, and today the weather was particularly vile. Alexa, Edwina and Donalda would not be pleased if anyone spotted their Christian Dior mascara making black tracks through their high-end blusher.

I was not wearing sunglasses. In my view, if you can't shed a public tear at the Remembrance Day ceremony, what the hell is wrong with you?

Next to me, my so-called office assistant, Alvin Ferguson, stood uncharacteristically silent, his bony shoulders hunched in his black leather jacket, his ponytail drooping, his cat's-eye glasses fogged, droplets of rain glistening off each of his nine visible earrings. A bit of advice to anyone running a small non-profit: if you wish to avoid a lot of headaches, don't allow your aged father to saddle you with an office assistant with the temperament and inclination of a performance artist, the office skills of a chimpanzee and the attitude of a minor dictator. Just a suggestion.

When the second boom marked the end of the silence, Alvin opened his mouth. Whatever he was saying was drowned out as the piper struck up the Lament and four CF-18s roared overhead in formation.

Alvin may be an accomplished pain in the backside, but he has his positive points. He thinks the world of Mrs. Parnell, and rightly so. The feeling, for some reason, is mutual.

As the sound of the planes faded, Alvin said, with a catch in his voice, "Violet loves to see the planes."

"True enough."

Alvin nibbled on a finger nail. "Do you think she's okay? It's a long way to march. And this is such friggin' revolting weather. What if she loses her balance?"

"We've been over this, Alvin. She's not going to trip. She's been doing strength and balance exercises and yoga for months just for this chance to march. She's in better shape than she's been in years. I'm really proud of her."

"Yeah well, in this rain, she might get pneumonia." In the last couple of months, Alvin had become extremely protective of Mrs. P. It's weird, considering he's in his twenties and singularly lacking in sensible behaviour, and she's well past the eighty mark without any help from anyone, thank you very much.

"She'll be fine. Mrs. P. is as keen on battle as she ever was."

Alvin sniffed. "They have ambulances here. If anything happened, they'd rush out to get her. Wouldn't they?"

"Nothing's going to happen. She waits for this moment every year. The ceremony puts a spring in her step."

"She sounded upset last night when I tried to talk to her."

"Really? I didn't notice that she was upset."

"You've been so busy crabbing about your house and your boxes of files, you haven't even seen her this week."

All right, so that was true, although I'd called her practically every day. Alvin's not the only one who thinks Mrs. Parnell is something special. She'd saved my life on several dramatic occasions, and she's an entertaining conversationalist to boot, not to mention a first-rate strategist. What's not to love?

I lowered my voice. "This is a special moment. Don't spoil it by getting yourself all worked up over nothing, Alvin."

Alvin continued to obsess in that irritating way he specializes in. His voice got higher with every sentence. "I thought she needed someone to walk with her. I offered to do it. She turned me down cold. She wouldn't even accept a drive. She took a cab to the meeting point."

"Alvin, your concern is commendable, but Mrs. Parnell has been having the time of her life lately. We can't hold her back. She's getting exercise and fresh air. Been on trips, been up in balloons, might I remind you."

Alvin said, "Been shot at trying to rescue you."

"The last time was months ago, and anyway, I think she kind of likes that sort of thing. Takes her back to the war. Besides, she wasn't hit. She loved the adventure. She keeps re-enacting it for anyone who'll listen."

"I still say it would have been way better if I had been marching with her."

"Shh. Listen to the speeches."

"Hey, I wonder if I can get a good look at the Governor General's hat from here," Alvin mused.

I will never understand that boy.

The speeches are always short and heartfelt, but if you ask me, all everyone wants is to see the planes fly over, to hear the gun salutes and the pipers and to applaud the vets. It's our opportunity to think about how goddam lucky we are.

"Every year, it's a smaller number of vets," Alvin said before honking his nose.

I didn't answer. I was clapping for the passing vets along with everyone else. Anyway, what could I say? My father and Mrs. Parnell were both well into their eighties. I didn't like to think about where all that was leading.

"It's so sad," Alvin sniffed.

I already had a lump in my throat, since I thought I saw my father marching by. I imagined Alvin felt the same way. My father had lost two brothers in Sicily, and Alvin's grandfather was killed in the battle for Ortona. The uncles were real to me. I saw their pictures, I heard the stories of the mischief they got up to as boys. More than sixty years after the war, they were still important in my family.

People shouted "Thank you!" and clapped as groups of vets marched by.

Alvin slipped off his fogged-up cat's-eye glasses and whipped out black binoculars. They looked a lot like a pair I used to have.

"I don't see Violet yet. Where is she?" he fretted. "Will they give her a wheelchair if she can't keep up? She should have her walker at least."

"For God's sake, Alvin. This is Mrs. Parnell we're talking about. She's as tough as they come. There are lots of vets the same age, some are even older and much more fragile. Please, try to control yourself. They'll be here," I said. Not that I was relaxed. A woman with a red umbrella and a bad attitude kept shoving me in order to get a better spot. I wasn't keen to get too close to the edge, since it was a couple of storeys above the sidewalk. You can't really growl at someone at this particular time and place. Besides, I'm still working on my nice side.

"I think she's coming now." Alvin stretched up and out. He leaned forward and adjusted the binoculars as a small group of marchers passed by. "Lord thundering Jesus," he said.

"What?" I may have said that a bit louder than necessary since heads turned.

"Something's wrong with Violet."

"Hand over those glasses." I snatched the binoculars and peered through, looking for yet another opportunity to prove him wrong. There was an upside to our bickering as the crowd around us had shifted away.

I zoomed in on Mrs. Parnell. I could feel Alvin's anxiety, maybe because he was gripping my arm. I expected bruises.

I stared straight at Mrs. P.

"See what I mean?" Alvin said. "Look at the way she's holding herself. You know how fussy she is about proper military bearing."

"Please let go of my arm, Alvin."

"And she isn't keeping step. It's like she's not even aware of the other marchers."

"There's nothing wrong with Mrs. Parnell that a couple of Benson & Hedges and a tumbler of Harvey's Bristol Cream won't fix." I hesitated slightly, because Mrs. Parnell *didn't* appear to be keeping step with the other vets. I wondered for a second if I was catching Alvin's panicky behaviour.

He grabbed the binoculars back. "We have to catch up with her and find out what the problem is."

"We can't disrupt the parade. She'll be going to the Chateau Laurier for the vets' lunch right afterwards. We'll catch up with her then."

Alvin plunged right through the juniper. "We can't wait that long. Let's go."

Easier said than done. As we pushed our way through the crowds and down the stairs, things got worse. People were lined ten deep around the edge of the street. I couldn't even see where the vets were.

Alvin zigged and zagged through the mass of milling people, using his elbows as weapons. "Get the lead out, Camilla."

"For heaven's sake," I puffed, "if you don't stop stressing yourself out, you'll need an ambulance."

Most likely a lot of fuss about nothing, I told myself as I plunged through the crowd after him.

*   *   *

"Keep a cool head, Alvin. We don't want to ruin her moment," I said half an hour later when we'd finally managed to cross Wellington Street and push our way into the green-roofed Chateau Laurier. The hotel was holding a luncheon for hundreds of vets, and the marble hallways were jammed.

13

Excitement ran high. We shouldered our way through the sentimental crowd, everyone wanting to shake the hands of a vet and express their thanks.

Alvin paid no attention to me. He was still cheesed off that I hadn't leaped over the barricades to connect to the marchers. He craned his scrawny neck, ponytail flicking in anxiety, heading for the ballroom where the lunch was being held. A few people attempted to stop him. That was a mistake on their part. I spotted Mrs. P. outside the ballroom. I felt a flood of relief.

"There she is. Look. Now will you relax, Alvin?" I said, nudging a couple of people out of the way and pushing ahead of him.

Mrs. P. sat by herself, in her CWAC uniform, her cap in her hand. Maybe she was still recovering from the march, or maybe she needed a Benson & Hedges. Plus Bristol Cream might not have been on the lunch menu.

"Mrs. Parnell," I called, galloping toward her.

She looked up blankly.

"Mrs. P.?"

She said nothing, staring beyond me.

I whirled to see who she was looking at. There was nothing but a blank wall behind me. I said, "It's Camilla."

She blinked and shook her head. Her hair hung loose and straggly. Deep purple shadows ringed her eyes. Her skin was as grey and mottled as the marble floor.

I felt my heart begin to thud. Alvin was right. Where was the perky and upbeat Mrs. Parnell I'd expected? "Has something happened?"

Alvin pushed in like a leather-clad tornado. He screeched to a stop in front of her. "What's wrong, Violet?"

Mrs. Parnell seemed not to notice him, quite an achievement considering he was now on his leather knees.

I bent over and placed a hand on her shoulder. "Something wrong, Mrs. P.?"

Alvin blurted, "Violet, what's going on?"

She shook her head and blinked. "I'm terribly troubled by a dead man."

"What?" I said.

"Whoa," Alvin said. "How long has he been dead?"

"Too long."

"That's amazing," Alvin said.

Something flickered in Mrs. Parnell's eyes. "Precisely. You can imagine how it took me by surprise."

Alvin's mouth hung open. Not a good look for him.

I said, "Obviously, something's upset you, but I think you must be mistaken. Easy to make a mistake in a crowd like this."

"There's no mistake, Ms. MacPhee."

"This is crazy," I turned and whispered to Alvin.

"Like I wouldn't figure that out for myself?"

Mrs. P. scowled. "There's nothing wrong with my hearing. And, in this case, I would far prefer to be crazy than right."

I was formulating a sensible response when Mrs. Parnell gasped. The gasp became a strangled gurgle. Her hands gripped her chest. As Alvin and I stood frozen, her eyes rolled back and she slid from her chair into a heap on the marble floor.

Dear Violet,

I do hope you are able to receive letters. You are so far away, and you have chosen to take such risks. I know you are afraid of nothing, but I wonder if you have gone too far this time. The war is no place for a woman, and I think you should know that. It is bad enough that Perce has signed up and gone overseas. Now I have to worry about you as well as my brother. There is no one much to associate with in Chesterton, since Hazel is the only person from our crowd still around. She is sillier and more scatterbrained than ever. All she can think about is hats. I suppose she daydreams about men too. Mother says that's the one good thing about Perce going overseas. At least we don't have to worry about her, if you can read between the lines.

So many girls from Chesterton have married boys they hardly know, it is a scandal. These boys have signed up and shipped out, and now the girls are working in factories. Can you imagine that? What is the world coming to? I took your advice and decided not to postpone Normal School. I will be finished my education and back home in no time. Even so, I hated to leave Mother, as she is on her own, with just the maid, especially since it is so hard to get good help these days. She misses Perce terribly. How could the government take a man who is the emotional support of an ailing widow? That is truly appalling. Of course, Perce is so patriotic, he insisted on doing his duty. It is such a shame for a capable and ambitious boy like Perce (and Harry too, of course) to have to put his life on hold. As you like to say, we must all be brave. I remind myself that Perce has a lucky streak, although I realize that is just silly and superstitious.

I am beginning to settle in at the school. I have a nice furnished room with a very respectable family. Toronto is so large compared to sleepy little Chesterton. Some of the other girls are much too frivolous to spend time with. I cannot imagine how they think they'll make competent teachers. However, one or two seem quite solid. Time will tell if they will be worthy friends, as you have always been, Violet.

Yours truly,

Betty

Two

L ucky for us, there was no shortage of medical help at this particular gathering. Mrs. Parnell opened her eyes as the first paramedic approached. In a pre-emptive strike, she said, "There's nothing whatsoever wrong with me."

"We'll just confirm that, ma'am," the paramedic said briskly.

"I'll be the judge of how I am, young man."

I was relieved to catch a glimpse of Mrs. P. in her normal mode, but I sided with the paramedic.

"You have to be seen by a doctor, just to be on the safe side. It shouldn't take long. Alvin and I will come along for the ride."

"Ms. MacPhee, I do not need to see a doctor. The world will not stop because of a moment's lightheadedness and a bit of indigestion. I have things to do." She turned to the paramedic. "That will be all, young man. I'll be on my way now."

"You fainted, Violet," Alvin said. "You can't just walk away."

"Watch me," she said.

By this time, we were ringed by observers, veterans and visitors alike. A hum of comment surrounded us.

"But…" Alvin said.

Mrs. P. struggled to her feet. "I'm leaving now. You two can decide whose side you're on."

"What?" I said, not for the first or last time that day.

"We're on your side, Violet," Alvin squeaked. He looked truly, deeply distressed. I could sympathize.

"It's best if we get you checked out in the hospital," the paramedic said.

She said, "I can't be tied up for hours. I have places to go and people to see."

Dead people? I wondered. I decided to tough it out. "As soon as the doctor gives you the green light, you'll be on your way."

"No time to dally." She straightened her shoulders. "Everything's fine. Excuse me, please."

It crossed my mind that maybe Benson & Hedges and Harvey's Bristol Cream were also calling. Even so, I had to admire her sense of drama.

"Maybe she *is* okay," I whispered to Alvin, as we stood uselessly watching Mrs. Parnell clump with her cane toward the exit.

"Do you think?" he whispered back.

"She sounds like her old self," I said, "although she's a funny pasty colour."

"And her knees are wobbling. You can see them."

The paramedic was not as useless as we were. He followed her. "If you don't mind, we'd like to confirm that you are all right."

"I do mind." Mrs. Parnell fixed him with a look that should have terrified a lesser man.

He didn't even blink. "Won't take any time at all. And, I'll make sure you get some privacy," he said, giving us a dismissive glance.

* * *

"Well, you can't just let that go," my sister Alexa huffed over the phone line. "It sounds like the start of dementia to me."

19

"What are you talking about? Mrs. Parnell doesn't have dementia. But something's wrong, and I wanted to tell you Alvin and I are here at the hospital, because I know you're planning dinner. I don't know when we'll be out."

"Don't be silly. Dementia's extremely serious."

"Once more for the record, it is not dementia. She seems to have had some kind of shock. We haven't had a chance to talk to a doctor. Mrs. P. was whisked away, in case it was a heart attack."

"*You* said she was talking to dead people. I was a nurse, in case you have forgotten, and I can tell you when people are in their eighties and they start having conversations with those who have gone before, it's not a good sign. So just this once, don't argue with every word that comes out of my mouth."

"I'm not arguing," I said.

"Of course you are."

"Am not."

"As usual."

I massaged my temple, something I find myself doing in every conversation with one of my older sisters. It's not enough that I have to be the short, dark, stocky one in the family, the three of them get to be tall, blonde and elegant. Apparently part of the deal is that they have the answer to everything. Always. My sisters are very attached to the notion of being right.

On the other hand, I was working hard to be nice.

Alexa said, "Edwina wants to talk to you."

Great. Just what I needed. The supreme commander. "No time, I have to go right…"

"Now look here, missy…" Edwina began.

"Okay. Let's start again. I didn't call to have an argument."

"It certainly sounds to me like you did, missy."

"I wanted to let you know that I'm in Emerg with Mrs.

20

Parnell, and I may not make the family dinner tonight because…"

"What? You really are incredible, Camilla. You miss out on so many family events. You know how important this day is to Daddy."

I took a deep, soothing breath. "Daddy will understand. I have to stay here until we find out if she's all right."

Edwina sniffed. "Alexa has worked very hard to make this special dinner. She's livid."

I said, "Alexa doesn't get livid. You're the one who's always livid. Alexa does the guilt trips. Never mind. Put Daddy on the line. He really likes Mrs. Parnell. I'll explain."

"This is a very emotional day for him. You'll manage to upset him about this. I'll make up a plausible story."

"What do you mean make up a story? Just tell him the truth."

"Leave it with me. I'm sure you'll show up eventually."

Oh, what the hell.

*   *   *

"I'm a bit tense, try not to make it any worse," I said to Alvin. We both knew this waiting room too well. We had now been hanging around in useless mode for what seemed like hours, breathing in air heavy with body odour and disinfectant. Our backsides were numb from too long in the molded plastic chairs. Hours earlier, Mrs. P. had vanished into some examination room along with a pack of highly-focussed medical personnel. At least they had behaved as though sudden headache and collapse in a woman in her eighties was worth taking action.

Alvin said, "Me? You're the one who always makes things worse."

"Who used the word 'crazy'?"

"You don't really think that made her…?"

21

All right, I didn't. He just gets me going, and I was worried. Maybe Alvin had been right. Maybe I should have tried harder to talk her out of marching. At the very least, I could have stayed in touch with her more in the preceding week. A good solid Catholic upbringing equips you to wallow in guilt over many issues. I was wallowing big time.

In the few years since we'd met her, Mrs. P. had begun to dote on Alvin, who didn't get much of that from other sources. She'd also saved my bacon more than once. She'd ended up in the ICU as a direct result of some of our investigations. In a pinch, she was game to spend the night guarding a client who was in danger. At the moment your life was flashing before your eyes, you could count on her to pop into the picture brandishing her Benson & Hedges and the appropriate military motto. She'd provide you with a tumbler of Bristol Cream to help you get over whatever trauma you'd be facing. I couldn't imagine life without her.

Alvin reached into the inside pocket of his leather jacket and produced a brightly-coloured notebook. Unless I missed my guess, it had repeating images of Margaret Trudeau on it. Very Andy Warhol. He clicked a hot pink gel pen, bent his head and began to write.

"What's that?" I said.

"It's my journal. Do you like the cover? I designed it myself."

"It's very interesting, and I'm not surprised you designed it yourself, but since when do you keep a journal?"

"I just started. I'm using it as an ongoing process of self-discovery. Not that it's any of your business."

"Everything is my business, Alvin," I said, for no particular reason. Sometimes you just have to pick on the closest person. I'm trying to cut down on that sort of thing, but Alvin makes such a fine target.

Alvin said, without lifting his head, "I was going to write about all the wonderful things Violet has done for me, like dropping everything and driving to Nova Scotia when my brother, Jimmy, was missing, but now I'm making a note that although you were supposed to try to be nicer to people, you have failed miserably. I hope that will be a lesson to me not to be half-assed about my own personal objectives."

"I can see you're going to enjoy your voyage, Alvin," I said nicely.

He snapped the book shut. "I'm scared, Camilla. What's wrong with her?"

I refused to say the awful words that reverberated in my mind. Aneurysm. Alzheimer's. Dementia. Brain tumour. Stroke. Cardiac arrest.

Alvin poked me in the ribs. "I need a bit of reassurance. Is that too much to ask?"

What could I say that wouldn't make things even worse? Mrs. Parnell smokes a package of cigarettes a day and consumes sherry by the vat. She doesn't believe in waiting until the sun is over the yardarm to do either. She is eighty-three years old, she never sleeps, she drives too fast, and wholesome living is not in her dictionary.

Alvin chewed his nails. "Do you think it *could* be a heart attack?"

"Wait for the doctor. No point in jumping to conclusions."

I was saved from a further volley of Alvin's questions by a familiar and darkly handsome Emergency Room physician who attempted to slip past us without making eye contact.

I shot out of the molded plastic seat and sprinted after him. I caught up and grabbed him by the arm. "Not so fast, Doctor. We're waiting to hear if Mrs. Violet Parnell is going to be all right."

He stopped and frowned. "I know you," he said in the

23

Newfoundland accent I was expecting.

"Well yes, we have met, Dr. Hasheem. It's not about me this time."

"You're in Emerg a lot."

"Not really. Just when something happens."

He closed his eyes. "If I recall: concussion, concussion, smoke inhalation, shock, hypothermia. Am I missing anything? Another concussion perhaps? Oh, yes. Broken arm."

"I'm fine today. This is not about me."

"Correct me if I'm wrong, but you have a tendency to encounter dangerous people, places and things. That right?"

"At the moment, I'm avoiding danger in all its forms."

"You look like you've lost weight."

People kept commenting on that, and it was beginning to get on my nerves.

"I dropped a size maybe. I was quite dizzy and nauseated after the concussions."

"She forgot to eat," Alvin said, sneaking up behind me. "In all the confusion of being evicted twice."

"Thank you, Alvin. I'll handle this conversation."

Dr. Hasheem's handsome forehead furrowed. "After what you've been through, you really must avoid all this stress. There can be lingering problems after concussion."

"It's been two and a half months. I'm all right." This was true enough, except for a tendency to wake up screaming in the night.

"It's not very long in recovery terms," he said.

"Look, I don't want to talk about me. I want to know what's happening with Mrs. Violet Parnell. She's been here for hours. Has anyone even been in to see her? Why couldn't we stay with her?"

I guess Dr. Hasheem didn't get to his unenviable position

without demonstrating a certain stubbornness. "I'd say you have to take it easy for more like six months to a year. Moving is a big stressor. Maybe you should try not to get evicted again."

"Great advice. Let me repeat. Mrs. Violet Parnell was brought in by ambulance from the veteran's ceremony. Is it a stroke?"

Dr. Hasheem raised an eyebrow. "That's your diagnosis?"

I said, "Not that I would know."

Alvin added, "She collapsed at the reception for the veterans after the Remembrance Day ceremonies."

"Hmmm. And what relationship is Mrs. Parnell to you?" Dr. Hasheem asked.

"Grandmother," Alvin said.

"And to you?" Dr. Hasheem asked me.

Alvin blurted, "I mean, she's Camilla's grandmother."

"And her relationship to you?" he asked Alvin.

"Aunt. Great-aunt."

"Great-great-aunt," I said at the same time.

"Really great aunt," Alvin said.

"Any other family here?" Dr. Hasheem asked, massaging his temple.

"We're her only family." As far as I knew, this was the truth.

"I remember your sisters."

"They're not available.

"She should never have marched in that parade," Alvin said.

Dr. Hasheem said. "We're doing the diagnostics on that. She's a smoker? And a drinker?"

"Well, I wouldn't call her a drinker," I said.

"We're going by the information she gave us."

I said, "She enjoys life."

Alvin added, "And we enjoy her company."

Dr. Hasheem scratched his chiselled chin. "Sorry to break

this to you, but smoking and drinking are major factors in heart disease."

I said, "What's the prognosis?"

"We have to wait for the diagnostics. You have to take into consideration that she's an old lady."

Alvin said, "That's not a very nice thing to say."

I said, "She's so full of life. And she's sharp."

"That may be," Dr. Hasheem said. "At eighty-three, with that profile, and with her symptoms, she's a prime candidate for cardiac arrest."

Alvin said, "What will that mean? Will she be stuck in a wheelchair? She'll raise hell if she is."

Frankly, I thought it would take more than a wheelchair to hold back Mrs. P., but we were in unfamiliar territory here.

Alvin kept on babbling. "Although if it was a motorized wheelchair, she might like that. If it went fast enough."

Dr. Hasheem said, "The outcomes can vary. But we'll have to monitor her for a couple of days. The good news is she got here quickly. The first thirty minutes is what counts. Might have been different if she'd been alone instead of in a room full of people."

Alvin said, "I think it was the shock."

"Shock?" Dr. Hasheem said. "Did something happen to bring this on? We should be told in that case."

I said, "Something upset her. We're not sure what."

"She had trouble with a dead man," Alvin said.

"A dead man? Well, I think we can rule that out as a causal factor," Dr. Hasheem said. "Although, sometimes a blockage can cause people to appear to hallucinate."

I opened my mouth, but he'd already vanished in a puff of smoke. Or maybe it was behind the door of an examination room.

*   *   *

Eons later, we received an update. Not a happy update, for sure. Still, not as bad as it might have been. According to Dr. Hasheem, she'd need rest, medication and a mending of her ways. In hospital.

"No smoking. Alcohol in moderation."

"Sure, like that's going to happen," I muttered.

Dr. Hasheem overheard. "It better happen. And, she shouldn't be alone, it goes without saying. We'll keep her here for observation for a couple of days, run some more tests. When she's released, she'll either require a convalescent home or a twenty-four hour caregiver. She shouldn't be by herself. You might want to get started on those arrangements for your grandmother," Dr. Hasheem said.

As soon as he had snapped the file shut and vanished again, Alvin said, "Lord thundering Jesus."

"No kidding," I said.

"I don't think he really understands what type of person Violet is."

We were both trying to imagine the impact of Mrs. P. on some unsuspecting convalescent home.

"I'm surprised they let her back into this particular hospital after the last time," I said.

"Come on, Camilla, everyone's entitled to a couple of parties," Alvin said.

"They can be pretty stuffy in the ICU. Anyway, I don't think a convalescent home is right for her."

Alvin looked shocked. "Of course not."

"I think she'd prefer to be in her own home."

"For sure."

"Between the two of us, and a bit of help, we could

27

probably manage for a few days. What do you think?"

"Damned straight. Wait a minute. I thought you were taking a vacation with Ray Deveau."

"That can wait."

*   *   *

Not everyone was enthusiastic about the idea of postponing a vacation. By not everyone, I mean specifically not Ray Deveau.

I said for the second time, "I know you're upset, but there's nothing I can do about it."

A long silence drifted down the phone line. I hate long silences. Unless they're my own.

I said, "I realize you're excited about this trip."

"It's our kick at the can, Camilla. If we're trying to build some kind of life together, this isn't the time to start postponing it."

"As romantic as that may be, we'll have to kick that particular can some other time."

"This is the only time my sister can come down her to stay with the girls."

"I'm sorry. I just can't go to Mexico and leave Mrs. Parnell alone. We don't know what kind of convalescence she'll have or how long it will take. I'm asking you to wait a bit until we know."

"Can you get someone else to look after her? Just for two weeks?"

"Maybe you can find someone else to look after the girls later?"

"You don't know a lot about teenagers, do you?"

I hate it when people snort. "I rather hoped that was part of my charm."

"Well, it's not. So back to my suggestion. Why don't we try to find someone else to take care of Mrs. Parnell? From where

I sit, I think little old ladies are easier to handle than teenagers. Even tough and stubborn old ladies, in case you're planning to mention that."

"In most cases, I'd agree."

I suppose I should have said *I know how much this trip means to you. I know about all the planning and the deal-making and the books you've read and your total effort to make this be a wonderful holiday. This is a major chance to get to know each other better in close quarters without either of our families spoiling the mood and murderers muddying the waters.* In retrospect, perhaps I might have said how much I valued Ray and our new relationship.

I didn't say anything. The trouble is, I am lousy at relationships. I'd had nearly ten years to get used to the idea of my husband, Paul, being killed by a drunk driver. It was past time to move on. I couldn't imagine anyone better than Ray to move on with. I just needed to work on some new habits.

"Okeydoke," Ray said, eventually. "New plan needed then."

What the hell did he mean by that?

*   *   *

A couple of words about emergency departments. Don't think anyone you care about is getting in and out of one quickly. It was evening before I was able to trap Dr. Hasheem in another corridor. I didn't waste time on false pleasantries.

"It's been hours. Why keep my grandmother here, where we can't even see her? What is this, the Gulag?"

"For observation and stabilization. Your wait is not really out of line. We have to check her thoroughly."

"Wouldn't she be more likely to recover in a room?"

"Yes, she would."

"Then why isn't she?"

"They must be waiting for a bed to become available."

"Unbelievable. How can she get better in this chaotic hellhole?"

His eyes flashed darkly. He was definitely beautiful when he was mad. "I'd like to see you do a better job with the same resources."

"Okay, I realize you have resource problems. My job is to make sure Mrs. Parnell doesn't get lost in the system.

"Mrs. Parnell? I thought she was your grandmother?"

"She is my grandmother. I'm calling her Mrs. Parnell so you'll know who I'm talking about. Anyway, what I call her doesn't matter. The important thing is to get her out of this hellhole and into a room."

His skin paled to light coffee colour. "She's not in a corridor?"

"I don't *know* where she is. I think *you* should."

"I haven't seen her for…" He frowned in a way I didn't care for.

"I'll double-check," he said.

"Double-check what?"

He raced down the corridor until he gave me the slip.

Something was very, very wrong.

21 Frank Street
Chesterton, Ontario
October 10, 1942

Dear Vi,

I hope England is everything you thought it would be. I am quite envious! I know there's a war on, but still you will see lots of London! We've been getting news about the Blitz on the radio. It's hard not to think of you and worry. Be careful with those flyboys, I hear they're all scamps. I know that you are used to scamps, especially growing up around Harry and Perce. I hope you have a chance to meet up with them. Are there lots of dances? When you get back, you'll have to spill the beans!

Things have changed a lot here. It's hard to get anything. I left the kettle on the stove too long and burnt the bottom out of it. Mum was very understanding, although we haven't been able to find a replacement. As for the old Ford, it's hard to get gasoline. Everything has gone to the war effort. Never mind, walking is good for the figure.

Mum has decided to let the upper floor to tenants. It is hard for people to get a place to live. Even in Chesterton, it's a problem. Mum says we should think about others less fortunate than ourselves. We have more than enough room downstairs. I suppose I am less likely to break a leg going out the downstairs window!

Harry Jones's father was kind enough to make some renovations for us. He seems lost in his own world. It must be very hard for him, losing his wife two years ago and now having Harry overseas. I bet Harry's having adventures too, even though there's a war on. If you see him, say hello from me. Tell him I think you make the perfect couple.

I have some grand news! I was able to get a job at the Court House as a court stenographer. Who ever thought all that shorthand and typing would be useful? It's very interesting, the judges are real gentlemen. Judge Stiles especially is quite handsome, and I get to wear lovely hats to work. We can use a bit of money. This old house is hard to keep up, and we still need the kettle. Movies are expensive too, but worth it. I just loved "Sergeant York". You never know who is going to be a hero (like you, Vi!).

Love from your best friend,

Hazel

P.S. I hope you find someone to help you with your hair since I'm not there!

Three

W hat do you mean gone?" I yelped at Dr. Hasheem. Alvin gripped my hand.

"Gone where?" I pried Alvin's fingers from my hand while continuing to block Dr. Hasheem's getaway.

"Lord thundering Jesus," Alvin moaned.

"Try and control yourself, Alvin. Make it part of your voyage of self-discovery."

The doctor said. "Apparently, she just walked out. We don't know where."

"You were talking about potential heart attacks. You can't let her scamper off."

"Actually, we believe she *might* have had a cardiac event. The results were really inconclusive."

"Minor difference. The fact remains she's in her eighties, and something happened, and you were supposed to look after her, and now she's gone. That seems pretty irresponsible in the legal sense."

"I spoke to her, and she was obviously reasoning quite well."

"No one advised her to stay here?"

"Of course. She was told of the advisability of remaining here until we had run some more tests. However, she chose to leave. We couldn't hold her against her will."

Alvin said. "She's seeing dead people."

I took a deep breath. "You don't think she has some kind of dementia, do you?"

"She definitely seems sharper than most people." I could tell that included us.

"How did she leave?" Alvin said.

"I have no idea," Dr. Hasheem said. "I am sorry that no one let you know. If you'd had a power of attorney, they would have required your authorization to let her go. You didn't have a power of attorney for health matters, did you?"

"No," I said.

"There you go," the doctor said. "Nothing we can do."

"But she'll need proper care," Alvin said. "More tests."

Dr. Hasheem said, "No argument here."

I said, "She needs to be here. You said that yourself."

Dr. Hasheem shrugged. "You'll have to work that out with her, since she's already left. We'll certainly re-admit her if she comes back. Now if you'll excuse me…"

Alvin bleated. "You are talking about a heroic war veteran here. She doesn't get frightened."

Dr. Hasheem passed a hand over his brow. "Heroic war veteran. Okay. All right then, you might want to look into what's available for vets. The Perley-Rideau is a great facility. Maybe she'd be more comfortable there. And if you do get her in, she may need a psychological assessment in addition to having her heart monitored."

"There's nothing crazy about Violet," Alvin shouted crazily.

"I'm not saying crazy. That's not a preferred term. It could be physical too. I think I already mentioned that sometimes vascular problems can lead to a person seeing things that are not there. It's rare, but it happens. But we can't jump to conclusions. We have to check out the possibilities. One way

34

or the other, her behaviour is troubling."

"Something happened at that ceremony," I said.

"After she saw that dead guy," Alvin said. "I found that troubling, for sure."

"So did she," I said.

"I rest my case." Dr. Hasheem steamed down the hall, his white coat flapping behind him.

*   *   *

My cellphone rang as soon as I turned it on in the hospital parking lot.

"Okay, Camilla, I knew you'd answer eventually," Ray Deveau said cheerfully. "I've got a new plan."

"Bad time for me, Ray." I jogged through the drizzle to keep up with Alvin, who had commandeered the keys to my car. "Can I call you back?"

Ray paused, just briefly. "It will only take two minutes."

"Mrs. Parnell's absconded from the hospital. We've got to get to her place to see if she's all right."

Ray chuckled softly. "Absconded. She broke out? Just like her."

I hadn't thought of that. "I guess it is."

"Did you think she'd take being in hospital lying down?"

"Don't laugh at your own jokes, Ray."

"Somebody has to. You know what, I hope we're capable of absconding when we're her age."

He had a point. "I guess."

"Just listen to the new plan. Can't you do that on your way?"

"Yeah, okay, shoot."

"I talked to my sister. She'll stay with the girls whenever the time is right."

"She will? Well, that's great."

"Yup. I talked to my supervisor, explained the situation. No one else wants to book off time right now, so I can make arrangements on fairly short notice."

"Huh."

"It looks like I can get pretty good deals online no matter where we want to go. November's not the best travel month for most people, so that works in our favour."

"Hmmm," I said, opening the passenger side door since Alvin had taken over the driver's side.

"You make sure Mrs. Parnell is all right, and when you're good to go, we'll arrange our holiday. When you have a moment to think about it, give me a hint where you'd like to go and I'll get cracking."

This would have been a good time to say something lovey-dovish to Ray, something along the lines of how glad I was he was in my life. Too bad I was distracted by Alvin, who had turned on the hazard lights instead of the windshield wipers.

"Thanks, Ray."

My neck jerked back as Alvin accelerated out of the lot, tossing ten dollars at the attendant.

After another pause, Ray said, "You're welcome."

"Talk to you later, then," I said.

"Yup."

*   *   *

In the apartment foyer, I shook my wet hair and jabbed the bell for Mrs. Parnell's unit repeatedly and without luck. Alvin and I both had keys to Mrs. Parnell's apartment, although I'd had to turn in my building key when I'd vacated against my will, and Alvin was too rattled to remember where his was. I buzzed a few other apartments at random. That usually

36

worked. Not this time. The building management was on a security campaign, and it seemed to be working.

Normally, I would think security was a good thing. Tonight it was a damned nuisance. To make matters worse, my grouchy former neighbour pushed past us as we were making a desperate attempt to gain access. I was pretty sure that jerk was the reason I no longer lived in this building. Some people have no understanding of a dog's need to bark from time to time. I dug deep into my politeness reserves to get the right tone and called after him. "You know me, I was your next-door neighbour. I need to get in to check on Mrs. Parnell. She's your neighbour on the other side of the hallway in 1608. She's supposed to be in the hospital and…"

I was talking to the closed door by this time.

Alvin gasped. "Can you believe that guy? What is our society coming to?"

"You tell me," I snarled and went back to jabbing Mrs. Parnell's bell and the Super's. Without result.

"Are we wasting time here?" I said, "Maybe she's not even home yet. Maybe she's confused and wandering."

"Or, she is home, and she doesn't want us to see her."

"Don't even think that," I said.

"Here's our chance," Alvin said. He took advantage of a nice girl who was leaving the building and grabbed the door before it closed.

The elevator took about a year to get to the sixteenth floor.

Alvin and I careened into each other getting out of the elevator, and we thundered down the corridor. We almost knocked over a somewhat startled man who was heading for the elevator balancing a hefty cardboard box. This guy's suit was already rumpled, and it looked like he was going to collapse before he got to the elevator.

"Oops, sorry," Alvin said.

"It's all right," the guy said in a wobbly voice, as the down elevator dinged.

I didn't have time to worry about innocent bystanders.

"Okay," I said, as we reached her apartment, "if she's not here, we have to contact the Super, so that he can keep an eye out, and let us know if she shows up."

"The Super's not answering. And if she's not here, where could she be?" Alvin looked a bit more wild-eyed than usual.

We both stopped abruptly. The door to 1608 stood open.

"Oh," said Alvin.

"Great," I said. "She's home."

"Violet!" Alvin barrelled through the door.

No answer.

"Violet?"

"Mrs. P.?"

Lester and Pierre, Mrs. Parnell's evil peach-faced lovebirds, screamed. Mrs. Parnell's place is neat, state of the art and minimalist. High-end stereo equipment and the latest in television, don't ask me brand names. The furniture was simple: black leather sofa and two chairs. Brushed chrome and glass coffee table and end table. Euro style lamps. There is a complete absence of doilies, knickknacks or clutter.

"Lord thundering Jesus," Alvin said. "Was there a tornado here? Her CDs are all over the floor. And look at the books!"

I stepped toward the bedroom, my heart beating. "Mrs. P.? It's me, Camilla."

Alvin said, "And me."

"Silence implies consent." I strode through the door.

Nothing. And no one. The bed was made, military style. Aside from that, Mrs. Parnell's room looked like the contents had been dumped from an airplane.

38

"What happened here?" Alvin said.

I shook my head. "A burglar?"

"The stereo's still in the living room, and so is her new plasma TV." Alvin said. "Burglars love electronics. You should know that, you had enough clients who were burglars."

"Maybe we interrupted one."

Alvin mouthed, "Maybe he's still here."

"He'd have to be in the bathroom," I mouthed back and pointed.

"Or under the bed," Alvin gestured.

"Or in the closet."

"Behind the drapes."

"Cornered," I whispered.

"Whoops."

Alvin armed himself with the standing lamp, and I picked up a small metal chair. With his free hand, Alvin yanked open the bathroom door. I raised the chair over my head.

Alvin shook his head.

No one there. Somebody had emptied the medicine cabinet though, scattering toiletries into the sink and onto the floor. I reached over and whipped open the shower curtain. There was a crunch as I stepped on an empty container.

"Closet," I mouthed.

No one in the closet either. A few items hanging. A couple of hangers lay on the floor. Together we checked behind all the drapes. As a last resort, I dropped to my knees and peered under the bed. I scanned the room again, trying to make sense of things. A large red suitcase lay in the middle of the bedroom floor, unzipped and open, with clothing strewn over it.

"Violet has a set of this luggage," Alvin said. "She just got it. We were thinking of taking some trips."

My mind boggled.

He said, "There was a carry-on, with wheels, and a little toiletries case too. It had a place to hang her cane. The two cases hooked together, and they were lightweight, so that she could handle them. Although I would have helped her."

I said, "Well, there's only one here now."

Alvin checked my facts by peering into the closet.

I said, "Do you think a burglar would steal suitcases?"

"He could use them to stash stuff."

"Nothing's missing."

"Like you said, maybe he got interrupted."

"By us. Or by Mrs. P."

"But she's not here," Alvin said. "Do you think she even came home?"

I pointed to the open door of the closet. "Isn't that her uniform, hanging up there?"

"Ohmigod, she was wearing it when she went to the hospital."

"Right. And naturally, she must have worn it home. Obviously, she changed her clothes, and she hung up the uniform carefully. And then what?"

"She must have changed."

"Obviously, Alvin. But what explains all this mess in the apartment?"

Alvin swivelled around. "I still figure a burglar. I can smell his aftershave. Can you?"

"What is it? Not Old Spice."

"Well, hardly. No, something contemporary. Hugo Boss maybe."

"Okay, so we smell aftershave, and Mrs. P.'s not here. Where did she go?"

"Why would she go anywhere? She couldn't have been recovered from seeing the dead man."

"We'll leave the dead man out of it. Dead men don't wear aftershave."

"She's been kidnapped," Alvin said

"That's just ridiculous. Why would anybody kidnap her?"

"I don't know. It doesn't matter why. Somebody must have. Expensive aftershave. There's a type. You know what? I think that guy we passed had it on."

"Let's keep cool. It's unlikely that she was kidnapped. This is Ottawa. And that guy we passed didn't have her. She probably just went out. She's independent. Maybe she had to pick up something."

Alvin was on his way to the kitchen this time, flinging open the door to the fridge.

"There's food in here. Cheese. Bread. Wait a sec. Yeah. Lots of frozen sweet and sour chicken in the freezer too. Her fave."

I headed back to the living room and checked the small modern cabinet where Mrs. P. keeps her Harvey's Bristol Cream. Three bottles stood waiting. A full carton of Benson & Hedges sat near the bottles.

"It wasn't a trip to fetch booze or cigarettes. What else could it be?"

Alvin loped back to the kitchen and flung open a door. "There's lots of bird seed. And it looks like she just fed them."

"No need to panic. We should think logically."

"If there were kidnappers, they must have had a van," Alvin poked his head around the corner.

"Why on earth would anyone kidnap Mrs. Parnell?"

"Maybe she knew something that…"

"Forget it. Let's operate on the principal that she simply went out, Alvin. Like anyone would do on any normal day."

Alvin's beady eyes watered. He put his hand in his leather jacket and pulled out the book. Another storm on the voyage to self-discovery.

We both turned our eyes to the clock.

"Okay, so it's after nine. Most stores will be closed. What's she doing out at this time of night? She'd hardly go to a concert in her state."

"We should have asked the doctor exactly when she left the hospital," Alvin said.

"I don't think he knew. He seemed quite shocked when he figured it out. Remember? We were hanging around when she was long gone."

"It's not like Violet to be inconsiderate, even if she did leave us sitting there in those miserable plastic chairs. Why would she do that?"

"Let's chalk it up to shock." I didn't want to suggest dementia. I couldn't bear the thought of Mrs. Parnell, sharp as a tack, as cunning as any field commander, slipping into nightmarish confusion.

Alvin said, "Probably she didn't realize we were there."

I said, "More likely, she thought we'd object to her leaving the hospital."

"But why did she need to leave in the first place?"

"That's the question, isn't it, Alvin? What? What's the matter?"

"Wait a minute. How did she get home? Her car's here."

"Her car's here?"

"Yeah. Someone picked her up to go to the meeting point for the march. A volunteer."

"What are you waiting for?"

Three minutes later, our elevator reached the garage level, and we walked briskly toward Mrs. P.'s parking spot.

"Holy shit," Alvin said.

"I'll second that," I said as we stared at the spot where Mrs. Parnell's new Volvo should have been.

"Maybe the kidnappers took it," Alvin said.

"Are you residents?" a voice boomed behind us.

I stared at an oversized, uniformed and unfamiliar security guard. "Not exactly," I said. "We're looking for Mrs. Violet Parnell, Apt. 1608."

"Yeah, sure. Stay put," he said. "Let's see what the cops have to say about that."

London, England
March 14, 1942

Dear Miss Wilkinson,

It was a pleasure to meet you at the dance last night. I never imagined I would meet a Canadian girl over here in England. You certainly do have a way of putting your ideas across. I've never met a lady who could drive a truck before. If I had ever given such an unlikely circumstance a moment's thought, I never would have expected the same person to be charming and feminine and yet to have such strong opinions on politics and economics.

I hope to have a chance to meet you again and to continue our discussion about the relative merits of Russian composers. I have quite a different take on this Shostakovich.

I hope you will allow me to call you Violet.

Sincerely,

Walter Parnell

Four

I t's about time," I said.

Sgt. Conn McCracken, my brother-in-law, joined the crowd scene in the garage. The cast of this comedy was now made up of the security guard, two police constables, and the Super, who had finally shown up in his pajama tops and chinos with pajama bottoms peeping out at the ankles. He smelled ever so slightly of bubble bath.

I'd never seen the two constables before. They seemed impressed by the arrival of a detective from Major Crimes.

Alvin and I were the criminal centrepieces.

Conn gave me a dirty look.

"It's not my fault. I told you Mrs. Parnell disappeared. Vanished. The police should be looking for her, not wasting time pestering us merely because we don't happen to live here."

"Let's finish up this business of your trespassing in a building you were recently evicted from before we move on."

"What a crock," I said. "Sure, they asked me to move out of my apartment. So what? I did. It was a misunderstanding about a fire alarm, which I never pulled, and a neighbour complaining about Gussie, which was just plain petty. No one ever said I couldn't come back to the building. So what's this trespassing crap?"

Alvin said, "We had to go into Violet's apartment to see if she was there. It's like when the cops showed up here, they didn't even care about where Violet was. I don't know what society's coming to."

I spotted a small spasm in Conn's jaw. "Please, tell me you didn't go into someone's apartment when they weren't there."

"We didn't know she wasn't there. How could we?"

Alvin said, "Hey, I bet it was that neighbour. He closed the door right in our faces. He probably went back to his apartment and looked on the monitor and spotted us coming and called security. He knows we're not burglars."

"Is that what happened? That jerk made a complaint again?" I said to the super, who was standing around looking useless.

The Super blushed. "I felt bad, eh, you getting booted out like that. It wasn't me. I would have let you guys in if I'd known."

"No hard feelings, although you might consider answering your doorbell in the future."

Conn said, "Let's just get this settled. You were searching for your friend who disappeared from the hospital. You went to her apartment because you were afraid she was in trouble."

"We tried buzzing the Super."

"I was in the bathtub," the Super said, pinkly.

"That's unlawful entering," the guard said. "I know that. I'm taking Law and Security at Algonquin."

I said. "Even though the door was open, I have a key to Mrs. Parnell's apartment, and that's the equivalent of permission to enter." I didn't bother to mention I had a perfectly serviceable law degree and a license to practice.

The guard puffed up his chest. "Yeah, well, the guy in 1603 said you weren't supposed to be in the building. That sounds unlawful to me."

Conn shrugged. "This is a whole lot of crap about nothing,"

he said to the two constables.

"It's something all right. Mrs. Parnell is not where she should be, and she's in rough shape. Her apartment's been trashed, and now her goddam car is gone. Something's wrong, and I want to know what the hell the police are going to do about it."

*   *   *

"So the short answer is they're not doing much besides sitting on their hands," I said.

Ray Deveau said, "There's not much they can do. She's a functioning adult, and she can come and go as she pleases. I'm sure you're aware of that, what with your law degree and all."

"Go ahead, mock. I'm looking for support here."

I had to admit, Ray was in a pretty supportive mood when I called. He always was. I wish some of that would rub off on my other friends and relatives.

"Something's wrong. I know it. Conn wasn't much help."

Ray sighed. "Okay, we'll talk about the vacation at a more opportune moment. Where are you calling from?"

"Mrs. Parnell's place. I'm waiting here in case she comes back. Alvin's out driving around in the rain looking for her. We're taking turns. Is there any way to light a fire under the police? Couldn't they be on the lookout for her?"

"It's a bit early for a BOLO. The problem is, not much time has elapsed since she took off. Lots of people would have still been lying on a gurney in the emergency room corridor. The cops just think you are overreacting."

"Come on, Ray. The hospital staff were talking about heart attack. Add to that the weird talk of dead men and the fact she skipped out of the hospital, deliberately giving us the slip."

"Camilla, you don't have to convince me."

"Then there's the fact that her apartment has obviously been turned over by someone searching for something."

"You said that the officers checked that out."

"They didn't think it was such a big deal, but they don't know her. Her apartment is always in perfect order, like a showroom. She loves her music. She'd never scatter her CDs on the floor."

"Here are a couple of tips. Never mind telling them how well you know the person and how they wouldn't do this or that. I'm a cop, and I hear that all the time about so-called missing persons who just want to get away from the same someone who knows them too well. It's not even midnight. No wonder they're not doing backflips."

"She should be in hospital, under medical observation."

"I understand. Trust me, if you want the police to do something, you have to use whatever turns their crank. Dementia or Alzheimer's is a hot button for the media. They'll put out a bulletin. People will watch for her. Someone will spot her and call in."

"She doesn't have dementia. The doctor said she was…"

"Don't quote the doctor when you're talking to the cops."

"I get your point, but if Mrs. P. heard that, she'd have a fit. When there was a false bulletin out for me, I was really pissed off. And frankly nervous too."

Ray chuckled. "I heard you did some crazy things. Now you're asking for advice, and I'm giving it. If you play the dementia card, mention medication needed and inadequate clothing for weather conditions. That'll ratchet up interest."

"Maybe we can just allude to it. Say fears for her safety, that kind of thing. At the very least, they'll track the vehicle." I had a flash vision of Mrs. Parnell giving the cops a run for their money in a high-speed chase. I bet her Volvo could outrun those Crown Vics.

The next step seemed obvious, if unpleasant. Unfortunately, as a rule, your previous relationships with the police can have a big effect on how they treat you later on. I was all too aware of this. I got voicemail hell on the police line for routine enquiries. I struck out with 911.

I saw no choice. I picked up the phone and dialled Conn's cellphone. Luckily, I knew exactly where Conn was. I asked him to make the appropriate contact at Headquarters. I said I was sorry if I was interrupting whatever he was doing at the time and requested that he not indicate I was the one calling during the family dinner. I made a point of mentioning that his own wife had introduced this dementia worry, and if he had a problem with it, he should take it up with Alexa later. Like that would happen.

*　　*　　*

Alvin stomped through the door, shook his wet ponytail and slumped on Mrs. P.'s black leather sofa.

"Still nothing," I said before he could ask.

"I went by your place like you asked and fed and walked Gussie."

"Thanks, Alvin. I appreciate it."

"I fed the cat too. You think we should bring them over here?"

I glanced at Lester and Pierre. "Bad idea."

"I thought you said that if the police put out a bulletin about Violet, that someone would call in."

"Ray thought if we claimed dementia, that might speed things up. No guarantees."

"Someone should have seen her."

"This is Mrs. Parnell. She probably doesn't want to be seen. Maybe she's wearing a hat or something."

49

"They had the license plate number of the Volvo."

"Alvin, I'm getting a headache. Let's find something to do here instead of fretting."

"There's nothing to do. We've already searched the place twice."

"Let's search it again. Maybe instead of looking for something, we should concentrate more on what isn't here."

"What do you mean?"

"I mean, what did she take with her. We think she took the two small red suitcases, and we know she left her uniform. We should have thought of this before."

"We're rattled, Camilla," Alvin said. He certainly looked rattled. The ponytail was damp and bedraggled, the earrings drooped, and he slouched, paler than dust.

"Agreed. And we have a right to be. Now, let's get moving. Her walker's here."

"What do you think that means?"

"I don't know what it means. Where is her cane?"

Alvin zipped from room to room. "Nowhere," he said. "It's gone. She's got two of them, and they're both gone."

"So, maybe she was going somewhere where the walker wouldn't be necessary."

"Or maybe it wouldn't be convenient. Or it might be too noticeable."

"Like where, Alvin?"

"I don't know. A bus?"

"Why would she take a bus? She has the car. Okay. We need some kind of focus. Let's assume she's not just randomly driving around to clear her head. Why would she go anywhere in the first place?"

"And not to tell us where she was going, that's not like Violet."

"You're right, it isn't. So either she's behaving irrationally, or she had a plan we don't know about and chose not to involve us."

"I hate both those options," Alvin said.

"Me too, but I think we have to face facts."

"What if someone took her away?"

I felt a headache coming on. "We have no reason to believe that someone took her. Do you really think that Mrs. P. would just go off with someone without putting up a fight?"

"She wouldn't."

"That's right. Now look around you."

Alvin narrowed his eyes and scanned the room.

"Do you see any signs of a fight?"

"I see mess. Remember we thought it was a burglar?"

"No signs of a struggle, right? No chairs knocked over, no stuff broken, no phone off the hook? This is Mrs. P. She wouldn't go quietly."

"Maybe he had a gun."

"All right, before we explore the gun theory, let's work through the other much more likely reasons. First, that she was not thinking normally. What evidence do we have of that?"

"Just the conversation with the dead guy."

"Exactly."

"Your sister said that probably means dementia. That's got me all nerved up."

"We were with Mrs. Parnell. She was upset, not demented."

"Yeah, but she was troubled."

"Deeply disturbed. Definitely rational, as usual."

Alvin seemed to take some comfort in this.

I said, "So let's assume that she is her normal self, even if upset enough to give us the slip in the hospital. If she's gone somewhere under her own steam, the question is, why would she leave here in such a hurry?"

"To find something out? Information."

"She's a whiz on that computer. She can surf the net as well as you can, and she's way better than me. I think if she just wanted information, she'd do it here on her own."

Alvin furrowed his brow. "True, I guess."

"She took suitcases, Alvin. Kidnappers wouldn't take suitcases. I think she's headed out of town, under her own steam and with some kind of plan we aren't privy to."

Alvin dragged himself into the bedroom and stared at the large, red unzipped suitcase in the middle of the floor. I followed.

Alvin said, "Maybe she had something hidden in the suitcases. Maybe that's what the burglar was looking for. Or the kidnappers. Although it doesn't look like it had anything in it."

I agreed, although to be fair, we were grasping at straws here.

He said, "It's hard to know what's missing if you don't know what was there in the first place. I have no idea what Violet kept in her suitcases."

"Me neither. You raise a good point, Alvin. Something is missing. Something's not quite right. Look around. What do we not see that we should see?"

His eyes misted. "I don't know."

"We'll figure it out. Stay calm, that's our main tactic."

Alvin sniffed noisily. "If you can call it a tactic."

"It's what we have."

Minutes later, back in the living room, while I stood staring at the CD cases with my mind a perfect blank, Alvin said, "That's it!"

"What?"

"The photos!"

"Oh, right. Her war photos. Where are they?"

We both pivoted around.

Alvin said, "Do you think she just moved them?"

"They're always right here on the bookcase, place of honour," I said.

"Maybe she was looking at them before the ceremony. Perhaps she wanted to honour her old friends, and she just put them down somewhere. Let's take a look."

It doesn't take all that long to comb through a one-bedroom apartment, particularly if you've already checked it out several times within the hour.

"Not here," Alvin said.

"Okay," I said, "thinking strategically, which Mrs. Parnell would want us to do, there's probably some connection with those photos and her departure."

"Sounds good," said Alvin. "What do you think it is?"

"No idea. We have to start somewhere. It's better to be off-base than to sit staring at our navels."

"So maybe she went to see someone in the photo?"

"Yes. Let's operate on that principle."

"You're starting to talk like Violet," Alvin said. "What's that about?"

"I don't know. Back to business. Let's start with what we've almost got. Who was in those photographs?" I closed my eyes and tried to imagine them.

"There was one of her husband. Two actually," Alvin said. "There was another photo of some people in Canadian uniforms overseas, maybe in England. She never talked about them, though. I asked her once, and she changed the subject. She likes talking about the war, although it made her sad, I think, to talk about the people in the photos."

"I imagine that some of the boys in uniform never made it back from the war."

"Her husband came back, but he didn't live all that long

53

after," said Alvin. "She doesn't talk about him either."

"She talked to me once about being widowed and trying to move on with one's life. She was trying to help me, I think." I didn't mention that a large quantity of Bristol Cream had preceded the discussion.

Alvin said, "Okay, we still don't have much to go on."

"Hold on. Back to the photos. Either the person who broke in here took them, or Mrs. P. did."

"Who would leave electronics and take photos?"

"Good point," I said nicely. "We have to assume it was Mrs. P. Let's suppose she was going to see someone who was in the photo, and she just wanted it with her to show them."

"We still don't know who she was going to see."

"Right, so if we had even one clue as to who the people were, we could contact them to see if they've heard from her."

Alvin said, "She grew up in Chesterton, down past Kingston. Is that any help? I guess not, after all these years."

I slapped my forehead. "Of course, her address book. What is the matter with us?"

Alvin said, "There's nothing wrong with *me*. I already thought of that. Violet keeps her address book by the phone. There's no sign of it."

"She must have taken it with her."

I narrowly avoided being knocked over by Alvin as he sprinted to the phone. "Last call redial!" he yelled, as he picked up the receiver. "Remember when Violet used that to find you when you were in trouble?"

"I do." It hadn't been the only time she'd used technology to save me.

"Oh." Alvin's face fell. "It's my number."

"Check the Caller ID to see if anyone has called her."

Alvin clicked away. "You. Me. You. Me. You. Me. Me. Me.

And you. It's only us for the last twenty-five calls."

"Crap," I said.

"Agreed."

"Hey wait, the telephone book is sitting right there. Doesn't she keep that on the shelf as a rule?"

"She does," Alvin said. "She must have been looking up a number."

I flipped it open to see if any pages were marked or dog-eared. I checked on the tops of pages to see if she'd written anything. It was Alvin's turn to pace, while I worked my way through it. No luck.

"Face it, Alvin. We're stumped. Okay, what else can we do?"

Alvin slipped into the black chair. "We can't give up on Violet that easily."

"I'm not suggesting we give up. We can't stay stumped forever. So what would Mrs. P. do now?"

"Soldier on," Alvin said.

"Exactly."

"Sometimes older people keep stuff in drawers or chests just to protect it or keep it safe. Not that I think of Violet as an older person. With my grandmother, the more important it was, the deeper it was buried. Her china tea set that I have, you know the one, well, it was in a box on the top shelf of her closet, wrapped in paper. It was her most precious possession."

"My father's like that with his medals. So let's go through everything. I'll start with the dresser drawers. You take the closets."

Alvin stopped and said, "You think we're violating her privacy?"

"Like they say, Alvin, forgiveness is easier than permission."

"I like that."

I pulled open the first drawer and frowned. "Looks like

55

someone already went through them. I don't think Mrs. P. kept everything in a jumble. I can't tell what's missing. All Mrs. Parnell's clothes are shades of khaki or taupe. They all look alike."

Alvin stuck his head out of the closet. "Let me check."

"This feels weird. What if she marches through the door with a smouldering Benson & Hedges and a tumbler full of Harvey's and says what the devil are you doing pawing through my belongings?"

Alvin's eyes got misty. "That would be the absolute best thing that could happen."

"Right. Okay, let's think. Did she pack before the burglar or after?"

"Before," Alvin said. "She learned in the army that it takes less time to do something right than to rush through it. She would have straightened up her apartment if she'd come here after him. She wouldn't leave her place like this."

"Good point. Did she know someone would break in? How could she?"

Alvin stepped down from the step stool he was standing on. "I don't know. Lord thundering Jesus, Camilla, I just thought of something. Where are her laptop and digital camera? Do you think the burglar made off with them?"

"Or she took them herself."

Alvin said, "Unless they're with the stuff she sent over to my place yesterday."

I did not yell. "What stuff she sent to your place?"

"Just a box. She asked me to take it home and not to disturb the contents."

I took a deep, soothing breath. "Did that seem strange? With all the empty space Mrs. P. has?"

"She's my friend, so I was glad to do her a favour without

being nosy. You would have done it too, no questions asked. So just don't start with me."

"Use your brain, Alvin. She didn't want someone to find it."

Alvin goggled. "That means she knew it might happen."

"Exactly. Let's go get the box, Alvin."

"What if we bring it back and whoever broke in is watching?"

"Now that's just plain…" I stared at Alvin. "The guy in the hall."

"The innocent bystander," Alvin said.

I kicked the leather chair. "He was coming right down this hallway, carrying a goddam box. I never even gave it a moment's thought."

"Yeah, and his suit was all rumpled," Alvin said.

"Did you smell aftershave when he passed?"

"Holy shit," Alvin said. "He's the burglar! No wonder he looked like he was about to have a heart attack."

*　　*　　*

Alvin lives in the tangle of narrow streets in old Hull, now called the Hull sector of the city of Gatineau. Downtown Hull had been off-limits when I was a teenager. With the seedy bar strip, the tangle of old streets, the availability of drugs and booze, it was no place for a nice Catholic girl from across the river in Ontario. Naturally, I've always liked it. Alvin chooses to live there, finding a campy charm in the area. No one could have followed us, as we looped around the old streets, changing direction every time we went over a hill. We gave it one extra whirl before we parked behind Alvin's latest apartment.

"I'll stay here, in case he comes by and spots the car. Safer that way," I said. I was avoiding any decorating innovations Alvin might have made to his apartment. Could be an autumn theme with crackling leaves, or maybe a simulation of Flanders Fields, with wall to wall poppies and a hidden bugler playing Taps around the clock. Whatever, I just wasn't up for it at the moment. "Bring the box, and we'll check it at my place. If we have to hide it, I have a zillion other boxes to throw someone off the scent."

*　　*　　*

Half an hour later, we parked on Third Avenue in the Glebe and opened my front door. The house is new to me, as anyone could tell from the stacks of packing boxes from my apartment, the battered filing cabinets and the two government surplus desks from Justice for Victims which were squished into the living room. My old furniture was stacked on end in the hallway, so you had to inhale to get through. The living room was being converted to the new Justice for Victims office, which would solve my office eviction problem and keep me from rambling around in a house that had far more space than I needed. Since the upstairs was about the size of my former apartment, I planned to live there as soon as I got rid of the surplus furniture. I had a good, workable plan, but for a variety of reasons, I wasn't getting far. My favourite social activist, Elaine Ekstein, had located a battered women's shelter that needed the duplicate furniture, particularly the sofa stacked in the hallway, and the extra bed, chairs and dining room table. Too bad Elaine was at a women's issues conference in Australia, so that wouldn't happen until she got back.

For the moment, Alvin and I perched on the sofa, tuning out the chaos around us and ogling an unassuming cardboard box, about the size of a toaster oven, which it had once contained. Gussie, the large and fragrant dog, who is with me temporarily until Alvin or one of the other Fergusons arranges a permanent home for him, was sitting on the floor between us. Mrs. Parnell's little calico cat, also a long-term visitor, paraded on the back of the sofa, her long, expressive tail swishing our necks. It would have been quite the homey scene if we hadn't both been so wrecked.

"Go ahead, open it," I said.

"You open it."

"Fine." I scissored through the duct tape sealing the box and pried back the flaps. I lifted out a couple of smaller boxes, shoeboxes as it turned out. None of the boxes was big enough to contain Mrs. Parnell's laptop. "She sent you her shoes?"

Alvin lifted out the Rockport box from the top and lifted the lid. "Look at that. Letters. They're all tied up in bundles."

"Hey, they're still in their envelopes. Are they to Mrs. Parnell?"

Alvin snatched one of the bundles and ruffled through it. "Stop breathing down my neck. These are addressed to Miss Violet Wilkinson. Looks like a woman's writing."

"1940," I said. "That's incredible. The paper's all brown. And three cent stamps. Can you believe that?"

"I like that King. He looks so sad," Alvin said.

"This batch is from 1944," I said. "Different writing. Hang on, some are from 1945, too. And even later. Look, there's a few from the fifties."

"These here are typed," Alvin said.

Alvin opened another box. "These are 1942 and 1943. You can sure squeeze a lot of letters in one box."

"She kept these letters for more than sixty years," I said. "Why would she hide them now?"

"You think it's connected with this dead man she was talking about?"

"Maybe something in these letters caused her to lose her grip."

"She didn't lose her grip, Camilla. Remember what the doctor said?"

"I'm just trying to understand."

"Don't forget her place was tossed, and we did see that guy in the hallway."

"We don't know for sure that he's really connected. Anyway, we shouldn't get distracted. There's one box left. It looks like the one my Sorels came in. Remember when Mrs. P. gave me those boots? They probably saved my life."

"That's just one of about a million things she did for you," Alvin said as he lifted the lid of the Sorel box. Silver frames gleamed at us. The photos were intact. Alvin lifted the first one out of the box, then the others and set them on the coffee table. Clusters of people in military uniforms stared back at us. There were two shots of the late Major Walter Parnell, and one of Mrs. P. in her CWAC uniform.

"Violet told me those uniforms were considered really swell at the time."

I said, "Mr. Parnell wasn't bad looking, in an intense way. I'm not sure how I feel about the mustache."

"He sure doesn't look like a barrel of laughs," Alvin said.

"Who are these people?"

"I've never seen this one before. This picture is not even framed." Alvin sounded slightly miffed, as though Mrs. P. had been keeping secrets from him.

In the black and white photo, three young men and three girls were clustered around a leafy oak tree in front of a brick house. By the look of their clothing, it was late nineteen thirties or early forties, summer. There were a couple more taken on the same day, same people.

I squinted at the images. "I'd say it's small-town Ontario. See the pale brick on those buildings?"

Alvin discreetly wiped his eye behind the cat's-eye glasses. "Hmmm. Violet looks great, doesn't she? I love the dress."

"Is that …? Oh my God, she does. She looks…"

"Full of beans," Alvin said.

"I was going to say almost beautiful. And full of beans too, now that you mention it."

"She had a great figure. And the hair is definitely retro."

I said, "How the hell did they do those roll things? It must have been a lot of work."

"You know what, Camilla? Even though those other two girls are really pretty, the one you would notice and remember is Violet."

"Who are they? She never mentioned them to me."

"Me neither," Alvin said, letting the miffedness creep into his voice again. "The little blonde looks like she could have been in movies, musical comedies. Get a load of the legs. I can see her dancing."

"You're right."

"The brunette is sort of regal. She looks like she'd be keeping everyone in line. You know the expression, 'sucking lemons'?"

"Maybe the sun's just in her eyes. Get a load of those boys. They're so debonair," I said. "The tall dark guy with the spiky hair has a bit of a lantern jaw, not like the chiselled chins on the fair-haired guys. They look like heroes."

"Or old movie stars, not smalltown boys. I love the trousers. You think they could get any higher on the waist? I can't believe dudes that age would dress like that. You can tell they're cool, though. It's all in the body language." Alvin flipped the photo over. "It just gives a date. June 24, 1940."

"What else do we have?"

"I can't believe Violet had these photos and never mentioned them. I love old photos. She knows that. Why wouldn't she ever show them to me?"

"Maybe she didn't want to look back to that era."

"The letters might give us a clue."

"We can't read Mrs. Parnell's personal letters," I gasped.

"She'd understand."

"I would not understand if you found *my* letters and took it upon yourself to read them."

Alvin's eyes glittered. "Do you have a secret stash of letters, Camilla?"

"Don't change the subject. These letters are private."

"You don't know that they're private if you haven't read them," Alvin said.

"You'll have to do better than that, Alvin."

"We have to."

"I just had a thought."

"What?" Alvin said suspiciously.

"We didn't check her computer."

"I thought you didn't want to violate her privacy."

"She probably has an address book in it."

"Isn't that just as intrusive as reading these letters?"

I ignored the comment. "These letters are more than sixty years old. Mrs. P. is on that computer every day. I don't know why we didn't go through that earlier. We must have been punch-drunk. Let's have a look at what she's been doing. Oh, don't sulk, Alvin."

"I'm not sulking. Why do you turn everything into an argument?"

"We can check them in the morning. I can hardly keep my eyes open, and you must be bushed too. One of us should stay at Mrs. P.'s place, in case she shows up."

"I'll go over and crash on the sofa. I'll take the letters with me," Alvin said.

"Better leave them here, just in case our visitor comes back. And Alvin?"

"What now?"

"Be careful."

England
March 21, 1942

Dear Miss Wilkinson,

I am very sorry if I have offended you. I did not realize that you were engaged to Sgt. Harrison Jones. I will, of course, cease writing to you immediately.

I certainly do hope that you and Sgt. Jones will be very happy and that he realizes that he is indeed a fortunate man.

Should we meet again, I do hope that your engagement would not preclude a discussion of music. I would like to change your mind about those Russian composers.

Sincerely,

Walter Parnell

Five

Lester and Pierre screamed in outrage when I arrived at Mrs. Parnell's on the morning of November 12. I chose not to comment that Alvin looked exhausted. He'd have to point out that I looked even worse. There was a good reason for that. I hadn't been able to sleep and had spent the time between three and five a.m. driving up and down the streets of Ottawa, hoping to catch sight of Mrs. P.'s Volvo.

"Not a word from her." Alvin said.

"Any luck with the computer?" I said.

"I've been through everything. Every file, every directory."

"Did you try her e-mail inbox?"

He rolled his bleary eyes and headed back to the computer. "Well, of course I did. It's the first place I looked, and I've kept checking every half hour, in case she gets a message. It's empty, except for today's spam. But come over here. I want to show you her sent mail folder."

"Good thinking."

I peered over his shoulder as he clicked on the keys.

"Take a look at that," he said, pointing.

"It's empty. That's weird," I said. "Didn't she send you stuff all the time?"

"She did. Maybe she liked to keep her system nice and

clean. See? The deleted mail is empty too. She probably set it to empty automatically. Don't breathe down my neck, please."

"No need to be peevish, Alvin. What now?" I pulled over a chair and sat far enough away to keep Alvin happy.

He said, still peevishly, "Why don't we read the letters?"

"You know I don't feel comfortable about reading them. They're a last resort. Maybe you should feed the birds."

Alvin sniffed. "How about you do it?"

"Because they're the spawn of the devil. Have you forgotten what happened the last time? You do it."

"In a minute. I forgot to check and see what websites Violet may have visited lately."

I resisted the urge to jump up and lean over his shoulder.

"Hey, here's something. It's a website on war graves. She was in there yesterday."

"What else did she visit recently?"

"Some veteran's stuff, sites on Canadian army regiments."

"Not too surprising around Remembrance Day."

Alvin jumped to his feet, rattling the computer table and shouting, "Jackpot."

"What? What?"

"Expedia.ca and Travelocity."

"You're kidding. Travel sites? When was she checking those?"

"Yesterday."

"Must have been after she left the hospital. That probably indicates her mind was clear. Oh, unless she was researching before the ceremonies."

Alvin nodded absently. "And take a look at this site—it has to do with the Italian campaign. Whoa, Violet's been busy."

"Back to the travel one. Does she have a folder for travel?"

"I thought of that earlier. She doesn't seem to use folders. There's nothing about a booking anywhere. It's like she didn't want anyone to know what she was doing. She deliberately wiped out her sent e-mail messages and forgot about the history feature of her web searches."

"Let's concentrate. We'll figure out what else there could be. What about the printer?" I said.

"Good thinking."

I got up and leaned over the printer. "Nothing in the tray. If she printed something, she must have taken it with her."

"The red light's on. Maybe there's a printer jam."

I flipped open the printer lid. "I hate printer jams, although I'm prepared to love this one, because something's stuck there."

"Just wait. This is a delicate operation. You know what you're like with equipment, Camilla. You don't want to break the printer."

"Sheesh. You sound like my sisters."

"Just don't rip the paper."

There was a slight tearing sound. "Fine, you do it," I said.

Alvin has weird, long, artistic fingers, perfect for disengaging paper. He flattened the scrunched sheet, getting plenty of ink on those artistic hands and on Mrs. Parnell's sleek computer desk.

"What? What does it say? Hurry up."

He said. "It's part of a travel itinerary. That means she really did plan a trip."

"A trip? Where to?" I asked.

"It doesn't say. It's just the top of the last page. Part of the itinerary number is there. Not enough to read."

"When you book online, they send you all kinds of confirmation e-mails."

Alvin said, "That must be why she deleted everything. She didn't want anyone to know where she was going."

"Exactly. Including us. She knows we'd check."

"That's bad." Alvin said. "The only reason we know anything is because of this paper jam."

"Hey, wait a minute. It couldn't be an old one, could it? Just stuck in there?"

"No way. Violet used that printer all the time. She would have cleared the jam the minute it happened. She's really good with equipment. She believes in keeping her stuff in top condition. She probably wouldn't have gotten ink all over her hands either."

"Wait a minute. Forget the computer. Let's check her paper recycling and the garbage."

Alvin loped into the kitchen while I took the bedroom and bath. "Empty," he called out.

"These are too. She did that on purpose, Alvin."

He said, "She's pretty crafty. She knows us."

"She's being strategic." I didn't suggest that someone else might have emptied them. I wanted Alvin to be calm, since I wasn't.

"Well, we can play that strategic game, too," Alvin sniffed.

"Exactly. She may be determined to give us the slip, but we can't let her get away with that."

"We're on the case," Alvin said.

I found myself pacing. "Okay. Where is she going to go? And when?"

Alvin paced alongside me, his ponytail flicking from side to side. "Or has she already gone?"

"No point in contacting the online booking service. They won't give out that kind of information. Too bad we don't have the entire itinerary number."

"The cops could find out. They must be able to get a warrant for something like that."

"We haven't had much luck with the police so far. I suppose it's worth a call anyway. We'll cross that bridge later. We have to go."

"Go where?" Alvin stopped in his tracks.

"To the airport. She might just be sitting there now."

*   *   *

I dropped Alvin off near the passenger exit and watched as he loped past the glass door of the garage and across the street to the airport entrance. I inched through the parking lot until I spotted the Volvo tucked almost out of sight behind a pillar near the exit. I whipped my Acura into a parking spot and got out. I put my hand on the hood of the Volvo. Cold. Our bird had flown.

Half an hour later, Alvin and I were sure of one thing. Mrs. Parnell was not in the ladies' rooms. Not in the waiting rooms. Not in the coffee shops, unless she'd gone through security. Even though we'd already called the police to report finding Mrs. P.'s Volvo, we were less than a hit with security. Even with all our talk of heart attacks, the ticket agents looked at us with suspicion when we described Mrs. Parnell. The officer made a note of our names and our alleged problem and made a phone call. No way were we getting through those gates to the other side.

"You know, Alvin," I said, as we headed home, "We're going to need a good picture of her."

*   *   *

"I don't think it's quite so necessary for people to be so incredibly rude," Alvin said, as we splashed through the latest downpour and back into my house, which I still couldn't think of as home. "We're not trying to violate anyone's privacy. We're trying to make sure Violet is all right. I thought they were supposed to be public servants."

"Nothing like an official with a rulebook to make you realize your place in society," I said. "There was no way to get past security without a boarding pass. Oh, shit. How dumb was I?"

"Sometimes you're pretty…I mean, why?" Alvin said.

"Why didn't I just buy a ticket?"

"To where?"

"To anywhere."

"You didn't want to go anywhere… oh, right, I get it. With a ticket, you can get through security. Why didn't you?"

"Because I just thought of it now."

Gussie turned circles with excitement as he greeted us. No wonder. I figured he'd missed a walk or two in all the confusion. I grabbed his leash and my hooded rain jacket and we headed out, leaving Alvin to come up with a next step.

When we returned a short time later, a pot of hot orange pekoe was waiting, Mrs. Parnell's little cat had been fed, and a selection of dog treats was laid out for Gussie. By the time I got rid of my wet rain gear and dried Gussie's giant paws and sodden undercarriage, Alvin was fussing over the rumpled itinerary, trying to extract some information.

"I have to do something," he said. "It's not like the so-called police have offered any help. Nor has anybody else."

"We need more bodies working on this. I've been trying to think who could help us: everyone's out of town."

"What about that awful Mountie?"

"Merv. He's on an international assignment, guarding some politico. Hush-hush."

"P. J. then. He's a reporter. Maybe he can get us something in the paper."

"He probably could, but P.J.'s in the States doing a follow-up feature on the U.S. election. I can't even reach him. I left a message with the news desk. They should get back to us."

Alvin said, "Elaine Ekstein? She's always willing to help us.

She's a mover and a shaker. And she's fearless."

"Elaine's in Australia. And Robin's away at a wedding in Edmonton. That wipes out my friends."

"Maybe the other cop, Leonard Mombourquette."

"He took some additional leave without pay and went to Australia too."

Alvin said, "Australia? I knew there was something between those two."

I shuddered. "Don't hallucinate, Alvin. It's just a coincidence. That would be too bizarre to contemplate."

"So we're SOL?"

"We have to rely on each other. Nobody wants to be in Ottawa in November. Of course, there's always my family."

"Let's not go there. They haven't been much help so far, even Conn. That reminds me, you got voicemail," he said. "I didn't know your code."

"Just as well," I snapped. "Voicemail is personal."

"What are you talking about? We just checked out Violet's voicemail, and her computer, and that's personal."

"I'm not an eighty-three year old missing woman, so you don't get to listen to my messages." I should have said "any more". For most of the time Alvin has been "working" for me, my messages have been neither private nor interesting, and Alvin has heard them, and frequently failed to pass them along. That was then. Now, Ray Deveau's current vacation fantasy was emphatically none of Alvin's business. I picked up the receiver, tapped in the code and listened. Alexa and Edwina had left snappish remarks requiring urgent callbacks. I pressed delete.

Ray had left a very warm message, definitely not for Alvin's ears. I pressed 9 to save. I could listen to it again, a couple of times, at a better time.

"Any luck?" Alvin interrupted.

"Just my sisters," I said, lying nicely. "You know what they're like."

The next message took me by surprise. I fumbled my tea cup, and the orange pekoe splattered my clothes.

"Holy shit. Who is it?" Alvin said.

"Ms. MacPhee? Violet Parnell here. By the time you get this, I will be off and away. Please do not come looking for me. I am sorry to have shaken you off in the hospital. However, there is a matter I urgently need to take care of. I realize it's all terribly melodramatic, and I beg your indulgence. In the meantime, I would appreciate it if you and Young Ferguson would look in on Lester and Pierre and see that they are taken care of. You know where the bird food is. They do enjoy watching a bit of television from time to time. Nature programs. Nothing with cats. Thank you for assisting me with this. I will make everything clear upon my return."

I flopped into the chair and pressed "1" to repeat the message. I pressed the receiver to Alvin's ear.

"Listen to this, Alvin."

Alvin listened and paced.

"What do you think?" I said, afterwards.

"She sounds great. Like her regular self." Behind the glasses, Alvin's eyes shone.

"Yes," I said. "She's perfectly lucid and logical. Except for one hitch: she's an eighty-three year old woman at risk for cardiac arrest. She knows she's taking a risk. She's intelligent and capable, and yet she lit out of here and won't tell us where to. Or why. There's definitely something wrong with that."

"It's great news, Camilla. She's alive! She's okay. Maybe it is none of our business," Alvin said.

"It's our business, all right. There's something wrong, or why wouldn't she tell us what it is, so that we wouldn't worry?"

"She said she had to clear up a matter."

"And you tell me what happens with the three of us when we have to clear up a so-called matter?"

"We help each other. We work together. Okay, I get your drift."

"We drop everything, and we do what we have to to help the other person."

Alvin scratched his head. "She thinks we want to stop her. Why would we do that?"

"I don't know. She must have some compelling reason to keep us out of it."

"She's all about comradeship. She might be wanting to protect us. Keep us from being upset."

"I've thought of that. If she wants to protect us, then logically, there must be something we need to be protected from."

Alvin paled. "If we need to be protected, then it must be dangerous, and if it's dangerous, if we're not involved, then who's going to protect Violet?"

"Exactly. There is another possibility."

"What?"

"Maybe there's someone she wants to protect."

"You just said that. Oh, you mean, aside from us."

"Yes."

"Who could that be? Aside from us and your family, especially your father, and maybe the super, who does she see?"

"No one. We're it. Except, what's new lately?"

"Lord thundering Jesus. This dead guy!"

"You got it, Alvin."

"So how do we go about finding him?"

"I have no goddam idea."

*   *   *

73

"Ray?"

"Hmmm?"

I have to admit, I got a little tingle at the way he said "hmmm". This was hardly the right time for tingling.

"Thanks for your call. Sorry to bug you at work. I need to know if you can find out what plane someone took to go somewhere."

"As queries go, Camilla, that's not the clearest I've ever heard. Try again."

"Mrs. P. has taken off."

"You mean she hasn't turned up yet?"

"She called."

"Well, that's good."

"I don't think so. We believe she's involved in something dangerous. We have no idea where she went. We located her Volvo at the airport. If we could find out what plane she was on, we'd have a clue about her destination and it might save time."

"Dangerous?" A bit of his cop persona sneaked into his voice.

"We think maybe."

"If it's dangerous, you shouldn't get involved. Does the word concussion ring a bell?"

No point in getting him ticked off. "We'd make sure the police were informed, of course."

"Promise me you won't do anything foolhardy?"

"Don't be silly, of course, I won't. So can you find out about the plane?"

"I'll see what I can do. I'm surprised the Ottawa guys wouldn't help you out there. Oh, never mind."

* * *

"We're doomed," Alvin said, looking up as I put the phone

74

down and walked back into my box-lined living room.

"Wrong attitude, Alvin. Keep positive. What do you think Mrs. P. would do?"

"I think she'd read those letters and see if there's anything there."

"I'm not so sure."

"Are you the same Camilla MacPhee who will break into people's apartments when it suits you?"

"Never mind, I always have my reasons. This seems so much more personal and, really, I can't see how it's going to do any good. They're sixty years old. These letters must be important to Mrs. P., or she wouldn't have kept them. I feel uncomfortable reading private letters. Maybe that's my own hang-up as a result of having the world's most intrusive family."

I did not mention that I had many letters from my late husband, Paul. I didn't ever want some snoop eyeballing those. Ever.

"I seem to remember you creeping through people's bedrooms while they were sleeping when *you* needed something," Alvin said. "That's pretty private."

"Listen to me, Alvin. Let's try not to squabble all the time. We need to work together to find out what's she's up to. We waste energy on bickering. We have to work as a team."

Alvin's nose seemed more pointed than usual. His Adam's apple bobbed. "We've always been like this. Anyway, it's not really squabbling. It's just standing our ground. All right, if we have to, we can stop. I suppose. I'll agree to watch my tongue if we can read the letters."

Well, that didn't go the way I'd wanted. I sat scowling on the box with my arms folded trying to find another route.

Alvin, on the other hand, was quite perky. "This has to do with the war. Remember those websites. Even though Violet always talks about the war, she never mentions her part in it, does she? I don't even know where she went."

"We know she was in the Canadian Women's Army Corps."

"Sure we know that. And we know she went overseas in 1941."

"She served in England. Working on trucks and things. She really enjoyed it, although she said it wasn't all that glamorous and exciting. Not like the guys who fought in Europe. She was proud to serve her country in her own small way, and it was a great adventure for a girl from small-town Ontario."

"Right, well, I didn't even get that much out of her. When she talked about the war, it was always Churchill or Montgomery or Patton. We don't know about the people in her life, not then, not now. And when we met her, there was no one. Not a relative, not a single friend. Right?"

I had to agree.

"See? We have no idea. These letters might tell us."

"Fine. We'll read the letters from her friends."

Alvin seemed satisfied with that. He was already riffling through the letters at high speed.

"You sort," I said, picking up the phone and dialling. "I'll call Conn and try to get some action going."

Alvin said, "Don't consider this squabbling—maybe you shouldn't tell him that you got the message from her saying that she's all right."

"Good point. I might forget to mention it."

"Hey look, this letter's from her husband. Captain Walter Parnell." Alvin whipped the letter out of the envelope.

"Not that one," I said, stopping mid-dial.

Conn, of course, was not at his desk. I left a message, not too snippy, and rejoined Alvin for damage control.

Darling Vi,

Not a day goes by that I don't think about you. I would be much easier in my mind if you would confine yourself to tamer activities. I have enough on my mind without imagining you in an upturned truck, pinned down by enemy fire. Of course, I have known you all my life, so I realize you are not the kind of girl to stay home and knit socks. That reminds me, Hazel sent me a pair of socks that gave me blisters and a box of fudge that was just like cement. Heaven help her husband, if she ever finds one.

Things are going as well as they can be here, given the circumstances. Can't complain. A lot of fine fellows haven't made it this far. I saw Perce when we were on leave. Sure wish it could have been you, instead. That fella sure has a way with the ladies. The English girls think he is the limit. Everyone loves a flyboy. They are all crazy about dancing, and he is something to watch on the dance floor. I can't imagine how we'll get him back home when this damn war's over. I imagine he'll set the world on fire. He's always been a lucky dog. You can keep the adventures, I think I might have seen more than enough of the world. I am looking forward to dancing with my own gal when we're together. I know you love to jitterbug, but I keep remembering those waltzes.

If I get back in one piece, I plan to stay on the ground. I got a letter from my Uncle Fred. He's promised me a place in his firm when I return. I am thinking I would like to try my hand at university, anyway. The government is promising to help out with education afterwards. I'd like your opinion on this, as it would mean a longer wait before we could be married. I sure don't want to wait much longer! Of course, we can keep dancing, even if it's just in our memories now.

With all my heart,

Your Harry

Six

N ot that one," I said.

"I'm just saying, Camilla. Calm yourself."

"What else have you got?"

"Fine. Here's one from friends. Some from a Miss Betty Connaught, some from Miss Hazel Fellows. They all have Xs and Os on the envelopes. I found a lot from Captain Walter Parnell. Some say Major Parnell. I wonder why she doesn't talk about him much. I think she really loved him a lot."

"He's dead, Alvin. She probably has just compartmentalized those memories because they're painful."

Alvin's head jerked. "Like you did with your husband?"

"Yes."

"Do you think he died in the war?"

"No, it was later. I know that."

"You don't suppose…?"

"Suppose what, Alvin? You can make a person crazy." I hate the wounded look he gets on his face. "Okay, I'm sorry," I said.

Alvin said, "I wanted to say, since she's talking about dead men, maybe her husband was the guy she was talking about? He was important, and he's dead."

"I don't think so. She would have said 'my husband'."

"Okay, look, here's another guy writing to her. Harrison Jones. Way to go, Violet."

"We'll stick with the girls, Alvin. Hang on, I have to answer the phone."

*　　*　　*

Conn McCracken uttered a small yet accusatory sigh. He said, "I do care about the situation. Be reasonable. It takes awhile."

"It's serious. I think you should turn up the burner."

"Do you have to be such a pain in the ass about everything? We *are* taking it seriously, even though we're out on a limb because we don't have medical confirmation that Mrs. Parnell is not perfectly capable of making an informed decision about where to travel."

"I told you she might go into full cardiac arrest, and did I mention she had troubles with a dead man?"

"Yeah, yeah. And you never exaggerate."

"I'm not exaggerating this time."

"No family member has contacted the police…"

"She doesn't have any family, you know that perfectly well. Alvin and I are like her family."

"Nor do we have a doctor indicating that something's wrong."

"You want a doctor to confirm it? I'll get you a doctor."

"Listen. This takes time. We have to contact the airlines one by one and ask them if she was on the flight. Usually the airlines cooperate, but there are issues."

"We're stuck here, Conn. We can't go any further without a clue about where she went."

"Frankly, I'm out on a limb Camilla, because I don't know for sure anything is really wrong with Mrs. Parnell."

"Well, I do. And Alvin does. We saw her. We heard her. Something is very wrong with our friend. Just because we don't know exactly what the problem is doesn't make it any less real."

"I understand, and that's why I'm doing what you ask. I'm helping you. I have a pretty good idea what she means to you and what she's done for you. So try not to piss me off. Just this once."

"How many airlines did you talk to?"

"Even though I have a full load of work, I personally contacted every airline that had a flight out of Ottawa last night."

"And?"

"So far, no luck."

"She wasn't on a flight?"

"Not so far. One of the airlines had a computer snag, and I'm waiting to hear back."

"Oh."

"When I hear, you'll hear. Count on it. Three or four hours."

"Thanks, Conn. I do know this was a big imposition."

Fine. Hang up. See if I care.

Dr. Hasheem was unavailable when I contacted the hospital. I left a message on his voicemail asking if plane trips to unknown destinations would be harmful to Mrs. Parnell. Like I didn't know the answer to that.

*   *   *

Alvin grinned in triumph when I put down the phone.

I met his grin with a frown. "No luck with the flight information."

"I've been lucky with the girlfriends' letters," Alvin said. "I don't think we have a big problem with private secrets or anything."

He held out a letter for me. "These two girls really wrote a lot, and she wrote back to them too. It's obvious that they know all about what she's doing in England."

"I guess people couldn't just pick up the phone and call long distance if they wanted a chat."

"Sounds like when she first went overseas, it came as a surprise to her girlfriends," Alvin said. He stood up to make room on the sofa. I settled in. Gussie and Mrs. Parnell's cat got as close as they could.

Alvin waved a letter in front of me. "This one's from Hazel. Just read it." I capitulated.

"That wasn't so bad, was it? You can't help smiling, can you?" Alvin said when I'd finished.

"She seems so full of fun."

"The other friend is more serious. I guess it takes all kinds," Alvin said.

I held out my hand. "Okay, fine, let's see the rest. The ones with Canadian postmarks."

Alvin said, "So we have Hazel who stayed in Chesterton and Betty Connaught who went to Toronto. There was a bit of competition for Violet's friendship, I think. The letters are pretty upbeat, even though they talk about people dying overseas. I can't imagine that. Violet's fiancé didn't die, although I feel like killing him."

"You read his letter?"

"It was an accident," Alvin said, radiating innocence.

Twenty minutes later, I had read enough of the letters to get a sense of Mrs. Parnell's life and friends. I had plenty to think about and lots of questions. I also had an idea.

I said. "I hate to say it, but I think you were right. Conn may not come up with anything, but at least we have the names of people who knew her and cared about her. Maybe the men didn't come back. The women were in Canada. Why don't we try to track them down?"

Alvin shot across the room to the Justice for Victims computer in its makeshift home on the dining table. "Canada411! My fave."

"Chances are that the women have changed their names; it's still worth a try. They'd be in their eighties. I wonder if they're alive, and if they are, how they'd react."

"Violet's in her eighties. If you called her about something like this, what would she do?"

"She'd help. And she'd offer intelligent suggestions," I said. "And strategic options."

Alvin's fingers danced on the keyboard. "No luck with Hazel Fellows anywhere in Ontario. "I'm on to Betty. That's too bad, there's no Betty Connaught. Or wait a minute, no, not even a B. Connaught."

"Try Elizabeth," I said. "She might not still be Betty."

"I'm trying E. Connaught, anywhere in Ontario. They might already be in retirement homes, or even nursing homes."

I said, "Maybe their married names will show up in the letters. Oh come on, Gussie. It can't be time to go out again."

"My nose tells me it is," Alvin said.

When I returned, wiping off Gussie's paws and belly yet again, Alvin was doing a sprightly jig. His ponytail danced. If the light had been brighter, his nine visible earrings would have twinkled.

"What did you get, Alvin?"

"It's a list of E. Connaughts in Ontario. I printed it out from Canada411. There are none in Chesterton, so this is what we've got. You want to call them while I keep googling the rest?"

"Yup."

I settled by the phone with a pen and the list. It's surprising how rude people can be when they get a call from someone they don't know. Is this what telemarketers have done to our society? I scratched through name after name. I may have written a few rude words in the margin of the list. All things come to an end. Thank heavens for name number nineteen. E.M. Connaught, conveniently located right in Ottawa.

"Hello," I said, tentatively. "May I speak to Elizabeth Connaught, please?"

"This is she."

"My name is Camilla MacPhee, and I'm a friend of Violet Parnell's, and I am trying to reach some of her…"

"Violet Parnell? You must have a wrong number. I am not acquainted with…oh, of course, Violet Wilkinson. I never think of her as Violet Parnell. She was always just Violet to us."

"That's the one," I said.

Alvin's hands poised on the keyboard. His eyebrows lifted in hope.

"We were great friends in school back in Chesterton. I don't know how good a friend I've been since. I haven't even seen Vi since the forties."

"You knew her during the war, Ms. Connaught?"

"Call me Betty, dear. I must ask, since this call comes out of the blue, is everything all right with Violet?"

"Something strange happened yesterday, and it seems to have something to do with the war, although we don't know what. Do you mind helping us out?"

"How can I help?"

"I'm not really sure. Which probably sounds stupid. The point is she seems to have left town without telling any of us, although she should be in the hospital. It's not like her at all. You are one of the few names we have from her past, so I was hoping she might have contacted you after yesterday. She was talking about seeing dead men."

"I'd have been most surprised if Violet called me after all these years. I would have been thrilled to hear from her. You said she left town without telling you. I'm sorry, dear, I don't know about hallucinations. I do know wandering off is one of the big signs of Alzheimer's. Is she still compos mentis?"

"Her mind is in better shape than mine."

"That's a relief. It would be a shame to have that happen to her, of all people. She was so clever."

"She still is, believe me. She had some kind of cardiac event, and we are worried it might get worse without medical help."

"At our age, these things happen. The last I heard, she married a Captain Walter Parnell and took up residence here in Ottawa. Poor Violet."

"I think she likes it here," I said.

"Yes, it's a lovely city. I enjoy it here very much, although it would have been much too prim and proper for Violet back in the fifties. I meant 'poor Violet' for marrying Walter. That came as a surprise. Of course, he died, not long after."

"Wasn't he good to her?"

"Who?" Alvin said.

"Shh," I hissed.

"I beg your pardon?" Betty said.

"Not you, Ms. Connaught."

"Betty."

"Right. Betty. It's just someone on this end who is trying to interrupt. Another of Mrs. Parnell's friends. He has a low frustration point."

"Ah. How nice that Violet has such good friends. Now that I am no longer an educator, I suppose sometimes a low frustration point isn't all bad."

"Was there a problem with Major Parnell?" I said, not wishing to be distracted by Betty's career in education.

"No. He was a gentleman always. Intelligent, kind."

"Fun?" I said.

"Fun? No dear. No one ever could have accused Walter Parnell of being fun. Or even having fun, now that I think of it."

"She *married* him."

"She did. But of course, he wouldn't have been her first choice, dear." Betty's voice sank to a whisper.

"Right," I said.

"You could have knocked me over with a feather when I heard. Vi was the smartest, bravest, most adventurous girl I ever met. But that's war for you. People make bad decisions. Everyone feels there might not be a tomorrow. And for many, there wasn't."

I didn't want to get sidetracked. "Have you heard from her lately?"

"No, not for years. You'll forgive me for saying so, dear, but Violet turned into quite a bitter person after her husband died. She certainly wasn't lucky in love. I don't believe she stayed in touch with anyone."

My mind switched to Mrs. P. when I first met her. She'd been nosy, argumentative, bitter and without friends, except for the super.

Betty cleared her throat. "You'll have to excuse me. My nephew has just arrived. He makes such a fuss if I'm the slightest bit behind schedule. Do yourself a favour, dear, and hang on to your driver's license as long as you can. Give me your number, and I'll call you back later."

I spelled my name, repeated my number twice and threw in my cell for good measure. "Please call back," I said. "I'd like you to think about who the dead man might have been."

Betty said, "He could have been anybody. At our age, dear, almost all of the men are dead. Certainly anyone that Vi and I knew. I will think about it. *Oh, stop fussing, I said I'm coming.* The doctor can wait two minutes for me for once. I've waited months to see him."

"Betty, one thing quickly, since we're already keeping the doctor waiting. Tell me about Mrs. Parnell's friend, Hazel Fellows. We couldn't find any trace of her."

"Oh, *Hazel.* Heavens. I suppose you might talk to her,

although she's a bit of a scatterbrain. She was always a terrible gossip, and I shouldn't say this, but she wasn't always the most truthful person. Take everything she says with a grain of salt. I wouldn't like you to waste your time, dear."

"We'll keep that in mind."

"She brought Violet some grief. They had a serious falling out to do with Harrison Jones, I believe. I imagine Violet told you about him."

"Maybe not everything." Or anything.

"Harry was Violet's high school sweetheart. Everyone thought they would marry when he returned. They seemed so suited to each other."

"And did Hazel go out with him?"

"No, no, Harry was much too fine a fellow for Hazel. She just wrote some things to him when he was overseas and ruined everything for Violet. He broke off the engagement. I wouldn't be surprised if that contributed to Violet pulling away from all her old friends. It won't be easy finding Hazel with all those husbands she's had. Married money each time, I imagine. I've lost track of her last names."

"And you have no idea where she might be?"

"None. We really had nothing in common except for growing up in the same town."

"Any idea who might know?"

"I don't want to disappoint you; she may not even be alive. She was such a wild and silly creature. I can't imagine her looking after herself too well."

"If you can suggest anyone else who might help, we'd really appreciate it, Betty."

"I will do my best, dear. I am *coming*," she said. "Young people are so impatient." I was glad I wasn't on the receiving end of that particular tone. "Please keep me informed about

Violet. I'll get in touch with you later. Goodbye."

"We're in your debt," I said to the dial tone.

Alvin gripped my arm. "What's happening?"

"Nothing. No damn luck at all."

"Oh. Well, at least you don't have to go through the letters again, Camilla. I googled Hazel Fellows and found a reference to Hazel Fellows Stiles Murphy Thurlow. In this article about balcony gardens."

"Great."

"I couldn't find the article."

"Damn."

"Have faith, Camilla. I found a H.S.M. Thurlow in Canada411, in Kingston. Here's the number. And this time, since we're a team, let me know what the person is saying." He held out the number.

I dialled and stood waiting, tapping my foot. "This whole thing is very frustrating. No answer, of course."

After a beep, a chirpy, happy voice said that Hazel would be back soon, and please leave a message.

"Well, why didn't you leave a message?"

"Because I am going to drive down there and find her. She's a gossip and a liar, with a tendency to change her name. She's still our best hope, because, face it, we don't have a goddam other thing to go on. I want to be able to look her straight in the eye."

"She's not home."

"She'll have to come back sometime. Anyway, I'm going crazy here. It's not like I have anything better to do. Conn said it would take a while. If her letters are anything to go by, I think I'm going to learn plenty from Miss Hazel Fellows."

"I'm coming with you."

"I have a job for you. Call forward Mrs. P.'s phone to your cell. You have Mrs. P.'s key. Head back over to the apartment. *You* weren't kicked out of the building, and most of the people on the sixteenth floor should recognize you after all these years. Talk to as many as you can. Find out if anyone saw her leave, or saw her talking to anybody. Whatever you can squeeze out of them will be good."

Alvin's leather shoulders slumped.

"Don't sulk, Alvin. You'll get wrinkles. This is really important. Talk to the Super. He doesn't have a problem with you. They've got cameras all over the building. Ask him what happens to the surveillance tapes in the building."

"That's brilliant, Camilla. They have cameras everywhere, the stairwells. And the garage. I remember you always used to make faces at them."

"Try to get a look at that guy who passed us in the hall. You might find something else relevant. I hoped they're not dopey enough to just keep the tapes on a twenty-four hour loop or something. You can see why you want to get over there soon. We don't know even when she left."

"The camera could pin that down."

"Good thinking. See if you can get the Super to hand over the tapes."

"You think he'd do that?"

"No, but it's worth a try. We have to get them somehow."

Alvin said. "Nudge nudge wink wink."

"I'm not suggesting anything illegal. Just making the point that we need those tapes. I'm heading out fast. I'll make sure Conn has my cell number. But just in case…"

"I know. Answer the phone. And take notes."

*   *   *

It's a nice enough drive from Ottawa to Kingston if you like the 401, with its big honking transports, and if chunks of

Canadian shield are your thing. Despite my coffee cravings, I didn't let myself stop at Tim Hortons, and kept a steady 135 klics all the way. Luck was with me, and I saw no sign of the OPP I hit downtown Kingston in well under two hours.

The address I had for Hazel of the many names turned out to be an elegant condo on the waterfront. Large windows and balconies faced a million dollar view of Lake Ontario. I did not have a unit number, the sole shortcoming of Canada411.

Never mind. Everyone knew who Hazel was. Soon I was lifting the brass knocker on unit ten.

Perhaps my luck was turning.

Hazel Fellows Stiles Murphy Thurlow answered her door. She was tiny, with the features of a china doll and soft apricot curls. She held an immense fluffy white cat, which didn't seem too pleased to be confined. She'd kept her trim figure, and the stretchy pale turquoise yoga suit with the white stripe down the sides showed her to advantage. It was hard to believe she was the same age as Mrs. P. She'd opened the door with such a look of expectation on her round pretty face that I felt a stab of distress. I managed a smile. The cat looked at me with contempt. I also positioned myself so that if she tried to close the door, my foot would be in it.

"Of course, I remember Vi. Like it was yesterday." The pretty round face fell. "That's the problem. I remember all the yesterdays perfectly. A heck of a lot better than I can remember the todays. Or the real yesterday, meaning Thursday. No matter what, I don't think I could ever forget Vi. Good grief, now what did you say your name was?"

I hadn't. "Camilla MacPhee. I am a very good friend of hers."

"You're lucky then," she said, with tears in her large blue eyes.

I stepped into the condo unit and found myself staring past the furnishings. The window revealed the vast expanse of Lake Ontario. Spectacular didn't come close to describing it. Of course, I hadn't driven like a bat out of hell to stare at the scenery. The room had a Florida feel, peach walls, turquoise and pale peach furniture with overstuffed cushions, the kind you sink into and never want to leave. Three soft, unremarkable framed prints covered the walls. The cat went nicely with the colour-scheme, although it could easily be missed in the white-pile wall-to-wall carpet. I pegged the decor at 1990. That had obviously been a good year for Hazel. It had been for me too.

Despite the summery decor, there was a fire in the fireplace. I've always wanted a fireplace, and this pale-cream surround, mantle and raised hearthstone seemed perfect. I wondered how Ray would look building a fire in it.

I shook my head. I had business to accomplish, and I was being distracted. Mrs. Parnell would have told me not to lose sight of my target. I kept that in mind as I made myself comfortable. I glanced at the cluster of about two-dozen silver-framed photos, crowding the glass top of the console behind the sofa.

The dominant feature was silver-haired men, although one bald gentleman beamed in a photo with a slightly younger Hazel. Three smiling couples in late middle-age. Two beautiful blonde girls smiled out in wedding pictures, a pair of babies stared at the camera in another shot. They were held by the same girls looking a few years older.

Hazel beamed. "My husbands. They were just grand, all three of them. These are my first husband's children. This one's Val. She lives nearby, and she's awfully good to me. Well, a bit of a mother hen, when you get right down to it. You'd think I was a child. I might be eighty-three, but I still like my independence. You never know when romance will strike. And these gorgeous gals are my second husband's children and *their* children. And the new babies, aren't they the cutest? I am blessed. The kids all treat me like a queen."

"I think they're lucky to have you."

She clapped her hands together. "What a nice thing to say, sweetie. I like you. Let's have G & Ts! It's late enough."

"Not for me, thanks, I have a long drive ahead. If you don't mind answering a few questions, that would be helpful. I'm sure you're busy, and I don't want to take too much of your time." My strategy was, get in, get info, get going, get home, and get some action out of the cops.

"I'd offer you coffee or tea, although I'm not supposed to plug the kettle in, just in case I forget it. The nice thing about gin. You can drink it and not burn the place down."

"You have one then. I'll watch the kettle for me if you want," I said.

"Thank you, dear. I did buy one of those that shut off automatically. I just felt like company."

"I'll keep your G & T company in spirit, so to speak."

Hazel might have had memory failures, but she hadn't lost her touch with perfect buttery homemade shortbread, or with the mixing of G & Ts, judging by the taste of the cookies and the look of her drink.

When we finally settled down, I took a good look at her. She could have passed for sixty. My sisters would have known if a cosmetic surgeon had helped with that. My guess was that her beautiful bone structure, crisp cheekbones, still clear jawline and lovely peachy skin were just good genes. And maybe, judging from the laughlines, knowing how to have a good time.

"What can I tell you, sweetie?"

"Have you heard from Mrs. Parnell lately?"

"Who?"

"I meant Vi."

"Right. Mrs. Parnell. Poor Walter Parnell. Poor Vi." Hazel got a faraway look in her eyes. "So sad."

It wasn't the time for yet another critique of the man Mrs.

P. had chosen to spend her life with, so I said, "Have you heard from her? A phone call?"

"No. Well, I don't think so." Her small shoulders sagged in her pretty sweater. "You know what they say? They say old age is not for sissies. For heaven's sake, what am I talking about? I have waited for so long to hear from Vi, I couldn't forget that. Ever!"

"Right."

"I've never been a sissy, you know. I've been frivolous, but I'm no coward. I was never afraid to go after what I wanted. And now, it looks like I'll have to leave my lovely home one of these days because they're all afraid I'll burn it down. Or drown in the bathtub. I don't really want to end up in a warehouse with a bunch of decaying old corpses, you know. I've had a fun life; I'd like to go out on a high."

I raised my coffee cup. "I'm with you there, Hazel."

"Here's to living life, Camilla." She raised the G & T.

"And your friend, Vi, lives life to the fullest too. We're just afraid that something has…"

"Who's we, sweetie?"

"My assistant, Alvin Ferguson, and I. He was very keen to meet you, but he's busy checking around Ottawa for Mrs. Parnell."

"Nice that she has friends who are so interested in her. I remember hearing that, after Walter died, she kind of kept to herself. That would have been a shame."

"Were you in touch with her then?"

She turned and stared through the window at the icy expanse of water. "I have to tell the truth. Vi and I had an awful falling out during the war, and we never got together again. I never met Walter. I just heard about him from other people. Even though Vi was my best friend, I never laid eyes on her after she left Chesterton."

"You would have spoken to her if she'd contacted you?"

93

"With pleasure! I was heartbroken when she cut me dead. Sweetie, I've buried lovely husbands with less grief than that."

The woman was full of surprises.

"The names we have from the past are you and Betty Connaught."

"Betty! Is she still around? Don't take anything she says seriously. Still bitchy, I imagine."

I thanked heavens that Alvin wasn't there, or he would have prompted Hazel for details. Old animosities between these women weren't going to advance my agenda.

"What about men?" I said.

"Men? They're like buses. There's always another one coming along shortly."

"Specifically, the men you both knew during the war," I said when I'd stopped laughing.

"The ones who came back, you mean?"

"I don't know what I mean. Before she disappeared, Mrs. Parnell said, 'I'm terribly troubled by a dead man.' It seemed to be in a World War II context, and I have no idea of how to find out who she meant. That's why I came to you. Betty didn't know much."

"She wouldn't, would she? She wasn't exactly the type you'd confide in. Miss Goody-Two Shoes. Does she still look like she's been sucking prunes?"

"We just spoke on the phone. She seemed nice enough and willing to be helpful."

"Oh, sweetie, now I feel mean. I shouldn't have said those things about her. She was pretty hard to take, even when we were girls. So preachy. Betty was all about duty. Vi was all about adventure. I was all about fun. I guess we all got the lives we wanted."

"I guess," I said.

My cellphone pealed out "Desperado", proving once again that you should never leave Alvin alone with a piece of your equipment.

"Sorry," I said to Hazel, "I know this is rude. I have to take it in case they've found her."

"Go right ahead, sweetie. I'll just get you some more coffee. I see you've enjoyed the shortbread."

Was it my fault I'd missed a few meals? "Hello? That you, Conn?"

Alvin's voice crackled over the receiver. "Camilla? They've found out where Violet's gone."

I jumped to my feet and shouted, "That's wonderful."

"Not really. Better get your butt back here. Fast."

Dear Violet,

Thank you for your lovely letter of condolence. I knew you were a special friend to Perce, as so many people were. I cannot believe that he will not be coming back. It does not surprise me that he died a hero's death trying to save his comrades. He was a very special person, and the most wonderful brother to me and son to my mother. I am able to bury myself in my teaching duties. However, I do not believe that Mother will recover from this terrible blow. She is a shadow of herself and rarely leaves her room. I have had to resign my teaching position in Toronto and return home to care for her. Now with the war finally winding down, and an Allied victory likely, it seems so unfair that Perce will not be coming back. He had such big plans.

I am sorry to have to say this, Violet. You must send a note to Hazel to tell her not to spread rumours about you. She's writing to several boys overseas, saying you have lots of beaux, including a handsome officer. What nonsense! She knows perfectly well that you are engaged to Harrison Jones. What will his father think if he hears such rumours from some other boy's parents? The poor man is like a ghost anyway. Hazel has no idea of the value of a person's reputation. I know you will think Hazel means no harm, but I'm not so sure she's not motivated by jealousy. I gave her a good talking to, and I think you should mention it too! Where will she stop otherwise?

This has been such a cruel, cruel war in so many ways.

Sincerely,

Betty

Seven

Hazel stopped in the doorway, her pink lipstick framing a hesitant, hopeful smile. I gave her a little wave.

"Where is she now?" I said into the phone.

"That's why you have to get your butt back here."

"Please, Alvin, give me a straight answer. Did you tell her we've been worried sick?"

"We didn't talk to her. That's just it. If you'd let me…"

"Well, did Conn talk to her?"

"No. Let me finish. We're a team, remember?"

I slumped back onto the sofa. "Has something happened to her?"

"I don't know, because she's gone to friggin' Italy."

"Italy!"

"She flew to Milan from Toronto."

"You're kidding."

Hazel topped up her G & T and listened wide-eyed.

"Can they have someone meet the plane and make sure she's okay?"

"They can't."

"Why the hell not? Is that just more bureaucratic pigheadedness? I hope you told Conn to make sure they did that. You'd think after all these years in major crimes, he'd be able to make a sensible decision."

"Calm yourself. I'm the one who gets hysterical."

"Okay, I'm calm."

"They can't meet her, because the plane has already landed, and she's deplaned. They don't know where she is," Alvin wailed.

"I'm on my way."

Hazel stood up, wringing her tiny, manicured hands. "What on earth has happened to Vi?"

"She's hopped a plane to Italy. Milan to be exact. She's gotten off the plane, and no one knows where she is."

Hazel managed a nervous smile. "Is that all? You had me scared to death, sweetie. I'd like to do that myself. Italy's a civilized country, and Vi's a sharp cookie. What are you carrying on about?"

I shrugged into my rain jacket. "She's not acting like herself. The doctor is worried about a full-blown heart attack. She's going to have to watch to ensure she doesn't do herself any harm."

"Sweetie, when you get to our age, and you stare down the long corridor and see your future, you think about doing things while you can. Don't be a party pooper. Let Vi have her adventure."

"She can have all the adventures she wants. I just want her to be safe. And if she'd spoken directly to us, we wouldn't be so worried. Why would she go by herself? To Italy, of all places. All those hills, that can't be good for her."

"Vi has the right to make these decisions, even if you don't like them, or don't find them convenient. Tough bananas. Anyway, that's Vi. She joined the army without a moment's hesitation. We were all absolutely flabbergasted."

"This is more dangerous," I said.

"Hardly," Hazel laughed. "At that time, Italy really was dangerous. A lot of our boys didn't come back from there. Including our friend, Perce. Now every wobbly old senior like me can stagger around snapping pictures and shouting at each other. I should know. I've been three times. The worst that can happen is that street urchins steal your passport."

I hesitated at the door. "What about this Harrison?"

Her face clouded. "You mean Harry Jones? He was seriously wounded, it was terrible. He made it through the war though. He was something special, so handsome. Very fine character. Except, of course, he jilted Vi and stayed over there in England. It was a shame really. It was the only thing he ever did that wasn't just lovely. I suppose this English girl just knocked him off his feet. Love can take a person that way."

This love chat was another one of those digressions I didn't have time for. I had to get the hell home. "Is he still alive?"

"I don't know. I never stayed stay in touch with him." Hazel had two little pink spots on her cheeks. Guilt or G & Ts? No way to tell.

"I hope you're right about Mrs. Parnell. Some people think we're overreacting."

She gave my hand a squeeze. "Vi is lucky to have a friend like you. Let me know what happens. I might not be able to ever sleep again otherwise. I'll help out any way I can."

"I'll call you," I said. "Thanks for everything."

*　　*　　*

A word of advice: if you are clocked by the OPP doing 145 klics on Highway 416, don't count on the fact that your elderly friend has disappeared in Italy to get you out of a two hundred and ninety-five dollar fine. The OPP officer might take unnecessary pleasure in pointing out you've just lost four points to boot. He might even smirk at the insurance implications.

Life's like that.

I burst through the door of my house, to be welcomed joyously by Gussie and the little calico cat. If you're ever feeling down about yourself, I recommend borrowing pets. Alvin might also have welcomed his returning team member, but he was too busy pacing.

"It was bad enough when we didn't know where she was *in Canada,*" he bleated.

"The message light is blinking," I said.

"Well, you refused to give me your code," he sniffed. "Not really team spirit, Camilla."

I keyed in the code and heard Ray's voice.

Beep. "Ray here. How does Costa Rica sound? Beaches, rainforests. I can get us a good deal. Listen, about tracking your Mrs. Parnell, I spoke to your brother-in-law, Conn. He said he got the info from the airlines. You probably already know she's in Italy. They'll track her down. Let me know as soon as she turns up, and I'll book our trip. And if you have to wait until she's in better shape, I'm good with that too."

Beep. "Dr. Hasheem here. I got your message. In my opinion, it would be extremely risky for your grandmother to fly anywhere, let alone overseas. She must not be under stress. In fact, she should be monitored in a cardiac unit. I can't imagine you would even consider air travel for her in her condition."

* * *

Here's a practical suggestion: make sure you keep your passport up to date, in case you have to sprint for the first available flight to Italy. I had mine. Alvin didn't. That explained why he was fussing.

My heart was still thundering since hearing the price of my return ticket. I needed one that was flexible in case I had to turn right around. You have to be prepared to pay for flexibility. Never mind. You can't take it with you. The first flight I could get was the next afternoon. Air Canada, connecting through Frankfurt on Lufthansa. When I saw the price, I figured it had to be business class. At least I could stretch out overnight. Silly me.

"Look," I said to Alvin for the fifth time, after I'd swallowed hard and booked my ticket online. "It's really a good thing. We need you here to talk to witnesses, try to track down her colleagues in CWAC, keep the lines of communication open, walk the dog, feed the cat and change the television channel for the lovebirds. It's a team effort. If you had your passport, you could go Italy, and I would stay here." This was an outright lie. Alvin let it slide.

"They bit me when I fed them. Ingrates. Look at that." He held out a finger with two triangular bite marks.

"Ouch. I know how you feel—the ticket is going to take a chunk out of my savings when the credit card bill comes in." I had money in the bank, legally mine, even though I wasn't comfortable spending it, for complicated reasons. I didn't mention it, but at the rate I was spending, with no income coming in, I'd need a job that actually paid something one of these days. It didn't bear thinking about. I never really got the hang of taking orders from people. Legal aid work beckoned, if I wasn't careful. Of course, this wasn't the time to be careful. This was the time to find my friend. No expense spared.

"I have a real physical injury, not a bite in the bank book. At least you have an account," Alvin said, still extending his finger. "Fine, I'll do my best for the team. You go to Italy, you find out about Violet, and I'll stay here and be torn apart by small vicious birds."

And dragged though the rain and sleet by Gussie and

maybe smothered by the calico cat, I thought. Instead, I said kindly, "Looks like that finger might get infected. You're way better here with Medicare."

"I hate being in Violet's apartment. It makes me too sad."

"Tell you what, bring the lovebirds to my place, Alvin. You can keep up with the Justice for Victims incoming mail, and you don't have to keep running from your place to mine to Mrs. P.'s. You'll be freer."

He sniffed. It's an unappealing sound, but you get used to it if you're around Alvin long enough. "Maybe if I can get the house settled a bit. It needs to be organized and decorated, and I'm very good at that."

"Please don't touch a single thing. I truly, deeply mean that. I'm still reeling from the Mikado theme in your latest apartment. By the way, what did the tapes turn up?"

"What tapes?" Alvin said.

I kept my voice nice and teamlike. "The security tapes from her building. The ones you went over to see."

"Right. I'm just distracted because I'm being abandoned here to do all the joe jobs, while you go waltzing through the great monuments of Italy. I studied that stuff, you know. I should be there with Violet. It's going to be totally wasted on you."

"I'm sure you're right," I said. "And you *should* go. Start by getting your passport. When you do go to Italy, I hope it won't be under these circumstances. I won't be visiting galleries and cathedrals. I'll be searching for Mrs. P. Now let's think about those tapes. They could tell us about the guy with the box."

"First of all, there are no tapes."

"What do you mean, no tapes? They have all those cameras. What's that about?"

"It's some kind of digital recording system. Goes right to the computer."

"Okay, that's no big deal. I thought you meant there was no record of who entered the building."

"The Super said he had to get permission from the building's management before he could show them. That would take time."

"Did he now."

I whipped out my cellphone and dialled. I'd spent many years in that building, and I knew the super's number by heart. I also knew what a wuss he was.

"Camilla MacPhee here," I said. "Look, I've got the press breathing down my neck. They've got wind of the fact that your building management won't let the family view the security tapes. How do you want to handle that?"

The Super squeaked in alarm.

I said, "You know what they're like. Hounds. They'll love the optics of 'elderly woman missing while wealthy, corrupt landlords impede search', that kind of thing. I'm no great lover of the building's owners, since I got turfed out of my apartment, so don't expect that I'll be standing up for them. I imagine you'll see the *Citizen* photographers showing up soon. What? Oh. I understand completely. I'm sure they are extremely busy people and really hard to get hold of. Of course, I'm a lawyer, and I do understand privacy issues. The media can be so unclear on them."

I smirked when I hung up. "I bet he hadn't even asked them yet. Let's give it an hour. He'll be putty in your hands, Alvin."

"I can't wait," Alvin said. "Staring at empty staircases and deserted foyers for hours on end, that will be almost as good as seeing Michelangelo's David up close and personal."

"What would Mrs. P. say, Alvin? Stiff upper lip."

"Do you have a plan for Italy?" Alvin said.

"Not yet."

"So you're just getting off the plane, and you'll just look around and scratch your head?"

"Hardly. I'll be in touch, and we'll take it as it goes."

"Violet and I are really kindred spirits," Alvin sniffed.

"We really need someone here to keep a finger on the pulse. You can get cracking on finding some women she served with. You can get in touch with the Legion, Veterans Affairs, try to track them down. It can be part of your voyage of self-discovery."

"That reminds me, did you move my journal?"

"Of course not."

"Well, I can't find it."

"It was by the phone when I called Betty and Hazel. Here it is, under this paper. Don't snatch, Alvin. I'll be happy to hand it to you."

"Look at that!"

"What?"

"I can't believe even you would do that, Camilla."

"Do what?"

"Well, look at it. See what you did to the face on my notebook? You gave Margaret Trudeau wrinkles."

I squinted at the cover. "Can't say I know what you're talking about."

He sniffed, "See those lines. You stuck your papers on top of my notebook and wrote on them."

"All I did was scratch out the names of the people who weren't Betty and Hazel. I didn't think it would damage your book." I didn't think it was such a big hairy deal, but in the interest of team spirit, I apologized. "Okay, I'm really sorry."

Alvin sniffed again.

"Hey, maybe it's a good thing," I said. "We didn't see any paper lying around at Mrs. P.'s, did we?"

"No."

"Chances are, she wrote something down before she left, made a note of a flight or a time."

"Is this connected to my notebook?" Alvin said.

"Definitely. We'd better check her books and magazines to see if we find indentations."

"That stuff only happens in the movies, Camilla."

"It just happened here."

"Violet doesn't keep magazines lying around. But you're right, I guess it wouldn't hurt to check."

"We'll drop in on the Super too. Take him by surprise."

* * *

The Super was standing in the foyer when we got there, which sort of ruined the surprise. He buzzed us in and wrung his hands. "I'm waiting for a call back."

"No problem. We need to see Mrs. Parnell's apartment. We have a key." I waved mine ostentatiously.

"I'll go with you, just in case there's any issue about it later. And don't be taking it out on me because of management's attitude, Camilla. I got nothing against you. I never wanted to see you tossed out on your..."

"It's history," I said.

"The phone book," I whispered to Alvin when we arrived in the apartment. Something told me we wouldn't be getting out of the building with anything belonging to Mrs. Parnell as long as the Super was with us.

"Roger, over and out," Alvin whispered back.

Naturally, there is no way to stash a phone book in your pocket. "You want to watch while I check the bedroom?" I said to the Super with what I hoped was a meaningful look at Alvin.

"Sure thing. I can't believe she would leave her place like

this," the Super said, shaking his shiny head. "It was always so perfect, eh."

"She didn't. Someone burgled it, which is why we are waiting to see those tapes. Have the reporters been by yet?"

He paled. "I left a message for the owners. They got lawyers too. In fact, I think they might be lawyers themselves. Don't quote me. Oh boy, somebody did a job in here too."

I stalled long enough for Alvin to check the phone book and any other magazines or books he found. There nothing in the bedroom.

"I wish I could have helped you stay in your apartment. The owners were pissed off about all the complaints about you. And the awful thing on the balcony a few years back. The false alarm in September was just the last straw."

"I didn't pull that fire alarm. Never mind, did these complaints come from different sources?"

"You know that's confidential."

"Oh, right, I forgot. Privacy. Yeah, yeah. People can complain about me, but I can't know who they are."

"You can be a scary lady."

"Know what I think? I think all the complaints come from the guy in 1604. You got a whole bunch of complaints from one gold-plated jerk."

He paled. "You didn't hear that from me," he said.

"I owe you one."

"Ready, Camilla?" Alvin called. "We gotta get back and walk the dog."

I grinned at the super. "We'll check in soon to see what got caught on the cameras."

*   *   *

We burst through the door of my place, and Alvin brandished the front cover of Mrs. Parnell's phone book. He slapped it on the table and covered it with a piece of printer paper. He scribbled over the paper with a pencil. I watched intently. It was just like being a kid with a puzzle from a cereal box. Words of a sort appeared. We read them out together, squinting. As far as we could tell, they said:

Berli

Pieve San Simone

Montechiaro

Alcielo

"There's another one too," Alvin said. "Maybe she didn't press as hard because it's hard to make out."

I squinted at it.

"O-R-F?" I asked

Alvin always likes the last word. "Not to squabble. I think it might be O-R-E."

"Let's make a list and check them all out. They sound like place names to me. And she is in Italy. Although with Mrs. P., that might prove to be a diversionary tactic. We'd better check them out anyway."

Alvin was already at the computer. "Lord thundering Jesus, the system's down."

"Crap. Keep trying, and I'll go pack. Who knows what we'll have to deal with tomorrow."

Gussie helped with my packing by flopping on the bed and sighing loudly. Some of the sighs were pretty stinky, so they may not have been actual sighs. Mrs. Parnell's cat helped by stretching out in the suitcase and licking her front paws. She varied this by also rolling languidly on the dark clothes I laid out and licking her back paws. Alvin helped by continuing to swear loudly at the online provider over the phone.

I already had the print-out of my e-ticket in my new

backpack style leather purse, black of course. My passport went in too. I dug through the boxes of books from my apartment and ferreted out my trusty old Italian phrase book and my favourite guidebook. I tossed them into the purse and added a notebook. So far so good.

I am not the most fashionable person, as my sisters would be happy to tell you. I do not use an entire closet, so naturally I don't have a separate travel wardrobe. I sure didn't want to spend time seeking laundry facilities in Italy. Although the November weather in Italy would be more pleasant than Ottawa's, it could be cool. I decided to travel in my jeans, black sweater, new jean jacket and broken-in black running shoes, with a hooded raincoat for insurance. I dusted off my rolling carry-on luggage and packed black wool pants, my good black leather loafers and a charcoal blazer that was warm yet presentable. I squeezed in a long-sleeved turtleneck, three pairs of warm socks, a couple of T-shirts in case of warm weather, a toiletry kit and all the clean underwear in my drawer. None of my sisters would leave home without a little black dress and pashmina, neither of which I own. As a concession to their voices in my head, I added a red silk scarf, a Christmas gift from Edwina. The Christian Dior Graffiti Red lipstick Alexa had given me for my birthday went into the little black backpack. You never know when you have to look respectable for someone in authority. In Italy, appearance counts.

My closet was almost bare, and I was good to go. Less than twenty minutes. Whatever I'd forgotten to pack, I'd just have to live without. It was too late at night to call Ray and tell him about the trip to Italy. Alvin gave up on the system and headed back to Mrs. Parnell's to keep the night watch. Just in case.

It was late, and I was fried. Still, I stayed awake for a long time reading Mrs. Parnell's letters. What the hell was she up to?

*   *   *

After my morning coffee, I dragged Gussie off through the rain-soaked streets. I splashed home and made myself presentable. I didn't have a lot of time to spare before my three o'clock flight, and I didn't want to waste a minute. I was banking on the idea that a retired school principal would not be lying in bed on Saturday morning.

I picked up Betty Connaught's address and Mrs. Parnell's photos, which I protected with bubble wrap and a plastic bag.

Twenty minutes later, I pulled up in front of an imposing condo-style building on a fine old street in Sandy Hill. Luck was with me. Betty Connaught answered on the second ring. Five minutes later, I was sitting in her gracious living room.

"I hope I'm not catching you too early," I said.

"Not at all. I've already been out walking for an hour," she said, pointing to a walking stick. "Can't let the weather hold us back."

Betty was tall and spare, and she still conveyed an air of authority. Lines criss-crossed her face. Her cheekbones were strong, and her chin remarkably firm. She wore her silver hair in a sleek pageboy. The style suited her, as it probably had for fifty years. She wore smart-looking navy pants and a soft grey sweater set, almost certainly cashmere. She was so pale that I wondered if her visit to the doctor the day before had been for something serious. On the other hand, I had burst in on a Saturday morning before she'd put her lipstick on. Lipstick or no, there was no doubt she was the dark-haired girl in Mrs. Parnell's photo. She still had the dark eyebrows, and she used them to advantage. Her former students must have dreaded being sent to Miss Connaught's office.

I was not a former student, and I'd had the advantage of

growing up as the daughter of a high school principal. It has always come in handy.

"A nice pot of tea will help us both on this miserable day," she said. "Does Darjeeling suit you?"

I like to use the time when people are playing host to examine their environments. My sisters would have given this one high marks. Betty owned lovely antiques, oriental rugs on polished floors, cream custom millwork shelving, silk draperies. Her walls were a soft celery shade which suited the soft faded greens and beautiful backlight of the large oil painting on the main wall. Fine, delicate watercolours hung in tasteful groupings. Alice Munro's latest book sat on the coffee table, keeping company with a National Gallery publication on Jean Paul Lemieux. The room even smelled elegant and old-worldly. From the kitchen, the CBC radio news was a soft burr in the background. Betty's life in retirement was pleasant, agreeable to the senses; she had a comfortable as well as an elegant home.

I reminded myself to get those damn boxes unpacked when I got home. And slap a milk calendar up on the wall.

Apparently Betty not only believed in tea, she believed in silver and in keeping it polished. She seemed worried and slightly distracted. It couldn't have been the antique silver tea service, because that was gleaming.

"Well, dear. I'm sorry to say that I've been fretting about poor Violet since we spoke, was it just yesterday? I can't really think of anything to help. It's quite distressing."

"Believe me, I know."

"Of course, you're going through the same thing."

"Maybe you *can* help," I said, accepting my tea in a Crown Derby cup. "Does the name Berli mean anything to you?"

"Vardy? I think there's a doctor by that name."

"B–E–R–L–I. I think it sounds like 'barely'. Mrs. Parnell,

Violet, had written it down."

"It sounds Italian. Could it be a type of cheese? No, that's silly. This seems as though we're playing a trivia game, even though it's really quite serious. Anyway, food was never important to Violet."

"I thought it might be someone's name."

"Berli. I've never heard that name. We didn't know any Italians when we were girls. There weren't any in Chesterton. Even though my memory isn't as sharp as it used to be, I couldn't forget that. Of course, one meets Italians everywhere these days. I don't recall hearing of anyone named Berli in any connection."

"What about Pieve San Simone?"

She shook her head.

"Montechiaro?"

"Monte Carlo. Of course, dear, who hasn't heard of that."

"No, this is Montechiaro. Or it might be Claro."

Betty frowned. "Perhaps it was a misprint."

"How about Alcielo? I think I'm pronouncing it right."

"I would have no idea how to pronounce it. I'm afraid I'm not much help to you."

"I thought it was worth asking. It looks like Mrs. P. has headed off to Italy."

"Italy? What, by herself? Didn't you tell me she's had some kind of a heart attack?"

"Something like that."

"That's serious. She wouldn't want to find herself in a foreign country at the mercy of some other medical system."

We weren't the only people who thought this trip was a bad, bad idea. "I'm heading to Italy to find her. My assistant, Alvin, will be looking after things here. You can contact him if you think of anything that will help. And there's voicemail."

"Off to Italy to look for Violet? My heavens. Do you know Italy, dear?"

"I've visited several times. I took a year off after I got my undergraduate degree and roamed around Europe. Italy was my favourite country. I even spent my honeymoon there."

"Do you think she's heading for one of those places you mentioned?"

"Possibly. We're flying blind, really."

"Do you speak the language? It's not easy to make yourself understood, although I suppose most people speak some English."

"I've taken a course or two over the years. Before I go, I want to show you some pictures." I slipped the photos from the bag.

Good thing I hadn't whipped them out when I first got there. Betty Connaught was the last person I would have expected to dissolve into tears.

"Forgive me," she said, wiping her eyes. "It's just seeing this photo. Perce was killed in 1944. I have nothing left of him. He was the greatest loss of my life. I adored him."

"I am so sorry to bring this up," I said.

"Just let me pull myself together. You would think that after sixty-one years, I'd be able to talk about Perce. All right, your photo. I remember the day this was taken. Violet and I, and Hazel Fellows had just finished high school, although I'll never understand how Hazel got through. The boys were older. Look how devil-may-care they are."

"They're very handsome. Which one is this?"

"That's Harry Jones. He was Perce's best friend. They enlisted together. And he was Violet's beau. Then something dreadful happened later in the war. He broke off his engagement to Violet and married someone else, and she married that Major Parnell, shortly after the war. He was a bit of a cold fish. I still can't think of her as Mrs. Parnell. Maybe if she'd married Harry, she wouldn't have shut everyone out of her life. Although, perhaps she had her reasons."

"And Harry Jones was injured, not killed, is that right?"

"He made it, thank heavens. He married an English girl, Dorothea Brockbank. She was from a wealthy family, and he went into her family's business, something to do with furniture, I believe."

"You don't hold that against him? Breaking off the engagement and marrying someone else, just like that?"

"I didn't. Of course not. I imagine it was hard on Violet, although she was such a strong girl. War can have a terrible impact. Harry was a wonderful boy. He'd been horribly injured. He'd seen so many friends die. He was vulnerable, and Dorothea was a lovely, gentle person."

"He didn't bring his wife back to Canada?"

"She had family money, as I mentioned, and both her brothers died in France, I believe. Harry went on to run the family business. He did very well. I stayed in touch with him. I have tea at Brockback Manor whenever I am in England. He's all I have left from my life in Chesterton. Harry had no reason to come back here. His father died while he was overseas. Another tragic family. I lost my own mother before the war was over, you know. I believe it was heartbreak in both cases. People have no idea what we all went through. I still think of my brother. Such a golden boy. This year, with the sixtieth anniversary of VE day, the war's all over the papers. I keep wondering what he would have been like. A grand old man! Such a waste." She wiped her eyes again.

I said, "Truly tragic. Do you think I could contact Harry Jones?"

She stared at me. "Contact him?"

"Yes, in England."

Her eyes brimmed again. "Oh, dear."

"Is he dead? I'm sorry."

"He's almost eighty-six now, although that's hard for me to imagine. He has advanced Parkinson's. He's very fragile and finds it hard to talk. He's in a nursing home, a very exclusive one, of course. Still, it's sad. I am bracing myself to get over to England for one last visit. It won't be easy to see him deteriorating. Harry was a wonderful, valiant fellow, the last of our boys. I always admired him. I'll just have to stiffen my spine and do it."

I had to admire the resilience of these women, Betty and Mrs. Parnell, and even Hazel. I sure hoped I had half their spirit when I hit my eighties. Maybe surviving a war helps.

It was time to get moving. I pointed to the third young man in the picture, the tall, dark one with the long jaw and the lively hair. "And who is this person?"

She squinted at it. "I wonder what he was doing there. He wasn't even from Chesterton. He was just passing through the area, footloose and fancy-free, and the boys met up with him. You can see that Hazel making eyes at him. I remember him flirting like mad with Violet. She used to tease him about being black Irish. You know that dark hair and the startling blue eyes."

"What happened to him?"

"Isn't memory funny. His name was Guy Prendergast. He's a bit of an odd-looking duck, isn't he? At least compared to Perce and Harry. They were both so handsome and well-built. Elegant really. Anyway, I haven't thought about Guy Prendergast for years, although I found him strangely attractive at the time. Of course, he was RC, and mother would never have tolerated me seeing a Catholic boy. Just as well he only had eyes for Violet. I heard later that he died in the battle of Ortona. I seem to remember Perce writing me about it. I could be wrong about that. After Perce died, I often got confused about things. The death of someone you love so much can destroy your ability to concentrate."

Didn't I know it. I glanced at my watch. I had run out of

time, and I felt bad that I'd upset Betty. At least I knew who was in the photo.

*   *   *

Back home, I kept a close eye on the time and gave Hazel another call. I wasn't sure she got up early, but I figured she'd have a peach or turquoise phone by her bedside. Hazel sounded very happy to hear from me.

"Vi always liked a little nip, you know, maybe they're wines." Hazel chuckled. "'Course, wine was never her first choice."

I imagined Hazel recumbent in a king-sized bed with a mountain of satin pillows behind her head, enjoying coffee with a little nip in it, while the white cat purred on the next pillow.

"You don't recognize any of those names?"

"Gosh, I don't think so, sweetie. Monte Cassino, Ortona, the Liri Valley, I remember those from the radio. A lot of Canadian boys died in places like that. I'll call you if anything happens in this silly old brain of mine."

"Thanks, Hazel."

"I'm a bit jealous, you know."

"Jealous?"

"Well, sure, that Vi gallivanting all over Italy without a care in the world. Just like her. I'm glad she still has an adventure or two left in her. All I'm getting is Florida again this year. I can't say I'll mind getting out of Kingston. This cold rain is going to be the death of us."

"I'm surprised you're still up here."

"You have to be careful. You can't be away more than five months, or it affects your health coverage. Trust me, at my age, that matters."

"At mine too," I said. "I owe you, Hazel. You just reminded

me of something I have to do. Before I go, do you remember a fellow named Prendergast?"

She paused. "Prendergast?"

"Yes, he's in a photo with you and Betty and Mrs. Parnell. Harry Jones is in it and Perce Connaught."

"Really?"

"Betty says it was just after you graduated. Maybe that same day?"

She laughed, a lovely low throaty chuckle that gave you a clue what all those husbands had seen in her. "Harry and Perce, they were really something, weren't they?"

"Yes."

"I'd forgotten that other fellow's name. Prendergast, that's not a name from our area. Dark hair. Long drink of water, right? Not too hard on the eyes."

"Right."

"Well, sweetie, I had such a terrible crush on Perce Connaught, although I wouldn't admit that to anyone at the time, even myself, that I didn't notice anyone else. It was totally unrequited. Perce could have had any girl he wanted."

"Betty remembered."

"She would. She didn't want me with her brother. She probably got the boys to bring Guy in as a distraction. Betty liked to run the show. I had to keep a step ahead of her."

"You never saw him again?"

"They were all gone so soon after. Chesterton had nothing but old men and women and girls and little boys left. The war was awful. I cried for a month when Perce was killed. I bet Betty was glad I wouldn't end up in her family.

"Better for me in the long run. Now I realize that Perce had such a big opinion of himself, didn't really care about anyone except Perce."

"Oops, look at the time," I said. "Thanks, Hazel. Got to fly."

*   *   *

"Jackpot, Camilla!" Alvin yelled, as he walked in the door waving a printout and a map. "I got tons of references. They're Italian towns all right. You're right. Berli's in the mountains south of Milan."

"Why would she bother to write that down?" I said.

"I have no idea."

"Maybe the Canadians were there during the war."

"I don't know. Let's take a peek." Alvin spread out the map of Italy and pointed.

"Right."

"And, look, I found Montechiaro, Pieve San Simone and Alcielo. They're all in Tuscany."

"What about Ore?" I said. "Did you find that?"

"Nothing. Nothing for Orf either. Maybe that's someone's name."

"Ore is the Italian word for hours. That doesn't help us, does it?"

Alvin kept pecking at the keyboard. "Nope. I'm trying to find something about these towns that will link them in some way."

"You know what?" I smacked myself in the forehead.

He glanced at me, eyes narrowed behind his glasses. "What?"

"I'll need a car to visit these places."

"Are you sure you want to drive over there? I've heard about those Italian drivers. Can't you just take buses and trains?"

"No way, if I'm heading to a bunch of mountain towns in different parts of the country. Are you turning into my sisters, Alvin?"

"Remind me to laugh."

"I'm heading over to the CAA in Lincoln Fields to get my travel health insurance, an international driver's license and a couple of other things. I'll book a car through them. I know it's cheaper if you make your arrangements before you leave Canada. There's a currency exchange out there too."

"You have fun," Alvin said. "I know, I know, someone has to stay here and work."

"By the way, I may as well take those letters to Italy. I'll have plenty of time on my hands, I can study them in more detail."

Alvin paled. "They're important to Violet. What if something happens, and you lose them?"

"Relax. I'm not going to lose anything."

"Your luggage could go missing."

"What luggage? My little carry-on? My purse? Lighten up, Alvin. We have enough troubles without hallucinating new ones."

"Have it your way," he said. "You're not getting the originals. I'll get you copies. And some copies of a picture of Violet. I should make a poster."

*   *   *

I was well behind schedule when I got back home. I'd arranged for a car rental pick-up at the Milan airport, plus taken out health insurance, picked up a road guide and purchased stick-on Canadian flags, large enough to be noticed, for my carry-on. One major item remained. I straightened my spine, called Ray and spilled the beans.

Ray said, *"Where?"*

"Italy."

"Huh. Well, Italy's not actually on the list of the places we can get deals on."

"Okay, I feel like a crumb, but I have to find Mrs. P. No choice.

We can take a vacation together when we're not facing a crisis."

"Don't know how to break it to you, Camilla: there hasn't been a crisis-free zone since I've known you. Unless you count the two months this fall when you were recovering from a concussion and couldn't get into any trouble. I was on sick leave. I guess that wasn't facing a crisis, because all the crises had already happened."

"We should have recovered in Mexico or something."

"Another missed opportunity."

"Come on, I'm sure we'll have nice uneventful trips. Think about it. This isn't the ideal circumstance for a relaxed holiday."

"Guess you got that right."

"I managed to get a seat on Air Canada, leaving this afternoon and connecting through Frankfurt. I get to Milan tomorrow morning. I should be at the airport already."

"You're leaving now? It's hard to keep up with you. I can't believe you planned an entire trip and called when you're leaving for the airport."

"Thanks, Ray, for understanding. You know I owe my life to her."

"Stay in touch and avoid situations."

"Don't worry."

"I won't be able to stop worrying. Do you have a plan for when you get there?"

"I'm sure I will have."

"Dear God," he said.

"It will be a very good one. It's a long flight."

"I don't believe this."

"I appreciate your concern, Ray. We've already lost Mrs. P. What else could go wrong?"

"About a million things."

"Hold that thought," I said. "Gotta leave, or I'll never get through security in time."

14 Bridge Street
Chesterton, Ontario
September 23, 1944

Dear Violet,

I am so terribly sorry to hear about Harry's dreadful injuries. It is almost impossible to imagine this added tragedy so few months after Perce's death. They were like brothers. I cannot close my eyes and picture one without seeing both of them, so full of boyish high spirits. I only hope Harry will make it. Perce would have wanted that. They both had so much to offer us and the world. One of them has to go on.

We both know Harry is also a valiant man and a great fighter. He will overcome this adversity. No matter how much the burns will have affected him physically, he will still be one of our golden boys. He is very lucky to have you on his side. It must be very difficult not to be able to see him now when he needs you most.

The new school year has started, and I have a large class of children. The girls, with a few exceptions, are eager to learn and well-behaved. The boys are a different matter. It is hard to get the enthusiasm to instill knowledge into their thick heads when you think that in a few years a war may claim them in a foreign country. I shouldn't say such things, I realize. However, this ghastly war has cost us all dearly and continues to do so.

You are in my thoughts. I can take some comfort in the fact that you have stayed in England, at least, and not gone off to the continent to be killed alongside our poor fighting men.

Sincerely,

Betty Connaught

Eight

The minute the wheels touched the tarmac at Linate Airport, everything changed. People smiled. They called me *signora*. I'll take *signora* before Ma'am any old day. I might have been crabby after flying all night and attempting to work my way through forgotten Italian words, but I wasn't.

The first part of my plan involved picking up a car. The second part of the same plan involved finding someone who recognized Mrs. P. I submitted my papers to the dark-haired man behind the counter, where I'd expected to arrange to pick up my car. This resulted in a waving of hands. There were many rapid words too. I had no idea what they meant. I reminded myself I was in Europe and responded with a magnificent shrug and matching hand gestures. For added emphasis, I stabbed my finger on the papers and said, *"Già pagato in Canada. Pagato! Pagato!"* Already paid in Canada.

The dark-haired man said, "Is mistake. We don't have thees car."

"Fine," I said, "give me another one."

There was such a flap behind the counter that I figured they must be paid by the word.

"Un'ora," he said. "One hour. We have, *signora.*"

I didn't wish to expend any energy on a temper tantrum, so I said, "All right."

I slumped on the plastic bench nearby and asked myself what Mrs. P. would do. Of course, I already knew she'd come up with a strategy. I fished through my papers and pulled out the nice little poster Alvin had done up, with her photo, her name, age, and MISSING written across the top with bold lettering. He'd put my phone number and his e-mail address. In the poster, Mrs. P. was smiling and jaunty, her grey hair in a neat bun, her hand raised in a salute. That was before she'd started seeing dead people.

I found a washroom, where I cleaned my face, used some bottled water to brush my teeth and slapped on a layer of the Dior Graffiti Red. I managed a half-hearted attempt to tame my hair and made tracks back to the rental counters.

I started at the next car rental and flashed my lipsticky smile at them. I answered to *"Signora, buon giorno."* Next I pointed at Mrs. Parnell and asked in my best Italian if the clerk had seen her.

Smiles, spectacular shrugs. The woman at the first counter said, *"Sua nonna?"*

I shrugged again. The translation part of my brain was still asleep.

The woman stared at me. The woman standing next to her said in perfect English, "She asked if this is your grandmother?"

I blinked. "Yes! It is! *Mia nonna!*"

That went over well. Everyone smiled.

"Have you seen her?" I asked the English-speaking woman.

"We see so many people."

"Her name is Violet Parnell," I said. "Does that help?"

A quick check of their computers showed that it didn't.

"Sorry," the woman said. "Not in our system. Good luck, *signora.*"

I thanked her and moved off to the next counter. I slapped

down the picture again and tried in English. "This is my *nonna*," I said. "Mrs. Violet Parnell. She is sick and lost. I need to find her. Big emergency." At that counter and the next two, the language barrier raised its head. Everyone was friendly and pleasant, but all I managed to produce was a look of bafflement.

I stopped to consult my dictionary. I looked up the words sick, lost and family emergency. Nothing to lose. I returned and tried with *La nonna è malata, La nonna è perduta,* and *è un' emergenza per la famiglia.*

Zero results, lots of sympathy. In fact, I left behind me a trail of workers who obviously loved their nonnas to bits and felt my loss. Despite their wishes, I was feeling pretty low by the time I got to the last counter. I did my intro one more time.

"Certainly, *signora,*" the man behind the counter said. And then, "Sorry, no record of her in our system."

At that moment, we were joined by the woman from the first counter. She had a printed paper in her hand. "We have found your *nonna!*" she said.

"That's wonderful."

"She was here yesterday. We didn't recognize her from this photograph. Was it taken a long time ago?"

"In September," I said. "Before she started to get sick."

Everyone nodded sadly. One woman bit her lip.

"Do you remember how she seemed?" I said, straining unsuccessfully to see the paper. "Was she understanding everything?"

"No, she seemed very intelligent. She spoke some Italian even, more than…" She stopped herself abruptly and looked at me. "Everything appeared normal." I caught the implication that I came up short in that department myself. Maybe I needed a better phrase book.

The girl next to her uttered a rapid-fire sentence. Everyone laughed

"What?" I said. "What's funny?"

"She went outside to have a cigarette. Our grandmothers would not do that. They probably wouldn't rent an Opel and drive off into another country either."

"She's definitely in a class of her own," I said. "By any chance, did she happen to mention where she was headed to next?"

"Not to me, *signora.*"

"She was thinking about Berli, Pieve San Simone, Montechiaro and Alcielo," I said.

"I don't remember her mentioning any of them. We mostly talked about relatives. I have a lot of cousins in Toronto. That's where I learned to speak English. She had a conversation with my colleague too. *Momentino,* I'll ask."

She turned and directed the question to the girl next to her. A staccato conversation ensued. I leaned forward, but I couldn't make out a single word.

"She said she was looking forward to seeing the mountains," the woman said.

"Me too," I said.

"So I think it must be Berli, that's in the Apennines."

"Is it a big place?"

"I imagine it would be just a mountain village. It's not really on the tourist track. Most of the clients who would go there would be people with relatives in the area."

"How far?" I asked.

One hour later, in addition to the best wishes of the two women, coupled with greetings to Mrs. P., I had a map with the route out of Milan marked in yellow highlighter. I had a second map with the route to Berli clearly indicated too. I was on my way in something called a Ka, which is a vehicle made by Ford slightly smaller than my sister's new dishwasher. I was hot on the trail of my alleged grandmother who, unlike me, was travelling in style in a silver Opel. I had to hand it to her. Mrs. Parnell might have been losing her marbles, but not her sense of occasion.

*   *   *

Let me set you straight about Italy. Outside of the cities, it is very green, and much of it is situated on forty-five degree slopes. Imagine vineyards marching up and down. The roads are dotted with snazzy cars doing two hundred kilometres an hour. I should also mention there are a zillion silver Opels going almost as fast. My Ka, on the other hand, just chugged along a little faster than a roller blade. On the *autostrada*, there were no English signs, and apparently no speed limit. If it hadn't been for the toll booths, some cars might have become airborne. I was damned glad to get off it. The smaller roads were a bit better, if you didn't count the narrow lanes, blind corners, steep hills and complete lack of guardrails.

The further south I drove from the urban industrialization and design mecca of Milan, the more the countryside changed. Soon enough, the roadway was surrounded by vineyards snaking up hillsides.

I was making good progress towards Berli when I found myself heading for a ditch. I swerved back on to the road. The Ka would have fishtailed, if it had had a tail to fish. What was wrong with me? It occurred to me that I might need to eat. Perhaps that's why I was feeling lightheaded. I gripped the wheel and drove until I passed an old stone building with a sign indicating it had a small hotel and a bar-restaurant. That looked promising. A large shambling dog wandered outside. It reminded me a bit of Gussie.

I had a glass of the proprietors' own red wine, a bottle of mineral water and a plate of fragrant local salami, salty cheese and warm crusty bread. It was hard not to care about that food, although my eyelids kept thumping closed. The hostess pressed a second glass of red on me. If I understood her, the offer came because I was Canadian. I did my best to resist, which isn't easy in Italy. Even the first glass wasn't such a good idea in retrospect. The last thing I needed was to relax.

I don't know why I was surprised, after two sleepless nights and a head full of worry, the high-octane *vino rosso* caught up with me. My eyelids kept closing. The hotel had rooms available, which came as no surprise, and they seemed unconcerned that I only wanted to crash for a couple of hours. I was *canadese,* therefore, they expected me to be nice but weird. They were used to Canadians. They had cousins in Moose Jaw. As long as I was paying the day's rate, I could do what I wanted.

Si, signora. Va bene.

These were fast becoming my favourite words.

I produced the picture of Mrs. P. No one had seen her. Oh, well. I stumbled up the stone stairs, heaved my carry-on and my purse onto the single chair and pitched headfirst onto the small hard bed. I have no memory of hitting the feather pillows. Nor of any dreams. I think that was a good thing. When I finally opened my eyes, the sky was a strange grey. It took a couple of minutes lying there, hearing a man and woman sharing an apparently hilarious exchange from downstairs before I figured out where I was.

I stuck my head out the window to encounter fog. Solid, almost impenetrable, from the ankle up. I couldn't see the Ka parked ten feet away.

I wasn't going anywhere.

* * *

My cellphone did not care for this particular location in the Italian hills. In fact, it had been uncooperative since I got off the plane. I was forced to fall back on Plan B, which was to use the Canada Direct number on a pay phone and bill the call to my calling card number. On the bright side, it was a much cheaper option. The drawback was it meant finding a public phone whenever I needed to check in with Command Post Alvin. After three tries, I got the hang of it.

"Uh-oh, Camilla. You better call Ray," Alvin said.

I don't know what I was expecting. How was your fourteen-hour trip, maybe?

"Of course, I'll call him. He knows I'm in transit. Tell me, any luck so far?"

"He's pretty insistent. He says he can't reach your cellphone."

"It's not working over here. I'll call him. Fill me in first."

"I haven't found anyone who'll give me information about Mrs. Parnell and the people she served with. I keep getting voicemail. I'll keep at them. Maybe everyone needs a rest the week after Remembrance Day."

"Could be. How's it going with the surveillance stuff?"

"The Super let me in. I have to look at the images on his computer. Mostly they're residents and regulars, like me. I got to know a lot of people since meeting you and Violet. After a while, you can't concentrate any more. The Super had to go out, so I'm going back later."

"What about this guy who passed us when we were heading into Mrs. P.'s place, after she left the hospital?"

"He's there. I can't see his face clearly."

"It's just that the timing's right. He has to be the one who was searching her apartment, and he decided to leave when we started to ring the bell. I bet that box had her missing laptop and camera."

"Unless she took them with her. Anyway, the Super thinks he's seen this guy before, so I'll watch a bit more and see if he shows up again. Did you learn anything? You distracted me from Violet, the most important thing."

"She was all right when she rented her car at Milan airport. No one noticed anything odd about her behaviour, except that she was smoking. They think she was heading for the mountains. They loved the idea that she was taking this car around Italy, by herself."

"Cool," Alvin said.

"Well, it will be cooler when we find her. I'd better get on the road again."

"Call Ray," Alvin said.

*   *   *

"And just where *are* you?" Ray said.

"Somewhere along the road to Berli."

"You don't know the name, or how long you'll be there?"

"What's with the tone, Ray? This an inquisition?"

"If you didn't want an inquisition, you shouldn't have mentioned swerving all over the road because you're exhausted and you're in a strange country, and I believe you said you were driving a lawn mower."

"It was a joke. I'm driving a Ka, which is also a joke, I guess. Look, Ray, I've been to Italy before. I know what I'm doing. And don't sigh, Ray. You sound like my sister Donalda. Not a good thing."

"I could meet you and help you look for Mrs. Parnell."

"I'll be fine."

What the hell was wrong with me? Here was a police officer, with all those useful police skills, who refused to be thrown off by snide remarks and crabby behaviour. I knew first hand what a warm heart he had. So why didn't I just say yes?

"Hello? Are you there, Camilla?"

"I'm here."

"Okay. I can take a hint. You want to be alone. You can just say that right up front. You don't have to drag it out over long distance."

"Sorry, Ray. I'm being stupid. I admit it. I'll be in touch, okay?"

"Not so fast. Where are you going? Now."

"I thought I told you. When the fog lifts, I'm on my way to Berli. It's in the mountains a couple of hours south of Milan. I hope to find Mrs. P."

"Based on what? Intuition?"

"Sure, it could be a wild goose chase. It's better than staring at my navel."

"Not that there's anything wrong with staring at your navel. In fact…"

"Goodbye, Ray."

"Camilla?"

"Hmm?"

"Stay in touch."

"I will."

"Make sure you do," he said gruffly.

What a tough guy.

Okay, I didn't need to spend a year on a shrink's couch to tell me Paul was at the root of my reluctance to have Ray join me. I knew damn well if Mrs. Parnell had chosen to vanish into the south of France, I would have been panting for Ray to come to the rescue. It had been too many years since my husband Paul was wiped out by a drunk driver. I knew it was time to get on with my life. Paul would have wanted that. And I was ready. I even knew that Paul would have liked Ray's sense of humour, would have appreciated his unflappability, would have approved of his commitment to his family and the way you could count on him, no matter what.

None of that mattered here. How could I go with another man to Italy? The last time I'd been in the country, I'd been the passenger much of the time, a woman on her honeymoon, thinking about the next laughing dinner over a litre of red wine and the next room for two overlooking a garden courtyard in a small hotel where people smile at newlyweds, wink and nudge each other, and sidle over to their tables bearing glasses of flaming Sambuca, on the house. In case the lovebirds hadn't had enough booze.

Paul's face has been fading in my memory. I keep his photos, of course. On these roads, I didn't need photos. I saw him in the reflection in the osteria window. Wherever I went for a first trip with Ray, even if it was searching for a missing person, I owed it to him not to make it a threesome.

* * *

The fog lifted at dawn. I spotted that right off because I was sitting up in bed, awake and staring. I had been for hours. Thanks to my ill-advised sleep in the afternoon and the six-hour time difference, I'd tossed and turned all night on the narrow, hard bed, thinking about Mrs. Parnell, fretting about who might have broken into her apartment, and what was happening to her. I spent the hours from two until five re-reading the letters. The men were dead: Walter Parnell, Perce Connaught and, most likely, Guy Prendergast. Harry Jones was close enough. So many choices of possible dead people to give Mrs. Parnell trouble, to say nothing of the thousands of others she would have come in contact with. Given the foggy circumstances, this was the best use of my time, although I didn't come up with any answers.

I didn't allow my thoughts to turn to Ray Deveau or Paul. Focus, that's what Mrs. Parnell would have advised me if she had been there, although if she'd been there, I wouldn't have had a problem.

I peered out the window and was delighted the Ka was visible. My room didn't have a shower, so I gave myself a quick swipe with a facecloth, brushed my teeth and hair and nixed the lipstick.

The owner intercepted me on the way out. She apparently required no sleep. She was smiling and efficient. Her hair was nicely arranged, and she was dressed to take on all comers. She told me Berli was still another hour's drive from there, apparently straight up. She insisted that I have a caffè latte and a *brioche* for the road.

That morning, the bar-restaurant was full of customers, mostly elderly men, enjoying breakfast and each others' company. The odd one had a glass of wine.

This far from the urban areas, I didn't expect anyone to speak English, although you never know when someone will have a cousin. I used my phrase book and smiled a lot. I learned to say *Basta!* for enough. I was on a mission. I didn't really intend to come back from Italy looking like one of those Genoa salamis I enjoy so much.

I didn't want to waste an opportunity though. I pulled out the picture of Mrs. Parnell and slapped it on the wooden table top.

"Mia nonna," I said, enthusiastically.

"Ah, la nonna. Che bella!" I took this in the spirit it was intended. Although Mrs. Parnell is a stalwart companion and an irreplaceable friend, and she has splendid military bearing,

131

she's less than conventionally beautiful.

I did my best to ask if the woman had seen her there on her way to Berli. I emphasized sick and lost. *Ammalata e perduta.* I also threw in the silver Opel for good measure. *Macchina d'argento! Opel! Opel!* I sounded quite deranged. Maybe that's what set off a blizzard of chatter. *"Sì?"* I said. *"Sì?"*

"No."

My shoulders fell. More chatter. Some shrugs. If anyone even slightly unusual, and Mrs. P. would certainly qualify, had come through a village in this part of Italy, word would spread ten miles before you could say *un espresso, per piacere.* Oh well, it had been a long shot anyway, and I got a decent *brioche* out of it.

I was just polishing off my second espresso when there was a ruckus at the door. A very elderly gentleman was escorted in by two slightly less elderly helpers. A young man handsome enough to be a model for upmarket jeans followed them. Everyone became very excited about the old man, not the gorgeous kid.

I approved. It spoke well of a society where the arrival of a tiny old man sparked a lot of interest. Who needs plasma TVs and Blackberries when people in a community find each other so fascinating? Not that I would want to be the subject of such close attention from my neighbours and family, mind you. Still, the old gentleman didn't seem to mind.

Before my wondering eyes, he was steered toward my table. By this time, he was surrounded by a cluster of people, all talking at once. I wasn't sure who was listening to all this talking. It wasn't me, since I only caught the odd word. There was a buzz in the air.

As far as I could tell, the old man's name was zio Domenico. Uncle Dominic. I shook his hand. I shook the hand of his two companions.

Everyone else seemed to want to shake my hand too. That was fine.

The companions picked up the photo of Mrs. Parnell and showed it to zio Domenico. He squinted. He paused. He leaned a bit forward. He squinted more. He paused again. I had to admire his innate sense of drama. I looked around. Everyone appeared to be holding their breath.

"*La nonna?*" he said in a quavery voice.

"*Si,*" I said.

"*Molta bella.*"

"*Grazie.*"

The young man stepped forward. I imagined the girls he went to school with had a hard time concentrating when they spotted the curly dark hair, electric blue eyes and golden skin. I won't even mention the cheekbones and chiselled jaw.

"My name is Dario," he said, showing teeth that most people would kill for. "I study the English in school, so that I can visit my cousin in Hamilton. They say your grandmother is sick?"

"Yes," I said, "she may have had a heart attack. And she's seeing things."

"Ah," he said. "*Pazza.*"

I knew that *pazza* meant crazy. "No, no. Not crazy, *sick.* I believe she went to Berli. I hope so, otherwise I have to visit Pieve San Simone, Montechiaro and someplace called Alcielo."

"Berli is a long drive from here. Not as far as these other places," Dario said. "It is dangerous to drive today because it is...*nebuloso.* Sorry, I do not know the word."

"Yes, very foggy."

"You should stay here with us, *signora,*" he said flirtatiously.

Flirtation's not my thing. "Has this gentleman seen my grandmother?"

"Zio Domenico? No. Do not worry. She will be fine, I think. Yes."

I could tell he wanted to help. "My grandmother might be

driving up the mountain in the fog. As you said, it's very dangerous. She might be sick. She needs to see a doctor."

"Your father will find her."

"What?"

"Your father."

"My father's not here."

"Your uncle perhaps? He was searching for your *nonna*. He stopped here yesterday, and he asks about her."

"You lost me, Dario. Who did?"

"Her son. I am trying to explain. Zio Domenico didn't see your grandmother. He saw her son."

Brockbank Manor
Hampshire
United Kingdom
January 26, 1945

Darling Vi,

This is the hardest letter I will ever write. You cannot imagine how war changes a fellow. The Italian campaign was beyond imagination. I lost so many fine colleagues. Especially Perce. I feel I should have been able to save him. I still see his shattered face in front of me in my nightmares.

Now that I am back in England, everything seems different to me. For a while, it looked like my face and hands might heal, but the doctors were certain I would lose my right arm. I have outfoxed them, it seems. I have had a wonderful volunteer hospital visitor in the course of my recovery. Her two brothers were killed in France in the early days, and she has been doing her best to help out with the morale of those of us who made it back. You used to call me a handsome devil. Although my face is healing, you couldn't say that any more. It is more than my damaged appearance. All those months of crawling through the mud in the Italian countryside have changed me. Perhaps it was always being under German fire, sleeping in a slit trench and having your ears rattled by exploding shells, losing your friends, in the worst cases, feeling their blood wash over you. I am no longer the happy-go-lucky fellow you fell in love with. That is one of the reasons why it has been so hard for me to write to you before now.

I got a letter from Hazel, and she mentioned that you had been courted by a dashing officer named Parnell. I believe I've run into him a few times. Hazel thought I would be jealous, but that makes what I am going to tell you a bit easier. What I am trying to say is that I have fallen in love with my hospital visitor, whose name is Dorothea. She is a very fine, serious girl who wants nothing from life except a husband and children and peace, of course. This is very hard to break to you this way: Dorothea and I have been married.

I hope some day you will forgive me, Violet, and that you will live a very happy life. You will always have a special place in my heart.

Harry

Nine

I stared. "She doesn't have a son."

"Si, si. She does, *signora,*" Dario said. *"Certamente.* Hundred per cent. He had a picture of your *nonna.* He was going to Berli too."

"My God," I said.

Dario said, "No problem! If she is in Berli, he will have found her. That's good. He will look after her. It will be fine, *signora.*"

I didn't think so. My head swam. Hold on, I thought. Perhaps this was one of those bizarre disjointed dreams you have while travelling in foreign countries. Too much espresso and salami, not enough sleep. It messes with your head. I decided if it wasn't a dream, I'd better behave strategically because something was very, very wrong.

"Please ask your zio Domenico what this man looks like?"

Dario regarded me oddly. "You do not know what your uncle looks like, *signora?*"

"Actually, I don't have an uncle."

"Your father?"

"No."

"He said…"

"Probably it's just some misunderstanding. But I am worried now."

Dario said, "Zio Domenico is almost blind, that is why everyone helps him."

"He's blind? But he said she was *bella.*"

Dario grinned. "Zio Domenico loves women. It runs in the family. He sees them in his mind."

"Then how does he know about this man who says he's her son?"

"He heard him speaking."

"And he was speaking English? Asking for my *nonna*?"

Dario turned and fired off a volley of questions. He got a variety of answers. I heard *l'Americano, il Canadese, l'Inglese* and Parnell.

The Parnell part made my heart race. American, Canadian, English. I guess we all look and sound alike. *L'Americano* seemed to win the day.

"Your uncle, he spoke American."

"You mean not like a Canadian?"

Another series of questions.

"Maybe," Dario answered after a very long while. "Zio Dominico doesn't know any Canadians, just one cousin in Montreal, and that one speaks French. He thought your uncle was from United States. What does he know? He is a simple man."

"Did anyone else see anything? Can anyone describe him? And what kind of car he was driving?"

"I will ask the others."

Dario turned and held an intense conversation with the two men who had helped zio Domenico into the bar. After a lot of arm-waving and shouting, Dario turned back to me and shrugged. "He looked like an American. He had dark hair. Maybe fifty years old."

At the end of a lively discussion, Dario translated enthusiastically, and warned me to keep an eye out for someone not too light, not too dark, eye colour indeterminate, medium build, although he may have been large or even small. He was middle-aged, although some thought he might have been a bit older. No distinguishing characteristics, except for his overcoat. Then again, that may have been a raincoat, or possibly even a jacket. One trembling fellow with cataracts suggested a sweater. He was quickly put in his place.

A small, wizened man with tobacco-stained fingers gave Dario a look and elbowed him out of the way. Dario elbowed back.

Dario said, "Mercedes-Benz." He made the international finger gesture for expensive.

"Mercedes?" I said. *"Certo?"*

He frowned as if I had questioned his intelligence. What were the chances that someone claiming to be Mrs. Parnell's son roared through this town in a Mercedes?

"Nera," he said.

The wizened man hopped up and down with rage. He shouted, *"Stupido, stupido, stupidone."* Dario ignored him.

"Crazy old man," he said to me in a whisper.

My mind was on the black Mercedes. There are lots of Mercedes all over Italy. Had I seen a black one recently?

"Did anyone notice the license plate number?" I said.

Dario translated, and the old man shook his fist. No one else had seen a license plate number.

"Grazie," I said and meant it. I dodged the wizened man. I shook zio Domenico's hand. I accepted a big hug from Dario.

Whoever my new uncle was, he had done all right for himself. I excused myself from the group and headed for the pay phone. I didn't know where the hell Alvin was. I hoped it was somewhere important. I left him a clear and forceful message that he should not flip out when he heard this. Now his urgent task would be to find out if Mrs. Parnell had a son she had never mentioned. I tried to do this without shouting, because everyone in the room was listening.

I pulled out my stash of Euros and bought a round of whatever anyone wanted. *Espresso, vino,* didn't matter. I got off kind of easy, because it was morning. I made sure to thank everyone for their help. I promised to return with my grandmother for a special meal. Zio Domenico seemed especially keen. Dario gave me another huge hug.

"Ciao, ciao, bella," he said as if he meant it.

Eventually, I tore myself away. It had started to rain softly as I hurried out the door to my Ka. I waved to everyone gathered in the door of the bar and drove off up the mountain, wondering why I hadn't packed anything for a goddam headache.

* * *

If you're heading to a mountain village in the Appenine mountains, be prepared to abandon the highways and drive in a zig-zagging pattern up steep, narrow passages that barely qualify as roads. Twice I pulled over to the side. I had my fingers crossed that nothing would come barrelling up the hill and ram the back of the Ka. Or down the hill and slam the front of it. There wasn't much metal between me and meeting my maker.

Problem two lurked on the edge of every road. In this part of Italy, the roads ended in steep falls, a long way down to the rock-strewn pastures below. Naturally, there were no guardrails. Best not to dwell on that.

I kept my eyes open for a silver Opel and a dark Mercedes. The Ka might have been small and slow, but it had a tiny turning radius, and I was prepared to rely on that.

No one passed me on the road, and eventually I made it to Berli. Peering through the fog, I concluded the town couldn't have more than fifty houses, perched on the glossy green hillside, some seeming to defy physics. Most were built out of rough gray stone, probably lugged by hand from the surrounding fields generations earlier. The stone houses had new roofs, doors and windows. A few attached stucco houses had a newish look to them. Every dwelling had a small car parked in front of it, the sign of the new Europe. No silver Opels, no Mercedes.

The fog was lifting a bit. I navigated along the main street, which had mostly houses, interspersed with small businesses: a hairdresser, a barber. On a two-storey stone building, at a sharp corner, I spotted a battered sign: Bar-Hotel Natalia. It would have to do. I parked and made my way on foot up and down the rutted side streets, avoiding potholes deep enough to swallow the Ka. These streets were just a few years away from the subsistence farming communities they'd once been. I knew from previous trips to Italy that the lower levels of some of the cute stone houses had once been the stables, with the families living above on the second floor. There were no animals now, except for one dog energetically announcing my presence. I saw no one. Most of the houses were unlit, shutters closed.

The back end of the building was crumbling, although the wheelbarrels and materials near it indicated a rebuilding of some sort was underway. There was new money in Berli, I was sure of that.

I took a deep breath and pushed open the door to the bar. In Italy, bar is used to mean a café restaurant, the place you get your sandwich or grab a quick breakfast. Of course, you can always get wine there. Or whatever. You're quite likely to get homemade food. Usually you'll find a few kids running around. The Italians aren't too hung up on booze restrictions, like some places I could name. Later in the evening, they turn into pleasant drinking establishments.

The room was full of people, again mostly elderly. Everyone nodded at me when I came in. The noise level was high, boisterous, happy. Or maybe just trying to drown out the large-screen television mounted in the corner and going full-blast. I'm not sure what gives with Italian television, and I don't want to find out.

I began by greeting the burly woman, possibly Natalia, who was using her muscles to polish glasses that already gleamed in the low light. *"Buona sera, signora."*

Her eyes narrowed, her mouth turned down. Maybe that was deep suspicion. Maybe she'd just had a very bad day. I could sympathize.

I smiled. This wasn't as easy as it sounds, since I had just crawled up miles of winding, foggy mountain roads on my way to a godforsaken place where no one would speak English. I had practiced my piece and managed to ask in my fractured Italian if she had seen my grandmother. I produced the photo of Mrs. Parnell and mentioned the silver Opel.

I smiled again for good measure. She folded her arms across her chest and shook her head emphatically. New wrinkles sprouted at the downturned corners. I pointed at the picture again. "*La nonna*," I said, soothingly.

"No," she said.

"È malata."

She shook her head.

I wanted to ask about the so-called son in the Mercedes. I gave it a shot with *figlio* and Mercedes. That merely caused her to turn her back on me. She half-turned her head when I ordered a glass of red wine and a plate of cannelloni. I was feeling ridiculously fatigued and hungry. Both of which I found irritating since I couldn't really enjoy a meal until I tracked down Mrs. Parnell. Then we could eat and drink

142

happily together, and I could help her with whatever she was trying to do here in the remote mountains of Italy.

The wine came immediately. Just because I wasn't an instant hit didn't mean I wouldn't have a drink in my hand. A basket of warm, rustic bread was plunked on my wooden table, along with a bottle of olive oil. The cannelloni arrived shortly after and was plunked down without a word from the burly *signora*.

I sat alone, aware of the glances of the crowd in the bar. Who cared? It wasn't like I was looking for a new social group. I just needed information about Mrs. P. I ate in solitude and tried to figure out what to do next.

A glance out the window told me that the fog had descended again. Every few minutes, another small car emerged from the fog just feet from the window. Not much chance I could drive down the mountain without killing myself or someone else.

As far as I could tell, this bar was the only game in town. The proprietor had quite obviously taken an instant dislike to me. Not that I would care, as a rule. However, I needed cooperation.

I asked about a room, and she hesitated. A short, round man I took to be her husband gave her a quick nudge in the ribs.

"*Si,*" she said, citing a ridiculously large number of Euros.

Five minutes later, I tossed my little backpack on a double bed with a puffy duvet that looked very inviting on this damp miserable day. The pillow-cases on all four pillows had obviously been ironed. The room was bright and comfortable, with a fine view of the fog. Better yet, it even had a small new-looking portable heater in the corner and a shining white wastepaper basket. The heater had already been turned on. I found the bathroom next door in a dark green hallway. There seemed to be no other guests. The towels were large, bright

143

white and fluffy. Maybe the little round husband took charge of guest hospitality. I figured the *signora* was in charge of clean.

I brushed my teeth, had an overdue shower, fixed my hair as well as I could, changed my T-shirt and put on the black pants and my sweater. I rinsed out my undies in the sink. I hung them to dry in the shower, picked up the photos again and headed back downstairs.

The proprietor was replacing a freshly polished glass. She stopped mid-task, gripping the glass, and stared me down.

I gave her a cheerful wave and started at the first table. A group of men paused in their card game.

To do them credit, I got a *"buona sera, signora,"* from each of them. I passed around Mrs. Parnell's picture. They all took the time to look at it.

No luck. Everyone shook their heads. No one looked sympathetic. No one said, *"Oh, la nonna!"*

I thanked them, picked up the photo and moved on to the next table. I repeated this at every table in the bar. Something was wrong though. The atmosphere didn't feel normal.

I'm not sure why it took so long, but eventually it dawned on me. The bar had become too quiet. Where were the competing voices? The raucous stories, the shouts of laughter? This was more like a morgue than a gathering of Italians.

When I reached the last table and had received the last negative shake of the head, I glanced at the proprietor. She shot back a triumphant smirk.

Great. I was fogged in on a mountain, with no clue about what had happened to Mrs. Parnell, trapped until the morning, wasting precious time. I turned back to the room full of strangely quiet people. I knew she had been there, and what's more, I knew that they'd seen her.

I said in my fractured Italian: "That photo is my

grandmother. She is more than eighty years old. She is sick, and the doctor says she may die if she doesn't get medicine. I know she came here. I think you should help save her life." I searched my mind for the word for shame. It eluded me.

The room remained silent.

I gave up. Time to go back to my room and think of a new and improved plan. I turned. I stopped. *"Vergogna,"* I said. Shame on you.

People turned away from me and reverted to nervous whispered conversations. I headed back up the stairs and kicked the white wastepaper basket.

Five minutes later, I had a new plan. Probably a waste of time; still, better than staring at the ceiling until morning. I was warm and well fed, and although I was bone-tired, I didn't intend to repeat my mistake of falling asleep too early. I put on my grey wool socks and slipped my jean jacket over the sweater. I checked my phrase book for a few more useful tidbits. I wrapped the scarf around my neck, applied a bit of Graffiti Red in case and slipped down the stairs and out the side door, without bothering to make eye contact with the useless lumps in the bar.

I pulled up my collar and made my way to the first house with a light on. I banged on the door and waited. When the door opened, I gave my best Italian greetings and started on my sick *nonna* story. I added my newest phrase: *Una situazione disperata.*

I can't say I really blame people for the way they looked at me. I probably wouldn't have opened the door myself. Door after door, the results were the same. Still, it beat twiddling my thumbs. I came up empty on Via Garibaldi, the main street.

What the hell. I had nothing to lose. The fog was getting thicker. While you couldn't see any distance, you could still avoid large obstacles, and you could tell by the lights if people were awake in a house. I made up my mind and headed down the Ruella Cavour. I thought I heard a scuttling behind me and off to a side. A dog? Too quiet for a dog. Dogs are not known for their subtlety. A rat? No point in giving in to the heebie-jeebies, I decided.

Fog can have that effect on you. This might have been a foggy alley with five hundred-year-old dwellings tilting on either side, but it was also in a tiny close-knit village that probably had zero crime, I reminded myself.

My self-pep talk didn't stop the hair on the back of my neck from standing up. Anyway, I had a job to do. There were two houses with lights still on. No one answered at the first door. I could hear a television or radio blaring irritating Italian pop songs from within. I banged a few more times, waited and then decided to cut my losses.

Was I imagining the scurrying noise? I clutched my backpack in a way that might be useful for smacking a rat. I walked quickly to the last remaining house with lights on.

After a lot of banging, a stooped woman with thin white hair in a bun answered. She stared at me. Listening in apparent astonishment to my bizarre Italian, she gaped at the photo of Mrs. Parnell and grabbed my hand.

"La poverina," she said.

I couldn't imagine anyone ever referring to my Mrs. P. as a poor little thing. It was the first bit of sympathy I'd received here in Berli. To my horror, my eyes filled with tears. This was so not like me. Maybe it was the time difference, lack of sleep, the red wine, the fog, the worry. I hauled out a tissue, blew my nose, said *"Scusate, signora,"* and pulled myself together. Despite the promising start, after a few moments of my pathetic Italian, I realized she had not seen Mrs. Parnell, or the

Opel, or the black Mercedes, which I tossed in to the conversation for good measure. She was pleasant and sympathetic. She offered me something to eat and, when I declined, suggested a little glass of something. I had to turn that down too, because the fog had thickened yet again, and it was going to be tough enough stumbling back up the hill.

I thanked her profusely, and she squeezed my hand. I felt her good wishes and was damn glad to have them as I hit the fog.

I made tracks, trying not to trip into potholes in the road. A burst of sound through the swirling mist caused me to step back and gasp. Five people, arms linked, chatting and laughing, emerged a few feet in front of me. I recognized one of the family groups from the bar. They clammed up immediately when they spotted me. The women shrank back. That didn't make sense. Why would anyone be afraid of me?

I felt their eyes on my back as I negotiated the holes in the road and made my way back up the hill. As I got close to the bar, a silver-haired woman, who looked to be in her sixties, passed me, walking quickly and confidently. Her collar was pulled up around her neck. She stared hard at my face before turning her head and disappearing into the mist. I kept going toward the bar with its light, heat, red wine and much-needed public telephone.

*   *   *

"How may I direct your call?" Alvin said.

"Very funny. What news do you have?" I said.

"What is this craziness about Violet having a son? Lord thundering Jesus, I almost died of shock."

"You and me both. Definitely unlikely and baffling. There's someone making the claim, and he has a picture of her, so there's a definite connection. We have to follow up."

"Are you in Berli now?"

"It's pretty small, and no one seems to have seen our grandmother or the guy who says he's the son. They are extremely unfriendly too. Everyone else I've met, since I've been in Italy, has tried to be very helpful."

I glanced around. I was on the public phone in the bar. Something about the body language of the remaining customers told me that they were paying attention to my call. That shouldn't have made a difference, since no one appeared to speak English. Even so, I was cautious. Everything about Berli seemed so strange and creepy. Maybe excessive fog just brings out the paranoiac in me.

Alvin said, "Our grandmother? Oops, I get it. Is someone listening?"

"Who knows?" I said. "She was supposed to come here. Perhaps she changed her mind and went somewhere else."

"Jeez, I hope not," Alvin said. "What would you do then?"

"Our uncle was also looking for her. Maybe he found her."

"Our uncle? Oh, you mean the guy who says he's Violet's son? That's weird and scary."

"It is."

"You're worried, right?"

"Puzzled for sure."

I was petrified. I didn't want to tell Alvin that my biggest fear was that, in the morning, as I made my way down the mountain, I would catch a glimpse of a silver Opel, lying crumpled in a rock-strewn field, having slid off the foggy-bound mountain road, while a Mercedes sped off.

I couldn't even let myself think about it. I promised myself I would creep down in the Ka and stop to check every possible site on the way down.

"Now you got me all worked up," Alvin said. "And I'm

148

stuck over here. I can't do anything."

"What about the project, Alvin?" I said.

"What project? Why are you changing the subject?"

"Our joint project, the *visitor* project. Did you get the images yet?"

"Not really."

"Does that mean no?"

"Yes."

"Well, keep at it. It's important."

"I have plenty to do here, Camilla. Lester and Pierre are no piece of cake. And Gussie ate something that didn't agree with him, and the cat won't come out from under the bed, and your sisters keep phoning all the time because they can't get you on your cell."

"The damn thing doesn't work here. Tell them I'll call them when I get settled. Let them know I'm all right."

"They were upset you left without telling them, and they seem really steamed because they don't know if you took the right clothes."

"That's so far from anything I'm concerned about. Tell them I did. Make up something. Anything."

"I have to tell you I'm really getting frustrated trying to find someone who served with Mrs. Parnell. It's not easy when I'm stuck here being a pet sitter and receptionist."

"You're equal to the task, Alvin. I'm counting on you. Conn should be able to find out if there was a son. Call him right away."

"There couldn't have been a son. Violet would have told us. Wouldn't she?"

"I think so too. I suppose there could have been a falling-out."

"She would never lose contact with her son." Alvin sounded on the verge of hysterics. "Her son. Family. *Never.*"

149

"Take a deep breath, Alvin. I can't imagine it being true. We still have to pursue it. People have seen this guy. Remember, he has a picture of her."

"Do I have to call Conn? He's always rude to me."

I glanced around. Everyone in the room was watching. I made no effort to keep my voice low when I said, "And in the event you do not hear from me, I am currently at the Bar-Hotel Natalia in Berli for the night. I have found the locals to be uncooperative and unresponsive. As if they are hiding something. It may be worth it to ask him to contact the Italian authorities."

"As if," Alvin said.

Was it my imagination, or did some of the shoulders shift? Did eyes meet? Did the proprietor turn away to hide the expression on her stumpy face? A woman at a nearby table stood up and began pacing not far from where I sat. To make her point, she stared at her watch, then glanced up at the wall clock. The international gesture for get the hell off the phone.

"Promise you'll do it, Alvin. I'll keep you posted. I have another call to make, and someone is waiting for the phone."

I turned my face away from the woman, hung up and dialled Canada Direct again. My next call was to Ray Deveau. Not that it made any difference.

I got a busy signal at his home, most likely the result of having a teenager tying up both lines at once. Not the first time that had happened to me. There was no answer on his cell, so I tried his work number.

His message was clear. "This is Sergeant Ray Deveau. I will be away from my desk for the next two weeks. If this is an emergency, contact the main number. Otherwise leave a message."

Well, thanks a lot. I slammed down the phone. Why the hell bother?

21 Frank Street
Chesterton, Ontario
December 20, 1945

Dear Vi,

It's my birthday today. I am writing again in the hope you will find it in your heart to forgive me, especially since there's not much to celebrate here. Betty calls herself Elizabeth now, as it's more suitable for a teacher. She walks right by me with her nose in the air. Well, she has the right nose for it, and she wasn't the easiest person to get along with before. Even so, I feel bad.

I miss you and wish you would answer my letters. We have been friends since we started school. I know that I betrayed your trust and our friendship just for idle chatter. I meant no harm. I was enjoying the idea of this officer pursuing you. I thought it would be fun if Harry was jealous. I will regret my foolish words all my life. Every single day I wish I could undo what has been done.

Mother is not at all well. Her cough is very worrying. I am afraid she'll end up in the San like so many other people. I am sure you knew that Harry's father's house burnt right to the ground. Mr. Jones was never the same after his wife died and Harry went overseas. He fell asleep with his pipe still lit. There's nothing left except the foundation. A lot of people turned out for the funeral. I wonder if people realize that the parents and families of those at home are also suffering and in some cases dying, perhaps of broken hearts. Even friends.

Oh, don't mind me! I know it must be much harder for you, even though I imagine you living in a castle somewhere and sipping champagne with officers and aristocrats. At least I got to see "The Bells of St. Mary's" at the Vogue.

Even though the war is over, perhaps you are not in a position to write yet. Whether you are or not, remember it is the Christmas season, a time for love and forgiveness. I hope you will find it in your heart to answer my letters.

Love always,

Hazel

P.S. Some lovely velvet hats have arrived at Adams' Ladies' Wear. Just in time for Christmas services!

Ten

F ine.
It takes more than that to get rid of a MacPhee. I pulled myself together and went back to Canada Direct. I ignored the waiting woman, who had been tapping her pointed leather shoes. I tried Ray's cellphone again. I decided that it must say something for our developing relationship that I knew all these numbers by heart.

The customer I was trying to reach was not available.

"Why aren't you available, Ray? I'd really like to be able to talk to you. For the record, I am stuck in the fog in the mountain village of Berli. I have learned some bizarre things, and I would like to talk to you, even if you have decided to take your vacation by yourself. If you get this tonight, I am staying at the Bar-Hotel Natalia in room *Uno*." I read out the telephone number and added, "Don't forget the country code for Italy. It's about eight our time, if you get this within the next few hours, I'll still be up. Tell the proprietor you want to speak to me, and I'll call you right back. I wish you were here, and not just because it's so goddam creepy."

I surrendered the phone to the foot-tapper and looked for a table. Every shoulder in the place seemed to shift as I walked by. I found a spot in the corner, where I could observe things, and settled in to watch the locals and hope for the phone to ring. My competition didn't stay on it long. I figured she'd just wanted to annoy me, although I couldn't imagine why. I chose espresso rather than wine. Even so, my eyelids soon began to droop. By nine, which was only mid-afternoon Canadian time, I decided to leave the party.

I did my best to explain to the proprietor that I might get a call, and I would like to be informed, even if she had to wake me up.

She shrugged.

I asked for a wake-up call in an hour.

Double shrug.

I could tell my business was really important to her. I headed up the stairs to my room. I opened the door and looked around. It was as I'd left it. I flung myself on the amazing feather bed and conked out. So much for personal grooming and hygiene issues.

*   *   *

I was jerked out of sleep by a soft knock on the door.

I leapt up and stared around. It took a minute to figure out where I was, even if I had fallen asleep with the light on. I staggered to the door and yanked it open. I was expecting the bitchy proprietor to be standing there with her arms crossed and an expression like an executioner, telling me that I had a phone call. Instead, I faced the woman with the silver hair who had passed me in the fog.

I gawked at her wordlessly.

Finally, she said in English, "May I enter, *signora?*"

I stood back to let her pass. She glanced into the corridor as if to check it was clear and slipped into the room.

I pointed to the chair. She sat on the chair, and I plunked

myself on the rumpled bed and waited. I had no idea what to expect.

"My name is Orianna Preto. I live here in Berli," she said.

"You speak English," I said stupidly.

"Yes," she said.

"You speak very well. Do you have cousins in Lethbridge?"

Of course, she looked surprised. "I spent many years working in England. I remember quite a bit of the language. It comes back when I need it."

"That's great," I said. "I'm having a lot of trouble expressing myself, and I need help."

"I know," she said. "You are looking for your grandmother. You knocked on my mother's door in the Ruella Cavour."

"Yes. She was very kind. She offered me…"

She laughed. *"Un bicchiere.* A little glass of something."

"Never mind, it was the first civil thing anyone in this town said to me. Why didn't you come to the door?"

"I live two houses further up. She called me to tell me about your visit. She was glad to see someone."

"Two houses up? I knocked on that door too. The lights were on. You didn't answer."

She gave me the national shrug. "My husband is away in Cremona this week. I am a woman alone, and a stranger was knocking at my door. I'm sure you understand."

"Your mother answered."

"She has always lived in Berli. She doesn't worry about crime or bad people. She's always been lucky."

"She's very kind too."

"A saint. She said you seemed very sad, and that she believed you really were who you said."

I blinked. "Why wouldn't I be who I said I was?"

"We were told not to believe anyone who came looking for

155

the other *signora*. We were told people would lie about who they were."

I leaned forward. "Who on earth would tell you something like that?"

"Well, the *signora* did, herself."

I jumped off the bed. "She's here!"

"Shh. She was. I believe she is gone."

"And she told you not to believe... I don't get it."

"My mother thinks it was not you she was speaking about."

"Do you know who she was speaking about?" I said.

"She did not mention anyone in particular."

"Someone's been following her. A man. And I'm sure she wouldn't have expected me to arrive from Canada."

"My mother believed you were worried about your *nonna*. She believed your tears were sincere."

"Is that why no one will speak to me here in this village? All I feel is hostility."

"Yes. They think you mean the *signora* some harm."

"What harm could I mean her? Let me explain: a few days ago, she had a shock. She thought she saw a dead man. She collapsed not long after, and the doctor thought she might have had a heart attack. She could die if she's not careful. In spite of this, she left Canada and made this sudden, mysterious trip to Italy. She needs medical treatment and observation, so you understand that I must find her. Plus there is a man claiming to be her son who is also following her. But she has no son."

Her hand shot to her mouth. "That is frightening. Nobody in Berli would help him."

"That's good. Now, do you know anything about her? About why she came here?"

"I will start at the beginning. She wanted to talk about the plane crash."

156

"I'm sorry, what plane crash?"

"It was 1944. The Allies were flying missions over Italy. I was a child growing up in this village. The Germans were still in the mountains, they rounded up people. They were beginning to retreat to Germany. They forced skilled workers to travel with them. They shot villagers. They took our food. Everyone was terrified of the SS. They were known for brutal reprisals. In our village, a lot of men had deserted the army, and there were partisans hiding out all over these hills. They would attack Germans, sabotage trucks, that kind of thing. The SS would have reprisals, and villagers would be killed. It was very dangerous. The people in Berli did not want to attract the attention of the Germans."

I nodded to her to continue.

"A plane crashed on the mountain, in a meadow a bit higher."

"There's something higher than Berli?" I said. "Unbelievable."

"Just grazing land. For goats."

"Go on," I said.

"I was only seven years old. I was in the pasture gathering sticks for firewood, and I came across the plane wreckage."

"Did you know what it was?"

"Oh yes, of course, people had been whispering about seeing it smoking and falling from the sky. Everyone kept that secret, because of the Germans. We did not want the Germans searching our homes looking for injured Englishmen or Americans. They might have found our fathers and uncles who had deserted. Perhaps they would have raped the women, or they might just have taken everything we had to eat. It was such a terrible time."

"I can only imagine. So you saw the downed plane?"

"I crept close to it. It was completely burnt out. The

ground around it was burned. The wings had broken off and scattered. You could see the burned skeletons of the men inside. I still have nightmares after all these years."

"What happened then?"

"I ran back to the village and told my father. He and a few other men came up all night and buried the wreckage. It would have been hard work, because the soil is very rocky here, but they didn't want the Germans to find it. They buried the bodies—they were just burned bones. They marked the spot. There wasn't much to be salvaged from the plane. People took the bits of metal; they were very useful. When the Germans left the area, the mayor sent word to the Allies. The plane was dug up, the soldiers were identified, as all their tags had been buried with them. Their bones were taken away to be buried in the military graveyard. That was the end of it. I suppose the families were notified. We still get family members here visiting the site from time to time."

"That is what you told Mrs. Parnell, I mean, my grandmother?"

"Yes. That is what she came to find out. She talked to many people in our village. She drank sherry with them, and she smoked a lot of cigarettes. She talked about the war with the old men. Everyone liked her very much. She even spoke some Italian. Quite a bit more than you do."

"That doesn't surprise me. So she wanted to talk about the plane. And she found out what she wanted to."

"Well, this is what I need to tell you. I wasn't going to talk about it, because it was so long ago, and she seemed satisfied with what she heard. My mother is a good woman. She said I must go to her and tell her the truth."

"And what truth was that?"

"The truth about the parachute."

"There was a parachute?"

"Let me explain. I was just a child. I didn't even know what it was, this wonderful billowing white silky fabric. You must understand, we had nothing. The economy was devastated by the war. The Germans took the food from our kitchens. We barely had clothes on our backs at that point in the war. Some people didn't have shoes in the winter. I had never seen anything like that wonderful fabric. I wanted it. The men were dead, so it didn't matter to them. I gathered it up, and I hid it under some stones at the edge of the field. I wasn't foolish enough to hide it in the house because, if the Germans came, they would think we had something to do with the dead airmen. There was nothing we could do for them. I hid it, and I kept quiet, but I didn't forget it was there. When the war was over, I uncovered it, and my mother used it to make me a confirmation dress. That's how I learned to sew. My mother taught me. I made my living that way. The parachute never mattered until now. It was just one of those strange and tragic things that came out of that terrible time."

"Of course, it did make a difference."

"No one wanted to talk about these things at the time. I wasn't even supposed to know about the plane. After so many years, I never thought it would matter."

"What did you tell my grandmother?"

"That I had found the parachute."

"Which meant that someone must have parachuted before the crash. Did she ask you if there was a body found outside the plane?"

"*Si*, she did ask. There wasn't."

"So someone may have walked away from the downed flight."

She shrugged. "Who can say? At the time, of course, no one spoke of such things to children. We couldn't be trusted not to blurt something out to the soldiers."

"Point taken. What did she do after you told her about the parachute?"

"She was terribly shocked. She turned as white as your pillow case. She had to have a glass of sherry and rest. She closed her eyes. I admit I was worried. I thought I'd made a mistake by telling her." Orianna bit her lip.

"Then did she leave Berli?" I had a horrible vision of Mrs. Parnell, brimming with sherry, pale with shock, plunging off the mountain road into the foggy night.

Orianna looked up again. "After she spoke to me, she returned to talk to all the old men of the village, and she asked them more questions."

"And do you know what they said?"

"I do not. I was not there. I have told you everything I know, *signora.*"

*   *   *

Orianna left without revealing anything else, although she had given me plenty to chew on. It was nearly midnight; the bar was closed, so there was no way of dragging anything else out of anyone. The crabby *signora* had vanished into her personal accommodations, most likely to polish her own possessions. Fog swathed the street. I offered to drive Orianna home. She laughed at the idea.

"I think this short trip will be much more dangerous in a car. We might end up in someone's *salotto*. There's nothing much to worry about. I can't see anyone in this fog, and no one can see me."

She had a point.

I accompanied her halfway home, then walked quickly back. Naturally, I was wide awake, no doubt because of a combination of the provocative information she had given me, the creepy quality of the fog, and the fact that, by my body clock, it was still late afternoon.

There had been no message from Ray. What kind of day was he having that he couldn't pick up the phone?

I navigated the tables in the empty bar to the public phone.

This time, I reached Ray's home answering machine on the first ring. I suppose that was an improvement. I left a message. He still didn't answer his cell.

I looked around the bar. In the pale light from the hallway, it was a ghostly place. The bistro-style chairs had been upturned on tables for ease of sweeping. In the gloom, they took on a menacing look. When had I turned into such a wuss? I jumped once, when I thought I saw someone sitting in the corner, but it was a merely a stack of chairs. A trick of the light.

I was well and truly stuck. There was no one to talk to. Nothing to do. Nowhere to go in the goddam fog. At the same time, I had plenty to worry about. Who was the man who was following Mrs. Parnell? Had he found her? What did he want? Where had she gone next? And most important, would she end up with a full-blown heart attack on her own in Italy, maybe even behind the wheel on a winding mountain road.

I checked my watch for the umpteenth time. Alvin wasn't answering and, more pertinent, even if he did pick up the phone, he wouldn't have had time to discount the nonsensical story that Mrs. Parnell had a son.

I helped myself to a glass of the house red and left a couple of Euros on the bar. I needed a good plan, and I stomped back to my room to make one. The big issue: the next step. I had wanted to head out after Mrs. Parnell as soon as the fog lifted. Now I had to try to get a group of hostile villagers to tell me what they had talked about. I was glad Orianna had agreed to help me. I spent a bit of time studying the map of Italy. I had no idea what to do next, and the wine was no help.

What would Mrs. Parnell do?

I lay there thinking of Mrs. P. spouting her favourite military catch phrases. Did any of them apply to this situation? *Don't fire until you see the whites of their eyes. Bombs away. Know your enemy.* That one seemed to fit. Orianna had mentioned that Mrs. P. warned the villagers not to give any information to anyone who followed her. That told me she was wary. And that was good news. But was she also wary of me? Could she know I was following her?

What else would she say? *Once you know your enemy, keep him guessing.* That worked. There were three more towns on my list. Pieve San Simone, Montechiaro and Alcielo.

A logical route would be straight south to Pieve San Simone, then directly across Eastern Tuscany on back roads to Alcielo. After that, a northeast turn would lead to Montechiaro. Mrs. P. knew me well enough to be sure I would want to take the logical route. I would never start with Montechiaro, because it was not in the logical loop and would mean doubling back and extra distance.

Okay. Montechiaro it would be.

Eventually, I fell into a troubled sleep, my dreams full of swirling fog, faceless men driving Mercedes, downed planes in gardens and little girls wrapped in billowing white silk.

*   *   *

I did a double-take as I walked into the bar at ten o'clock the next morning. I'd had a lousy rest and still managed to sleep late. The old men were waiting for me. The glowering looks were gone.

I smiled, and the world smiled with me.

"Buon giorno, signora," the proprietor said. A grin creased her heavy-jowled face.

"Buon giorno," I said.

The old men nodded. Some went so far as to smile gap-toothed grins. Something had happened to change everyone's attitude. My money was on Orianna.

For some reason, I was starving. Maybe fog does that to you. And speaking of fog, the village was still shrouded. I wouldn't be going anywhere in a hurry. I settled down to a caffè latte, and fresh crusty bread and cheese for breakfast, then turned my attention to the gentlemen. I was more than a bit relieved when the door swung open and Orianna appeared, looking much more rested than I did. And, even better, ready to translate.

The old gentlemen were all pleased to talk about the war. The trick was not in getting them to talk, rather in getting them to focus. I couldn't have done it without Orianna, for sure.

"Ask them if they think that someone actually escaped from the plane." I sat back and waited. This question created a great deal of loud talking. I felt a buzz of excitement too.

"They think it's possible," Orianna said.

"How would someone survive under those circumstances? Where would they hide? You mentioned that the Germans were searching the villages."

"Partigiani," was the answer. The word echoed. Everyone said it at least once. Everyone nodded vigorously when anyone else said it.

Partisans.

Orianna extracted key bits from the bubbling talk and distilled them for me.

After a volley of information, I said, "So the partisans were hiding in the mountains?"

"Yes, they led the resistance against the Germans. It was very dangerous. They had other people with them, sometimes infiltrators from the Allies, soldiers who were separated from their platoons, escaped prisoners. Americans, British, Canadians too. Even Russians. I don't know really all the details. I was just a little girl. And these men here," she looked around, "they were not partisans, they were poor farmers, hiding in the root cellars or in the woods until the war was over. They would hear rumours. They wouldn't know for sure."

"What happened to the partisans after the war?"

"They went home, back to their lives, I imagine. They were young, adventurous types."

"Were there any from your village."

"A few, yes. They are all dead now."

"Do you think you could find someone who would have been a partisan hiding in these mountains?"

"I could try. There is probably someone who would love to talk about those old adventures. It will take some time. I will have to talk maybe to the librarian and see whose names they have in documents in the city hall."

"Thank you, Orianna. I'll be on the move around Italy. I'll stay in touch and see if you've found anyone."

"I will do my best."

"Okay, now please ask these men about the so-called son. Did anyone see him?"

"What does he look like?"

I sighed. "Middle-aged. Maybe dark hair. Maybe wearing a raincoat. That's the best I can do."

A minute later, Orianna shook her head. "Except for your grandmother, you are the only stranger who has been asking questions around Berli."

That was good news, unless by some far-fetched connection,

the so-called son was known in Berli, and they were covering up for him. What were the chances? Poor, I decided.

* * *

The fog lifted by noon, leaving a soft, glistening green behind on the mountains and pastures and the odd wisp of mist. I prepared to set out with a packed lunch from the now friendly *signora* and many good wishes from several of the good people of Berli.

I was surprised Orianna hadn't been there to say goodbye. She'd done so much to help me, and I wanted to thank her one last time. I decided to trot down the ruella and knock on her door. As I tossed my bag and backpack into the Ka, I spotted her.

She was running up the steep road, scarf flying in the wind like a victory flag. I straightened up and waited.

"Grazie a Dio," she said. "I was very afraid to miss you."

"I wouldn't have left without saying *ciao.*"

She threw her arms around me. "I have wonderful news!"

My dear Miss Wilkinson,

I hope that my attentions have not been in any way responsible for the termination of your engagement to Harrison Jones. If I have contributed to this, I apologize profusely. However, I would like to add that Sgt. Jones turned out to be a most shortsighted and foolish man, if you will pardon my unsolicited opinion.

I would hope that, at some time, we will find ourselves in a congenial setting where we might resume our discussions about music. Although you are a most intelligent woman, I cannot share your view of the works of Shostakovich, and would appreciate an opportunity to make my case more fully on the topic.

Yours very sincerely,

Walter Parnell

Eleven

Y ou found her?" I shouted.

Oriana's face fell. "Sorry. But I have found a *partigiano* for you. Someone who was here in the war and who was connected to everything that went on. He was connected to many partisan brigades. My mother remembered some people who knew some other people, and we were finally able to locate him. He is eighty-seven years old. I spoke to him on the telephone, and his mind is still very clear."

"Thank you. This might be just what I need." Of course, it might also be a total waste of time. I didn't say that. If Mrs. P. had been there, instead of on the run, she would have shouted, "Onward into the breech!"

"I hope so. His name is Luciano Falcone. He was a famous partisan. They called him *il Falco.*"

"The Falcon. I'll write down the information," I said, reaching for my bag in the car.

"I have already written it, with his address." She handed me a small piece of paper, with neat European style handwriting and a name, address and telephone number. "He is expecting to hear from you and will be happy to talk about his time in the mountains here."

"He's in Florence?" I said.

"Yes. Firenze. Is that a problem?"

"Of course not," I said, although I had a plan, and Florence didn't figure into it. No point in disappointing Orianna after all her efforts. I'd just keep going south to Montechiaro and head back up to Florence afterwards if I didn't locate Mrs. P.

"It is just a few hours from here," she said. "You Canadians are used to long distances."

She had a point. What was a couple of hours? Florence it would be, after I'd exhausted the towns on my list. After a final round of hugs and cheek-kisses, I got into the Ka and turned the key. I gave a wave at the send-off party, a cluster of ancient farmers, Orianna and the still smiling proprietor, who reached through the Ka window to give me a bearhug.

Italy always took a bit of getting used to. I pulled away to a chorus of *ciao! ciao! ciao!*

I soon whipped past the tiny main street and headed down the steep and winding mountain road. As I had promised myself, I pulled over and stopped at every point I could on the way down. I found no skid marks and no silver Opels lying crumpled at the foot of rocky hills.

I was surprised at how soon I was passing through the nameless village, where I'd spent the first night. I'd forgotten there was a cross-roads. I pulled over, checked the map, and concluded after some poking around, that if I took one road, it could knock some mileage off my approach to Montechiaro.

A small group of cars was clustered outside the bar, and people were standing around enjoying the absence of fog and the presence of sunlight. That dashing young man about the village, Dario, pulled up behind the Ka in his red Alpha Romeo. I waved, and he hopped out of his car, looking like a billboard ad, all that bedhead to go with the bedroom eyes. Good thing my affections were committed.

"Bella!" he shouted. What the hell, maybe he'd heard something. I got out of my car, and he greeted me with a triple cheek kiss. He made a valiant attempt to entice me into the bar to eat something.

"No, thanks." I remembered to get back into character. "I was wondering if you'd heard anything about my grandmother. Did she drive through here on her way from Berli?"

"Sorry, I didn't see her. I am not on this road all the time. Just when I am *fortunato.*"

"Can you ask these people, please, Dario. Remind them she was driving a silver Opel."

"Of course."

No one claimed to have seen her on the road. It had been foggy, they reminded me. And it was still nippy, even if the sun was shining. Dario said, "They told me to tell you it's a good day to be inside drinking grappa with your friends. They think you might want to try that too."

"Not a chance."

I knew enough about grappa to stay away from it. There are potent drinks, and there are really potent drinks, and then there is grappa.

I was distracted by a minor fuss. A tiny old man, bent nearly double, was jabbering at Dario, in a high-pitched whine. I didn't remember this man from my visit the day before. He wasn't a type you could forget easily.

Dario nodded and nodded and laughed.

Everyone else laughed too.

I waited. Finally I could wait no more.

"What did he say?"

"He said he saw an old woman driving very fast. Like a Formula One driver.

"That's my *nonna*," I said proudly. "Which way did she go?

169

Dov'è andata?" That was one of my better Italian phrases, and one which I figured I would get to use again at some point.

Dario pointed to the road that went south, the one I would take if I were to head to Pieve San Simone.

This seemed to enrage the tiny man. He jumped up and down, and shouted at Dario. He gave him a whack on the backside for good measure. The crowd howled.

"Scusate, zio," Dario kept saying, laughing.

The small man turned to me and pointed emphatically in the other direction.

"Grazie," I said and stammered out something in Italian that was supposed to mean "Did you see a Mercedes following her?"

No results there. I was at the end of my useful Italian. I turned to Dario. He shrugged. He was going to end up with a lot of wrinkles on that pretty face if he kept using those expressions.

"Please, Dario. Ask him again. I really need your help."

He ran his hand through his hair. "Sure, for you, *bella,"* he grinned and turned to the elderly man.

A torrent of Italian followed. Everyone joined in. A few more people, who had been inside drinking grappa, emerged to join the chaos. The Mercedes excited a lot of chatter.

"What are they saying?" I asked Dario.

"Different things," he said. "What would you like to hear? You can have your many choices."

I nodded in the direction of the small, fierce gentleman. "What does this man say?"

"Now he says a car stopped in the fog. He doesn't know what kind of car, and he doesn't know which way the car went. He says maybe someone else in the village will know. If you are not in a hurry, he will ask everyone."

I kept a straight face. "Thank him very much for me, but I

have to leave right away. I have an appointment. I guess it means the Mercedes..."

"...with your uncle driving," Dario added helpfully.

"Yes, I guess it means he didn't see where my grandmother went."

"I think that is true," Dario said.

"Well," I said, keeping the grin of relief from spreading across my face.

I thanked the old man and shook his hand. Dario beamed on the sideline. He sidled up next to me and said, "Do you have a *cellulare, bella?*"

"My cellphone doesn't seem to work in Italy."

"I will give you my number. I will let you know if we see your *nonna* again. I will find out for you."

"Terrific. I'll check in with you later."

Dario scribbled a number on a piece of paper, and I dropped it into my purse. I was eager to get away, especially since Mrs. P. was driving like a race driver. I hopped into the Ka before I got another hug. I'm not all that huggy and kissy as a rule. Even without Ray in my life, I wouldn't have been looking for a weekend romance in a strange country. If I read Dario's body language right, that's what he had in mind. I'm not the girliest girl, and I wouldn't have thought that an unglamorous widowed lawyer wearing running shoes would be his type, but I didn't have time to fret about that. The old man seemed certain about the direction she'd driven off in. Southeast, unless I was mistaken.

I thought about it as I turned the key. None of the towns on our list were in that direction. Was Mrs. P. just trying to give her so-called son the slip? That made sense. It didn't give me any guidance about where to go next. The profound feeling of relief I'd experienced evaporated. Italy might be small compared to Canada, but it was still a hell of a lot of territory to comb looking for one very fast and tricky elderly lady who definitely didn't want to be found.

Of course, a new thought came to me.

Southeast would lead me to Florence.

Firenze.

The home of Luciano Falcone. Ridiculous coincidence? Or belated stroke of luck?

The thought of driving in Florence made my stomach hurt. Florence was a spectacular medieval city renowned for its art, architecture, magnificent piazzas, jaywalking tourists, gouging prices, suicidal scooters and other frenetic Italian drivers, not to mention five-hundred-year-old streets that switched from one-way to two-way at whim. I was going to have to negotiate those ancient streets in my mobile dehumidifier. And for all I knew, Mrs. Parnell could have just waited to give that Mercedes the slip and headed for one of the other destinations.

Any decision was better than no decision, I knew that. There was no way to be sure I was doing the right thing. It was important to do something. A new thought dawned on me, as I thought about Florence and the navigational chaos I would encounter in the middle of the city. There was something else in the middle of Florence.

The letters O, R and E. ORE, the one word we hadn't been able to figure out on the list on Mrs. Parnell's telephone book. To hell with Pieve San Simone, Montechiaro and Alcielo.

My decision was made.

* * *

During the trip, my brain worked overtime. I tried to think like Mrs. Parnell. What would she do after she gave this guy the slip, which I was sure she had? Was this direction just a diversionary

172

tactic? Did she still intend to visit the other towns? Had she ever intended to visit them? Did he have the same list of towns? If so, it was just a matter of time until he found out where she was. The first thing she'd do would be to ditch the Opel, which was large and noticeable. She'd decide on camouflage.

Florence was a major centre, and I knew from personal experience that all the car rental agencies had offices in the city. It would be easy enough to switch cars, even if you had to pay a penalty. Mrs. Parnell is always willing to pay for what she wants. If my memory served, the car rental spot I needed was not too far from the railway station and near the highway leaving town. Knowing it and finding it were two different things, of course.

Eventually, tired, cranky and unbelievably lost on the outskirts of town, I parked the Ka and sought out a small, pleasant *trattoria*. I asked for a telephone book along with a menu. I gobbled a calzone without tasting a bite. I found the address for the car rental Mrs. P. had used and picked up a flurry of conflicting directional advice from the staff and the other diners. I was on my way.

No one said it would be easy, and it wasn't. After a ridiculously long time, I wedged the Ka in a half parking space and scoured the area on foot. I was hot and tired, when I found what I was looking for.

"Hello." I smiled brightly at the middle-aged man behind the desk. He looked tired, irritable and bored, in equal parts. "I hope you can help me. I believe my grandmother planned to exchange her vehicle for one that was easier for her arthritis. She was renting an Opel from you. Her name is Violet Parnell. I am hoping to catch up with her before she leaves the city. She needs a bit of help with her trip. I can just wait around if she hasn't been in yet."

The rental agent didn't seem to have any concern with checking out the information for me. I'd learned that a grandmother is the one key that opens all doors. He nodded, and after a few taps on the keyboard, I had my answer.

"Sorry, *signora*. We have no one by that name."

I felt myself deflate. Had I been wrong in assessing her strategy? I didn't think so. She would have to use her real name. She'd probably had to show her passport. I now knew her maiden name since reading some of those letters. No harm in trying. "Sorry," I said. "I meant to say Violet Wilkinson. Parnell was her husband's name."

Bingo.

Pretty sneaky, Mrs. P. Two can play sneaky games. She had indeed returned the Opel, the agent told me. Her new car wasn't ready yet.

"I'll wait," I said.

"Domani mattina, signora." He smiled. *"Scusate,* it will not be ready until tomorrow."

"Tomorrow?" I said. "That's fine. I'll just check in with her at her hotel. She's at the Paris Hotel, is she?" I gave the name of the hotel Paul and I had chosen on our honeymoon. I held my breath to see if he would fall for this new ploy and reveal the place she was staying. My usual concerns about the value of privacy were well overwhelmed by my need to know and know fast.

He frowned at the screen. *"Strano.* It seems we do not have a local address. She will be picking up the new vehicle at one o'clock."

"That's fine," I said. "I'll find her. What kind of car was she able to get this time? Was it a Ka, by any chance?"

"Ma no, signora! A Ka! *No no no no. No.* She selected a Volvo sedan. Very nice. *Molto elegante."*

"She likes those," I said.

I left the office and ambled along the sidewalk. There were hundreds, if not thousands, of places to stay in and around Florence, so there wasn't much chance I could find her hotel.

I decided I needed a place to stay. I could use the time to check out the partisan, signor Falcone, then pounce on Mrs. P. at the car rental. Since it had been a what-the-hell kind of day, I decided on the Hotel Paris. It would be a nice treat and a trip back in time. I allowed myself plenty of time to find the hotel, counting on being lost. It took even longer. Lucky me, there was a room available. That's the nice thing about the foggy old off-season.

I got a reasonable deal on a room on the fourth floor and dragged my sorry ass up the stairs. I had fond memories of the historic mansion with high ceilings and casement windows that opened over the narrow street outside. The decorations were vaguely Florentine, with frescos and curlicues. The bed was welcoming. I conked out seconds after getting into the room and slept for a while. That was one bad habit I'd need to drop, and soon.

I spent a half hour in the shower and emerged, shampooed, clean and rested. I changed from my jeans to my black pants and jacket. I slipped on the leather loafers, because a woman wearing running shoes would not get taken seriously in Florence. I fiddled with the silk scarf until it looked right and finished with a slash of the Graffiti Red. I was ready to deal with the Florentines.

I used the hotel phone to call the number for L. Falcone. No answer.

Okay. No problem.

The Paris Hotel was within easy walking distance of the historic centre of Florence. I had plenty to keep myself busy until someone answered. Just to be on the safe side, I headed downstairs and double-checked with the front desk. Could they show me how to get to this address?

I left with a map. The route to Luciano Falcone's house was marked out in yellow highlighter. No more than a forty-minute walk. A piece of cake compared to five minutes behind the wheel in this town.

First, I headed along the street to find a payphone to check in on the home front.

*　　*　　*

Alvin took seven rings to answer the phone. I reminded myself that we were being nice to each other and said, "Glad you could bring yourself to answer. Have you heard anything from Mrs. Parnell?"

"That means you haven't either."

"No luck so far."

"That's so bad. Where are you?"

"I'm at the Paris Hotel in Florence, if you need to reach me, and, believe me, I'm thinking of nothing else but finding her."

"Florence? You're in friggin' Florence? With Violet at death's door? You're at the Paris Hotel? Sounds *very* cushy. Too bad you're not here answering the phone, and I'm not over there trying to find Violet. It's not like we got all the time in the world to find her, before she has a heart attack. I don't really want to be planning a funeral." Alvin's voice went up at least an octave during this.

I kept my own voice level. "I know it's urgent, Alvin. You don't need to remind me about that. And I am not in Florence on an art tour. Mrs. Parnell is here."

"Florence wasn't on the list."

"Remember that fragment? Ore. Think about it. There's a man here who might be able to help. Anyway, any luck on

176

tracking down the son?"

"That's another thing, all that stuff about the son. She doesn't have a son. I spent all day checking. Your sister Alexa got Conn on it. It was a crazy idea anyway. He came up empty. No big surprise. How could Violet have a son and us not know a thing about it?"

"Of course, she would have told us if she had a family. But we had to check it out. If he's not her son, then he's pretending to be her son. He can't be up to any good. Anyway, we have to follow up on whatever we find out on either side of the Atlantic, no matter how weird it might be. I have something else for you. And don't sigh like that. Now I need you to find out about the crash of a bomber in 1944 in the mountains, near Berli. The information would have surfaced after the war."

"Okay, sure, downed planes in 1944. What's the connection to Violet?"

"I don't know. She was in that village, and that plane seems to have been a big secret deal during the war. Someone told me that she was very upset about it."

"You mean that could be connected with the dead guy Violet was talking about?"

"Maybe. I don't know. See what you can turn up. See who was on it. Any luck with the security images?"

"Not so far. Do you have any idea how long it takes to watch twenty-four hours worth of images on six separate cameras?"

"Stiff upper lip, Alvin. Talk to you later."

I called Ray Deveau next. No answer at home. No answer on the cell. So much for romance.

*   *   *

I tried the telephone number for Luciano Falcone once more.

177

No luck there either. Then I did a little calculation. He would have been a bit older than my father. My father often doesn't hear the phone ringing these days, especially if he's chosen to leave his hearing aid in his dresser drawer.

The address was in Oltarno, the other side of the Arno River. According to the reception clerk, it was not too far past the Pitti Palace and the Boboli Gardens. Paul and I had ambled along that route together on our honeymoon. I didn't let myself dwell on that.

I strolled through the narrow medieval streets, crammed with tall stone buildings housing small shops, restaurants, businesses and homes. I deliberately chose those streets off the beaten track to avoid the tourists. I also gave the Ponte Vecchio a miss. Too many memories. Instead I took the Ponte Santa Trinità, the next bridge down. There was less foot traffic on that one, and it had a great view of the river and the city on both sides, if you cared about the view, which at that moment I didn't.

After several wrong turns on foot, I finally found the address. signor Falcone lived behind a door-sized gate in faded black. Two black metal pots with geraniums flanked it. I rang the doorbell next to the name Falcone. No answer. I rang again. A curly-haired boy of about twelve opened the door. He could have rivalled any cherub in any painting in the Uffizi gallery. This was a modern-day cherub though, wearing a long-sleeved soccer shirt and expensive-looking running shoes which made his feet look huge. Apparently, I scared him. He squeaked, ducked past me, skittered along the curving street and disappeared around the corner. I put on a burst of speed and caught up with him. I managed to trap him in a corner. I did hope that no conscientious Florentine would call the *carabinieri*. What was the matter with the kid? He squirmed and whimpered. There was no reason for him to look quite so terrified.

I said in garbled Italian, "I am looking for signor Falcone. No one seems to answer. He is an old man. Do you know if he is at home?"

He stared at me. "Signor Falcone?"

"*Si!*" I shouted joyfully.

"*È morto.*" His lip quivered.

"*Morto?* Dead? That can't be."

"*Si. È morto. Certamente.*"

His huge luminous dark eyes filled with tears. Was signor Falcone his grandfather?

"I am sorry," I said in my best Italian.

He rubbed his nose on his sleeve. He shook his head.

"He was expecting to hear from me," I said.

"*Aspetti, signora.*" The young man turned, ran back along the narrow curving street and vanished into the house of Luciano Falcone. I hurried after him, thinking no matter how horribly inopportune this death was, it was obviously a personal tragedy as well. As I reached the black door again, the boy emerged with a woman. She was tall and voluptuous, like Italian film stars of the fifties, with the same dark hair and luminous eyes as the boy. Hers were rimmed in red. He rattled on in Italian, pointing to me. She blew her nose and then nodded.

"*La mamma,*" he said to me, in explanation, "*parla inglese.*"

She introduced herself as Maria Martello. "I am speaking English only a little bit."

"Already I can tell that your English is much better than my Italian."

"Thank you, *signora,*" she said. "How can I help you?"

"Your son tells me that signor Falcone is dead."

She choked up as she spoke. "*Si.* A car hit the *signore* in the street. He was just going to the Bar 45 for a *caffè corretto.* He went every day. He would have a beautiful lunch, a little nap.

Then he would walk to see his friends. He was very old. Perhaps he fall down in front of the car."

Caffè corretto, I knew from happy experience, was espresso "corrected" with a shot of grappa. I also knew it could knock your socks off if you weren't used to it. Most Italians seemed to have adapted well to the correction. It was only tourists who fell over as a rule.

"You think he fell?" I said. "What a shock that must have been for you."

"It was a *tragedia.*"

"Signor Falcone was your father?"

"No, I am the housekeeper. He was wonderful man, very good to me and to Fabrizio, my son. He is very upset."

"When did this happen? Recently?"

"*Oggi.* Today. This afternoon."

"This afternoon? I can't believe it."

She began to weep. "Why now, when he was so happy?"

"Now, when he was so happy? Why was he happy now?"

"Because after all these years, the telephone was ringing and people were coming to ask him about the war. He loved to talk about the war," she wailed.

"What people?"

"A *signora.* An old woman. The age like signor Falcone. She came to see him."

I fished in my backpack and pulled out the battered poster of Mrs. Parnell. "Is this the woman?"

"*Sì.* This one."

"And she was here today."

"*Sì.* This afternoon."

"And what happened?"

"They talked and talked. They laughed a bit, they talked some more. I make them lunch," she sniffed. "They did not eat much, they drank some sherry. They talk and talk more."

"What did they talk about?"

"I did not listen too much. I had much work to do, and I was glad signor Falcone had someone else to talk to this time."

"You said people wanted to talk about the war. Do you think that's what it was?"

"Yes, the war for sure."

"Did they seem sad? Upset?"

"Signor Falcone was a big partisan. Sometimes it makes the old people cry to remember the war. Not signor Falcone. He had funny stories. I have heard them all a thousand times. They are not quite so funny after a while."

"And the *signora?*"

She stopped to think. *"Sì,* perhaps whatever they talked about made her sad, but something made her *furiosa."*

"You didn't hear what she said?"

"Just her voice. Very angry. And signor Falcone trying to make her cheerful again."

"Did he succeed?"

She shrugged. "I was not really listening."

"Do you know where the *signora* went after?"

"I do not know." She turned and spoke rapidly to Fabrizio, who was leaning against the wall scuffing his feet. He answered just as rapidly.

His mother turned back to me. *"Scusate, signora.* We do not know. To her hotel, I think," she said.

"Did she have a car?"

The woman shrugged again. "I did not see her arrive."

"You said that *people* came to see him. Who else?"

"Sì. Look you are here."

"Besides me."

"No one else came. A man called on the telephone, and he

was going to meet the *signore*."

"And then the man didn't come here?"

"He make an *appuntamento*. He did not come yet, because the *appuntamento* was for five o'clock and by that time, the *signore* was already…"

I touched her sleeve and said, "This must be very hard."

"*Sì*. I don't know what we will do."

"Did you see what happened?"

She reached for her son. "Fabrizio saw it. He is very upset."

I glanced at the boy. The kid was definitely shaken, all right. And more than just shaken.

"What about the car that hit him? Was the driver arrested?"

"They did not find him. He left signor Falcone to die on the road. *Disgraziato!*"

I gave her a minute. "Did anyone see the car? Did anyone tell the police?"

She said, "Of course, the police were called. I heard my neighbour crying. I thought it was Fabrizio. I ran out and…"

"And the car was gone?"

"*Sì.*"

"Your neighbour saw it happen?"

"She found signor Falcone lying in the middle of the road."

"Maybe she knows what kind of car?"

"I don't think so."

"That information might save someone else."

"But why?" she stopped and stared. She brought her apron up to her mouth. "*Dio mio!*"

The boy turned as white as marble.

"Was the car a black Mercedes-Benz?"

Fabrizio tore past me and raced along the street and around the corner. I said, "He's understandably upset."

I would have chased the kid, but I wanted to talk to the

neighbour, and I needed his mother with me. Half an hour later, I'd had a long conversation with the woman who'd found signor Falcone. We stood in her doorway, our conversation translated by the *signora*, including the hand movements, tears and words of lamentation which needed no translation. At the end of the conversation, I had no new information. A fine and generous old man had been killed. No one knew quite how. No one had seen anything. Everyone was stunned. I knew since neither woman invited me in and forced food on me, that they must have been in shock.

"And the police?" I said, winding up the conversation.

They both shrugged, implying what was the use of police?

Maria Martello said, "Of course, police officers came, lots of police. Photographers too. The ambulance took signor Falcone away."

A remnant of red and white police tape still flickered in the breeze in the spot the women had pointed to, although the police had obviously come and gone. I didn't know how the Italians handled these things as a rule, but these narrow streets couldn't be completely blocked off for any length of time without chaos.

"I need to talk to one of his friends. Someone else who might have been in the mountains near Berli as a partisan."

Maria Martello spread her hands, a silent entreaty. "*Signora*. It is very hard for me to think of anything today."

"I realize that this is a tragic day for you. It's important for his memory. Can you think of someone, maybe not here in Florence? Anywhere in Italy. Anywhere, anytime."

She paused. "There might be someone. I will try to check his papers. He has photographs and names in the apartment. There is one old friend. Maybe I can find that."

"Thank you. Did you see photos? Photos of when he was a partisan?"

"*Sì.*"

"Could I have a look at them?"

She hesitated.

I knew she was wondering about the rightness of this, as I would have been myself. That was not my problem. I needed something to move forward on. I tried to smile sadly, in a trustworthy fashion.

"It would help so much," I said.

The *signora* might have been distraught, but she was not stupid. I could tell that she was starting to wonder about me and what I really wanted. Perhaps she was processing the idea that, if the death had not been an accident, and since people wanted to talk to him about the war, there might be some connection. She seemed like an honest and transparent person. I could imagine her thoughts written on her face.

"I must go to my son," she said. "He is very upset. Later, I will look."

"Please give me your address and telephone number, *signora*," I said.

She looked surprised. "This is my home. Fabrizio and I live here, with the *signore*."

"I didn't realize that," I said.

"I do not know what will happen to us now."

"Did signor Falcone have any children?"

She shook her head absently. I hoped that the kind and generous old man had made formal provisions for Maria and Fabrizio, since they were pretty damn ripped up about his death.

As I left, the *signora* went off in search of her boy, pausing briefly to lock the door.

"Firenze is full of thieves now," she said, meeting my eyes.

I tried not to take it personally.

Toronto, Ontario
June 12, 1946

My dearest Violet,

What excellent news to hear that you plan to attend Queen's University. I think you will make an excellent mathematician, and it would be a waste not to take advantage of the government's education program. Perhaps you will be able to teach it after you graduate. If you were a man, I'd say you would make a first-rate lawyer, but teaching is a very fine job for a woman. As it is, I would like to be a fly on the wall in your classes. You will give the boys a run for their money and probably your professors too.

I am continuing my own studies. I have been accepted to medical school. It will be good to put one's energy into saving lives instead of taking them or watching helplessly as one's colleagues fall.

The next few years should be quite demanding. However, Kingston is not so very far from Toronto. It is easy enough to get the train between the cities. I hope we would be able to get together. Perhaps next Christmas would work out for both of us. I certainly hope so.

Yours very sincerely,

Walter

Twelve

I trotted off towards Bar 45, which turned out to be two winding streets away. Fabrizio's mother ran in the opposite direction. I could hear her calling her boy's name until I rounded the corner.

Just before I reached the bar, I glanced through the front window of a small convenience store as I passed it. Fabrizio was there, flashing a wad of Euros. I stopped and watched. A nasty thought flickered in my head. Fabrizio's mother had been signor Falcone's housekeeper. Fabrizio was very well-dressed, and now here he was, a young boy with a lot of money. Did he have a new source of cash? Could his mother afford to indulge him this much? I asked myself whether someone might have slipped that boy a bundle to let them know when the late signor Falcone was about to cross the small street for his *caffè corretto*.

An ugly question. The answer was possibly even worse. Fabrizio jumped when my hand landed on his shoulder. He whirled and squirmed. I held tight until he slumped and hung his head. His plump lower lip quivered.

The proprietor rolled her eyes. I guess she'd seen a bit too much of Fabrizio and, anyway, she already had his money. She wagged her bony finger at him. *"Cattivo ragazzo."*

Bad boy.

I gave him my most wolfish smile. I fished out my pocket dictionary and pieced together the phrase, "I will keep your secret."

Tears filled Fabrizio's eyes.

I handed him a tissue to blow his nose.

I said in Italian, "Did someone pay you?"

"No," he said, *"no, no, no."*

"Sì," I said. *"Sì, sì, sì."*

"No, no, signora."

I checked the *dizionario* again.

"Sì. I know what you did. I have proof," I said or hoped I said in Italian.

Fabrizio began to wail. I was able to piece through his blubbering that a man had called, the man had paid him, he loved signor Falcone, his mother loved signor Falcone, he thought the man was a friend who would surprise signor Falcone, he never thought it was so bad to do that. A little surprise, a nice thing, and so many Euros to buy treats.

I said, "It's not your fault, Fabrizio. The man tricked you."

Before Fabrizio became too much more upset, I tried to get a description of the man. "You are sure you didn't see him?"

He shook his head, sending tears flying.

"And the car, was it a Mercedes-Benz?"

That triggered another bout of sobs. *"Non l'ho visto,"* he said.

Okay, as far as I could tell, he hadn't seen the man or the car. After listening to him blubbering for a bit, the best I could understand was that the money had been tucked behind a flower pot.

"You must tell the police, Fabrizio," I said.

I couldn't really follow his distraught response. It contained lots of *mammas* and sobs.

I managed to more or less convey the following: "You must do it for signor Falcone and for your mother. You did something a little bit wrong, but someone else killed your old friend, and you have no choice. You have to be a man, Fabrizio. For your mother."

Fabrizio sat straighter, dried his eyes. *"Per la mamma."*

I said, *"Anche per signor Falcone."*

Fabrizio swallowed hard.

I handed him another tissue to mop his dripping nose and moved on before it got too late. I could have called the police myself, but something told me that would just slow things down. Time was what I didn't have. I also didn't want to have to explain holding Fabrizio against his will, even for a minute.

*   *   *

I needed help. A sane voice. Advice. I checked my watch and made for the nearest public telephone before continuing on. The phone was picked up on the first ring for once.

"Is Ray there?" I said.

"Nah." Ashley, the second daughter.

"Do you know when he'll be back?"

"Nah."

"Do you know where he is?"

"No idea."

"Okay. This is his friend, Camilla. We have met."

"Yeah."

"I'm calling from Italy. I really need to speak to him."

"He's not here."

"He's not back in the hospital, is he?"

"Why would he be in the hospital?"

"When he had his appendix out in the fall, he ended up in

ICU. I wondered if that was it."

"Oh, yeah that."

"So he's not sick?"

"I don't think he's in the hospital. *Brittaneeee!!* Is Dad in the hospital again? Wha'? Okay. No, he's not in the hospital."

I massaged my temple with my free hand. "Is it possible to talk to your aunt?"

"Look, Carmella, can you call back later or something? I'm on the other line and it's, like, real important."

*   *   *

Fine. You win some, you lose some.

Alvin didn't answer when I tried calling again, and the machine did not pick up. I was in Florence without a clue how to find Mrs. Parnell among the million or so tourists who still thronged the city in November, despite the crappy drizzle. I had eighteen hours to kill.

I needed to organize my thoughts for a few minutes before I talked to signor Falcone's friends. Just to clear my head and make sure I asked the right questions. If you need to amble around somewhere in order to think straight, I highly recommend this area to do it. At one time, Oltarno was the wrong side of the river. Then in the sixteenth century, give or take a hundred years, upstart rival bankers had constructed the Pitti Palace to thumb their noses at the Medici, and things began to look up in terms of local real estate.

I'd been to the palace and the gardens. I really liked the curving narrow streets of the surrounding community, the houses without an inch between them, the way they loomed over you, flush with the sidewalk, blocking the sky. Aside from the occasional glimpse of a stubborn potted plant, they gave no clue about the lives lived behind the massive wooden doors. I liked to imagine medieval lifestyles.

Churches crept right to the edge of the sidewalk. No long lawns or high wide stairs here. I stopped outside the English Church of St. John. I'm not big on churches. I tend to avoid them, except for weddings and funerals. I try to avoid weddings and funerals too. I was tired of walking, my head was buzzing. I needed to sit and think. I pulled out my travel guide and set it on the middle step. I pulled out my notebook and hunkered down. I added Fabrizio and Maria Martello's names to the others in the book. That reminded me to copy in the dashing Dario's cellphone number. I wasn't so sure that Dario might not be more distraction than help. Just in case, I wrote it down underneath Hazel's, Betty's, Orianna Preto's and Luciano Falcone's.

What a day. signor Falcone was dead. Mrs. Parnell was dashing all over Italy, evading capture. The reports of her driving like a racer and talking to villagers had been a bit reassuring. It might have even been amusing if I'd known what was compelling her to take this trip despite her condition. Maybe the condition was causing the problem. How had I let her get away from the hospital? Dr. Hasheem's words echoed in my brain. What if I didn't find her in time? What if she had a cardiac disaster? What if I'd really screwed up?

A whippet-thin woman emerged from the church and, with a foxy smile, handed me a piece of paper promoting a concert inside the church that evening. It named a tenor and a pianist and included a list of the music to be played, mostly Vivaldi. I remembered this about Florence, you might find a string quartet playing Vivaldi's Four Seasons concerto on a street corner. A dizzying number of evening concerts took place in churches and other quasi-public spaces.

I stood up and thanked the woman profusely. I grinned like a fool. She took a couple of steps back.

I dusted off my black wool pants, tucked the guidebook into the backpack and went on my way with a spring in my step. No wonder I felt grateful. Who in the world liked concerts better than Mrs. Parnell? Shostakovich was her weakness. She'd only attend a performance of Vivaldi pieces as a last resort. There'd be plenty of other options in Florence. I turned back and asked the woman if she knew of any concerts featuring Russian composers that evening.

She glanced at the door and said in a crisp British accent, "I suggest you consult your hotel concierge, madam."

"Good thinking," I said.

It was nearly five thirty, getting dim. I still had time to check the Bar 45 before I found out about concerts. Signor Falcone had gone to the same bar every day, so there was a chance someone at the bar might know about his partisan comrades. Someone might even have heard about the appointment with the unknown man. With any luck, I could extract information from these elderly, grief-stricken and probably unilingual Italian friends of signor Falcone. I reminded myself to be calm and sympathetic and not to scare off the witnesses.

Bar 45 was jammed with people. I approached the server and asked her in fractured Italian where signor Falcone used to sit. She pointed to a corner where two old men were huddled together, leaning on the small wooden table, laughing uproariously. They had obviously moved past *caffè corretto* to straight grappa, and beyond grief to affectionate memory. There were few tables in this bar, typical for a fast food and drink spot, but I could see the regulars got special treatment.

I rehearsed my Italian as I approached. I stuck out my hand to the first old gentleman, introduced myself and said I had come to Florence to speak to signor Falcone to learn about his experience as a partisan. I said how shocked I was to hear of his tragic death. At least, I hoped I said something remotely like that.

They both regarded me with astonishment. Perhaps my words had been quite different from what I had intended. Maybe I'd said the world was flat or the plague was about to rip through the country. That can happen when you're limping along on a rusty vocabulary of about three hundred words, most of them food, drink or toilet related.

One of the old men stood up and gave me a courtly bow. He was a long-faced fellow, about my father's age, with a full head of thick wavy silver hair and a sharp dark mustache. He sported a red scarf even jauntier than my own and a crisp crease in his grey trousers.

"Sit down and have a little something, signora Camilla. I am Vittorio Ralli. Luciano Falcone was my oldest friend. We were just telling stories of his exploits during the war. Luciano had a superb knack for drama and a wonderful sense of humour. He will not be equalled."

I sat down and pulled out the notebook and wrote Vittorio Ralli promptly. For one thing, I had too many Italian names dancing in my head to keep them straight without a written record.

The second old man had a strangely tilted orangy-brown toupee, unlined skin and twinkling bright blue eyes. He howled with laughter as Vittorio Ralli spoke.

Ralli scowled at him and turned back to me. "This is my friend Giuseppe."

"Does Giuseppe speak English too?" I asked, as the man continued to chortle merrily, his blue eyes swimming with tears of merriment.

"Unfortunately not. Forgive him. He is not himself today."

"You speak very well."

"I should, signora Camilla. I was a prisoner of war in England."

"Ah." I was at a loss for the proper comment to make about that situation. What would Miss Manners recommend?

"Revolting food. At least I didn't have to be slaughtered in the service of that madman Mussolini, and I learned another language and met some lovely English ladies." He winked flirtatiously. Something told me this wasn't the first time Vittorio Ralli had ever flirted.

Again, he had me at a conversational impasse.

"How can we help you, signora Camilla?" he asked, waving the server over and ordering a glass of red wine for me, since I was apparently looking pale. He must have had special status in the Bar 45, since in most Italian bars the customer orders from the bar. I accepted, not wanting to seem ungracious. I told him what I wanted, mentioning everything I knew about the plane crash, the pilot and Orianna Preto in Berli, who had suggested the first connection with the partisans. I filled him in on the background: Mrs. Parnell's absence, the black Mercedes-Benzes and the late and obviously lamented signor Falcone and his fatal appointment.

"Any information that you might have about any of those might help," I said, as my generous glass of Bardolino arrived.

"You are in luck, *signora.*"

"I am?"

"Yes. We don't know anything about this appointment, so it must have just been made. Luciano mentioned yesterday that a Canadian lady was coming to see him to talk about the war. He was very pleased. Apparently he likes Canadian ladies. Now I can see why. Was that you, signora Camilla?"

"Yesterday, you said. No, it must have been my friend. She is the one who is missing now."

"Ah, yes, and that is very serious. For her heart, you mentioned."

"Yes, it is. And I believe her visit, and the other appointment, have something to do with signor Falcone's death."

"You must go to the police, *signora*, even though they are incredibly stupid and quite useless."

"Hmm." I hadn't wanted to get the police involved, mainly because I didn't want them to pick up Mrs. Parnell and possibly trigger a heart attack, the very thing I needed to prevent.

He gave a wicked and perceptive grin. "There are channels, of course. They take time. There is politics. Perhaps you'd better steer clear of those fellows, after all. I should know. I was a policeman myself until I retired. Of course, that was nearly thirty years ago."

"Maybe I will try again," I lied. "First, you said I was in luck?"

"*Si.* Yesterday, when Luciano was talking about his visitor, he said they discussed an old friend who had been a partisan with him. Someone they both knew."

I had too many Italian names whirling around in my head, mixing themselves up at that point. I reminded myself that Vittorio was silver hair and flirtatious, while Giuseppe was toupee and twinkle. And unfortunately, Luciano, the Falcon, was dead.

I said, "Was Giuseppe a partisan too?"

Giuseppe nodded, giving the toupee a workout. He seemed to have understood that question.

Vittorio said sadly, "No, he wasn't. He spent the war in the hospital with tuberculosis."

"Oh, but…"

"He has good days and bad days. This is a bad day. He might think he was a partisan. He was not."

"Okay. Does he remember the name of the other partisan that he and Luciano Falcone knew?"

Vittorio shrugged. On him it seemed flirtatious. "Today he wouldn't remember his own mother's name."

"Mamma!" Giuseppe shouted.

I took a swig of wine.

Vittorio smiled approvingly.

"Giusep'," he shouted and asked the same question three times in Italian. I caught the words Lucian' and *partigian'*.

Tears formed in Giuseppe's empty azure eyes.

Vittorio said, "We don't want to upset him. If we talk of other matters, he might remember. I'll get him a bit more grappa. Would you like another glass of wine?"

Somehow I didn't think grappa would be the answer to Giuseppe's memory lapse, but I was new to the culture. I still had plenty of wine, so I turned down the offer of a second glass, before I had lapses of my own.

"By any chance, would he remember the town signor Falcone's friend lives in? Or maybe you overheard them talking?"

Vittorio shrugged. Giuseppe joined him in the shrug, even though he didn't understand the question.

I looked straight at Giuseppe and asked loudly, "Montechiaro? Pieve San Simone? Alcielo?"

A look of unbearable sadness passed over his face.

Vittorio said, "We mustn't push him, *signora*. He is having problems. The slightest stress only freezes his memory, and he feels very bad, very inadequate. We must talk about other things. How much we liked our old friend. I will tell him you said something nice about Luciano. What will it be?"

I thought for a minute. "Although I never met him, from what I have heard, signor Falcone was a fine and generous man."

I could tell from his face the comment was well received. A fast

195

conversation ensued. I listened and didn't understand a word.

In the middle of it, Giuseppe shouted, "Stagno Toscano."

"What's that?" I whispered. "A wine?"

"Benissimo!" Vittorio said. "He remembers the town."

The good news: he remembered. The bad news: I had another town to add to the list. Never mind, I told myself. It's better than nothing.

"And the name of the person?" I said.

Vittorio gave me a reproachful glance.

A half-hour later, Giuseppe still hadn't remembered the name. I was beginning to feel desperate. I wouldn't be able to put off another glass of local red forever.

"Signor Ralli," I said.

"Vittorio," he said flirtatiously.

Fine. "Can you ask him if he has told anyone else about this other friend who was with signor Falcone?"

I gathered from the resulting injured looks and what sounded like recriminations that no one else knew about the friend. No one. No one whatsoever. Absolutely no one! A lot of denials. Was Giuseppe lying like a rug? Had he already told the mysterious visitor? Or did he really not remember? I made no more headway. In fact, when I persisted, both men developed pouts. I put Stagno Toscano, wherever that was, on the list just ahead of Montechiaro, Pieve San Simone and Alcielo.

Vittorio leaned forward and whispered, "Tell me where you are staying, signora Camilla. I will contact you when Giuseppe has a memory breakthrough. I will get you the name. Trust me."

I did. In fact, I was sufficiently grateful for their efforts that I bought a round of grappa for the two of them. What the hell, I decided to have one myself. Paul and I had had a memorable evening consuming the potent beverage. I'd forgotten how much like floor cleaner it tasted, and how it

196

raised the top off your skull and made your eyes water. Never mind, I was on foot, and if no one lit a match near me, I would probably survive the two-mile walk back to the Paris Hotel.

*   *   *

As the old saying goes, too soon old and too late smart. I was whistling my way along the ancient curved streets, heading back to the bridge over the Arno, when I caught sight of Fabrizio and his mother.

"Hello, *signora!*" I shouted, in the manner of one who has had a snootful.

Maria Martello's striking face contorted. *"Strega!"* she screamed.

Strega?

I was pretty sure *strega* meant witch. That didn't make any sense. I'd never been called a witch. Other things, yes, witch, no.

"Pardon me?" I said.

"Ladra!"

Thief?

Now just hold on.

"What are you talking about?" I said.

"I am kind to you, I let you in to my home, when I am in terrible grief, and what do you do! *Ladra! Ladrona!*"

"Stop screaming," I said. "I am not a thief, and I am definitely not a big fat thief. What on earth do you think I did?"

"You know what you did."

"I have done nothing. I have been at the bar with the *signore's* friends."

"You have been in our home to steal signor Falcone's photographs and papers!"

I have to admit, the grappa on top of the red wine and my

197

enduring jetlag made it hard to deal with this bizarre accusation. I told myself to keep calm and not to make things any worse. Didn't matter, they got worse on their own.

"You mean someone broke into your house?" My head whirled dangerously.

"You did!"

"Not true. I didn't break into your house."

"Pfff. I have called the police already. I hope you die in jail, you witch."

"What did they take?"

"Ha! You already know. Thief!"

"Why would you even think I had anything to do with it?"

"Because you wanted the photos and the information about the other partisans."

"You said you'd give them to me. Why would I steal them?"

"Maybe you couldn't wait."

"Why do you think it was me?"

"You were seen. That is proof."

"Seen? Who could have seen me?"

From behind his mother, Fabrizio smirked.

I gasped. Of course. The little creep. First, I sympathize with him for inadvertently causing the death of his benefactor, then he tries to frame me.

The gloves came off.

"And did I get the photos and information?" I asked, expecting the answer to be no.

"Of course you did. That is why I am so angry." The *signora's* nostrils flared. She stood with her hands on her hips, very voluptuous, very Italian, and, I realized, very dangerous.

"Well, I did not," I said. "And I will be happy to tell the police that."

"Of course you deny it."

"I will tell the police they should talk to your son about where he got the money to buy that expensive soccer shirt."

"Signor Falcone gave him the money."

"I don't think so. I think a man gave him the money to say when the *signore* would be going to the bar. I think that same person asked Fabrizio to get the photos and letters. I also think that same man will kill the *signore*'s friend next. That's a lot for one *cattivo raggazzo* to be guilty of."

Fabrizio was struggling to understand our conversation in English. He picked up on the *cattivo raggazo* all right.

"That is not true! Fabrizio is not a bad boy. He would never do such things." The *signora* glanced fondly at her darling and hesitated just a blink.

"I don't expect you to believe me. I think the police would think that Fabrizio could have been an innocent child used by a killer in signor Falcone's death. Of course, if something happens to the second man, Fabrizio's in deep, deep trouble. Do they put children in jail in Italy?"

She clasped her hands on her capacious bosom and howled. The woman clearly had missed a career on the stage. She had the body for it and all the right dramatic impulses. Plus a voice that could really project.

I continued, "Go ahead. Talk to the police. I sure intend to."

I pivoted and strode off. The stress of the situation coupled with the grappa caused my head to spin, but I think I made a dignified exit. One thing I knew, I had to get to Stagno Toscano quickly, before someone else did.

First, I raced back to the café and spoke to Vittorio and Giuseppe. I grabbed Vittorio by the arm and blurted out about the break-in and the theft of the letters and photos.

"We need to find Giuseppe's friend and warn him. And warn his family."

Vittorio stared at me with his mouth open, grappa glass suspended. "Signora Camilla! Please slow down. Sit, sit. Here," he gestured to the waitress, "have a glass of wine to calm yourself."

Oh, sure. I'd had more than enough wine. I opted for *aqua frizzante*. I did sit and repeat the story a little less breathlessly, as I sipped my mineral water. It had the desired effect.

I said, "Where is this place, Stagno Toscano? Show me on the map. If he can't remember, I'll go to the town and ask them who knows about partisans. Is it a small place? Couldn't I just ask around?"

"It is only about an hour from Florence, southwest of the city. It is too big for everyone to know who was a partisan and anyway, young people today don't want to hear about the war."

"He has to watch out for a man in a black Mercedes."

"Giuseppe still doesn't remember. Soon though, any minute, I am confident, it will come back to him. I will do my best to find out for you. I give you my word."

I took a good look at Giuseppe, whose toupee appeared to be turned backwards by this time. I figured he was as high as any transmission tower, and the required remembering just might not be happening. I'd really helped that along with my gift of grappa. What a dope.

Vittorio insisted he would call me when Giuseppe recalled his friend's name. Giuseppe had begun to sing a happy peasant song. Something about birds.

*   *   *

I bustled through the door of the Hotel Paris, hoping Maria Martello hadn't swallowed her fears for Fabrizio and phoned the police, and in turn, that the cops hadn't located my hotel. I was grateful that I hadn't written my name down for Fabrizio's mother. I checked for messages. Vittorio still hadn't called with the name of the friend in Stagno Whatzit. Oh well, it wasn't like I had nothing to do. With luck, I'd find Mrs. P. surrounded by emotional Russians.

I asked the concierge about concerts in churches and was loaded up with flyers. I freshened up in the room and took a couple of Tylenol to overcome the grappa headache. I swiped on some Graffiti Red, re-swirled the silk scarf around my neck and headed out for the nearest phone booth. I tried Alvin one more time. He was gasping for breath when he finally answered.

"What are you doing?" I asked.

"Nothing."

"Nothing is not a good answer. Have you heard anything from Mrs. P.?"

"Have I? You mean you spent the whole day in Florence, and you still haven't found her?"

"And what have you found out during your day?"

"First of all, it's just getting started."

"I need to know about the security cameras, Alvin."

"Oh, yeah, I almost forgot. Last time, I found another image of that guy who passed us just as we were coming into the building. You can see his face better this time, and it's obviously the same person."

"You did? That's great. You can ask the Super who it is."

"Like I never would have thought of that. Since we looked at him together on the screen."

"Right. Sorry. What did he say?"

"He'd seen the guy around, only once or twice. He doesn't know who it is. And if the Super doesn't know him, he couldn't live in the building, or even be a regular visitor. We still have some more stuff to view. It's so boring, you have no idea."

"You're the one up on technology, Alvin. Is there a way to

201

get the image to me? Spend whatever you have to on it. I'll reimburse you."

"I'm on it," he said.

"Keep up the good work. I'm off to church. Find a solution. I'll call you in the morning."

"You're going to church? Wait a minute," he said, but it was too late.

*   *   *

Armed with the list of church concerts, I turboed along the streets of Florence, pushing my way through Florentines dressed elegantly in well-cut black wool coats and classy leather boots. I was jostled by flocks of tourists wearing candy-coloured scarves from market vendors. I ruled out concerts with Mozart or Chopin, too tame for Mrs. P. The concierge had suggested a couple of possibilities and written down directions. I pushed against the tourists thronging the piazza in search of the most likely concert, needless to say featuring works by Shostakovich.

An hour later, having been lost and turned around at least three times, I had peeked into three churches and come up empty. For once, I wasn't running into people who'd worked in England or the USA. No one could help. Where were all the people with cousins in Canada when you needed them? My Italian was getting a workout, although my brain seemed to be on strike. Finally, I approached a young woman playing her flute on a street corner. To my relief she answered in English with a distinct Scots burr. I asked if she knew of a concert that might appeal to someone with a love of Shostakovich. She suggested I try a nearby church.

I dropped a couple of Euros into her open flute case and hustled my butt. It was nearly nine o'clock on what had been a long, tiring, confusing day which had also included too much wine and grappa, and no dinner. I had no time to eat. As it was, any concert would be nearly over.

The church she suggested was like dozens of also-rans in Florence, not old enough to be historically significant, attractive, not beautiful. Who cared? Inside it sounded like a string quartet was doing right by Shostakovich. I paid my two-Euro ticket, nodded to the woman at the ticket desk, and slipped through the door. The dark woodwork and pews gave it a certain gloomy gravitas, although the frescos and gilded statues lifted the atmosphere. I had no idea who all those saints were. Of course, I had other things on my mind.

The concert was in full swing, the pews jammed with intent listeners. I stood at the back, leaning against a pillar, sniffing the churchy air: holy water, decades of burnt incense and beeswax candles. I craned my neck to see if I could spot Mrs. P. anywhere among the audience. I saw several dozen grey heads. No one was smoking or drinking, so the usual indicators didn't apply.

After five minutes, I decided to move around to get a better view. I sidled as far as the front on the extreme right side of the church. I peered down each row. Most of the people were listening raptly, although several glanced sideways at me with reproach.

I returned to the back of the church and made my way over to the far left. I began to edge toward the front, attracting dirty looks from people as I went. So what? I would never see any of them again and, more importantly, I was on a mission.

I was pussyfooting to the end of the aisle when I spotted a familiar hawklike profile at the far end of the third pew. Mrs. Parnell, shoulders forward, head tilted to hear better, eyes front, transported by the music.

I gave a quiet whoop of joy that earned me many glares and shushes.

21 Frank Street
Chesterton, Ontario
July 1, 1946

Dear Vi,

Guess what? I'm getting married. Imagine that! I believe I have mentioned Judge Stiles. He is quite the gentleman, awfully handsome, and also very kind and good to me. It is time for him to have some companionship, now that his wife has been dead for five years. I am sure his children will get used to the idea in time. They are older than I am, so I can't see why they shouldn't mind their own business, get on with their lives, and allow their father a bit of happiness. Regardless of what they say, for our wedding I plan to wear a smart little cream silk suit with pearl buttons and, of course, a matching hat with perhaps just a puff of cream veil. This has been the happiest Dominion Day ever for me! I even have a diamond ring.

Speaking of happiness, it would make me very happy if you would respond to this letter. I know that someday you will find it in your heart to forgive me and that I will find a way to make it up to you. I hope you will be home in Chesterton soon! We could find lots to do here. I still love the movies. "The Best Years of Our Lives" is playing the Vogue. It makes you think about men coming home from war and what they face. I don't know if it is the same adjustment for gals. It made me sad because so many boys we cared about have never come back. I'd like to hear what you thought of it.

With love from Hazel (the person who misses you and who will always be your friend!)

P.S. Betty (Pardon me for living, I mean <u>Elizabeth</u>!) has moved to Toronto and has a job teaching at some snooty private school. There's nothing for her in Chesterton now with her mother and Perce gone. And I have snagged the last eligible man!

H.

,

Thirteen

People sat crammed with shoulders touching in Mrs. Parnell's pew. I couldn't let that hold me back. I had found her. The entire purpose of this trip to Italy was fulfilled. Every inconvenience and bizarre occurrence was worth it. From her posture, she was fine. Probably better than I was.

I wore a silly grin on my face as I began to work my way past the listeners in the pew. It started well, but went downhill fast. These people were in a church, for Pete's sake, listening to music. So you'd think they could have been a bit more accommodating. The snarling reactions diminished my joy, but only slightly.

"*Scusate,*" I said for the eighth time, as I stumbled over a pair of stubbornly unmoving feet and grazed the knees of a scowling woman.

"*Permesso!*" I whispered to an elderly couple. I swear the husband stamped on my toes on purpose.

Never mind.

I continued to be polite. I am Canadian.

I was surprised by the increased muttering and hostile expressions my passage generated. I like concerts as much as the next person. However, this was an *emergenza,* as I kept saying to those whose feet got in the way. Where was Christian charity? And why the reluctance to stand and let me through? Was this the longest pew in the world? Halfway across, I realized it would have been faster to have gone to the back of the church and approached her from the centre aisle. Too late now. I would have had to retreat past the worst of the mutterers and foot stampers. I kept going and hoped for a more civil reception.

I was almost ready to reach out and touch her shoulder, when she turned her head and spied me.

Tears welled in my eyes.

She scowled.

I smiled broadly.

My smile was not returned.

"It's me, Camilla," I mouthed, pointing to myself. "I want to help you."

A chorus of shhs.

Mrs. Parnell got to her feet. The two people between us refused to budge. Something was very wrong. It was as though the person I was looking at was not Mrs. Parnell. Recognition, yes. No warmth, no welcome, no look of mischievous regret. No relief. Nothing. I recognized her face. I could have sworn that someone else looked back at me through those eyes.

I stopped pushing forward. I felt as if I'd been hit.

Years of defense work and helping victims should have prepared me for that look. I'd seen it in people who had nothing more to lose. I'd seen it in victims who had been pushed beyond their capacity to care. I'd never thought I'd see it in Mrs. Parnell. Had she had some kind of cardiac event that deprived her brain of oxygen? Had it changed her personality? You hear about these things. You can't imagine the impact when it happens to someone you love.

Mrs. Parnell whispered something to the people next to

her. Whatever it was caused quite a commotion. People leapt to their feet. A distinguished gentleman in an expensive-looking overcoat shoved me hard.

As Mrs. P. slipped from the pew, two sturdy middle-aged women grabbed my arms. I was trapped. I heard talk of *carabinieri*. I could see Mrs. Parnell hustling as fast as she could with her cane, down the centre aisle toward the church door.

I was stunned and shocked. Not to mention getting roughed up. And Mrs. Parnell was escaping.

Two can play that game, I thought.

"Aiutatemi!" I called. Help me!

The quartet stopped playing mid-melody.

The man holding on to me let go of my arm, shocked. It gave me the chance to jump over the pew to the row behind. I scrambled over people, ignoring the yelps, and reached the centre aisle.

"Interpol!" I bellowed. *"Polizia Interpol."*

It wasn't really a false declaration. I hadn't actually claimed that I was an Interpol officer, so it wasn't my fault if someone misinterpreted. It was worth the risk to stop Mrs. Parnell from disappearing.

I shook off a young man in a striped scarf who seemed determined to restrain me. I raced down the aisle. I never looked back to see if anyone was following. I shot out the door.

The music swelled behind me.

I stopped on the church steps and checked both ways. There was no sign of Mrs. Parnell.

I spoke to the woman at the ticket desk. *"Mia nonna è malata! Dov'è partita?"*

She shook her head. Perhaps she'd heard the sick grandmother story once too often in her time.

No time to argue.

Voices rose behind me. I sped down the stairs and into the street. No grey head in any direction. I picked the route leading toward the piazza and stormed on, peering from right to left. I left no corner unchecked, seeking her tucked in a boutique entrance, standing inside a restaurant door or flattened against the wall of an alley.

No luck at all.

I glanced over my shoulder and saw that no one had followed me from the church. Good. I leaned against a wall and caught my breath. Time to think. If I was out of breath, Mrs. P. must be too. She might be fit. Still, she was eighty-three. Since she had not come this way, she must have gone the other. She would have to be resting. I turned back and retraced my steps, scooting speedily past the church just in case.

At the next cross street, someone whipped around the corner at the end of a long curving block. When I reached the spot, I found no one. Just a dark, misty, damp Florence streetscape in November.

I kept prowling just in case, around blocks, doubling back, continuing to peer into alleys and gated courtyards, although she could hardly have vaulted the gates. She could easily have been staying at one of the small hotels cunningly tucked into this part of the city. All she needed was a key.

Where the hell had she disappeared to?

And why didn't she want me to find her?

*   *   *

An hour later, I let myself into my hotel room and flopped on the wonderful bed. I was relieved that the police still hadn't come looking for me to discuss the theft at signor Falcone's place. If they got a complaint about the church incident and put those two together, life might not be too good.

For a scary moment, I pondered the fact that the hotels have to register foreign visitors with the Italian authorities. Would the police be able to connect the fracas in the church with me and roust me from my ochre-coloured, high-ceilinged room at the Hotel Paris and slap me into a cell? Would anyone have called them? Anything to do with the police was bad. I didn't want to have my movements restricted. On the other hand, it might work in my favour if I went to them and asked where Mrs. Parnell was staying. She would have to be using her maiden name, Violet Wilkinson, as she had at the car rental office, so maybe they'd fall for the sick grandmother story.

In the end, I decided against it. I figured there was plenty of bureaucracy to slow me down and way too much to do me any good. I'd likely end up being questioned and wandering through the rigmarole you'd expect in dealing with police in another country and grovelling for help from the Canadian consulate. My main concern hadn't changed. If Mrs. Parnell found herself in any confrontation with the police, even an interview at the station, it might provide enough stress to trigger a heart attack.

Anyway, I needed time to make a plan. I had one stunning piece of new information: Mrs. Parnell was in full control of whatever was happening. Judging by her quick-witted escape, her mind was working just fine, thank you very much. I worried about what that speedy departure might have done to her body.

I couldn't shake my reaction over the look in her eyes. What did it mean? Mrs. Parnell was no criminal. She was a person of great spirit and integrity. She never gave up. She was always ready to devise another tactic to solve a problem. She wasn't a victim either. Of course, there were things that we didn't know about her, but she always seemed so in control. It couldn't be that she didn't care about me. She had risked her life to save me more than once. She was the most loyal person I'd ever met. She must have had some compelling reason for not wanting to see me. And I was pretty sure it was something I wouldn't like.

I made a list, scratching out things, adding things, scratching out the added things, adding some of them back until I was left with:

She thought she'd encountered a dead man.
She came to Italy with a plan.
Her plan seems connected to the plane crash in Berli.
She has something she wants to accomplish.
She'd visited a former partisan who turned up dead.
She knows exactly what she is doing.
She does not want me involved.
Even though her heart might do her in without medical attention, she won't stop until she gets what she wants.

All this told me whatever she was up to either wasn't legal or wasn't safe. Maybe both.

I also still had one nameless partisan in Stagno Toscano who was possibly in grave danger, one fibbing little boy, four towns left to visit, some kind of false son, who was almost certainly the hit and run driver and who might or might not have been the furtive visitor who got to Mrs. Parnell's apartment before us, a whole lot of Italians whose names sounded quite a lot alike, and a bunch of letters that offered poignant glimpses into Mrs. P. as a young woman, yet shed no light on our problem.

I had one other kick at the can: I would intercept Mrs. P. at the car rental garage the next day at one p.m.

While I was making lists, in my personal life I had: one useless assistant, one unreachable love interest, too many

211

disturbing memories of Florence and a case of jetlag that just wouldn't quit.

* * *

I awoke with a start, fully clothed. I yanked open the heavy velvet curtains to face a grey day. It was just before seven in the morning, and I was ravenous. I wasn't sure when I'd last had a meal. I needed something so that I could at least think straight. The breakfast room would be opening in a half-hour. I showered, changed and tossed my notebook into my backpack.

I pulled my wet hair into a ponytail, slipped my jean jacket over the sweater and headed to the pay phone down the street.

* * *

"Who is this again?" The Cape Breton accent was clear on the line. It would have been one in the morning there. I knew that was prime time for the Deveau girls.

"Camilla MacPhee, your father's friend. We have met, Brittany, although you may not remember. And I spoke to your sister, Ashley, yesterday."

"Oh, yeah. She said that. Something about a hospital. Dad's not in the hospital today either."

"Can I speak to him?"

"I don't know where he is."

"He seems to be on vacation from work."

"Yeah, that's right. He is on vacation from work."

"He's not home now?"

"No, he's not."

"Do you know how I can reach him."

"I don't."

212

"All right. Any idea when he'll be back?"

"No idea. My aunt might know."

"That's great. Can I speak to her?"

"She's in bed."

"Should I call later?"

"It's your money, Carla."

I thought hard. I needed to get something out of one of these pricy phone calls, besides another headache. I tried a variation on the theme.

"Is your father in town?"

"No, he isn't."

"Okay. You don't know where he went?"

"He's on vacation somewhere. He was talking about like Costa Rica or Mexico and places like that. I didn't pay too much attention."

"But…"

"Look, that's my boyfriend on the other line, I gotta go."

"Wait! Is there a number where I can reach him?"

"I don't *know*. He went with a friend. Some lady."

I hung up with a sick feeling in my stomach. Ray had lost patience with me and gone off to a bird sanctuary in Costa Rica or a beach in Mexico with another woman. Who could blame him? It wasn't like I was much of a companion. On the other hand, what else could I have done? I'd had no choice but to try and find Mrs. Parnell. What kind of guy couldn't deal with that?

*   *   *

Okay, I asked myself, what would Mrs. P. do? She always says that an army marches on its stomach. Good advice.

I headed back to the hotel and hit the breakfast buffet the minute the door opened. I managed to catch up on a day's

213

worth of food and stockpiled a bit for the future rough spots. The breakfast room had even higher ceilings than the bedroom, fourteen foot ceilings or more with lovely faded frescos, ancient stained glass windows, and a smattering of other guests who minded their own business. I helped myself to rolls and butter, preserves, cheese and ham and salami. I even had a yogurt and juice. I considered cereal but settled for fruit.

I avoided the coffee pot, where a dark mucky brew was boiling away in what was obviously considered to be American style, and headed for the smiling girl behind the bar counter. She was making cappuccinos.

I was happily sipping one when the desk clerk fluttered in with a message for me. A signor Vittorio Ralli was asking to see me. It was urgent. signor Ralli was waiting in the lobby. Was I available? To hell with cappuccino.

*　　*　　*

Vittorio delivered big time. He'd coaxed the missing name out of Giuseppe's memory and secured an address in Stagno Toscano. He assured me that this man, Stefano Braccia, was a noted partisan, with all his marbles, and unlike poor Giuseppe, he was rumoured to speak some English as well.

"Signora Camilla," he said, running his fingers through his thick silvery waves, "I wish I could come with you. I have promised to help with the funeral arrangements for poor Luciano Falcone. He deserves proper respect, and signora Martello is too hysterical to do a good job. That boy Fabrizio is quite a brat, and who knows, they may even lose their home. *Povera donna.* Not everyone can be *brava* like you. Don't worry too much, because Giuseppe tells me his friend can speak pretty good English. Of course, Giuseppe's a bit off his nut. Let's hope it is the truth."

We left the hotel lobby together and barely avoided a pair of police officers sauntering through the front door. Their uniforms looked like something out of a Gilbert and Sullivan production.

"Don't worry about them," Vittorio said. "They're just *carabinieri.*"

I was still a bit skittish as a result of events earlier that fall, so I did worry about the police. I couldn't afford any delays if I wanted to meet this Stefano Braccia and be back before Mrs. Parnell showed up to pick up her new vehicle at one o'clock. So I was out of there as fast as I could.

Fifteen minutes later, I was in the Ka, trying not to close my eyes. I gripped the wheel and prayed to avoid humans, vehicles and buildings on my way out of town. I should have prayed not to get lost, not to drive in circles, and definitely not to choose one-way streets, which inexplicably and heart-stoppingly changed direction mid-intersection.

Never mind, I was rested, well-fed and glad to get out of Florence alive.

*　　*　　*

You have to get lucky sometime, and I got lucky with Stagno Toscano. The town seemed fairly modern and straightforward. I found the address easily by turning off Via Garibaldi and driving straight for two blocks. Vittorio had given good instructions.

The house was a good-sized, two-storey stucco, with the same type of terra cotta roof tiles seen all over Italy. It had the ghost of a vegetable garden on the side. It sat in a line of newish residences and was surrounded by a fence and a locked gate. A minute after I rang the bell, a woman popped out onto the second floor balcony and waved.

"I am Camilla MacPhee," I shouted up. "I would like to speak with Stefano Braccia."

She waved both arms. *"Momentino!"*

Seconds later, she flung open the front door. She clutched my hand and gave me a huge and unexpected hug. She ushered me up a set of narrow marble stairs and into a large kitchen. The kitchen was a surprise: dark cupboards, built-in huge gas oven and six-burner cook top, microwave, cappuccino maker, large fridge, freezer, double-sink and dishwasher. In the middle of the slate floor was a table that could seat a dozen people. On the far wall, a large-screen television flashed soundless images of half-dressed performers.

The modern appliances stood in contrast to a sofa covered in a ratty quilt. An old man sat there, with another quilt covering his lap. His small dark face was criss-crossed with tiny lines, as if he'd shrunk. There was something lively, almost mischievous, in those faded eyes.

She spoke rapidly to him. I couldn't really follow her staccato Italian, but I got the sense she was telling him to behave himself.

"Signor Braccia," I said.

He nodded.

I introduced myself again, mentioning Vittorio Ralli and Giuseppe, whose last name I'd never heard. I smiled.

He spoke to the daughter in the same rapid-fire manner.

"Si, si, papà! Un po' di vino, signora?" she said.

"No, grazie." I had to be on top of my game to get back to Florence by one.

"Grappa?"

I shook my head and managed a gesture to indicate that

grappa would make me dizzy.

She said, with some anxiety. "Espresso? *Caffè ristretto? Corretto?*"

I agreed to espresso, just to get things moving.

"Please, sit down," the old man said.

"I'm so glad you speak English," I said. "My Italian is quite limited."

"Let's see how much I remember. It's been a long time since I lived in Canada."

"You lived in Canada?"

"For a couple of years in the early sixties, working in construction. Lotta people went over. Some stayed, some came back home."

"Great," I said. "I bet you have a few cousins there."

"Out west. Can't stand that bunch. I got these teeth in Canada though, and I always liked them." He tapped his large white incisors.

"Great-looking teeth," I said. "So, where did you live in Canada?"

"Mostly Toronto. Had to move back to Italy to get some good food," he said with a wicked chuckle. "I hear it's better over there now."

"Still can't measure up to Italy," I said.

That was well received.

"Allora, signora. Vittorio tells me some tall tale about planes and missing women. He says these all have something to do with the death of my old friend, Luciano Falcone."

I took a deep breath. "I am very sorry about your friend."

"Forget about it. At my age, everyone's dying. You get used to it. Luciano was a bit younger than me, only eighty-even. He was still enjoying life, not being kept in prison by his family." He flashed a look at the daughter.

"It all sounds crazy, and maybe I'm wrong, but I believe there is a connection between signor Falcone's death and my missing grandmother. I hope you can help."

"We'll see about that. I am glad you came. It's boring here. There's not much for an old man with no legs to do, except watch my daughter cook, and watch the *porcheria* on the television."

"You'll find this interesting, at the least," I said.

The daughter had produced a feast on the table. In addition to the three kinds of cheese, bread, ham and prosciutto appeared by slight of hand. I couldn't identify everything. I thought I saw fresh ricotta cheese and homemade fig preserves. She gestured toward them with a shy smile.

"Please, you eat," she said.

"My daughter doesn't remember much from our time in Canada. At least she retains the right words."

I filled him in while his daughter helped him from the couch to the table. She filled a large tumbler of homemade wine for him.

"Salute," he said, raising his glass.

The daughter said something in that staccato manner I was getting used to.

"Mariella wants you to know that our family makes this wine. She hopes that you will try just a lil' bit."

"Only a splash," I said. I didn't bother to say because it isn't even noon yet. That kind of thinking gets you nowhere in Italy.

"Not this wine," he said. "No headache, very pure."

"They tell me you were a partisan during the war," I said, wanting to get back on topic.

"I was. Garibaldi brigade."

"What I need to know is if you can recall meeting an

218

airman who escaped from a bomber that went down in Berli back in 1944."

"Sure. I met a lot of downed airmen," he said.

"A lot?"

"Sure. There were all kinds of people hiding in the hills in 1944. Allies who had become separated from the units, pilots who had bailed out, infiltrators, spies, English, American, Russians, you name it. I even met an Indian from India. He was a mule driver."

"Really? And Canadians?"

"Canadians too, of course. Canadians were big in Italy during the war. That's one of the reasons I went over in the fifties. I knew some guys."

"You don't remember meeting any specific Canadian airman in that area?"

"Well, sure, I do."

I got it. I was the most fun he'd had in years. He was trapped in the kitchen of his daughter's house. He couldn't walk without assistance. Then I show up, wanting to talk about what was probably the most exciting time of his life. Who wouldn't want to drag that out? I understood, but I still had to get back to Florence by one.

I smiled conspiratorially. "What do you remember?"

"I remember that everyone died on that plane, except the one guy."

"Were you surprised that anyone could get out of a plane like that?"

"We had learned not to be surprised by nothing. The world had been crazy for years. You could be happy one of the good guys beat the odds, that was it. One day at a time."

"I hadn't thought of that. I had wondered if there was some controversy about the crash."

He shrugged. "Never heard nothing about a controversy. The villagers hid it, couldn't blame them. Didn't want the SS snooping around."

"So you didn't think there was anything suspicious about him?"

He threw back his head and laughed. "For sure, we didn't."

"Why do you say that?"

"Because if we did, we would have killed him on the spot."

"Killed him?"

"You surprised, *signora?*"

"Yes."

"Shouldn't be. It was war. People killed each other all over the place. For a pair of earrings, a dirty look, a rumour. We were partisans. We risked our lives and the lives of our families every day. We all seen people murdered, friends, family, innocent people. Shot in front of us back in our villages. My next-door neighbour was Fascist, he watched while my father got killed in 1936. You know why? Because my father believed in socialism. So a man he knew all his life watch an innocent man get kicked to death. That's why we were in those mountains fighting. We knew the kinds of tricks the Nazis played. And the *fascisti.*"

"Right."

He said, "It was a dangerous time. For everybody. Most of us did things we lived to regret."

I knew he was speaking from experience. I decided not to inquire about what happened to the Fascist neighbour after the war.

"Where did this airman go after he left you?"

"He didn't go anywhere for a long time. He was hurt bad, burned a bit too. It took a while for him to get well enough to leave."

"Did your group look after him?"

"Well, a bit, I guess. We gave him shelter and a bit of food. Someone set his broken arm. One of the girls nursed him. We didn't have medicine or painkillers, except if one of us managed to get some grappa."

"Ah," I said, "grappa."

"Makes a pretty good disinfectant as well as a painkiller," he said with a chuckle.

"And emergency fuel for a vehicle, I imagine. Did he recover?"

"Yeah, sure. I seen a lot worse than him."

I resisted the urge to drum my fingers. "When did he leave your group?"

"When it was okay to. We were on the move, too. The area was crawling with Germans in 1944. They were heading back to Germany, marching prisoners and forced labourers with them. We were doing our best to blow up their transport."

"Did he stay on with your group until the Germans troops were gone?"

"We were a brigade."

"Your brigade then. Did he stay with you for the rest of the war?"

"No, no. He left as soon as he could."

"Do you know where he went?"

"Back to one of the Canadian units, I suppose."

"How would he do that?"

"Probably we gave some names of contacts to help him get back to the Canadians. They been fighting their way north, breaking through the German defensive lines. In '44, they been moving up toward the Gothic Line."

"Were there any Canadians around where you were?"

"They been east of here. Not far, by Canadian distances. It's different when you're on foot in winter."

221

"People knew where the Canadians were? I thought they would be trying to be, I don't know, inconspicuous."

He laughed out loud at that, showing the Canadian teeth. "They had a big army. You could not miss them."

"So he could have made it alive?"

"This guy? Well, sure. He spoke pretty good Italian, he had nerve, for sure. Lotsa charm. The women were crazy for him. Tall blond guy like that. They been fighting over who got to look after him."

"I don't suppose by any chance you remember his name?"

He smiled. "Maybe."

I waited in silence. Two can play these games. He was certainly enjoying it more than I was.

"Some more wine, *signora?* Mariella! *Vino per la signora.*"

The daughter rushed forward with the bottle.

I covered my glass with my hand and shook my head at Mariella. "No, *grazie.* Just the name would be good for me, please."

"I am an old man. I like to have fun," he said.

"Can't blame you for that," I said. "Still, I need to know the answer."

"Forgive my little jokes," he said. "At my age, things come and go. The name is gone. I hope it will come back."

"Oh, boy. I hope so."

"He was RCAF. I remember the symbol."

"While you are trying to remember, I need to tell you something. You have been very kind to me. Your friend Luciano was almost certainly killed by someone who wanted this information. Can your daughter make sure you are in a safe place? Can you go visit friends?"

"I'm not going nowhere," he said, making two fists. "Let them try."

I turned to the daughter and attempted, in my fractured Italian, to tell her that her father might be in danger.

"Madonna santa!" she said, making the sign of the cross. She had picked up the phone before I'd finished talking.

He said, "Now you've done it. Now I gotta go visit my son. I can't stand his wife. She's a stupid bitch and a lousy cook, not like Mariella here. She can work miracles with food."

Mariella, hearing her name, turned away from the phone and stared anxiously at her father.

He lowered his voice and muttered, "Don't tell her I said that. I don't like a conceited woman."

Mariella's mental health was not my immediate concern, although I did get the urge to boot Stefano Braccia's mean old butt.

"You should spend a few days there anyway. It's a dangerous situation, because we don't really know why your friend was killed."

"I'm gonna take the risk."

"It won't take long. It's just to sort things out. A day or so won't hurt, I'm sure."

"You get to my age, every meal counts." He barked something at Mariella.

She said, *"No papà, no papà, no papà."* Finally, she put her hands over her ears. *Papà* was quite a handful. He must have really been something back in the war.

"Now look what you done. I'm gonna have to go there. My son is a policeman. Serves him right to marry a lousy cook."

"Sorry," I said. "Maybe Mariella will pack you some food to take."

"I will go on a hunger strike. Like Gandhi."

"Gandhi's dead. Tell me, would any other partisans remember him? Did Luciano Falcone know him?"

"For sure. You know, it mighta been Luciano Falcone helped this guy get back to the Canadians. Luciano liked him a lot. Everybody did. Especially the women."

"You mentioned that. Tell me, has anyone else asked about him?" I asked.

He shook his head. "Nobody."

"That's good. You are safer that way."

"Safe," he snorted. "Who cares to be safe? I need some excitement in my life."

"Maybe you can tell your son about the connection with Luciano Falcone, find out what happened there. Suggest that it was suspicious. That's a good idea. I'll call and see what you've learned. That would be exciting."

"Humph," he said. "He don't want any extra paperwork. None of those cops do. Lazy bums."

I could tell Stefano liked the idea. The proof came when he wrote down the telephone number at his son's place and handed it to me.

"And I'd appreciate if you'd try to remember the guy's name," I said.

"That's the trouble with us old dogs," he said, tapping his head. "Memory."

I thought back to Giuseppe at the Bar 45. If he could do it, anyone could. "Keep trying."

"You know what? It sounded something like this movie star. That makes sense. It was an exciting time. Like the movies, except not always with a fake ending."

"Like what movie star."

"Sure, you know the one, Indiana Jones guy."

I thought for a minute. "You mean Harrison Ford?"

"That's the guy."

Of course. It was close enough. Harrison Ford. Harrison Jones.

Harry Jones.

Harry, who had been engaged to Mrs. Parnell, the same Harry who never came back. Harry had escaped from a downed bomber. So what? Why would Mrs. Parnell find that so strange? Was it because he bailed out while his comrades died? Never mind, at least I knew who if not why.

"You're a hero, Stefano Braccia," I said.

56 Oak Street
Chesterton, Ontario
September 14, 1956

Dear Vi,

I hope you remember me: I am Hazel Stiles now. I was very sorry to read of your husband's tragic death. Of course, I never met him, but I read about all those military awards listed in his obituary in the Globe and Mail. He must have been very special. What a shame to lose a doctor so young. It must be a terrible loss for his patients too as well as for you. I hope you won't let it make you nervous about driving.

I am sure you will find yourself feeling quite lonely. I certainly did after my husband died nearly two years ago. Of course, in our case, it wasn't an accident. He had three heart attacks, and then he just didn't pull out of it after the last one. He was courtly and kind right to the end. I miss him very much and, as you know, black was never my colour. Also, I am stuck with this rambling house, way too big for one person.

Perhaps now that we're both widows we can get together again to talk. We have something in common, even if it is a sad thing. Remember how much we loved the movies? Of course, they're not as good as they used to be. I did enjoy "The Ten Commandments" though, especially Charlton Heston. That's not how I imagined Moses.

I have decided to move to Kingston and start over. What a shame that you have already moved to Ottawa. I can't imagine you with a job in the civil service. I heard about that from Mrs. Reverend Dornan, who heard it from Betty Connaught. Betty's way too important to talk to me any more. She's the assistant headmistress now, I hear.

Anyway, I hope Ottawa is not too boring for an adventurous girl like you. I must say, I don't like the sound of all those politicians. Oh well, I suppose you get to wear some lovely hats, what with your career and all.

Your friend forever,

Hazel

Fourteen

I did my best to drive like an Italian. I used Mario Andretti as my role model. I needed to be back in Florence by one, and I was behind schedule. On the other hand, I was hampered by the Ka, which may be small and easy to handle, but is not built for the racing circuit.

I tried to recall what I'd learned about Harry Jones from his letters. For sure, both Betty and Hazel thought he was special. And Mrs. P. had been engaged to him. Now she was interested in this crash. Damned if I knew why. If I pulled over and took the time to reread the letters, I'd miss my best chance of catching up with her when she collected her new rental car. The letters would have to wait. A glance at the fuel gauge told me I couldn't put off getting *benzina*. I pulled off the *autostrada* and into a service station. As I was getting the Ka filled, I spotted a black Mercedes accelerating out of the opposite side. I would have followed, but I was blocked in by two other vehicles.

There are almost as many black Mercedes in Italy as there are red Fiats and white Alpha Romeos. So probably nothing to worry about. I headed into the station, found the pay phone, consulted my notes on signor Braccia's number and made the connection.

Mariella answered. *"Pronto!"*

I did my best to remind her of possible danger, including shouting *"Pericoloso! Molto pericoloso!"* a couple of times and *"Mercedes-Benz! Nera!"* to round out the picture. I raced back to the car. The surrounding motorists seemed to feel I had taken too much time. I tossed some euros to the attendant, who shook his fist at me. I hopped into the Ka, pausing just long enough to employ one of the gestures I'd picked up from other drivers in Italy. I left Ka tracks on the asphalt as I peeled out of the service station.

*   *   *

The drive back through Florence was a nightmare. I found more blocked streets, lunatic motos, jumbo SUVs, jaywalking tourists and blocked streets. In fact, I found more of everything except space to drive. The buildings seemed to lean further over the narrow winding streets. Once I'd crossed over the river, the zillion or so pedestrians were all walking faster than I was driving. I did my best to ignore their sneers.

According to my watch, it was five to one, which apparently was the magic time in Florence when all the parking spaces turn into pumpkins. I was still a block from the car rental location. Finally, in desperation, I tucked the Ka into a ridiculously small space. I set out on foot, running. I'd nearly reached the car rental office block when it dawned on me that I'd forgotten to lock the Ka doors. So what? I decided. If someone wanted to steal it, they could just pick it up and walk away.

It was too late to turn back. Mrs. Parnell has a military respect for punctuality. She would be there at precisely 1300 hours as scheduled with the car rental agency. I peeked into the office. No sign of her. Probably in the pick-up area. I puffed up the ramp and into the garage, bent over and gasped for breath.

Three young men were busily vacuuming the interiors of returned cars. They all had on what looked like Mp3 players and seemed caught up in whatever they were listening to. Excellent hip movements.

An Opel with its doors open sat waiting in the return area. I glanced around, and my heart soared. Mrs. P. emerged from the glass-fronted office on the far side of the garage. She was engaged in an intense conversation with a short, bald man with an immense moustache and a rental agency logo on his shirt. She spotted me a second after I spotted her. I stood there with a big honking lump in my throat and felt something sting my eyes. I raced toward her. She nodded curtly to the car guy and turned to me.

"Thank God, you're all right," I babbled. "I've been so worried. I won't hold you back. I'll help you with anything you're doing."

"Leave me alone, Ms. MacPhee."

"What?"

"This is none of your business."

"Of course, it's my business. I am your friend. I need to know that you're all right."

"I do not require your help. Cease harassing me."

"Harassing you? Are you joking?"

"I am very serious," she said.

"Well, I'm serious too, and I won't stop until I find out what the hell is going on. I know about Harrison Jones and the downed aircraft. Are you aware that your apartment was broken into? Do you know that some guy in a black Mercedes is driving around Italy claiming to be your son, and that Luciano Falcone has been killed by a hit-and-run driver, probably by that same guy? How's that for serious?"

Tough words. I could tell by the way her face whitened that I'd gotten to her. I felt a twinge. Maybe shouting about people she knew being killed wasn't the best way to keep her from having a heart attack.

"This is none of your business, Ms. MacPhee."

"Oh, it's my business all right. I have a right to know what you are involved in before anyone else gets hurt."

"You have no such right."

"You may as well get used to the idea and fill me in. I want to help you."

She lit a Benson & Hedges, although this was a distinct non-smoking area. I felt strangely reassured. She regarded me through narrowed eyes and blew a few smoke rings.

"I can be part of it, whatever you're doing," I said. "You've helped me so many times."

"You are correct, of course, Ms. MacPhee," she said. "I will indeed fill you in."

"Great."

She looked around, her gaze flitting from one oblivious car maintenance worker to the next. She lowered her voice. "Not here. We can't be too careful."

"No problem," I said, glancing around. I was pretty sure none of the guys with the vacuums in their hands and the music in their ears had anything to do with anything. Was this part of the paranoia problem?

I said, "Where?"

She nodded in the direction of the back wall.

I decided to humour her. "Sure."

She moved stiffly, but with purpose. Her cane thumped on the cement floor. I followed. We ended up by a wall with a fresh Ka poster and a faded Opel poster. We stopped in front of what looked like a large supply cupboard. Mrs. P. turned around again, narrowing her eyes suspiciously at the young men busying themselves with a Ka at the other end of the garage. I reminded myself that signor Falcone hadn't been paranoid, and someone had flattened him. Maybe Mrs. Parnell was on to something.

"Come here," she whispered, sidling into the storage closet. What did she think? That they could read our lips? Never mind. I followed her. We'd soon get back to our usual cordial comradeship. Anyway, if we did have to worry about being overheard, better be safe.

She held the cigarette in her left hand and put her right fingers to her lips. "Shh."

I nodded.

She pointed to the interior.

I looked.

"Inspect this, Ms. MacPhee," she said. "I think you will be most surprised."

"What?" I said, staring at a pile of rags and a stack of cleaning products. "What am I inspecting?"

"Move carefully. Soon you'll understand."

I moved carefully toward the pile of rags. I was still puzzled. Was there something underneath? I lifted the first rag and the second and found more rags.

"What is it?" I whispered, peering back over my shoulder. Mrs. P. was already out the door, which gave a metal bang. I sprang forward in time to hear the latch click shut.

"Mrs. P.!"

I turned the handle and pushed. It didn't budge.

I banged. "Hey, not funny!"

The light went out.

I banged and hollered seriously at this point. What were

the chances that the guys at the other end of the garage would hear me over the vacuums and their music?

I hammered on the door until my hands hurt. Then I slid to the floor and swore long and hard in the dark.

Once again, I had plenty of time to think about what the hell was going on.

*   *   *

What can you ever really know about a person? How had I been so wrong about Mrs. Parnell? From early in our relationship, she had symbolized bravery, spirit, honour, loyalty, unflappability. And more recently, the spirit of fun and adventure. So many admirable qualities in one woman. And now, in an underhanded move, she had locked me in a stifling foreign closet and, perhaps, left me to die. All right, it was November, so it wasn't exactly stifling. It was definitely foreign, and it stank of ammonia and car wax. It didn't take long before I decided the guy who invented air fresheners for cars should be locked in a closet with them for the rest of his wretched life.

The worst part was that I'd been betrayed by my friend. If I reflected on the letters, it wasn't the first time either. She'd dropped her friend Hazel too, over a bit of gossip apparently, and no amount of begging and apologies had made her change her mind. I had hours to ponder, what was Violet Wilkinson Parnell really all about?

Speaking of unreal, what about my so-called relationship with Ray? That had ended up with him hightailing it to a Mexican beach with some bimbo. Not even leaving me a voicemail message to say "so long sucker". Then there was my so-called assistant, Alvin, busy being useless in my house and on my nickel. Okay, so I wasn't actually paying him, and he was probably doing his best, but how hard could it be to find a couple of CWACs, or to confirm the identity of an intruder?

It was a perfect time to fume.

*   *   *

At three o'clock, one of the dancing cleaners opened the door and shrieked in alarm. I barely dodged the pail of filthy water he dropped. In return, I nearly mowed him down getting the hell out of the supply cupboard. Escape first, explain later. That's always been my motto.

The garage manager spoke English far better than I spoke Italian. He had lots of cousins, all over Canada, although that didn't help me any. He offered no information about where Mrs. Parnell had gone or what she was now driving, despite my impassioned pleas. He seemed to feel I had been trespassing in his supply cupboard.

"Look, my grandmother has a blocked artery. Something terrible could happen to her. Do you want to be responsible?"

"Sorry, *signora*. I cannot tell you anything about another client. Perhaps if the police request it." I have to say, he didn't look sorry.

"It's a matter of goddam life and death," I shouted.

He shrugged.

"Don't shrug at me. I hate shruggers! Surely you can do something."

A second shrug. Grander this time. Italy is crawling with shrugsters. It was starting to get on my nerves.

"Fine," I said. "Just tell me if she decided to switch cars again? Did she stick to the Volvo? That's all. I'll find my grandmother without any help from you."

"And we would never consider giving out that kind of

234

information, even if we could provide different cars at a moment's notice. Surely you can understand that."

"I understand I was held hostage here in your garage. You and your staff were definitely negligent by allowing that to happen. I can report that to the police. Have you thought about that?"

This time he produced a world-class shrug. Maybe he'd had special training. "I will tell them that our client specifically asked us to be on the lookout for a person of your description. You have been harassing her. You say you are her granddaughter. Frankly, I am beginning to doubt that."

I had to admire his command of the English language, although I didn't bother to say so.

"You haven't heard the last of this," I said. Might as well sound like the villain in a B movie.

I headed back out into the chaotic, crowded streets and stomped all the way back to my illegally parked Ka. The good news was that the Ka hadn't been ticketed or towed. The bad news was that it had a flat tire.

I had plenty of time to kill while I waited to get my tire changed. That was all right. I had people I needed to talk to.

*   *   *

"Well, I'm sorry, Camilla. I haven't been able to find those colleagues of Violet's. The people at Veterans' Affairs and at the Legion keep talking about privacy concerns. I'm working on it. I'll find them."

"What's that banging noise?"

"What banging?"

"It sounds like a hammer. What's going on?"

Alvin interrupted, "Before I forget, you gotta get in touch

with Ray Deveau. He seemed pretty anxious to talk to you. Don't forget."

If he wanted a distraction, he got it. I wasn't about to share with Alvin my failed attempts to contact Ray, let alone my feelings about him and his trip to somewhere exotic with another woman.

He didn't stop anyway, "So have you any idea where Violet is?"

"I found her all right, and she gave me the slip."

"No *way*. Are you kidding? What's the matter with you?"

"She locked me in a closet, and I think... Are you laughing, Alvin?"

"For sure."

"This isn't a game of hide and seek and may the oldest player win. This is serious. May I remind you that you were worried about her health?"

"If she could give you the slip, it sounds like she's her old self, and that's the best news. She must be okay."

"She's definitely not herself."

"What's that supposed to mean?"

"It's like there's someone else looking out of her eyes."

"That's just plain creepy. Have you been watching Italian horror movies?"

"Fact, Alvin. She wasn't happy to see me. She did everything she could to get away both times..."

"Both times? Hey, did you say both times? You let her get away twice?"

"Leave it, Alvin. The point is that there was no warmth in her response. She was cool, collected and very determined."

"Even if you're embarrassed, the main thing is we have Violet back."

"Will you listen to me? We don't have her back. She's

changed. She's like another person. She's on some kind of mission, and she doesn't want us involved."

"She's okay, right. That closet thing sounds kind of playful."

"It damn well wasn't playful," I snapped, remembering the stench of the air fresheners in the darkness.

"Doesn't sound too bad."

"It was and, pay attention, you didn't see her expression. She meant business. And I got no help from the car rental people. For some reason, they all love her and they hate me."

"You can be pretty abrasive. Maybe they don't realize you only want to help."

"That's what I said to Mrs. P. So why would she turn on me?"

"So do you have any other brilliant ideas to find her?"

I did have one idea. I wasn't ready to share it with Alvin. He wasn't ready to hear it. It was a good time to change the subject.

"Change of topic, Alvin. I need you to do a couple of things: first, see what you can turn up about Harrison Jones. He ended up in England after the war, married to a wealthy girl and running some kind of successful business. Furniture, I think."

"You mean the guy who wrote the letters? That rat? I don't think much of him."

"That's the guy. She seems to be retracing his steps in the war. He walked away from that downed flight I asked you to find out about. The one in Berli."

"I haven't found anything yet. I have feelers out about it. It would help if I knew what kind of plane it was or when it went down."

"I know he was on that plane that went down. I don't know what else that means. Mrs. P. went to check it out."

"He must be the dead guy."

"No, he's eighty-five and still alive, as far as we know. Betty said he's in an exclusive nursing home now, very ill with Parkinson's. And he's sure had a long and prosperous life. Dig around and see if there's anything about his war service. Whatever."

"He dropped Violet for someone else, Camilla. By mail. What kind of creep would do that?"

"It appears to have been out of character. Betty and Hazel both thought the world of him. Anyway, I can understand, he'd been injured. Maybe he thought she'd be better off without him. He's connected somehow."

"I'll get on it right away."

"And this is easy: read me the telephone numbers for Betty and Hazel. I want to ask them a couple of questions. The numbers are by the telephone."

"I don't see them. The place is a bit of a mess."

"Check carefully. Otherwise, you'll be looking them up again."

I drummed my fingers on the phone and listened to scrambling, rustling sounds for a bit while my bill mounted. Eventually Alvin came back. "Oh yeah, here they are. Are you really going to call them from Italy? Are you going to wait until three in the morning?" Alvin said after he had read out the numbers and I'd copied them.

"Camilla?"

"Please don't whine, Alvin."

"You won't tell Violet's old friends about Violet, will you? I mean about the look in her eyes and everything?"

"Of course not."

"We've been through so much together. You still feel she's our friend, don't you?"

"What's the matter with you? Of course she's our friend. Nothing could ever change that."

"You said…"

"Look, Alvin. I'm afraid she's on a dangerous path. She's up to something."

"But…"

"And she doesn't believe I'll condone it."

"You? You're the one that always plays fast and loose with the law."

"What? That's not true."

"Sure it's true. What does she want to do? It must be something awful if you wouldn't go along with it."

I took a deep breath. "Revenge, Alvin. She's seeking revenge."

Fifteen

I called Hazel next. I reached her answering machine. I tried again a few minutes later, with the same result. There's no point in leaving a message when you're calling from a payphone in Italy.

Luckily Betty was home and answering.

"This is Camilla MacPhee. I hope I'm not calling too early."

"What a surprise, dear. And a pleasant one. It's not early for me, I just got in from my morning walk. Are you planning another visit?"

"No, I'm in Italy. I do have a question for you."

"For heaven's sake! Are you really calling from Italy? Did you find Violet? I hope this isn't bad news about her."

"I need to ask you about Harrison Jones."

"You're calling me from Italy to ask about Harry Jones? Goodness."

"Bear with me. Mrs. Parnell, I mean Violet, has been to see the site where he was shot down, she has visited the partisans who sheltered him, and she's still on the trail of something. Was there any kind of unusual story about his plane being shot down?"

"Not that I know of. What sort of thing do you mean?"

"I'm not even sure. Only one parachute was deployed. Maybe that was it. Do you ever hear any negative stories about Harry Jones?"

A headmistressy chill drifted down the phone line. "I certainly did not."

"I wondered if there was anything odd about his escape with the partisans."

I still felt the nip in Betty's voice. "I know that sometimes people do things that they wouldn't do at home. Harry was a wonderful boy, valiant and patriotic and very loyal. I think the only thing he ever did that didn't measure up was to jilt poor Violet. That's just my opinion, but in my career, I needed to be a pretty good judge of character, and Harry was, and is, very honourable."

"Okay, it was just an idea."

"You should be careful what you say, dear."

"Sorry, just trying to make sense of this situation."

"Even so, you must do that without causing harm. I can't believe Violet would want that."

I felt a knot in my stomach, and not just because of Betty's preachy tone. Dr. Hasheem had warned about possible paranoia and personality change. What if Mrs. P. was not in danger but dangerous? I chose not to mention that to Betty.

"Point taken," I said.

"I'd be happy to try to help. If I think of another reason for Violet to inquire about Harry, I'll certainly let you know."

"Thanks. I'll be back in touch."

I waited a bit and tried Hazel's line for the third time. I got the answering machine again. Hazel was obviously a woman on the move.

By this time, my tire was fixed, and I could get the hell out of Florence. Hazel would have to wait.

241

*　　*　　*

Mrs. Parnell's traits, like loyalty and comradeship, might have been on hiatus, but she could still give lessons in strategy. I was disadvantaged by not knowing what she was seeking. And therefore, I had no clue where she'd gone. I was back to speculating about the list of towns. I puzzled over the map, calculating distances to each of these places from Florence.

Whatever she was looking for, she would still want to avoid me. She knows the way I think. Would she conclude that if I could track her down in Florence, and if I knew about Berli, I might also know about the other towns on the list? If so, she'd want to outwit me. She'd put herself in my mind. Normally, I'd head for Pieve San Simone, because that was closest, although it wasn't far from Alcielo. Mrs. P. could safely assume I would never opt for Montechiaro, because it was in the middle. That was a compromise and not my style.

Decision made. Montechiaro it was. I edged the Ka into traffic and aimed for Montechiaro, even if it did seem just plain wrong. According to my calculations, it was less than two hours south east of Florence.

During the drive, I kept looking through my rearview for signs of the black Mercedes. Even though the only thing I saw was a small bright blue Citroën, which had been behind me for a long way, I couldn't let down my guard. People can change cars. I put the accelerator to the floor and shot forward. The Citroën kept pace. In fact, it seemed to be trying to overtake me. The driver kept honking his horn and waving his arm out the window. Under the circumstances, I didn't plan on putting myself at some stranger's mercy. Since I was in a strategic mode, I whipped off the *autostrada* at the next exit, without signalling. I raced along the secondary road until I came to a village. Just over the crest of a hill was a cross-roads with three choices. I made a plan. I made an illegal turn and tucked the Ka behind a stone building. I watched as the Citroën slowed at the crossroads, then sped off in the wrong direction, raising dust in the late afternoon sky.

*   *   *

Montechiaro is the opposite of Florence. I found no traffic, no tourists, few buildings and not a whole lot going on. A few scattered farms with crumbling stone outbuildings, a half-dozen chickens pecking here and there, and a dusty road leading to a prominent hilltop villa. Vineyards snaked up the hill to meet the building. A pair of goats hung around. No big deal, as far as I could see.

The sole farmer I met did not speak English. Probably had no cousins in Canada. He stared as I tried my missing *nonna* routine on him. As far as I could tell, he hadn't seen Mrs. P. or the Volvo or a black Mercedes. No sign of a pesky Citroën. I pointed up the hill and asked about the villa. Turned out I should have called it il Palazzo. Well, pardon me.

I hopped back into my Ka and prepared to storm the palace. I chugged up the long road to il Palazzo Degli Angeli. As I got closer, I saw that this was no mere villa. Four stories high in the centre, the building was layered like a wedding cake, with pillars that would do any classical Greek proud. A spectacular ornamental pool at the approach set the tone. Classical marble statues watched over the shimmering pool and immaculate property.

If Alvin had been there, he would have said Lord thundering Jesus. I just gawked.

I parked the Ka next to an elderly, dust-covered Fiat 500.

The two cars looked like a pair of dinky toys left outside by some royal child. I felt pretty small myself approaching the massive door at the top of the wide marble staircase. My sisters would say it had serious curb appeal. It felt like the setting for a fairy tale except for the lack of passing peasants and the presence of the security sticker by the door. As I raised my hand to knock, the door swung open and a most elegant man said *"Buon giorno, signora."* He was about forty, long, thin and slightly lopsided, giving the impression he'd been painted by Modigliani. On him, it looked good.

I trotted out my well-worn missing *nonna* tearjerker, repeating the word for cardiac crisis three times. I flashed the poster. He switched effortlessly to English with a hint of Oxford and enough Italian inflection to make it sexy. If you could bottle that and sell it, you'd make a fortune.

"Come in, please. I am Claudio Degli Angeli," he said.

"Camilla MacPhee." I extended my hand and gave him my firmest handshake. He winced. Too bad. You never want to let the palace-dwellers get the upper hand.

"Let us go into my office, and you can sit and explain your problem in comfort. Your grandmother is missing and ill? How dreadful. Have you contacted the authorities?"

"No luck there yet," I said.

I followed him through a grand hallway flanked on both sides by vast sparsely furnished rooms and twelve-foot shuttered windows. Our footsteps echoed on the marble floors. I spotted a grand piano in one of the rooms as we swept past. You couldn't complain about overcrowding here. Cheap reproduction prints of Renaissance paintings hung on the walls. Maybe that was typical palace chic. How would I know?

When we reached a much smaller room off to the left, he stood back to let me pass. At least this one had armchairs with faded, comfortable-looking upholstery. A high, antique secretary-style desk with many drawers and stacks of paperwork dominated the room. I took the seat I was offered, and Claudio Degli Angeli stayed standing.

"Nice place," I said.

He shrugged. "What is left of it. It was once very splendid. May I offer you an *aperitivo?*"

I had begun just to say yes to all offers of food or drink in Italy. Refusals, even polite refusals, just slow things down.

He poured a bit of cognac from a crystal decanter and handed me a delicate snifter. He was definitely not the kind of guy to pop beer caps with his teeth.

He bent elegantly into his chair and raised his own glass. I raised mine back at him. After a graceful sip, he said, "Yes, I have seen your grandmother, although aside from needing a cane, she did not appear to be suffering from any physical or mental impediments."

"Trust me," I said, "she's in big trouble. What did she want here?"

"She warned me about people who might follow her and pry," he said.

"I bet she did. She doesn't want to be found. And you're right, she's in good mental shape. She is also in danger. She has a blocked artery. Plus someone is pursuing her."

"She's not really your grandmother, is she?"

"Possibly not. Grandmothers get attention here in Italy, and as they say, when in Rome…"

He laughed out loud. I think we were both surprised by that laugh. It seemed to do the trick.

He said, "Of course, we are not in Rome."

"Nevertheless, someone really is after her. Someone with a black Mercedes who has killed a partisan." I paused. People who lived in *palazzi* could quite easily drive Mercedes-Benzes. Great. Here I was in the bowels of a building in the middle of nowhere. My Ka could be disposed of in an outbuilding, and no one would ever know what happened to me. I took a swig of the cognac. What the hell. Too late to back out. "So," I said, "what was she looking for?"

"She wanted to know about the Palazzo."

"Did she ask anything about the second World War?"

"Yes."

"About the Canadians?"

"That is correct."

I looked around. "Were they here?"

"Very much so. They commandeered the Palazzo during the offensive. The officers used the Palazzo as Headquarters."

I gathered from his tone this was not a good thing.

"What happened?"

"It killed my grandparents. Indirectly, of course. They lost so much. They could never return here. Even after many things were recovered."

"Was the Palazzo bombed? It doesn't look like it's been rebuilt."

"Not bombed. Stripped."

"What?"

"Furniture, artwork, china. Rugs. All worth a fortune, family heirlooms. Gone." He snapped his fingers.

"You mean looted?"

"Of course, I do."

"You said many things were recovered."

"Larger things, furniture. The grand pianos. Much of the china. The artwork and the silver, pffft."

"That's unbelievable."

He shrugged. "It was war. I can understand that. Those

246

men had been crawling through icy mud, sleeping with corpses, having shells explode next to their sleeping trenches. War erodes the veneer of civilization in many individuals."

"I am sure that the Canadians were never involved in looting."

He smiled at me, a sweet, sad expression.

"*Signora,* let us agree to disagree."

"Did she mention any names? Did she mention Harrison Jones."

"I had no way of knowing names. My grandparents wouldn't have known names either. They weren't even here. They took refuge in Switzerland until after the war. It was safer there. They heard about what happened from the staff who survived the war."

"The staff, that's an idea. Would any of them be alive now?"

"They are long in their graves. No one around here remembers anything. In fact, there are very few people in the area. Most have moved to cities, you must have noticed it's very sparse. It's hard to get good help nowadays," he said with a sly smile. "I don't suppose you'd like a job?"

I returned his grin. "So you couldn't tell her anything."

"On the contrary, I was able to tell her quite a bit."

Why does everyone find it necessary to play stupid games? I felt like booting his skinny aristocratic backside.

"Perhaps you could just tell me what you told her, and then we can save ourselves some time and aggravation," I said.

He chuckled. "My apologies. Your friend wanted to know what had been taken from the Palazzo. We had extensive records of what was taken, what was definitely or most likely destroyed, and what my grandparents believed to be stolen."

"What was that?"

"Mostly paintings, small sculptures, objets d'art, religious

247

articles. Silver, as I mentioned, although that could be melted down easily. The paintings were cut from their frames and rolled. I have read that the soldiers hid them in their bedrooms, then mailed back to Canada."

"That's terrible. I can't believe it."

"What can I say? It could be worse. My family survived the war. The Palazzo was still standing and continues to stand. We lost almost everything. We managed then, and we continue to manage. The Palazzo is a lovely spot for a wedding or a special event or party. We can support corporate functions beautifully. State of the art electronic access, of course."

"Did she show you any pictures?"

"Yes. They didn't mean anything to me."

"Do you know where she's gone now?"

"I have no idea. Would you like your drink topped up?"

"I'm good to go," I said, getting to my feet. "I have a long drive in something called a Ka. I'm thinking of upgrading to a Mercedes. What kind of vehicle do you drive?"

"A Fiat 500. You parked next to it in the driveway. When I have the choice, I prefer to walk."

*   *   *

The trip to Pieve San Simone might have been a beautiful drive in the daylight, but it was a least two hours south west of Montechiaro. As my trip wore on, it was getting too dark to be driving comfortably on unfamiliar secondary roads. It wasn't too dark to see a Citroën show up in my rearview though. I spotted the headlights; the blue body might have blended with the night. Were there blue Citroëns all over Italy? Just in case, I used a few evasive manoeuvers, being grateful in one way for the tangle of unpaved back roads in

Tuscany. I sat in the Ka, behind a cluster of trees, until I felt confident. I was getting tired and hungry. Pieve San Simone was far enough away that, finally, I took my chances and roared off. I found no trace of my pursuer on the way. Maybe it had just been all in my mind.

When I finally got there, Pieve San Simone was an unremarkable small town. Of course, unremarkable in Tuscan terms is still pretty damn amazing to a Canadian. I'd been on the road a long time and hadn't stopped to eat, or find a bathroom. I was starving, cold and miserable.

I scanned the cars parked at the periphery of the Pieve San Simone piazza. I didn't know what kind of car she had taken in the end, although my money was on a Volvo. There were plenty of Fiats, no Volvos. On the bright side, there was no sign of a black Mercedes or a pesky Citroën. The piazza is the centre of community life in Italy, and all around the Pieve San Simone piazza were shops for food and clothing, services, now closed until the morning. More important, there was a *trattoria*, an *osteria* and two *gelateria*s, and they were hopping. When you want information, go where you find food.

First, I found a bathroom. Then I went to the payphone in the piazza and called Hazel. Still no answer. Alvin was next on my list.

"Did you get any better results from the security cameras?" I said.

"I'm fine, thank you very much, Camilla. I did get to finish going through them. I wish that on you some time. Six cameras going twenty-four hours a…"

"Get to the point, Alvin."

"Okay, I tracked down the Super, and we found some more shots of the guy we saw in the corridor. And get this, he was caught on the camera at least three times. You can see his face

249

clearly. Anyway, I got the best shot printed out. Maybe the best thing is to fax it to you."

"Great, let me check my car fax."

"Doesn't your hotel have a fax?"

"I don't have a hotel. I'm in Pieve San Simone—it's not the most cosmopolitan place in the world. I don't even know if the hotels will have private bathrooms."

"Pieve San Simone? Hey, that's good, because…"

"I'll find a hotel, and I'll call you with the fax number. If they have one, which I doubt. In the meantime, keep trying Hazel's number. She's not answering, and she didn't mention going away or anything."

"Wait, Camilla…"

"I'll call you back later. Gotta eat or I'll die."

When I pushed open the door, the *osteria* was jammed with people, chatting away, drinking red wine and beer. I knew the food would be fast and plentiful and most likely good. I chose the lasagna, a green salad and a glass of red wine. I settled into a rough wooden chair at a wooden table and wolfed my meal. I was lucky I'd picked this place.

Afterwards, I had an espresso and asked about a place to stay with a fax. Everyone seemed to think the Albergo Maxim would be the best place for me. The Albergo Maxim was not far, up the hill from the piazza.

"Very good hotel for Americans," someone said.

I wasn't sure what that meant. Not good for Italians? Expensive? Lousy food?

"I'm Canadian," I said, pointing to the flag sewn on my backpack.

"Even better for Canadians," was the answer. This was repeated in Italian so everyone could have a good laugh. Anything I can do to entertain. I put on what I figured was a good-natured grin.

After I listened to the location of everyone's cousins in Canada, I said, "Maybe my *nonna* has checked in there. We got separated in Florence. I am trying to catch up with her. She's been sick."

The official English speaker translated that to the group. Everyone looked interested. *La nonna* continued to be magic.

I pulled out the picture, which made its way around from table to table. *O la nonna*, people said. *Poverina.*

No one seemed to have seen Mrs. P. The consensus was that I would almost certainly find her at the hotel.

Ten minutes later, the nice young woman at the reception desk of the Albergo Maxim shook her head, making her silver and crystal earrings sparkle. Tears glistened in her eyes.

"I haven't seen your grandmother. We're not supposed to give information about guests, but if you are looking for your *nonna*..." She shrugged to show that where *nonna*s are concerned, all bets are off.

I smiled encouragingly.

"Sorry, no signora Parnell here. Perhaps she is staying at a pensione, or in another town?" Her forehead creased with concern at the thought of the wayward *nonna*.

"How about signora Wilkinson?"

She gave me an odd look and shook her head.

"Don't worry," I said soothingly. "I'll find her."

I got the fax number and checked in.

"You have a nice room," the woman beamed. "Beautiful. It is on the third floor. Very big bed. Unfortunately, our elevator isn't working tonight."

Oh, well. I hauled my stuff up the three flights. One way to work off the vino, although I was glad I travelled light. The room was opulent in a late sixties kind of way, all red velvet and dark polished wood. I resisted the urge to lose myself in the seductively large bed. Instead, I took a quick shower, changed, and slashed on the Graffiti Red as a concession to the relentlessly groomed Italians.

I made my way to the first *gelateria*. There were three in close proximity, and to my surprise, they were all doing business, despite the fact it was November. Suited me. I like ice cream. I love *gelato*. I had a *nocciola* in the first one. No one there had seen Mrs. P.

I tried *gianduia,* a mix of praline and milk chocolate, at the second spot. Strike two on the Mrs. P. front. The *gelato* was world class, though.

In the third one, which was full of teenagers, lots of booze bottles on the wall and a blaring television, I hit pay dirt. I ordered a pistachio. You have to get your greens somewhere.

Everyone seemed anxious to practice their high school English. A young man came forward.

He took the photo and stared at it with a look of importance on his handsome face. He turned to his friends and asked all the right questions. This triggered a storm of responses and a half-dozen parallel conversations. I did my best to concentrate on the conversations. People pointed. Unfortunately, they pointed in all four directions and some minor combinations, such as south south west.

After five minutes, it became apparent that some of these young people had seen Mrs. Parnell. A consensus emerged, and the young man made the announcement with pride. That afternoon, Mrs. Parnell had been seen up the hill, although not the same hill as the Albergo Maxim.

"Great!" I said. "I think she may be visiting a friend. I don't have the name of her friend."

That struck them as odd. Not knowing the names of your *nonna*'s friends was apparently peculiar.

"She was here during the war," I said. "I have heard the stories many times. I wish I knew her friend's name."

That had the ring of truth to it, I suppose. A few more comments were offered. None of them useful.

"You've helped a lot," I said. *"Grazie a tutti,"* I added to the group.

No one seemed to remember exactly which street Mrs. P. had been seen on, only that she had been on foot, using her cane. This was not seen as anything unusual, since everyone in town walked everywhere. Someone had noticed her pausing to smoke a cigarette, which got a chuckle from the crowd, then she'd set off again, full of energy. A quiet girl piped up and said she'd seen the old lady driving a Volvo on the road near the top of the village. That got a laugh too.

I poked around town looking for her and her Volvo, because what else could I do? There's plenty of life in Italian towns in the evenings, and this evening was cool but dry, no nasty fog. People were still calling greetings to each other. Finally, after showing the photo to everyone I met, and walking till my feet hurt, I figured I wouldn't find her that night. I crossed the piazza to the payphone again. I got my own answering machine on the first ring. I left the fax number at the Albergo Maxim for Alvin.

As I crossed the empty piazza again, I noticed three black Mercedes. Maybe it was a convention? Maybe this was the most popular car in the country. There were just as many Fiats, and now, a blue Citroën, with no sign of the driver. Time to head to the hotel. That luxurious bed seemed like the best and safest idea.

There was nobody at the front desk when I crossed the lobby and headed up the stairs. I reached the landing and stopped. What was that? Someone was puffing up the stairs behind me.

Holding my key, I raced up the stairs two at a time. Footsteps thundered behind me. I reached my door and fumbled with the key. Sometimes adrenaline works against you. I managed to open the door when the voice yelled, "Slow down." I fell back against the door, and we both tumbled into the room. I only managed one gargling scream. Then I recognized the middle-aged, sandy-haired man who had landed on me.

I got to my feet with some dignity and shouted, "What the hell are you doing here?"

He picked himself up off the rug.

"You bastard," I added.

Ray Deveau caught his breath. "What did you call me?"

"You heard me. Running off to Mexico with some bimbo."

"What? What is the matter with you? Did I make a wrong turn? Is this Mexico?"

Of course, at that moment, I began to see a small hole in my theory.

"Why didn't you call me?" Ray dusted off his knees and sank onto the bed.

"Do you have high blood pressure?" I said. "Your face is all red."

"No diversionary tactics, please."

"I did call you," I said.

"You didn't."

"Did. Umpteen times. At home, at work, on your cell."

"It doesn't work over here."

"Mine neither. Your work message said you were on vacation, and your daughters said you went to Mexico with some woman."

"They said what?"

"Well, they implied it. I guess."

"And you believed that?"

254

"You had to be part of the conversations to understand. It made sense at the time."

"A tip for the future. Don't let teenage girls be your major source of information. Particularly if the girls in question have lost their mother not that long ago and aren't interested in the old man finding anyone to replace her in his affections."

"Okay, point taken. What are you doing here, Ray?"

"What do you think? You're racing all over Italy, reporting murders and hit-and-runs and attacks. Alvin can be really irritating, by the way."

"You think so?"

"I know so. I've been calling him regularly. That's how I found out you were here. He was supposed to tell you to get in touch with me."

"I guess he did, in his own Alvin way. Maybe I wasn't listening. Never mind."

"I've been on your trail since Florence."

"By any chance, have you been driving a blue Citroën?"

"I knew you were trying to give me the slip."

"I didn't realize it was you. I'm sure glad it was."

"Well, that's good. I'm really glad to see you too. Especially alive. Hey, is this a queen-sized bed?"

"Yes," I said, flopping down on it. "That's romantic."

"Yeah, good luck finding a waiter with a margarita in this burg."

*　　*　　*

"I didn't realize that you snored," Ray said in the morning.

"Right, like you don't."

"How would you know? You were sawing logs all night. With your mouth open too. That some kind of test for me?"

The day had gotten off to a good start. It felt great having Ray there. He was bound to have theories about the best way to find Mrs. P., and since he was a cop, I was less likely to get arrested in the process.

Over breakfast, I filled him in on everything that had happened from the time I'd arrived in Italy. I didn't even skip over the embarrassing incident in the car rental garage. I told him what I'd learned and what I'd concluded, which was not much.

"It must have something to do with this Harrison Jones. Alvin is working on getting information on him. He's going to try to find Hazel. She's a gossip, and she might have something interesting to add. Alvin has a few things to do. It's better to keep him busy and, face it, we need all the help we can get," I said.

"Let me make some calls after breakfast," Ray said. "We'll find out about this guy."

Who needs margaritas on the beach when you have a guy who'll make a call without being badgered?

We were on our third espresso when the young woman from the front desk rushed into the dining room waving a piece of paper.

"This is great. It's the fax from Alvin," I said to Ray.

We leaned over to get a good look at the two faxed pages.

"Well, it would be great if you could make out the image," I complained.

"No kidding. Just a blob, and this must have used up most of the ink in the hotel fax machine," Ray said.

"So we're no further ahead. So much for digital images. They're always a bit fuzzy anyway."

"Digital? He has it in digital form?" Ray's eyebrows shot up. "Why doesn't he e-mail them to you?"

"How am I supposed to get e-mail in Italy? I can't even get my cellphone to work."

"Internet cafés are all over the place. There's one right on the piazza."

"Really? I guess I didn't notice."

"I'll do it for you." Ray scribbled on a piece of paper. "Give Alvin my e-mail address, and we're in business."

"I'm glad you're on the team, Ray."

Ray might have been on the team, but when I got to the payphone, apparently Alvin wasn't. No answer. I left a voicemail and hoped Ray's e-mail address didn't get mangled.

Ray was leaning against the wall in the hotel lobby when I rejoined him. His arms were crossed, and he looked a lot more relaxed than I felt. He said, "Where to next?"

"We'll be knocking on doors here, trying to find out if anyone saw Mrs. P. in town. After that, there's only the one town left. Alcielo. It's not far from here, the next town of any size. If we don't find her there, I don't know what to do."

At least the weather had turned. Ray and I were heading into a mild, sunny November day, no rain, no fog, just perfect. Ray had already checked us out. I suppose he'd updated the records, paid the double rate and settled up for our breakfasts. As I passed, the desk, the girl with the twinkly earrings waved and called out, "Signora MacPhee, I have made enquiries about your *nonna*. Someone suggested she may have been visiting the American gentleman staying at the Villa Rosa. Of course, it might be someone entirely different." She stopped and shrugged. If she wondered where Ray had come from, she never mentioned it.

"Where's the Villa Rosa?" I said.

She beckoned us over to the desk, drew a map on the hotel stationery and offered a few tips on not getting lost.

"Do you know this man?"

"No."

257

"Are you certain he's American?"

"No, he's not from here for sure. Not English either. He is very rich, and he speaks Italian with an accent. I thought…"

"Is his name Harrison Jones?"

The earring swayed as she shook her head. "I do not know his name. One of the maids has a sister who keeps house for him. Wait here, please, I will ask."

"This could be it, Ray. Let's get over there. And we'll take the two cars. She can't get away from both of us."

Ray chuckled. "I still can't believe the old girl tricked you like that."

"Glad someone thinks it's funny. She won't succeed with a stunt like that again," I said with more confidence than I felt.

Our helper bustled back in two minutes, waving another piece of paper. She said, "Here it is. I have no idea how to pronounce it."

Ray and I stared at the neatly printed name.

"Who the hell is this Guy Prendergast?" Ray said.

I felt a flush of excitement. "He's a man from the past. And you know what? I think he might be dead."

*   *   *

Perhaps the Villa Rosa was named for its soft Tuscan pink colour. It was one of many reconstructed farm houses that dot the hills in Tuscany, surrounded by olive trees and ancient cypress. Although this villa stood on a hill, at the end of a tangle of dirt roads, with the map and travel tips, we had no trouble finding it. Up close, the villa was smaller than most. I glanced around the property for a Mercedes. I saw only a battered green Rover.

Ray scanned the property while I banged on the rustic

wooden door until a very tall, stooped man opened it. His brilliant blue eyes were still bright and alert. And his spiky white brush cut, overdue for a cut, contrasted with leathery skin the colour of cognac. He had leather sandals on his feet, a glass of red wine in his hand and a Peter Robinson paperback tucked under his arm. He peered at us over half-moon reading glasses. I recognized the long jaw from the old photo.

Ray stuck out his hand, "Ray Deveau, how you doing."

"And my name is Camilla MacPhee," I said, "Are you Guy Prendergast?"

"Sure am. It must be my lucky day to have two English-speaking visitors." He had a firm two-fisted handshake, just a slight tremor in the thin fingers. Something told me he was not surprised to see us. Had he had a call from the hotel? Or had Mrs. Parnell warned him I might show up? He kept up the pretense of an unexpected visit as he ushered us through the house, an interior of cool tile floors and rough walls in the soft Tuscan pink.

"Don't mind the mess," he said with a slight quaver in his voice. "I've developed the bad habits of a single man. Perhaps if I'd known you were coming, I might have cleaned up a bit, but probably not."

Of course, I liked Guy Prendergast's casual approach to housekeeping. Books lay stacked in piles, a half-dozen empty wine bottles clustered in a corner. My guess was his housekeeper spent most of her time in the kitchen and cleaning, since everything that could gleam gleamed. She'd have orders to leave the books alone. As we passed through, I noticed the walls sported some very nice artwork, elegant oil landscapes, which fit in well. We filed past a large rustic wooden table with an open suitcase on top. A second heavy wooden door led to a stone patio, nestled against the vine-covered back wall.

"Have a seat," he said, pointing to mismatched wooden chairs. There was nothing casual in the way he kept his plants. Well-tended rosemary, thyme and basil still grew profusely in the raised herb garden. Hibiscus trees hugged the walls. I sniffed the air and found it hard to believe it would ever be winter anywhere. Guy Prendergast seemed very pleased at our visit, although we hadn't given him any idea of what we wanted. He hadn't asked.

Ray and I declined the offer of red wine. Ray relaxed and leaned back in his rickety chair and gazed out at the view of rolling hills and vineyards. I kept my eyes on our host. I wasn't so sure we could trust this foxy old fellow. I sat forward and whipped out the fragile, faded photo of the six young people.

"Will you look at that," he said shaking his head and chuckling. "What a bunch."

"Do you remember these people?"

"Who could forget them? Betty Connaught was a bit hoity-toity, too good for the likes of me. The kind of gal who'd say one thing and mean another. Now we'd call her passive-aggressive. Now that Hazel Fellows was a pretty thing, always up for a party, loved to laugh. And Violet Wilkinson, she was the best, just splendid. Never met anyone like her."

"Me neither," I said.

He said: "Hasn't changed a bit. After all these years. Still has that look in her eyes. Not to be trifled with, Vi wasn't, then or now."

I blurted out, "Did you stay in touch with her?"

His eyes flicked away. "Not really. I carried a torch for her all over Europe, but she had her heart set on Harry Jones, that's this fellow here." He pointed to the first golden boy with the debonair grin. "So there wasn't much point in hoping."

Something told me there was still a spark left in that torch, even after more than sixty years. Guy Prendergast continued, "By the time I found out that fool Harry had jilted her, she was going out with this Parnell fella. I knew him a bit too. Stuffy as all get out, but he was stubborn. He wouldn't have given up like I did. My own fault. What is it the kids say nowadays? You snooze, you lose?"

"I'm sorry," I said.

"I tried again after that Parnell fella died. Wrote to her, hoping to get things going. I never heard back. That time I took the hint and found myself a nice girl, got married and turned my attention to making money and raising kids."

By this time, I'd decided the quaver in his voice was age or illness rather than emotion or nervousness.

"Mrs. Parnell is in Italy now."

He peered at me over the half-moon glasses.

I said, "She's investigating what happened to Harry Jones in the war. She's visiting people who might know something about him."

"Really?" he said, taking off the glasses and slipping them into his pocket.

"Yes. And we've been told she came here to see you."

"Have you. Well, you can't keep secrets if you're a foreigner in Italy. The locals know everything. Walk into the bakery, and everyone behind the counter is already up on what you had for dinner last night."

I fought down a flash of impatience. "We'd like to get to the point. Mrs. Parnell needs medical help. We have to find her before something bad happens. I want to know what she was doing here."

"Medical help? What kind?" That was news to him. The dark leathery skin paled at least two shades.

"She's in grave danger of having a cardiac arrest. Her doctor is outraged that she would even consider flying to Italy in her condition. I don't care if she told you to stonewall anyone who came looking for her. She needs help, and you'd goddam well better help us." So much for the well-mannered guest.

Ray looked more than a bit surprised by my outburst. Guy Prendergast took it in his stride. Maybe someone had prepared him to be yelled at. "I didn't know she wasn't well. I should have guessed from the look of her. Not herself at all. Can't say I blame her. Thing is, we were all so wrong about Harry, weren't we? It had to come out some time."

"What do you mean?"

"I mean, no one would ever have expected it. He seemed such a fine fellow, way better for a fine gal like Violet than a layabout like me. Something changed him. He…"

We were on to something new now, and I couldn't stop myself from interrupting. "Changed him how? Please get to the point."

"War does strange things to people. It can wreck your mind and heart. Some never get over it. Some rough and ready fellas grew up on the front lines, came back stronger and tougher. Others hear screaming shells and the shrieks of dying comrades all their lives. They end up wrecks of human beings. Nervous breakdowns, drinking." He raised his glass and chuckled. "Who am I to talk, with my *vino rosso* at ten thirty in the morning?"

"One last time, how did Harry change?"

"Well, if you ask me, Harry just plain went bad."

Ray had been quiet up to this time. He said, "Bad? What kind of bad?"

"First of all, Perce was shot down, then Harry was seriously injured. I guess you know that. They were together all their lives. Harry was always the good influence, and Perce was the wild one, he was always in trouble, some of it serious. I don't think Harry got over Perce dying. Never was the same afterwards."

I frowned. "I never heard anything about Perce being in serious trouble. Hazel alluded to childhood pranks, that was all. Are you sure? I thought he was such a heroic guy."

"Well, it would depend on who you asked. His family thought the sun shone out of his arse, if you'll pardon the expression. And Harry did too, always bailing Perce out. He'd have done anything for his buddy. Not everybody felt the same way. Perce was skating pretty close to the wire when he died. Maybe Harry snapped. Maybe he took over where Perce left off."

"What was Perce involved in?" A cop's tone edged into Ray's voice.

"I couldn't really say. No proof." He gestured toward the green hills that surrounded the villa. "Wouldn't like to lose all this in a lawsuit."

I looked him straight in the eye. "A lawsuit will be the least of any of our problems, if you don't start to treat this seriously. We're trying to keep someone we care about alive. You say you care about her too. Tell us what you know."

He let out a long sigh. "I've already caused enough harm. All right, Perce got mixed up with the wrong people, shady types. The kind who get court-martialed. Or shot because they find themselves in the wrong place at the wrong time. Black market shenanigans, contraband, that sort of thing, back in England. At the time of his death, he was supposed to have been under investigation for some serious activities. That's what I heard from some of the RCAF guys I ran into after the war."

I butted in. "Let me guess. Did the bad stuff have to do with the looting at the Palazzo Degli Angeli?"

263

Guy Prendergast picked up his wine, sipped it and frowned thoughtfully. "I don't know about that. There were rumours about looting at the Palazzo. Never saw any of it myself. We were busy trying to stay alive in 1944 and 1945. Having our friends bleed to death in our arms. Wasn't a shopping expedition, let me tell you. Canadian troops were high calibre. Even though the rumour was that the people who owned that Palazzo…"

"The Degli Angeli family," I interjected.

"That's the name. They were supposed to have been very hospitable to the Nazis. I'm not so sure they really were. Some of the fellas might not have been too sympathetic if they did hear that kind of gossip. Anyway, none of the officers I encountered tolerated any monkey business."

"Perce could have been mixed up in it?"

"I don't see how. He wasn't anywhere near there. He was an airman, flew bombers."

"Mrs. Parnell went to the Palazzo. Must be some kind of connection."

"Sure there was a connection, and the connection wasn't Perce, it was Harry. I told you he went bad afterwards. His regiment would have been moving up through that part of Italy, not all that far from here really. I'm pretty sure he could have been involved in looting fine artwork and other valuables from there and other places too. Wouldn't be surprised if that's what got him started doing so well after the war."

"Did you tell Mrs. Parnell this?"

I knew the answer before he opened his mouth.

"Oh, God, what the hell did I start?" He lifted the wine glass and drained it in one serious gulp.

"Okay, so you did. How did she track you down here?"

"I found *her*. It was awful lonely here after my wife died. Never stopped thinking about Violet. Perhaps I should have kept my mouth shut and let her have her memories. I was hoping maybe she'd have a place in her heart for me, I suppose. Two lonely people. One independent woman, one foolish old romantic with more money than brains. Did pretty well out of my business, and then got lucky with some investments. Bought up a few old farms around here years back, and they've paid off well too. Timing is everything, and the Brits are crazy for this area. I figured the right art can give you a good return too, and, even if it doesn't, you get to enjoy it. So I started buying pieces, some good furniture, a few oils. A while back, I bought a lovely landscape that would suit this place. You walked by it on the way out here." He pointed toward the house. "I dealt with an associate of Harry's. Figured you could trust a boy from back home, and the people he dealt with. Fella I got to know in the appraisal business dropped a hint my painting has a very iffy provenance. He hinted it might have been stolen from a church. He turned up his nose when I mentioned Brockbank & Brickle. I had gone through Harry's company for more than one purchase, and let me tell you, I was pretty steamed. I dug around a bit more, the lost art registry, that kind of thing, turned up a bit of mucky business about Harry and his lads. I never had enough solid stuff to go the police, especially here where there are a lot of hands in a lot of pockets." He peered at us to see if we got the point.

We had. This was something unexpected. I found my eyebrows up. Ray's jaw tensed.

Prendergast said, "What I learned made sense of some of those wartime rumours."

I bit my tongue. Guy Prendergast sure liked to drag out a story.

He said, "I knew Violet would have nothing but contempt for any dishonest dealings. Vi was all about King and Country.

Duty. Straight as an arrow. I always kept tabs on her. I wrote her a letter letting her know I wanted to visit her. No response. I called her, and she said the past was the past. She didn't want to see me." He stopped and chuckled. "Lots of spirit, that gal. Finally, I figured it was my last kick at the can. Not too many Canadian visits left in the old fella, far too comfortable here at Villa Rosa. To make a long story short, I made a trip to Ottawa, and I just dropped in on Violet, caught her unawares. I hauled out everything I knew about Harry and spilled the beans. I even had some photos of him and his boys in later years, with an Italian dealer known to be a slippery customer. I showed her that to prove Harry's no matinee idol now. Vi and I had been friends back in Canada, and I was hoping once she'd let me through the door, maybe one thing would lead to another, you know. Thought that might be more likely to happen if she didn't still half-worship that damned scoundrel. I figured I didn't have anything to lose, except the plane fare, and that's only money you can't take with you. I must have been nuts."

Ray was sitting forward on his rickety chair, drinking in every word. He'd be registering it all in his police officer's brain. Sixty years of unrequited love. There seemed to be quite a bit of that going around.

I said. "What happened when you told her?"

"She threw the photo into the garbage and tossed me out like last week's trash. Not physically. She said I had nothing to go on. Talked about slander, libel. Threatened me with her cane. Still quite the woman. You never want a gal like that to get mad at you." He chuckled sadly.

I didn't dare glance at Ray.

"When was this visit to Canada?"

"Just got back, not even a week ago. I'm not unpacked yet,

suitcase is still on the table. Evelina never would have put up with that."

"Then Mrs. Parnell turned up here last night."

"Yes."

"And what happened?"

He chuckled again. "Vi's not the type to turn down a glass of sherry. Not like you young pups, no staying power."

"Why did she come here to see you, if she was so angry?"

"She'd given it some thought. Said she did a bit of research and decided I might be right after all. Wasn't too happy about it. Needed to know more about what he'd gotten up to. Wanted details, names."

"Is she still in Pieve San Simone?" I glanced at the house. What if she were hiding in it? There'd been no sign of a car.

"She went on to Alcielo. Next stop. If I were that miserable bastard Harry Jones, I'd be shaking in my boots." Guy Prendergast threw back his head and guffawed.

"He's near death in an English nursing home."

"That a fact?"

Ray said, "Any idea where in Alcielo?"

"Annalisa's, I imagine. Wouldn't be surprised if she had a word with Sergio either."

Before I jotted down Sergio and Annalisa at the end of my long list of Italian names, I asked. "Do you have last names?"

"Sorry. Alcielo's a small Italian town. Everyone knows them. Sergio's in restoration. Well, Annalisa's got a finger in a lot of stuff. Well, she did. She's getting on now, as we all are."

I leaned over to Ray, "People might be on Mrs. Parnell's trail. Alcielo's not that far from here. I'll go ahead and find her. You stay here and get Mr. Prendergast to fill you in on Harry Jones' sins."

"That won't be happening, Camilla," Ray said. "We'll stick

together. We'll be back to see Mr. Prendergast as soon as we make sure Mrs. Parnell's safe."

"I'm not going anywhere," Guy Prendergast said, struggling to his feet. "Hold on, what people might be on her trail?"

"We don't know. Whoever they are, they're connected somehow."

He slumped back. The chair rattled and came close to tipping. "Thash terrible. Maybe I should come along too. I know Alcielo, and I speak the lingo."

"No," Ray and I blurted together.

I added, "Thank you. We'll be back if we need more information. Please be careful, and don't let anyone in."

Ray glanced meaningfully at the empty wine glass. "In fact, don't drive anywhere."

*   *   *

Alcielo, when we finally squealed into it, turned out to be a medieval fortified hill town, plunked in the middle of the sprawling tobacco fields. It had an almost magical quality. Alcielo meant something "to the sky" or "to heaven". That fit the place. Too bad I wasn't there to be charmed. I pulled the Ka into the piazza, stepped out and stretched as Ray parked the Citroën next to me.

"You ask around for Sergio and Annalisa," Ray said. "There's an internet café right across the piazza. I'll see if Alvin sent that guy's photo. Don't go off by yourself."

"Of course I won't."

"I mean it. Do not. And don't bother to get huffy either. You ask in the shops. As soon as I check this, we'll head to the police station and see if we can get some help with finding

268

Mrs. Parnell without alarming her. Maybe we'll have some luck on the Harry Jones front too. I want to take that photo image with me. The police will know who Sergio and Annalisa are too.

I said. "You know what? I'm not sure I trust and believe this Guy Prendergast. Maybe Mrs. Parnell's not here after all. What do you think?"

"I'm a cop. We don't really trust anyone."

"That's a bad attitude. Do you trust me?"

"To do the most cautious and sensible thing, no. To go right out on a limb regardless of consequences, absolutely."

"Sorry I asked. Okay, I'll make a phone call while you check the e-mail. Considering the circumstances, I don't think it's too early to call Canada. Alvin and I have been trying to reach Hazel. She seems to be out all the time, so early morning might do the trick. She might remember something more about this Guy Prendergast. I'll run the Harry Jones stuff by her too for a reaction. I'll try Betty too."

"Sounds harmless."

Betty's answering machine picked up. Since I was unreachable, there was no point in leaving a message. The phone rang on and on in Hazel's house, no answering machine this time. Just as I was getting ready to hang up, a breathless voice answered.

"Hazel?" I said. "Glad I caught you at home. We've been trying to reach you. Look, there's something I need to ask you about. It has to do with Harry Jones."

"Who is speaking, please?" The female voice sounded middle-aged yet oddly shaky, although I figured that might have been the phone line.

"Camilla MacPhe," I said. "Who is this?"

"Val Desrochers. I'm Hazel's step-daughter."

"Oh," I said, surprised. "May I speak with Hazel?"

"I'm sorry, she's…"

"Look, it's urgent really. Tell her it has to do with her old friend Violet Parnell. I'm sure she'll take the call."

"I'm sure she would if she could," she said.

"Let's let her make that choice," I snapped.

"She can't. She's in hospital. ICU. She's been there for a couple of days."

"ICU? What happened?"

"We don't know. One of the neighbours heard the phone ringing and ringing and eventually decided to check on her. He found the door open slightly. He came in and found her unconscious. They called the ambulance, then contacted us."

"I'm sorry. That's awful. She seemed so lively. Did she have a heart attack?"

"A head injury. She must have tripped and hit her head on the corner of the fireplace hearth."

I remembered that raised hearthstone in Hazel's living room. I shook my head at the image of pretty little Hazel crumpled against it with blood spreading on the cream marble.

I said, "That's terrible. It's a good thing the neighbour looked in." I figured the phone calls must have been from Alvin. Maybe a couple from me.

Val's voice choked up. I waited until she could speak again. "Yes, it was. We don't know how long she was here alone, but she was very dehydrated," she said. "We only got together once a week for lunch, and the rest of the time we stayed in touch by phone. I feel so guilty. She always insisted she didn't need a babysitter. She was so independent. She was getting ready to head for Florida."

"She mentioned she liked her independence. I can't

imagine anyone trying to interfere with her freedom," I said.

"I wish I had. She might have died here alone. Perhaps we should have insisted she move to a residence with more supervision."

"I'd like to keep in touch and see how she's doing. You may hear from me again or from my assistant, Alvin Ferguson. Is there a number where we can reach you?"

"MacPhee, you said? C. MacPhee?"

"Yes."

"Your name was on the phone display. Quite a few calls. We wondered who you were."

That must have been Alvin calling from my place. I'd been meaning to switch my new phone number to unlisted, but now I was glad I hadn't gotten around to it.

"When I visited Hazel, we talked about the war and some people we needed to contact."

Val seemed to have regained control of her voice. She said almost cheerfully, "Oh, the war years. She would have loved that. Sure, you can call me." She gave me her number, and I copied it down.

"Please let me know how she's doing," I said.

She said, "Will do. I have your number on the phone. We'll let you know how it goes."

"You'll have to leave a message. I'm out of town. And I hope everything goes well. Hazel seemed to me to be a very strong person."

"She is. If anyone can recover from this, she'd be the one."

After the phone call, I took a deep breath. I stood on the sunny piazza, thinking dark thoughts. The open door sounded a lot like our discovery of Mrs. Parnell's apartment. What if Hazel's so-called accident was a deliberate attack? My heart started thundering. Was Betty in danger too? Was it open season on elderly ladies who knew Harry Jones? I tried again. I left a message. "Betty, be careful of anything connected to Harry Jones or Guy Prendergast. Make sure you don't let anyone into your apartment. Please call my assistant as soon as you can. He'll fill you in. I'm in Alcielo in Tuscany, and I'll try to reach you later. Please be careful."

Of course, next I had to fill Alvin in. At least he answered the phone. "Listen carefully," I said.

"Me first. I have something to tell you."

"It can wait. Hazel's in critical condition in the hospital."

"Lord thundering Jesus. Critical condition!"

"Exactly. She was found unconscious. She'd hit her head on the fireplace hearth. The neighbour found her, because the front door was open, and the phone was ringing incessantly."

"That must have been me. I told you I kept calling."

"And it's a good thing you did. Otherwise the neighbour might not have gone in until too late."

"The open door, that's what happened with Violet."

"Exactly. And that's just creepy."

"That reminds me, Camilla…"

"Hang on, Alvin. Another thing. Betty doesn't answer her phone either."

"You think something happened to her too?"

"I have called quite a few times."

Alvin said. "You think the same person who ransacked Violet's place hurt Hazel?"

"I don't know. It seems like a strange coincidence. It might mean there is more than one person involved. We have bad things going on over here too. They might be connected."

Alvin said, "How?"

"Don't ask me, I've been wrong about everything so far. And there are liars everywhere, apparently."

"Wait a minute. I've got something to…"

"Hold that thought. First I need you to keep checking on Betty and make sure nothing's happened there. I'm really worried. Then, as soon as you can in the morning, get down to Kingston with that picture and talk to Hazel's neighbours. See if that creep was anywhere near her. You can get in touch with her stepdaughter, Val Desrochers, to see how she's doing. If Hazel's okay, and I sure hope she is, maybe she can identify the guy. I'll call you back when I have anything to add. Write down this number," I said, reading it out carefully.

"Got it, Camilla," Alvin said, after a bit of scratching. "Don't hang up. I have good news."

"What's the good news, Alvin? Were you successful in e-mailing the photo to Ray?"

"That's done. The big thing is that I found a lot of info on this Harrison Jones dude. He's a big deal in the art and antiques business. He was the Managing Director of a couple of English companies. Brockbank & Brickle is the main one. They're respectable international dealers. Art and antiques. Sort of like a smaller version of Christie's or Sotheby's. He made a pile of money from various things. His companies have diversified into different kinds of import/export. If the antique market's soft, then they have other interests. Lives in…"

"Hampshire," I said. "I knew that."

"He married into the Brockbank family, which had a solid business. That's about it. Not much help, really."

"Any scandals?"

"I didn't read about anything like that. They sound like very respectable people. Why do you ask that?"

"Today Ray and I met Guy Prendergast, who suggested Harry Jones may have 'liberated' some stuff, maybe lots of stuff during the war. That he'd turned into a sleazy sort."

"That's bad. But it's also a long time ago. This Harry Jones guy is in bad shape. I called the company and spoke to his personal assistant. I said I was doing a project for business school on international art dealers."

"What did you learn?"

"She doesn't think he'll live long. She started to cry when she was talking about him. She was really excited about my project and wanted me to talk to one of his sons. They run the business now. I guess they're in their fifties. Now that Daddy's sick, they're finally taking over."

"Sons. I hadn't thought of that. They might have something to lose if there was something fishy."

"Yeah, but they're middle-aged respectable business people. They wouldn't run off and start killing old people on two continents because of a few rumours."

For once Alvin was being sensible, and I had to agree. "You're right. These days it takes a lot of hanky-panky to have any impact. Even major firms like Christie's and Sotheby's have weathered scandals. I seem to remember smuggling charges in one case. I don't remember against which firm, which sort of proves my point. Anyway, it was serious stuff, but no one ran around killing people."

"It's true. Even if people do get convicted and go to jail, they still come out and get back to business. Some of them go on TV and make some more money." I could tell this was a sore point.

"Right again, Alvin. It would have to be something huge and awful. Nothing that Guy Prendergast alluded to would do more than keep the legal counsel busy. Hard to prove complicity. Face it, no one will arrest old Harry Jones if he's dying. And the Jones sons wouldn't even have been born until

274

after the war. They couldn't have been looting anything. I'll keep thinking about what this all might mean. See what else you can find out. And don't forget to check in on Betty and call Hazel's step-daughter."

"I'm on it. I think we're getting somewhere."

* * *

I met up with Ray outside the internet café.

"Hey, I see you managed to stay out of trouble for twenty minutes," he said. "Good going."

I let that slide. After all, the man had many excellent points. I liked the way his sandy hair ruffled in the breeze, and I loved that grin. I filled him in on Harry Jones and his sons, and the situation with Hazel.

Ray nodded. "I think we should find out a bit more about these people, without making too many waves. The cops have access to stuff that Alvin won't. I'll make some calls. I know a few guys with international connections too. It's a bit early to call Canada now. Let's give people time to get to work. Hey, you look pretty upset."

"Now I'm worried about Betty as well as Mrs. P. and Hazel."

"Let's go sit somewhere. We'll work on our plan." Ray put his arm around me as we crossed the piazza yet again. I was damned glad of that arm.

The midday sun was flooding the piazza, and people spilled out of homes and businesses. Tourists and locals alike took advantage of the good weather after the rain and fog. Everyone was sporting sunglasses. Ray stared in the window at some T-shirts his girls might like, and I took advantage of a small boutique to buy a pair of ridiculously pricy sunglasses for myself and a pair for Ray. I figured we had to bring something back from Italy in addition to Mrs. Parnell. We found an inviting *trattoria*. The waiter was setting up patio tables for lunch, and it was warm enough to park ourselves and soak up the November sun. We snagged a table with a good view of the bustling square and ordered lunch. Ray suggested a glass of Chianti was what I needed. He decided he'd have one too. The wine arrived almost immediately. Despite the weather, the presence of Ray, and the prospect of food and drink, I was not in the mood to waste time. I hauled out the poster of Mrs. Parnell and showed them first to the waiter and then to the other diners. While the poster was making the rounds, I studied the images that Ray had printed out from Alvin's e-mail.

I stared at a male face, late twenties perhaps, with dark thinning hair, slim build and beautiful chiselled bones. It was definitely the man with the box in the corridor near Mrs. Parnell's place. That must have been why he seemed familiar. Was there something else? A scrap of memory wiggled tantalizingly, yet refused to emerge fully. Alvin had sent three photos of him, once in the stairwell, once entering the front door and once in the elevator.

"He's wearing different clothing in each of these," Ray said. "Must have been there several times."

"Yes, Alvin said he'd been back three times. He was looking for something all right. There's something about him, I don't know what."

"Could he be the same man in the Mercedes? The one who was supposed to be Mrs. Parnell's son."

I shook my head. "I didn't see him. Anyway, this guy's in Canada, so that's not likely."

"Don't forget we were both in Canada a few days ago, and now, we're in Italy. It can be done. Plus the clothes that guy's wearing look kind of foreign to me. The cut of the jacket."

I stared at the pictures. All men's clothing looks alike to me. "Do you think they're Italian designs?"

Ray shrugged. "I don't know what they are, but I'm betting he didn't get them back home."

"That's a good point. Maybe he *is* Italian, and when he lucked out with Mrs. P.'s place, he followed her over here. I don't think he's the guy in the Mercedes. I got the impression he was an older man. They thought he might be Mrs. Parnell's son, so my father or uncle."

"I suppose it was a stretch anyway," Ray said. "How would he know she came here?"

"It could be because she began to contact people, and maybe one of them couldn't be trusted."

"I'll take these with me when I go to the police station. I'll also forward them to a colleague at home to see if he can get a lead on the guy."

"Very efficient. I might have to keep you on staff, Sgt. Deveau," I said. "Okay, I could take them to Dario. He could show them to the old guys in the village, and maybe Orianna, or someone else in Berli, might have seen him. That would help."

Ray studied his glass of Chianti. "Don't forget Guy Prendergast back at the Villa."

"Good point. Let me see, who else? That boy Fabrizio might be able to identify him as the person who bribed him about signor Falcone's whereabouts. If his mother would let me near him."

Ray leaned back as the waiter delivered two plates of tortellini with butter and sage, a dish that really should be revered the world over. He said, "But..."

"I know, I know, these people are all in different towns, and that will mean a lot of driving. Still, it has to be done. No choice."

"There's an easier way. We just forward them to anyone who has e-mail. That might cut down the travel."

"I should have thought of that. Pays to have a cop around," I said. "I'll call Dario and Orianna. Dario will have e-mail for sure. He's a modern guy."

"Great. Do me a favour. Drink your wine, finish your tortellini and then do it." Ray raised his nearly empty glass and smiled. "Five minutes more won't make any difference. I don't get that much of your time, and you won't be getting food like this back home."

I hesitated. What if five minutes did make a difference? "How about I make the calls first, then we can relax?"

"I realize there's no point in arguing." He signalled to the waiter for a refill. I like a man who takes things in his stride.

"Good. The phones are right over there," I pointed. "I'll be back in a flash."

I never made it. We were distracted by a flurry of activity. We had a bite on the *nonna* poster.

"Si. Si. Si. Si!" a girl squealed.

No question about it, our Mrs. P. had hit town. Several people had seen her. I listened to at least four exuberant Italian conversations at once. I had trouble following and Ray sat baffled. *"Restaurazione"* was the key phrase. That fit well with what Guy Prendergast had told us.

"A restaurant?" Ray said.

"Restoration." I asked the girl and her companions, "Is there a Sergio here? A restorer? And someone named Annalisa?"

A couple of lively conversations followed. I caught every tenth word or so. Sergio and *restauro* figured prominently.

I saw people shaking their heads when they spoke of Annalisa.

"Aspetti, signora! Aspetti," someone said. *"Aspetti qui."*

"They're telling us to wait here," I explained to Ray.

"Good. Eat your lunch while you're waiting."

We worked our way through the tortellini and the Chianti while someone else worked to track down Sergio, and, with luck, Mrs. P. Whatever they did would be faster than anything I could.

Ray was getting keen on *dolce* when a young woman arrived, escorted by two of the people who had been sitting in the *trattoria*. She was barely five feet, with wild corkscrew curls and jeans that must have been spray-painted on. Her fashionable square glasses would have looked hideous on most people. She was thin as a whippet. It was hard to imagine she had ever eaten a plate of pasta.

She held out her hand and smiled luminously. "I am Lucia Giansante. I understand you want to speak to my father."

"Is he Sergio the restorer?"

"Yes. Sergio Giansante of Giansante e Figlia Restauro."

"Giansante and daughter, that's nice. A family business."

"Third generation. My grandfather started it. It was an unusual occupation then. Now as you can see, Alcielo is a centre for restoration of all kinds. It is because of the special history of this town."

"I take it business is good."

"*Si,* restoration is a big business all over Italy now. We are starting to realize what we have and how we must preserve and protect our heritage. We are learning to be more respectful. What we have been as a society is reflected in our buildings and our artifacts, our art. We have lost so much."

Interesting enough, but I didn't need another digression. I

pushed the picture of Mrs. Parnell toward Lucia. "I'm told you may have seen my grandmother."

She hesitated.

I nodded in Ray's direction. "Sergeant Deveau here is a police officer."

She paled slightly. "Earlier today, she came by."

I jumped to my feet, "Is she there now?"

"She did not have an appointment, and my father has gone to Milano to meet suppliers."

"Where did my grandmother go?"

She stared at me, her eyes huge behind the square glasses. "I told her he would be back tomorrow morning, and she could see him after lunch."

"And?"

Lucia continued to stare. "She said she would return."

"We have to be there too. She needs to be seen by a doctor. She has a heart condition, very serious," I said. "Do you know where she's staying?"

The curls flew as she shook her head. "Alcielo is a small place. Someone will know."

I didn't want to let go of this fluent English speaker. "Do you know someone named Annalisa? Perhaps also in restoration?"

Was it my imagination, or did she curl her lip slightly? "Of course. Annalisa Franchini lives in the village, in the upper part. Everyone knows her." Lucia gestured toward the top of the hill. "She isn't a restorer, though. Far from it. I haven't seen her for quite a while. They say she has been very sick for a long time. She may be away visiting her family in the mountains. Your grandmother asked about her too. Perhaps one of her neighbours will know."

Ray said, "We'd like to be there when Mrs. Parnell shows up."

Lucia shrugged. "No problem."

I said, "And we'd like to talk to your father too. Before she does. If you see my grandmother, don't mention that we're coming. I wouldn't want her to think we were alarmed. She's very independent."

Lucia gave me strange look number two. "I must get back and unlock the shop before I lose out on any business." With her wild curls blowing in the breeze, she hurried up the hill, made a sharp right turn and disappeared.

Ray said, "See, everybody lies."

"Did she lie? How do you know?"

"You did. Don't want your grandmother to think you're alarmed. Cute. So we've got time to kill."

The waistband of my jeans felt smaller than before lunch. "Not really. I need to move a bit to burn off this meal. We might as well explore the town. Maybe we'll learn where Mrs. Parnell's staying and find out about Annalisa while we're at it. First, I've got to call people about the e-mail."

I reached Orianna in Berli. She didn't have e-mail. She was keen to learn about what I'd found out. I took the time to fill her in. Vittorio didn't answer his phone, nor did Maria Martello. I felt a shiver when I thought today might even be signor Falcone's funeral. Signor Braccio's son, the police officer, would most likely have e-mail. I called the daughter and worked hard at the ensuing Italian conversation. Yes, she thought her brother had a computer, but she didn't know anything more than that. She suggested her father would love to hear from me, because he was very bored and unhappy. She was sending meals for him, even though her sister-in-law was going to be very offended by that. What else could she do? She gave me the telephone number. No one answered. I saved Dario for last.

"Ah, Camilla, *bella,*" he said. "How are you? Are you

281

coming back to see me? What's happening? Did you find your *nonna, la poverina?"*

I told Dario what I'd been up to. "No luck so far. Do you have e-mail? I have a photo attachment for you to show the people in your village."

"E-mail, *si, certamente.* Why don't you bring the picture yourself? I'd like to see you. Everyone would like to see you again." He dropped his voice to a husky whisper. "Or maybe I can come there."

Somehow I didn't think that would go down well with Ray.

"I don't know how long we'll be in Alcielo. E-mail's best. I'll see you another time."

"Sure, *bella.* Send it, send it. I will ask zio Domenico and everyone else," he said. He gave me the address slowly and carefully. I'd never heard anyone make an e-mail address sound sexy before. Some people just have the knack.

Ray handled the forwarding of the photo. As soon as the e-mail was dispatched, Ray and I left the piazza and began a labyrinthine trip through the centre of Alcielo, during which I could have sworn we doubled back on ourselves three times. There was no concept of a block, no space between buildings which all seemed to be three stories high, at least. Some structures seemed to have other buildings constructed on top of them. I wasn't sure I was seeing that right.

"Look at that," Ray said, pointing. "That overhead passage connecting both sides of the street has windows in it. And laundry hanging out."

"Obviously someone's home sweet home."

The streets split in unexpected locations, one going down, another going up. Some had stairs built into them, others felt like long curving ramps, vanishing into blind corners. The old-fashioned lamps seemed like electrified versions of the gas lamps from a hundred years earlier. We puffed up hills and down stairs and down hills and up stairs. At one point, we arrived at a solid, wooden door that must have been there for centuries. Behind the door was a shop with two wide windows filled with furniture and beautiful objects that would have made my sisters melt. The sign said Giansante e Figlia Restauro. An alley no wider than my shoulders ran between the building and its neighbour. I peered into it, half expecting to find Mrs. Parnell, however silly that may sound. Except for the pile of boxes stacked there, the alley was empty.

Ray and I meandered around, leaning into each other. We didn't find a single soul who spoke English, but my Italian was enough to confirm that no one had seen Mrs. Parnell, and that, *certamente,* Annalisa Franchini lived at the very top of the town. She was out of town. From the expressions, I gathered there was something special about signora Franchini. Whatever it was, nobody seemed to miss her.

At the top of the hill, a pair of elderly ladies gestured toward Annalisa's house. It was a narrow three storey, with a smartly painted front door, bits of brass, newly restored stone facing and cast iron pots of bright flowers on the steps and in window boxes. No one was home. *"È partita! È partita la donna!"* the ladies shouted helpfully.

Ray was still chuckling when we reached the centre of a reconstruction project on top of the hill, although work had stopped for mid-day. He said, "Enough fun for today. I'll head over to the police station, introduce myself, and see what kind of reaction I get. I realize you hate that idea and have been stalling me. Still, it's got to be done."

"I do hate that idea. They have a lot of different police jurisdictions over here. Do you even know whether you want to talk to the *carabinieri* or the state police? They're practically in competition with each other. Be careful, that's all I have to say. I've heard horror stories." I ignored the look he gave me. He is, after all, a cop.

Our first enquiry told us the *posto di polizia* was situated on the opposite side of town and up another serious hill. On the way down, Ray stopped to examine some official-looking signs, with the architect's renderings of the reconstruction work for the medieval fortifications. "There's access through the underground passages," he said.

"Gives me the creeps," I said.

He gave me a nudge. "Want to explore it?"

"We're not on holiday," I snapped. "Shoot, I'm being a jerk, but I can't relax. I wouldn't blame you if you had gone to Mexico with another woman."

"That's never going to happen. And I'm not in any kind of race, Camilla. I know Italy has a lot of memories for you, and that's on your mind too."

That came as a surprise, since I hadn't really talked much about being here with Paul, just mentioned we'd spent our honeymoon here.

He glanced down at me. "We'll do what we have to. I want you to think about this: your friend has played you like a violin. Is that going to affect the way you feel about her afterwards?"

I said, "I don't care. She'll have had her reasons. I just don't know what they are. Maybe I'll never find out. She is my friend, and she didn't ask me to chase after her. She didn't ask me to do anything. So I guess I deserve whatever I get."

He raised a sandy eyebrow but kept a straight face. "Even getting locked in the supply cupboard at the car rental?"

"I was never in danger of anything greater than embarrassment. Face it, I was a legal aid lawyer for years, I eat embarrassment for breakfast."

Ray's grin broke through. "Yeah, you criminal lawyer types. You've all got it coming."

"Don't push your luck," I said. "I'll just rub those Italian cops the wrong way if I go with you, so I'll mosey around town while you make contact."

"Thanks."

"For what?"

"Saving me the trouble of telling you that you'd only get under their skin. You have to be careful on other people's turf."

"Right. Careful's not my best thing. There will be someone who speaks English there. If you're stuck, you can find me and I'll go back with you to translate. I'll try to behave."

"Don't go far."

I continued to make the rounds with my poster. A woman with two string bags full of groceries frowned at the image of Mrs. Parnell. She smiled, showing shiny new-looking dentures. She pointed across the hill to the hilly part of the old town we had just walked all over.

Oh, just great. What was all this hobbling up and down steep roads going to do to her condition? Should I head up there again myself? Before I settled on a course of action, I spotted Ray stomping towards me. His mouth was clamped in a thin line.

"Need an interpreter?" I said.

"Nope. The guy I spoke to had a good handle on English. Cousins in Prince George, it turns out. They hung on to the poster. They'll keep an eye out for Mrs. Parnell. I've been firmly instructed to leave it to them."

"Did you tell them everything? About the hit and run and the attacks at home?"

"Well, sure I did."

"The black Mercedes?"

"Yes."

"Did you mention Sergio and Annalisa?"

"I told them everything, Camilla. And I was politely reminded I'm a foreign national. I was pretty well put in my place. They said I have to be careful not to defame anyone. Defamation's a pretty serious crime over here, apparently."

"I can see how that could be convenient in certain lines of work."

"No kidding. Anyway, he gave me the name of a few good restaurants, and suggested that we find one this evening."

"Like we couldn't find a restaurant in this place. There's a new one every ten feet."

"The point was that we should cool it and let them make enquiries. And that's what we'll do."

Speak for yourself, I thought.

Ray yawned. "They know the locals. Let's give them a chance. They also suggested the Hotel della Collina."

"That means the hotel on the hill. Hill number three actually."

"Figures. We'll get settled and have an early dinner. The time difference is catching up with me. Let's head for the payphone first. I'd like to touch base with my girls."

"I'd like to check in with Alvin once more. In case."

That was easier said than done. I left a message giving the name of the hotel.

The cop at my side didn't have any better luck. His home line was busy.

*   *   *

What the Hotel della Collina lacked in red velvet and dark furniture, it made up for with a huge modern bathroom. I enjoyed a long shower without actually touching the walls. I emerged some time later, towelling my hair, to find Ray crashed on the orange-patterned bedspread, snoring. Jet lag. You gotta love it. I decided to let him sleep a bit. I didn't feel like being cooped up in the hotel room though, so I headed back to the square and the payphone to try Alvin one more time.

People were still straggling through the streets making their way home from work and school. The lovely day had been replaced by the now familiar creeping mist. Off the square, you could see it swirl around the old fashioned lights. They shone eerily through the shadows.

The police hadn't told *me* not to do anything. I figured I could continue to ask these locals if they'd seen Mrs. Parnell. I hustled across the square, which was filled with cars, and headed to the side of the hill where she had last been seen. Ray and I had been all over the area, and I didn't really expect to see her out on the street. Never mind, I had to do something. I set off up the narrow street.

The dark doors and shuttered windows allowed no glimpse into who lived there, just the odd glimpse of warm light hinted at lives lived behind these stone walls, at people sitting down for dinner, or homework or television.

A young couple passed me, leaning into each other, laughing, glancing back at me and shrugging in unison. I felt a pang. I wished Ray were there with me at that moment. I could have happily leaned on him in the fog and gloom. As the young couple reached the top of the hill, I heard another burst of laughter. They rounded a corner, vanishing into the light and warmth of a restaurant.

It seemed a bit odd to be knocking at strangers' doors and asking in my bad Italian if anyone had seen my grandmother. I considered it anyway. I was low on choices.

Huxtable Hall
1 Huxtable Crescent
Toronto, Ontario
September 7, 1954

Dear Violet,

Please accept my condolences on the death of your husband. Car accidents always seem so senseless. How terrible for you that he was travelling in England at the time. I would have written sooner, but I just learned the sad news recently. You have always been strong and brave. You will weather this too, just as you did your war service. Do not let anger at your personal tragedy prevent you from living a productive life. I have seen that happen too often.

I know that you will be a dignified widow, unlike some. You have probably heard that Hazel, after creating the most awful scandal by marrying a man more than twice her age, has remarried again in Kingston. Someone in the military this time, a Murphy, if you can imagine. Who knows, with a name like that, he might even be RC! Tongues are wagging. Hazel wouldn't care about that, as long as she had a new hat to wear. Consider yourself lucky that you managed to move to Ottawa in time. With your education and interesting job in the government, you would find her most tiresome.

I have continued on with my own education, which has led, in turn, to a promotion to Assistant Headmistress here at Huxtable Hall.

Yours truly,

Elizabeth Connaught, B.A.

Sixteen

The streets were so disorienting that I had no idea where I was or where I had been. There was nothing to do except keep walking, now through a thin drizzle. I fished out my travel umbrella and flicked it open. A gust of wind yanked it from my hand. The umbrella tumbled down the steep, winding street. I bent to grab it and noticed a slight flutter of movement not far off. Something in the entrance to one of the houses. Or someone. I straightened up and stood still.

Was it Ray? Awake and irritated at my walkabout? Most likely just another citizen hurrying home to dinner.

I moved along the street, keeping an ear out, just in case. There's something about a foggy medieval town on a November evening that makes the hair on your neck rise. There. I heard something. Behind me. The soft splash of feet in puddles. I stooped and pretended to adjust my shoe. I peered over my shoulder. I was just in time to see someone wearing dark clothes duck into another front entrance. Definitely a he. I watched as he fiddled with a door. The door didn't open, because I could still see his shadow in the lamplight. I hustled my buns up that hill, turned a corner and ran like hell. I reached yet another crossroads and chose the left turn.

Two could play the same game. I hugged the wall of an entrance, thankful I was wearing basic black, always just right for hiding out in the fog. I held my breath.

The footsteps stopped at the corner, where yet another choice had to be made about which murky twisting street to check out next. He picked the same one I had and passed by my hiding place. I was pressed so tight against the wall that I could feel the rough stone wall surface through my jacket.

I could have reached out and touched him, but I couldn't make out his face. His body outline showed clearly, though, as he moved stealthily past the next street lamp. He seemed tall, slim, fit, maybe even athletic. Definitely male, although I wouldn't have expected anything else. From his confident stride, he appeared to know exactly what he was looking for. Was I just being stalked by a pickpocket? An opportunistic mugger or rapist who had just picked a convenient victim?

As soon as he moved out of sight, I ducked out of my hiding spot and dashed in the opposite direction. I splashed and puffed loud enough to be heard inside the houses as I ran past. I prayed my head start would get me back to the piazza before he caught up.

I hadn't gone far when I heard footsteps behind me. I picked up the pace. I had wild thoughts about banging on the many doors I passed. Too bad it was impossible to tell which houses had people at home. And whoever he was, he was gaining on me.

I put on the afterburners and ran like hell. I turned a corner, expecting to see lights and people in the piazza at the bottom of the long hill. Where the hell was it? I'd been running longer than I'd been walking. Had I gone around in circles? The footsteps were closer now. I darted left and took a twisty street that I'd noticed on my earlier stroll with Ray. One house had a narrow garden court that ended with a low stone wall. I glanced over my shoulder as I approached the wall at full speed. Just at the point where the street curved behind me, I dashed across the garden and vaulted over the wall. I hoped like hell my pursuer went straight.

I dropped onto the soft hillside below and rolled into another garden court, a half-street lower. A few stacked terra cotta pots clattered loudly around me. No lights flicked on in the windows of the house. I picked myself up, dusted my knees and kept going. This street had to lead back to the downtown area. I figured I'd shaken off my pursuer and stopped to catch my breath. My relief was short-lived. I realized that I had headed away from the downtown. I heard footfalls behind me, getting very close. Worse, the street appeared to be a dead end. I spotted a set of stairs that looked amazingly uninviting, but I was cut off from anything else. There wasn't even a door close enough to bang on. The stairs clanged a bit more than I thought they would. I wasn't expecting a metallic rattle in this world of old stone and wood.

I felt my way into some kind of tunnel. It was too dim to read the large signs on the side. It had to be part of the reconstruction site for the fortifications.

Aside from dripping water, the only sound was my own ragged breath as I felt my way along in the dimming light. Behind me, I heard the clang of the stairs. I was in my own personal horror movie, brought on by my own personal bad decisions.

The floor sloped, and I bumped my head on some protrusion from the ceiling. I ducked down and lumbered forward in a fast crouch, groping my way along the damp and slippery walls. Behind me, someone grunted in pain. He must have hit that ceiling too. It didn't stop him long. I stumbled and landed on my knees. I scuttled sideways, intending to press myself against the wall, hoping to hold my breath until he passed. But there was no wall, just a gap where the wall had been. Would I fall into some ancient cistern? Tumble into a sewer? In my head I heard Mrs. Parnell's voice. *Remain calm, Ms. MacPhee.* Right. I used my hands to try and find the extent of the gap, feeling to the left and right and then up. I inched forward to avoid falling into some unseen void. Just as the footsteps moved closer, I felt a solid wall about knee-height. I realized I'd been feeling around an entrance of some sort. I felt forward and encountered solid ground. Sanctuary. I crawled forward into it, banging my knees on what felt like broken bricks and jagged rock. I was cold, wet, shivering in the dark, breathing musty air. My knees and shins stung from being scraped by the broken bricks. I was scared shitless. Something slithered by my foot. The sinister foggy streets seemed very Martha Stewart in retrospect.

No one in the world knew where I was. Ray would wake up and feel annoyed, then bewildered, and eventually betrayed. He'd been counting on a holiday, and he was getting a dead girlfriend whose body would probably never be found. I hadn't said goodbye to him. I knew the hard way how not saying goodbye could haunt you years later.

My sisters would make new careers out of besieging the Italian embassy and bedevilling the Canadian Department of Foreign Affairs. They'd find a way to pester Interpol. Of course, it would be too late.

I sniffed a bit thinking about them. Although they drive me nuts, at that moment I longed to hear their piercing voices. I thought about my father. He'd never again say, "Oh hello, um, Camilla."

And maybe Mrs. Parnell was right, maybe I was too hard on Alvin. Something about him always brought it out in me. Still, I had to admit Alvin is loyal, resourceful and never boring. That's pretty good. I would have given anything to have him show up at that moment. He could be as irritating as he wanted. Of course, I wouldn't see Mrs. P. again either. I'd never learn what trouble had driven her to Italy, setting off this weird chain of events. Seeing dead men, that was weird enough for anyone. I wouldn't be able to help or protect her. And who would look after her little calico cat? What would happen to Gussie? He'd already been discarded by the Fergusons. My sisters would never let a dog inside their pale cream houses. Alvin's apartments never allowed pets. Would wonderful stinky Gussie end up at the Humane Society?

Ray would take them. Of course, he would. If only I could leave him a message. I dug in the pocket for a pen. I only located the goddam useless cellphone. I might have used the light from the cellphone to examine my surroundings if I hadn't thought even that tiny light might be seen. That left my lipstick. What good was Graffiti Red in this situation? Hold on, red graffiti might be just the ticket. I used it to scratch out "Love you, Ray, Camilla." He probably wouldn't be able to read it, in the unlikely event he ever saw it, but I knew it was true. That one fact surprised me as much as anything. It gave me a lift too.

I straightened up, as much as I could. It's not like me to go down without a fight. What's more, that wasn't going to happen. I could almost imagine Mrs. Parnell shouting, "onward into the breech." Of course, Mrs. Parnell was far too cagey to get herself get blocked in a place like this without back-up.

What did I have going for me? Cavelike opening, dark, dank, low ceiling, floor covered in debris of some sort. Impossible to see. Difficult to move around in. Definite weaknesses.

The cave wasn't really visible from the tunnel, so that was a strength, although it could be found by someone either crawling, such as I had been, or searching with a light. I was safe only as long as my pursuer didn't find the opening, or come back with a flashlight. I could have done with a bit more imaginary sympathy from Mrs. Parnell.

The damp from the earth floor seeped through my jeans. My thighs felt numb, my bum itched, my teeth chattered. I could hear them. Could someone else? The broken bricks and stones dug into my legs. I'd cut myself on a very pointed one. Hey. If it could hurt me, it could damage someone else. I scooped up the brick. I moved my arms to see how I could best deliver a projectile to disable someone crawling toward me. What if he had a gun? Broken bricks aren't much good against a bullet. If he did have a gun, wouldn't he have fired it at me as I was fleeing, when there was enough light to see? No one would have heard a thing. So no gun. A knife maybe.

Trying to be silent, I gathered brick bits and stones. My hand tightened on the brick with the sharp end as a splash sounded in the passageway.

I listened intently.

Something slithered past my back. I was getting used to that. This was different. Squish, squish. Footsteps, soft-soled shoes coming closer, stopping nearby. I heard a scraping, an ooof, and then the slow, measured sound of someone inching his way into the opening, moving toward me.

Adrenaline shot through all my systems. Fight time. Never forget the element of surprise, Mrs. Parnell whispered in my head.

His breath rasped. Or maybe that was mine. I thought my lungs might burst from trying not to gasp. Nice girls, even lapsed Catholics, are not programmed to hurl dangerous objects at others. That kind of thing is trained out of us in school, home, church. And a good thing too.

I needed to break free from constraints of law and decency. My pursuer had. He would not be expecting an attack. I lobbed my first brick. I followed with every piece of debris I could reach. The brick bits were lighter than the stones, but sharper. My fingers were so cold and stiff, it was hard to grip them. Keep going, I told myself, or you'll be colder than this forever.

I heard a grunt of pain.

Within seconds, I'd hurled every projectile in reach. I heard a yelp. Then nothing. Holding a stone in my hand, I crawled the short distance toward the spot where I hoped the opening was.

I bumped into a soft, inert form. I crawled over the warm body, trying not to vomit. Was he unconscious? Was he dead?

I felt for the opening and crawled through. I stood up in the passageway and gulped the air.

Who was lying there? I had no light. My desire to flee was tied with my desperate need to know. Of course, the useless cellphone! Was there enough of a charge left? I kept a rock in one hand, while I dug in my pocket and fished out the phone with the other. I flipped open the lid and fumbled to turn it on. The pale light on the small screen flicked off almost immediately. I bent forward, pressing keys to keep the light on. I gasped. I was expecting the dark-haired middle-aged man who claimed to be Mrs. Parnell's son. Or the balding, chiselled face of her burglar. Instead, I saw the dark trickle of blood that worked its way across the handsome unconscious features of Dario, my most flirtatious friend.

My cramped muscles screamed as I raced through the tunnel, stumbling many times. I kept looking behind me, half expecting Dario. I found the stairs and clattered up them to the deserted street. The mist turned to solid rain as I limped toward my hotel and Ray.

I lurched through the dark streets, slipping on the damp cobblestones. The piazza was dim, storefronts shuttered.

A black Mercedes sat among the Fiats and Golfs and Opels along the edge of the square. I stopped and stared.

Had Dario been the man in the Mercedes all along? But Dario drove an Alpha Romeo, and I could see it parked at a brazen angle on the edge of the piazza. Dario had been the one to tell me of the son. No one else had ever mentioned him. Dario had told me he was in a black Mercedes. At the time, I'd been quite appreciative.

The vicious little bastard. There'd never been a black Mercedes following Mrs. P. And no false son, just misinformation to get me off track.

I jerked my head at a shadow. A dark figure approached through the misty piazza. I yelped and raised my arms to strike out.

"Camilla. Where the hell have you been?"

I capsized into Ray's arms and burst into tears. How girly was that?

March 17, 1980

Dear Vi,

I think you could get off your high horse one of these days and answer some of the letters I have sent over the years. I go to quite a lot of trouble to find out where you are. I have lost my third quite lovely husband, a man who was kindhearted all of his life. He had a hard couple of years. I guess he's in a better place now. I sure hope so. My point is, we're all off to that same location sooner or later, so we shouldn't waste a single day on old grievances. Let's face it, the dead don't get out much.

I'd really love to see you and have a grand laugh about the good old days. For instance, do you remember the time that Perce managed to get that cow up on the roof of the school? Poor Harry got the blame for it, and him afraid of heights! I remember you told the principal you thought the cow on the roof must have been an act of God. I thought Betty would die on the spot when she found out her precious Perce was the culprit. She kept her mouth shut, though. Couldn't have the family lose face, I guess.

I have met a lovely widower from South Carolina. Sam Thurlow is his name, so I am about to become Hazel Fellows Stiles Murphy Thurlow now. Practically the whole alphabet. Sam is at loose ends too and very gallant. Unlike the others, he has no youngsters. That's all right, I have plenty of step-grands to love and buy presents for. I am happy to report that the Southern girls dress up a bit more than we do.

Don't go thinking that I keep writing to you because I have no life. I have wonderful friends, fine step-children, well the second and third batch anyway, and a lot of fun every single day, although I've given up on hats and there's nothing on at the movies. Even so, I am not about to take up golf like Betty!

Still waiting,

Your friend,

Hazel

Seventeen

You don't have to get so huffy, Ray. I'm a functioning adult. You were sound asleep. I let you rest. It wasn't even dinner time. I'm sorry I gave you a scare. It seemed safe to go out."

"Functioning adult, eh? Look at yourself. Where were you? You're covered with mud."

"Somewhere in the tunnel at the reconstruction site."

"Christ on a crutch."

"We have to send the paramedics down there. He could be dead. I might have killed him." I felt my stomach heave.

"Killed who?"

"Dario."

"You're shaking, Camilla, and no wonder, you're like ice. And your jeans have holes in the knees. We'll get you to the hotel. Then we'll deal with Mario, whoever the hell he is."

"Dario. I told you about him. He gave me information back in the mountains. He's the person who chased me."

"Oh, right, I really want to give him a helping hand," Ray said.

"Yeah, well, it's okay for you to talk tough. You didn't whack anybody in the head with a rock, even if it was for a good reason. I don't want to end up killing him. I don't even know what he wanted. What if he wasn't even chasing me?

What if he just wanted to tell me something?"

"You know what? You can talk to the police when you're warm and dry."

"I should talk to the police now. What if…"

"No what ifs. We're almost at the hotel. See?"

As Ray helped me limp through the foyer, he signalled to the unfamiliar desk clerk. *"Polizia."*

"Very good," I said through chattering teeth.

"It's the only word I know besides *vino* and *amore.* I looked up that last one."

The *polizia* took their sweet time. At first I thought it was good, since I needed a hot shower. I was still shivering after I'd dried myself. My jeans, sweater and jean jacket were fit for the garbage. Even the scarf was slathered in mud. I put on all my remaining clothes. Ray wrapped me in the blanket. He disappeared downstairs and returned with a glass of brandy. He pressed it into my hand.

"I'll have to go down there again and show them where he is," I chattered.

"Not a friggin' chance," Ray said.

*   *   *

I'm told I was snoring with my mouth open when the police arrived. One of them spoke English. Ray stepped out of the room and took it from there. I got the news update when I finally woke up.

Ray said, "Good morning. You can start your day right. This Dario's unconscious, but alive."

"I have to talk to him."

"That won't be happening, Camilla. First of all, the police will not let you in to see the guy who attacked you. I wouldn't

300

let you either. Call me crazy, I'm a cop."

"We need to know why he did it. What's Dario's connection to Mrs. Parnell? Or is it just me?"

"Give it up. This is the kind of incident that can blow up in your face in a foreign country. You don't want them to interrogate you at the police station. We don't know how their system works. Anyway, you're in no shape for that."

"I should be talking to them directly."

"Bad idea. Anyway, I've told them everything you told me. And I put a call in to the Canadian consulate in case Dario wakes up and spins a credible counter story, and the locals haul you in."

"Dario's not from around here. They'll need to locate his family."

"The police know who he is."

"You mean he's a criminal?"

"I mean he lives in Alcielo, Camilla. Right up the opposite hill over there."

"But why would he have been in the little mountain village outside Berli two days ago? It's hours from here in the middle of nowhere."

"I have no idea."

"Can't have been a coincidence meeting him. Maybe he was tracking Mrs. Parnell. I played right into his hands. I asked questions. He fed me wrong answers. He seemed to be related to people there. They all knew him. That is weird."

"Not really. You live in Ottawa, I'm in Sydney, a three-day drive apart. You still have relatives in Sydney. I'm hoping to have relatives in Ottawa someday."

"Holy crap, I sent him the e-mail with the guy's picture, and I told him I was in Alcielo. Wait, let me guess. Dario lives with his grandmother, signora Annalisa Franchini."

Ray nodded. "You got it. And Mrs. Parnell was going to

talk to her. We didn't make that connection earlier."

"There was no reason to suspect it. It's starting to make sense now. Annalisa Franchini's supposed to be visiting relatives in the mountains. I bet she'll turn out to be from that same village originally. Which is the nearest place to Berli."

Ray said, "And that's the spot where the plane went down."

"On the way."

"That's just too much of a coincidence. It has to be connected."

"Okay, so, Dario must have been watching for Mrs. Parnell and anyone else with her. In those villages, everyone knows when a stranger hits town. He missed her when she went through. Then I played right into his hands. He might have even paid a few people to keep their eyes open. I told him lots of stuff, where I was going, and the names of the towns. Everything. What a jerk I am. No wonder he was on to us."

Ray scratched his five o'clock shadow. "That means he already knew she was on the way. How could that be? He couldn't have been working alone. He must have had a source in Canada."

"Oh boy, and we e-mailed a photo of the source right to him."

Ray leaned forward. "You are not leaving my sight until we get a handle on this."

"Sure, sure. Can you go back to the cops and find out if this Annalisa Franchini was a partisan during the war? She might have been one of the people who found the airman who survived. That makes sense."

"They don't want me meddling. You know that. And they're tied up with some crime that happened outside of town. I'll have to wait."

It's not like Ray to look shifty-eyed.

"What is it?"

"Nothing to worry about."

"Then why won't you look at me when you're talking?" I said.

He sighed. "Okay, I guess you can take it."

"Take what? Oh, God, Mrs. Parnell. She's dead, isn't she? What happened?"

Ray put his hands on my shoulders. "Not Mrs. Parnell. Relax. Breathe deeply."

"Don't treat me like a helpless idiot," I said, helplessly and idiotically.

"I'm not. Sorry. It's just that you don't know what you've been like. You had nightmares, you tossed, you screamed a few times. I just thought you didn't need this right now."

"I don't need you to beat around the bush. What the hell happened?"

"When I was explaining what happened to my English-speaking contact at the station, I asked if they knew anything about Guy Prendergast. He's a decent guy. He made a call to Pieve San Simone. It turns out that Villa Rosa burned down last night. They were fighting the fire until morning. There's already a rumour that the State Police think it was arson."

I gripped his hand. "What about Guy Prendergast?"

He wrapped his arms around me. "They haven't found his body, the site is too hot."

It's not like me to blubber, especially twice in twenty-four hours, and I hate it when it happens. Ray's used to that kind of thing. He's had practice with the teenage daughters.

*   *   *

Eventually Ray agreed to go back to talk to his contact at the cop shop and find out more about Guy Prendergast. He said he'd nose around about Dario and his grandmother too. There were strings attached.

"I'm happy to grovel in front of them if you promise me that you won't go break into Annalisa Franchini's house, or interrogate the neighbours, or try to get into the hospital to grill Dario."

"Please," I protested, "give me some credit."

"Yeah, right."

"You have nothing to worry about. I'm going to spend a bit of time making calls. I've got to get in touch with Alvin as soon as it's late enough, and I'd like to give my family a buzz. How harmless is that?"

* * *

A stranger answered my phone. My heart thumped.

"Alvin, please," I said. Had something happened to him too?

A scuffling noise ensued, and a slightly breathless Alvin finally said hello. It was a bit hard to hear because of the background noise.

"What is going on there? Is that a drill I hear? Why is Gussie howling?"

"Don't know what you're talking about, Camilla."

"Grant me strength. What's the word on Hazel?"

"Good news. Hazel regained consciousness."

"That's a relief. Is she going to be all right?"

"She's not out of the woods yet. But she was very worried about her hair. I think that's a good sign."

"And was she able to identify the man in the photo as the person who attacked her?"

"Not really. She's confused."

"What do you mean?"

"She thought it was the guy in the other picture, the one of

304

Mrs. Parnell's group of friends."

"You mean Harrison Jones? There's some kind of connection with him for sure. You know what? I think it could be one of his sons."

"No. Not him."

I felt a shiver. Had we been led astray? Sent to Alcielo on a fool's errand? "Was it Guy Prendergast?"

"Will you let me finish?"

"Fine, finish."

"She said it was Perce Connaught."

"Perce is dead."

"I know. He died in the war. That's what I mean. She's still confused. Head injuries, right?"

"Holy crap," I said. I could almost hear the pieces clinking into place.

"What?"

"I think I'm starting to understand. We've been on the wrong path. Call Conn and tell him Hazel's in danger. She shouldn't be alone there, even in the hospital. Conn should light a fire under the cops in Kingston."

"I can go myself. I can stay with her."

"I need you to do some other things."

"Like what?"

"Like confirm how Harry Jones was wounded, and in what part of Italy. Guy Prendergast mentioned that Harry Jones' regiment was moving north through Eastern Tuscany in 1944. I didn't think much about it at the time; I don't think the RCAF would have regiments."

A long, loud whine echoed in the background, and Alvin raised his voice. "Squadrons, I think. Not regiments. I'll see what I can dig up online. Then I could pay a visit to the war museum. Don't hold your breath. I still haven't heard back about the other women that Violet served with."

I don't know if he heard my goodbye with all the racket in the background. Whatever was going on, I was better off not knowing.

* * *

If you have promised to be good, you might as well be in Tuscany on a day that has turned out to be dry and sunny. I put on my wool pants and blazer, slipped into my loafers and picked up my sunglasses. I told our worried desk clerk that I'd be in the piazza buying a new lipstick.

The locals criss-crossed the square, bustling in and out of shops, collecting groceries *bottega* by *bottega,* and stopping to talk with everyone they met. The air was full of happy chatter. I made my way to the small patio of the *trattoria* where we'd had lunch the day before. I kept an eye out in case I saw anyone suspicious. The cheerful server remembered me and was glad to practice his English. With a flourish, he sat me in the corner with the best view, or so he claimed, and I ordered an espresso. As I took the first sip, Lucia came striding down the hill from her shop with her wild curls flying in the light breeze. She joined a friend a few tables over. They ordered brioche, which everyone in Italy seemed to eat for breakfast. I waved, and she smiled and nodded. I hadn't forgotten we would be seeing her father after lunch and that was our chance to nab Mrs. P.

My waiter approved. "Ah, Lucia," he said, smiling fondly, "very nice girl."

"Good to her father, I suppose," I said, making vacuous conversation.

"And to her *nonno*. She takes very good care of him."

"Her grandfather?" First I'd heard of him. "Is he still alive?"

"*Sì*, he must be ninety. He is very fine old man, and Lucia sometimes brings him in here for a glass of wine. He is in a wheelchair now. She is very strong for such a skinny girl."

"I bet she is," I smiled.

Several cars eased into the square as I killed time making the espresso last. The small clusters of tourists made good watching. A half-dozen tall Germans were unsmilingly consulting maps. A pair of middle-aged couples in matching jogging suits, sneakers and American accents spilled out of their rental Opels and stretched. The women headed to the *gelateria,* and the men hit the internet café. Two tall, elderly ladies in flowered dresses and cardigans, and a tweedy old gentleman emerged from an ancient Morris Minor and began an animated discussion about the problems of getting a decent cup of tea on the Continent. They wandered off up the hill, the man arguing for a trip to the top of the hill, one woman insisting on the antique stores as the other had a fear of heights, and how could he have forgotten that? I chuckled at that and at a thin and stylish man and woman, standing by a Renault, shooting contemptuous glances at the jogging suits and the retreating flowered dresses. An Italian teenager made laughing faces behind everyone's backs.

Back in Ottawa, I'd have been indoors to avoid the wind and cold, and worse, would have been bombarded with relentless Christmas music and advertising. Italy in November would have been wonderful if things had only been normal, if I'd only been able to relax. I figured Ray would be back in a short time with some useful information, and we'd snag Mrs. P. at Sergio's. It was such a pleasant morning, and I was glad to be alive after the previous evening. I had plenty to think about. One phrase kept echoing in my mind. Fear of heights. Something about that, but what?

Villa Rosa
Pieve San Simone, Italy
November 1, 2004

Dear Vi,

I hope perhaps you will remember me from our youth. I have tried to follow your life. I have only recently found your newest address. It wasn't easy!

If you're wondering where I've been in the last sixty years, after the war, I went home and started a plumbing supply business outside Toronto, just in time for the post-war housing boom. Left me with a pretty good retirement income after I sold out to the competition. Let them tear their hair out dealing with the big box stores. I did okay out of the tech boom too and got out early and intact. I've always had good timing in my life, except when it came to a special girl from Chesterton. I'd like you to know, after things went haywire with you and Harry Jones, I tried to "run into you" quite a few times. By the time I found out where you were stationed in England, you'd already hitched up with Major Parnell. At least that's what he told me. In hindsight, I think I should have tried harder.

Never mind, I found myself a nice Italian gal in Toronto, and I've had a damned good life and better food than I had any right to for nearly fifty years. Evelina and I retired back here to her home town of San Simone. Can't say I miss the Canadian winters. Last few years, I've been picking up abandoned farm houses and getting them renovated. Keeps me out of trouble. Except for the lousy TV, Tuscany's the best place in the world to live. Up until Evelina died, I guess things really turned out well for me. Right now, the local widows are elbowing each other out of the way to fatten me up. You're probably asking yourself why this old fart is rambling on. Well, I'm just about to get to the good part.

The point of my letter is that a few months back, I decided to buy myself a small piece of art for the Villa Rosa. I've nothing to do in the evenings, except read and stare at the wall and I like to have good stuff and I can afford it. You can't take it with you, and after eighty, we're all on borrowed time. Bought myself a little beauty of an oil from a local dealer who was associated with Brockbank & Brickle, that's Harry Jones' firm. Bit later I had an art expert tell me my painting might have been stolen, maybe from a church, and the provenance faked. I'd heard some rumours about Harry dealing in smuggled stuff, some of it looted in the war. Harry's not long for this world. His two boys keep the cash rolling in. In fact, they even shipped his grandson, William, over to get the business going in Canada. I had the unexpected surprise of meeting another grandson while I was collecting my painting in Alcielo. A handsome lad he is too. There was a daughter born on the wrong side of the blanket. I guess Harry stuck by mother and child, although the daughter died a few years ago. He had a fondness for the Italian gals.

I'll be in Ottawa for a week in early November, looking up old friends and in your case, someone I wish had been more than a friend. It will probably be my last trip. Hope you will see me. I have some photos you'll find really interesting.

Yours fondly,

Guy Prendergast

Eighteen

A s I sat there pondering fear of heights, a bus disgorged a load of tourists at the edge of the square. Within minutes, everyone had slapped on their sunglasses and launched themselves towards the shops and boutiques. Lucia Giansante glanced up, then checked her watch. She finished her coffee, put down the rest of her brioche, tossed some money on the bill, and hurried off. I had a couple of questions for Lucia before we met with her father in the afternoon, and there is only so much espresso you can drink. Ray wasn't back, but what the hell. It was morning, Alcielo was crawling with locals and tourists, Lucia's shop was not far from the square, and somewhere nearby was a grandfather we hadn't been told about. Sergio. I wouldn't really be breaking any promises. The server agreed that if Ray showed up, he'd tell him I had gone to Lucia's. I was still pretty achy, so I meandered slowly up the hill, stopping regularly to wince. On one of the stops, I remembered who had been afraid of heights. I stood still when I realized what that meant. I could almost hear the other pieces dropping into place.

There were already customers gabbing in English, French and German when I hurried into Giansante e Figlia. The scent was a wonderful blend of beeswax, solvent, old wood and something else. Lucia was showing an American couple a beautifully restored table. Apparently the showing wasn't going well, because there were signs of stress on her fine features. The flowered ladies had joined a group clucking enthusiastically over some antique porcelain lamps in the corner. The Germans had donned reading glasses and were turning small objects upside down. Serious hunters and gatherers. I moved out of the way of the door, as yet another old lady in a floppy hat and a flowered dress entered, swinging a large bag with a loud chrysanthemum design. The bag barely missed knocking over a lamp before the woman joined the clucking crowd. I felt grateful for my black wool pants and dark jacket and promised myself I'd die before I ever wore clothing with chrysanthemums. How different these ladies were from Mrs. Parnell, always cool and collected in taupe or khaki. No flowers and floppy hats for her. I ambled around the shop, stroking the lovely woods, squinting at the fine china, fingering the silver candelabra, waiting for my chance to speak to Lucia. I stopped and sniffed the air. There was a large *VIETATO FUMARE* sign. Even so, above the hint of wax and solvent and the relentless lavender of the ladies, I caught the distinct scent of Benson & Hedges cigarette smoke. I kept calm and jockeyed for a chance to speak. Apparently the price of the table was so outrageous that, after a round of dickering, the disappointed purchasers left. The bell jingled as they slammed the door behind them. That cleared a few extra customers, frightened off by the minor conflict. Lucia ran her hand through her hair and said a rude word in Italian. The Germans seemed to take offence, and the door slammed again. Lucia raised an eyebrow when she saw me leaning against a huge carved sideboard.

"Tell me, Lucia," I said in a low voice, "is your grandfather around?"

Her bright lipstick stood out as she paled. She folded her

arms over her thin chest. "No."

Direct hit. "Where would I find him?"

"He is sleeping. He is not well."

"No problem," I said, pulling out my non-functioning cellphone. "My friend is at the police station now. I'll ask him to have the *carabinieri* drop in."

She bit her lip. "I will see if he is awake. Wait here."

"I'll come with you."

"That is not possible. He is in the workshop. It is not open to the public."

"I'm not the public, Lucia. I'm the person looking for my grandmother, and we both know she's here."

The British tourists had begun to look alarmed and whisper among themselves.

"You are lying," she blustered. "She is not your grandmother."

"Close enough." I pushed past her and opened the door marked *officina*.

An elderly man with skimpy wisps of white hair framing his shiny pink scalp looked up in surprise. He'd been parked in a wheelchair next to the long work table. The work surface was covered with paint and solvent cans, jars filled with brushes and tools. Some cans were opened, rags, paper and mats for painting lay around. He might have been in his nineties and confined to a wheelchair, but it appeared that he still had his skills.

Mrs. Parnell was seated in a half-restored ornate wooden chair, facing him. They had been deep in conversation. She turned and raised an eyebrow. She doesn't startle easily. Lucia turned back to me and shrugged.

"I almost got killed last light, Mrs. P.," I said, keeping my tone conversational. "By a beautiful boy named Dario who is almost certainly the grandson of Annalisa Franchini."

"I am most sorry to hear it, Ms. MacPhee. This is a dangerous situation. I did advise you to mind your own business."

"This is my business. I know what happened during the war. I believe everyone should be told about it."

"Cos'è, Violetta?" The old man quavered.

"Niente, Sergio," Mrs. Parnell said.

"Nonno," Lucia said, *"sta' tranquillo."*

"You can't do this on your own, Mrs. Parnell. Leave it to the police."

"The police have been less than efficacious over the years, Ms. MacPhee."

"I know about Harry. The police know all about him too. And I think I know something you don't."

"You're a very ineffective fibber, Ms. MacPhee. Now for the last time, this does not concern you. The next time you might be more than almost killed. I would not be pleased about that."

"Glad to hear it, Mrs. P. This does concern me, not only because I would like you to get proper medical care, not only because I was attacked, but also because signor Falcone, a nice old man I was planning to see, was run down near his home in Florence. You knew him too."

She kept the emotion off her face. Her hands were clenched, knuckles white. "Yes, poor signor Falcone."

"Now another nice old man, signor Braccia, has to hide out with his son." I held up my hand. "Don't interrupt me, Mrs. P. Your old friend, Hazel, was struck on the head and left for dead, and that really concerns me. I like Hazel a lot. Plus, the Villa Rosa in Pieve San Simone burned down last night."

She slumped in her chair. "I am distressed to hear it."

"As I was saying, it's my business, because I am your friend. No matter what. And so is Alvin. You're just plain stuck with that fact."

She recoiled. "Dear God, is young Ferguson here too?"

"He's at home. It's no safer over there, until we get this settled."

"I capitulate. Of course. We can meet and discuss this later, Ms. MacPhee. Will that satisfy you? I'll give you my coordinates."

I cut in, "Here's what I think happened…"

She slammed her hand on the work table. Jars and cans jangled. "I do not wish to hear."

I kept talking. "In 1944, a Canadian bomber crashed in Berli. On it was Perce Connaught. The rest of the crew perished. Somehow Perce escaped. Perhaps by luck, perhaps by engineering. Who knows. We do know that Perce was already in hot water because of his shady black market dealings. The rumour was out that he may even have been about to face a court martial. Then along comes this convenient crash. Perce parachutes out and tosses his dog tags into the smouldering wreckage with the bodies of his colleagues."

I glanced at her face and got no reaction. Of course, she already knew this. I kept talking. "You see, I thought it was Harry Jones in that plane. But Harry would never have joined the RCAF. He was afraid of heights. Harry joined the army."

Mrs. Parnell said, "Poor Harry wouldn't even stand on a chair."

I continued. "Perce, of course, was a lucky devil, everyone said that, always landing on his feet. This time especially. Nothing escapes the notice of the partisans hiding in the hills. They are more than willing to hide a Canadian airman. The women like him, even with the burns on his face and his broken arm, I guess. A girl named Annalisa from a nearby village takes a particular shine to him. Over a few months, she spirits him from the mountains near Berli to her home town of Alcielo, or nearby anyway. Annalisa is plugged in. She has connections through the partisan network. Perce will be able to get back to one of the Canadian contingents pushing the Germans up through Italy. I suppose we'll never know how he managed to meet up with Harry Jones. I suppose Perce would have been well aware of what regiment Harry was with, and the partisans would have been able to find out where that regiment was. Any arguments so far, Mrs. P.?"

"This is not the right time, Ms. MacPhee. I urge you to leave this alone."

Fat chance. "Then all of a sudden Harry is caught in a surprise ambush by a small group of Germans, or so we're told. Harry Jones barely escapes. His face is burned, and he's left with a broken arm. He is hidden by a local family, until he is finally able to get word to the Canadians using the Palazzo Degli Angeli as a temporary HQ. He never gets back to his original company. No one questions his story. Why would they? Harry Jones is a fine fellow, a good fighter, a good friend. It's obvious now what really happened. Harry Jones was lured out to meet Perce. Perhaps Perce used his girlfriend's connections to get a message to Harry. Perce is able to dispatch Harry and his colleague and to take Harry's dog tags. Harry and Perce were the same physical type, tall, fair, well-built."

"The golden boys," Mrs. Parnell said, a faraway look in her eyes.

"One more unknown soldier dumped in the Italian mud. Without tags, Harry's body will never be identified, and Perce has solved his problem. Meanwhile, things are going well for Perce. He's now installed as Harry in or near the Palazzo Degli Angeli. Must have felt like a candy store. Even better, because he's been injured, he'll be sent to England to recover and wait out the war, as Harry Jones, with whatever loot he can smuggle.

Most likely, he stashed some of it here with Annalisa, who was certainly in on everything. We'll never know all the details."

"I will. Even if it is the last thing I ever do," Mrs. Parnell said.

"You should know that Perce started using Harry's name while he was still in the mountains near Berli. A partisan who helped him get back closer to his regiment remembers that name."

She was quiet, stunned perhaps at the possibility that Perce could have caused the crash, in order to launch his plan to become Harry Jones, rather than merely taking advantage of a situation.

I said, "You'll probably never know for sure whether Perce had his eye on Dorothea Brockbank before he faked his death or not. Or was he just fortunate enough to come back and have a plain, sad, girl, mourning her dead brothers and her fiancé end up as his hospital visitor? Luck or cunning? Never mind, it's not a crime to marry a girl for her money or her family's art and antique business. Reprehensible yes, criminal no."

"I have my theories."

I said, "No question that it was a lucky break for a man who'd dabbled in the black market and who'd developed a knack for unloading paintings and objets d'art. Perhaps that's how they connected. Whatever. One thing leads to another and presto, they're engaged, and he's in her family business. I'm assuming some of the detail, but you can see how it would have been."

Mrs. P. stared back at me. I was close enough to see how haggard she was. She might keep her stiff upper lip, but I knew she was deeply affected by what I was saying, even though it was obvious she'd already worked it out for herself.

I said, "Of course, after the amount of cunning it would take to fake his own death and Harry's murder, and assuming

Harry's identity, hooking up with a lonely heiress would be a piece of cake."

Lucia stood staring at us, holding her cardigan tightly closed despite the oppressive warmth of the room. Her grandfather sat silent, hunched in his wheelchair, listening openmouthed.

"There's more, isn't there?" I said. "It gets worse."

Mrs. P. met my eyes. "Yes."

"There are two serious impediments to Perce getting away with being Harry."

She nodded.

"His fiancée, Violet Wilkinson, is dealt with firmly. She is the one person who will know instantly that he is not Harry Jones. And most inconveniently, she's stationed in England with CWAC. She's also enterprising, loyal and a whiz with a truck. Exactly the type to drop in for an unexpected visit. Violet would have no trouble getting past the fiercest of nurses. Harry has to drop Violet and make sure she stays dropped. Violet gets a crisp letter telling her she's no longer needed."

Mrs. Parnell absently picked up her package of cigarettes. The workshop with its open cans of solvent wasn't the right place to be smoking, but this wasn't the time to give a safety lecture. Anyway, I wasn't finished.

"Let's assume Dorothea never knew what she was getting in to. I understand she died in a car accident along with her parents, foggy night, winding road, that kind of thing. Perce, of course, was on full public view in London at the time, as Harry Jones. Did he tire of Dorothea? Did she come to realize the kind of person she'd married? There are plenty of car accidents and falls in this saga. Fires too. By then he had people to do his work, guaranteeing he'd always have an alibi. The man calling himself Harry Jones now becomes the head of Brockbank &

Brickle, respectable family firm, with international connections and impeccable credentials, doing a lot of business here in Italy, where his lover is, and I imagine by this time, her child. I would assume that that child became the father or mother of Dario. Something to be confirmed. All in all, Brockbank & Brickle is still going strong, despite the odd whiff of scandal. Of course, these days it's hard to get people worked up about scandal. But the law still takes a dim view of murder. He may be dying, but his sons would need to bury this story."

Mrs. Parnell nodded slowly.

"I suppose I'm missing some details. But you figured it all out after Guy Prendergast contacted you. Guy thought he was doing the dirty on his old rival when he showed you the picture of Harry and his boys meeting with someone he considered to be disreputable."

"You're right, Ms. MacPhee. He had no idea."

"But you worked it out as soon as you saw the photo. The grandson, William, was the spitting image of Perce Connaught, except for the thinning hair. Must have got that from poor Dorothea. That's the face that Hazel recognized too. I can see what you meant by being 'troubled by a dead man'."

"Full marks, Ms. MacPhee."

"It made you sick. You weren't faking that faint. Now I can understand why."

She opened her mouth to speak.

"Let me finish," I said. "You decided to do something about it. You thought that Alvin and I would try to stop you. Why was that? What were you planning?"

"Sergio is a man of honour and integrity, but he has some information that will help. He knows everything there is to know about trade in antiques and art in this area. He has been troubled by aspects of this business."

I said, "Ah, Annalisa Franchini's activities, perhaps, and those of her grandson, Dario. A very handy connection to funnel art and artifacts, with iffy histories, out of Italy."

She said, "He will help me wrap things up. Then we can approach the authorities. I don't believe he will give me that information when you are here, so I must ask you to leave."

"Sergio's not going anywhere. You can come back later. We have plenty to go on. I think enough people have been hurt. My friend Ray Deveau is in Alcielo too. He knows most of the story. He's talking to the local police right now."

"Do what you must, Ms. MacPhee. Regrettably, you will find the police think you're a crank. So long ago, so little evidence. Such important people, those wealthy Joneses of Brockbank & Brickle. Some minor functionary may possibly give you the time of day, may even be intrigued, but they will not put any amount of effort into it."

Maybe she was right. So far the locals had been useless, if not worse.

Mrs. Parnell said, "I must insist that you leave, or Lucia will make a complaint. She may even hint you have been light-fingered. That will be very inconvenient for you, spending hours at the *posto di polizia* before that silly misunderstanding has been cleared up."

Lucia was leaning on the door back to the shop, scowling at me. I think she liked the idea of shopping me to the police. She hadn't liked the lie about my grandmother. Perhaps it was time for a strategic withdrawal. I planned to be back with Ray, and some local police presence, before Mrs. P. could finish up. I worked hard at looking defeated.

"Fine. There's nothing more I can do."

I took the back exit into a dark, narrow alley, barely wider than I was. The key scraped in the door behind me. I navigated around boards and boxes and debris and found my way back to the street. It would take me a couple of minutes to find Ray and the police. I admit I was angry and puzzled. What was I missing? How many car accidents and accidental falls and fires would there be before it was all right to pounce on the Jones boys? I stopped just as I emerged from the alley into the cobbled street. A small workman's van whizzed by on the narrow cobblestones, and I pressed myself against the wall to avoid being squashed.

Too many car accidents. Way too many. Another puzzle piece clinked into place. Walter Parnell had died in a car accident in England in 1954. Both Betty and Hazel had sent condolences.

I stopped, my head spinning. Walter Parnell had known Harry Jones, it said so in his letter. Had he also known Perce Connaught? I tried to remember from the letters. Was this the thing that I didn't understand? Was Mrs. Parnell seeking revenge for her husband's murder?

I had to know.

I turned back into the dank alley, but, of course, Lucia had locked the door when I left. That left the shop entrance.

The sign on the door said *CHIUSO*. The shop was empty. Why would Lucia close it? I peered through the glass into the shop. No customers, but a large chrysanthemum tote bag leaned against the side of the desk, almost out of sight, telling me just how stupid I'd been. How much time did I have? Not much if history was anything to go by. Not enough to run for Ray. I twisted the door handle, holding my breath. Yes, closed but not locked. Lucia would have that key, but she would never leave the shop unattended. I slipped inside. The door to the workshop was open a few inches.

I reached for the phone on the desk and dialled the number

for *EMERGENZA 113.* Luckily for me, Lucia had it pasted on the phone. Would it do any good? How could I get the attention of the police quickly in this part of the world?

"Aiuto," I whispered. Help. *"Fuoco! Fuoco! Restauro Giansante e Figlia."* I figured a fire call would bring everyone. In this dense part of town, a fire could be a true disaster, despite all the stone. There was plenty of old wood and other flammables in these buildings. I left the phone off the hook and padded toward the workshop door. I grabbed a heavy silver candlestick and crept closer. I knew who I'd find. My stomach was knotted. I'd led the trail right to Mrs. Parnell. I crept up to the door, froze and listened to the voices.

"You've been most clever, Betty," Mrs. Parnell was saying, cool amusement in her voice. No more of the quiet, heartbroken old woman. Had she been planning this encounter all along? Had she known Betty would show up? My head swam with the possibility. My old friend had done everything to keep me out of it, to keep Alvin out of it and to keep me from leading Betty or Dario or the Jones sons or grandson to anyone she knew or cared about. But I am not one to listen.

I leaned forward to hear better. I was rewarded by hearing Mrs. Parnell, sounding like her old self. "Allow me to congratulate you."

"Ah, I remember that sarcastic tongue of yours, Violet. I regret to tell you it won't be enough to get you out of this."

"You have so much to regret, Betty. Surely, you don't think you'll get away with this. Three people in the middle of town. What if one of us gets out alive?"

"That won't happen."

Lucia's voice rose with a note of hysteria. "What will not happen? Who is this woman? Why does she have a gun?"

"I have a gun so that you will be quiet. Which you will be,

dear," Betty said in her best headmistress voice.

Mrs. P. said, "Come now, Betty. Answer a few questions. Where's your sense of sportsmanship? And that weapon is so gauche after those elegant falls and car accidents. And let's not forget the fires."

"Please, let my *nonno* go," Lucia sobbed. "He is old."

"See what you've done, Violet?"

"What I've done? What you've done defies belief. Poor old Mr. Jones. He was always so kind to us children. He always liked you especially, Betty. Was it hard to set fire to his house? Did it cause you to lie awake nights? I am curious."

"Fire is an excellent tool. And no, I did not lie awake nights."

"You always had a tendency to gloat, Betty. Tell me about Dorothea and her parents and their tragic accident at the very moment when Harry, or should I say Perce, was in full public view in London."

"It's a shame you didn't just stay away. You would have lived longer."

"Had Dorothea become suspicious? Had she found out about Annalisa Franchini and her child over here in Italy? A divorce would have had your poor Perce out on his lazy manipulative rump."

"I will not tolerate that kind of talk. Perce had the courage to do whatever he had to. He's a wonderful man who deserves his success."

"You love your brother. As I loved Harry and later my husband, Walter. I've lost a lot because of you and Perce. Walter was on his way home from visiting Brockbank Manor, wasn't he?"

Betty said, "He wasn't as smart as you thought he was, your precious Walter. But even so, he took us by surprise coming by the house. Very bad manners that, showing up at the Manor without an invitation. Perce worried that Walter had recognized him, since his face had healed a bit. Walter asked sly questions, but he gave himself away. Never mind, he'd had quite a bit of Perce's fine port by the time he left. Perce was so generous with the drinks. An unfortunate accident for an inebriated tourist. I didn't think it was worth taking a chance with him, and I don't think it's worth taking a chance with you."

"All those letters you sent letting me think Hazel was responsible for Harry breaking off the engagement. You didn't want us to get together and talk."

"It couldn't have been much of a friendship, if you gave up on it so easily," Betty sneered.

"There are three against one here, Betty. And you're no spring chicken, in case you don't know it."

"Nor are you and Sergio. That snivelling girl isn't likely to take a chance at getting shot."

"You can't just shoot us. Bullets show up easily."

"A tragedy of course. Elderly man, early stages of dementia, naturally depressed, uses the pistol he'd had as a partisan to finish himself off and take his granddaughter with him. You, Violet, were simply in the wrong place at the wrong time."

Mrs. Parnell said, "A pistol belonging to a partisan? You don't think the police will be able to trace that to Annalisa?"

"That damned tramp," Betty spat out. "She's at the root of our problems."

I recoiled, almost as shocked by the venom in her voice as I was by her cold-blooded discussion of wiping out the trio in the room.

Mrs. Parnell gave a throaty little chuckle. "Perhaps Annalisa had better start looking over her shoulder too."

Betty managed to regain her cool. "Make noise if it suits

you. No one will hear through foot-thick walls."

I edged closer to the door. This was my chance. I had to act. Nothing in life really prepares you to sneak up behind an elderly woman who you'd have tea with and clout her with a candlestick. Even hitting Dario with the bricks seemed easy in comparison. I knew I had to act, but my body seemed frozen. My mouth still worked, though. "You were too affluent for a retired headmistress of a girls' school, the condo worth close to a million dollars, the paintings on your walls would have been beyond your reach. I wasn't the only one who noticed."

Betty whirled. "Well, look who's here. Very good. That saves me going looking for you afterwards."

"It's over." I gripped the candlestick tightly behind my back.

"For you it is," she said, gesturing with the gun. "In you come. Don't believe for a moment that I won't shoot you. The police in Alcielo are thicker than these walls. And no one knows I'm here."

"On the contrary," I said. "I have told several people."

"Nice try," she smirked. "I wasn't a headmistress for years without spotting a brazen lie. I don't think anyone would piece together what's happened. It's been too well organized. I know what I'm doing, and I have the right kind of help."

"The so-called Jones sons? They stand to lose everything."

"They are respectable middle-aged businessmen who can account for their presence at any time it might matter."

"I think they might have to account for their involvement selling stolen art and artifacts," I said. "Then there's the nephew you mentioned when I called you."

"William has nothing to do with any of this."

"William? Is that his name? William Jones, I imagine. He must be Perce's grandson, since you had only one brother, and you never married. He's been caught on camera in Mrs. P.'s building and identified as Hazel's attacker. Hazel's under police protection now, so no point in thinking you can send in reinforcements."

"Bravo, Ms. MacPhee," Mrs. Parnell said.

"You will not live to harm Perce or his boys, or William for that matter. And don't try to distract me with your cheerleading, Violet. I've had plenty of practice hunting at Huxtable Manor. I'm a crack shot. I'll get your little friend here. Then I'll get you and the other two." Betty stared me down.

She meant business. I knew it, and I believed Mrs. Parnell did too.

Betty gestured to me. "I said, get in here."

Damn. Betty was enjoying this. She'd kept the secrets of the very clever Connaughts for sixty years. She was obviously exhilarated at finally being able to brag to her doomed listeners.

Mrs. Parnell looked away from her. "Of course, you can't continue to get away with it."

"I can and will."

"Killing a fellow soldier and assuming his identity will get your precious Perce arrested, no matter how old and frail he is."

Betty laughed. "It could never be proven."

"A scrap of DNA is all it takes," Mrs. Parnell said.

"Unfortunately for you, Harry's relatives are dead."

Mrs. Parnell said, "But Perce's relatives are not. You are not, Betty. There is easily enough evidence to prove that Perce has misrepresented himself as Harry Jones all these years. There's plenty to link his sons. And his Italian grandson, who I believe gave Ms. MacPhee a spot of trouble."

Betty said, "Dario is like his wretched grandmother, a lower life form, but useful in doing business in Italy. But it doesn't matter if you link Dario to Harry Jones. Harry could easily have had a bastard son by an Italian woman. There's no crime in that. Even in polite English society, that wouldn't dent Brockbank & Brickle."

"There's still your DNA, Betty, which will be enough to link Perce and his sons and Dario and to prove that Perce faked his own death, murdered Harry Jones, and took on his identity. Brockbank & Brickle is a business built on murder and fraud."

"You're not in a position to obtain my DNA, are you? And do you not think I realize you are all stalling? You seem to have forgotten that I'm the one with the pistol."

Mrs. Parnell said, "I am well aware, and as a condemned woman, I feel entitled to one last cigarette, since I don't see any blindfold." She extracted a cigarette from her package and flicked her lighter. I wished I felt as calm as she looked.

Betty said, "Filthy habit." She turned back to me. "I will count to three. Either you're in here by then, or you're dead."

"Fine. But you must let Lucia go." I moved forward awkwardly, holding the candlestick behind my back with one hand, hoping she wouldn't see it.

"You're hardly in a position to bargain," Betty said. "Let me make that clear." She twisted around and fired off a shot toward Lucia. Lucia reeled as a red stain spread on the arm of her green cardigan. She uttered a high, piercing wail.

Betty said, pointing the pistol toward me. "And now watch this." Another deafening shot rang out. I felt something whiz by my ear. The smell of cordite filled the air.

Sergio roared, *"Dio mio, no.* Lucia, Lucia."

We had nothing to lose at this point. I swung the candlestick, narrowly missing Betty's arm, as she glanced at Sergio. Betty whirled and took aim at me.

With remarkable speed, Mrs. Parnell reached out with her

cane, using the curved handle to hook Betty's ankle, throwing her off balance. As she moved forward, her cigarette fell from her cigarette holder to the floor. I swung again with the candlestick and missed. Betty staggered, firing wildly. How many shots now? How many shots? I asked myself, as I slammed the candlestick into her shoulder.

Sergio roared again, raised himself from his wheelchair and lobbed an open can of solvent toward Betty. The edge struck her temple. She sank to the floor. We watched, frozen, as the solvent spilled, rippled toward Mrs. Parnell's cigarette, igniting it.

Lucia's wail rose higher. The red stain had spread.

Sergio shouted and reached forward, trying to reach his granddaughter.

"Get out," I screamed to Mrs. Parnell. "This place will go up like a munitions depot. Lucia, move your grandfather out fast."

Betty lay still, blood trickling from her temple, the pistol fallen from her hand. Flames licked at her flowered dress and caught. I threw my jacket over the burning dress and rolled her. Flames danced past us along the floor and lapped at the stacks of wooden frames. A pile of wrapping caught, and smoke began to billow.

I know way too much about fires. "Get moving. If those flames hit the varnishes and solvents, we're finished."

Lucia shoved past me with Sergio in the wheelchair, her hair swirling, dark blood spreading on her arm, tears streaming down her cheeks. She thrust the wheelchair through the door. The door swung behind her and nearly closed.

I grabbed Betty by the shoulders and pulled.

"I can't leave her to burn," I said, looking Mrs. Parnell in the eye.

"Neither can I," Mrs. P. said. "Although I'd damn well like to."

"Get yourself out of here fast."

The first can of solvent popped.

Mrs. Parnell, pale and trembling, bent over to help. "Please go, get out of here," I said, pulling Betty's dead weight with all my strength.

"Divided we fall, Ms. MacPhee. At least, let me hold the door."

Mrs. P. held the door, as I dragged Betty's dead weight, as far as I could into the shop. From outside, we heard Lucia shrieking, Sergio still roaring and feet thundering amid shouts. Through the shop window, I could see Ray Deveau, shoving his way past a resistant police officer.

Firefighters pushed their way through, brandishing hoses.

"We're here!" I yelled, from my moving crouch. "Someone's injured."

I turned to Mrs. P. "Welcome back," I said, with a lump in my throat.

I collapsed in a heap, as the first fireman picked up Betty. Someone pulled me to my feet, and I was propelled out the door to the street. Paramedics were already attending to Betty. Mrs. Parnell allowed herself to be helped away. Firefighters steered the gathering crowd from the building, forcing everyone to the safety of the piazza as the hoses opened.

Ray held his ground. He was right where I needed him.

Nineteen

The early evening light bathed the hills surrounding our new digs in the Villa Verdi. I sat in silence with Mrs. Parnell, Guy Prendergast and Ray. We watched the sun sink below the horizon in an explosion of crimson and gold. From the hillside courtyard, you could still see the cypress and olive trees silhouetted by the dying light. Snatches of opera wafted from the open windows along with the scent of roasting tomatoes, rosemary, veal and porcini mushrooms.

The air had begun to chill after yet another unusually warm November day, but no one showed any inclination to move inside. The evening sky and the ambiance were irresistible following our hellish first days in Italy. Forty-eight hours had passed since the fire that claimed the Giansante e Figlia business and left Betty Connaught clinging to life with third-degree burns and other injuries. Our long hours in Italian hospitals and police stations were behind us. We were just beginning to unwind.

Well, three of us were unwinding. Ray continued to do his duty. He moved off to the far corner of the patio, engaged in an intense telephone conversation on the Villa Verdi's portable phone. He kept his hand pressed to his ear to drown out the noise as our conversation picked up again.

Guy Prendergast bent his tall body and expertly applied a

corkscrew to a fresh bottle of Chianti. He grinned at Mrs. Parnell, who was comfortably ensconced with the best view. I was happy to note her hair was neatly arranged, her clothing crisp and her colour normal. She was as good as ever, with a clean bill of health from the Italian medics. Go figure.

Guy said, "Couldn't have you folks stuck in a hotel when this was available. Villa Verdi's usually a great little money maker. I'm darned glad it wasn't rented this November for once. Needed a place myself."

I said, "Not everyone has a spare villa in Tuscany. Definitely comes in handy." I wondered if he had villas in every shade. "It's a shame about Villa Rosa though."

"Easy come, easy go," he said, splashing yet another refill into my glass. "Lucky I ran out of *vino rosso* that night, or I'd have gone up in flames with it. All the same, it was only a house. I have plenty of those."

"We're glad you're alive," I said.

He took the chair next to Mrs. Parnell. "Gave myself a scare. Brought it on my own head, and on everyone else's. Should have kept my mouth shut instead of trying to impress you, Vi."

Mrs. Parnell shook her head at the offer of Chianti and took a long pensive sip of her Harvey's Bristol Cream, before putting the glass down. She took her time lighting a Benson & Hedges, and frowned. I held my breath. I bet Guy Prendergast did too.

"How could you have known?" she said at last. "Who could have imagined the intricate conspiracy that Betty cooked up to save her precious Perce? Once that was threatened, nothing was safe. And none of us."

Guy spoke with the now familiar tremor in his voice. "But that Falcone fella in Florence would still be alive, and poor Hazel never would have ended up with a cracked skull, if I hadn't stuck that photo under your nose, Vi."

I leaned forward. "You couldn't have known what you were going to unleash."

"Perhaps not, but I still wish I'd done things differently. Hope I can make it up to you."

Mrs. Parnell shrugged, indicating to me that she'd been in Italy too long already. "It really wasn't your doing, Guy. If I'd been more civil to you much earlier, some of this could have been avoided. I have always avoided anyone connected with Harry."

I butted in. "One thing, Mrs. P., without Guy, you would never have found out that it wasn't the real Harry who broke off your engagement."

"I should have realized it myself. Harry would have found a way to make the break face to face. We were both in England at the time. I should have twigged that something was wrong as soon as Harry called me Violet in that letter. He'd never once in his life called me Violet."

Darling Vi. I remembered the letters. I felt a deep sadness for Mrs. Parnell, and for what might have been if the real Harry Jones had come back to Chesterton after the war. Maybe she really would have ended up as someone's grandmother, the happy centre of a large family. Hard to imagine. I kept that speculation to myself.

"I should have treated poor Hazel more kindly," she continued. "I blamed her for the break-up. I didn't even open most of her letters. Betty fanned that division, of course. She couldn't have us getting together and comparing notes, having some little oddity not add up, questions being asked."

Over in the corner, Ray ended his calls. He made his way back to us and his full glass of wine. He joined us at the small table, reached over and raised his glass in a toast. "To the end of the Connaughts, Betty and Perce and his two sons and his grandsons, William *and* Dario. May they do no more harm."

Guy said, "Don't count the English side out yet. I've got the British papers here, and those sons already have lawyers. They've got the money to pay for the high-priced help for William in Canada too. They might get away with it."

"I don't think they'll get away with much," Ray said. "Too many crimes, too many people in the know. I made a couple of calls. The Ottawa guys have William in custody for the attack on Hazel. They have a positive ID from Hazel, and at least one of her neighbours, who saw him in the building. No bail for him either. Flight risk. That's worth another toast, if you ask me."

We were happy to raise our glasses.

Guy said, "Maybe that will work here too. The Italian papers are blustering about the war hero *il Falco* being murdered. They're talking about a witness. With any luck, they'll get Dario for that, as well as the attack on you, Camilla."

"The witness is probably that kid, Fabrizio," I said. "He'll cave under questioning. And Lucia and Sergio Giansante will be able to testify about everything Betty said in that workshop. Betty's gloating will come back to haunt Perce for as long as he lives. Maybe they'll get Annalisa Franchini too, as part of the conspiracy."

Mrs. Parnell said, "But the fact is, Betty was pulling everyone's strings. I should have realized that as soon as I saw that photo. Perce could never have pulled all that off by himself."

"We all played right into her hands."

Guy said, "Especially this old fool. I called Betty after you gave me the bum's rush that night, Vi. Didn't know how to reach Hazel, but I knew Betty was in Ottawa. She never changed her name. I didn't realize what I was doing, but I blabbed about everything I'd told you. Of course, I thought Harry Jones was the bad guy. Never occurred to me Perce was living life as Harry. You figured that out as soon as you saw that photo of the grandson, didn't you, Vi?"

Mrs. Parnell gazed off into the darkening sky. "When I saw his face, I couldn't let myself believe it right away. Because the implications were simply too horrible. The Remembrance Day march sent me to hell. All I could think about was our wonderful Canadian boys, and our women too, who perished under such awful conditions. It magnified Perce's heinous crime. I knew, of course, that I had to do something. I knew he must have had allies, confederates, including Betty, of course. Perce had turned into a very dangerous man. Much too dangerous for me to involve the people I cared about. As it turned out, I was right."

She kindly didn't mention Guy Prendergast blundering about, or me, making waves.

She continued to stare into the distance, sorrow etched on her features while Guy Prendergast chattered on. "Guess I'm lucky to be alive," he said. "Betty invited me right over, but I'd had a bit too much of the good stuff at my hotel, so I took a rain check. Supposed to go for lunch the next day. Instead, I hightailed it back to Italy and my Villa Rosa, to drown my sorrows."

I said, "That probably would have been your last lunch. You were in line for a fall, or an accident. Or a fire."

"Sure didn't take long to torch the Villa Rosa."

I said, "I wonder if we'll ever know who did that? Dario was in the hospital, after I hit him on the head. Annalisa perhaps?"

Mrs. Parnell turned her gaze back to us and lifted her glass again. "My money's on Betty herself. She would have blamed you for the whole thing, Guy. Wasn't her first fire."

"Still blame myself," Guy said.

I said, "Please don't. We all played into her hands. I left her messages with everything she needed to know. William must have been picking up Betty's messages when he wasn't ransacking apartments and bashing people on the head. We're lucky no one burned down my house with Alvin and the pets in it. This reminds me, I wonder what William stole from your apartment, Mrs. P."

"I had my laptop and camera with me. I imagine he was looking for photos and letters. As soon as I fully understood what might have happened, I packed up everything like that and left it with Alvin for safekeeping."

"Good thing you did, or we wouldn't have had a thing to go on."

"I didn't *want* you to have anything to go on, Ms. MacPhee. Perce Connaught was such a vicious scoundrel. I never really understood why Harry was such a good friend. But once I realized that he'd..."

Murdered Harry, I thought.

Mrs. Parnell fell silent.

"Well, who could imagine something like that?" Ray said. "I'm a nasty suspicious cop with twenty years on the force, and it wouldn't have crossed my mind. Although from the sound of this Betty, she probably would have wiped out anyone who threatened Perce."

Mrs. Parnell said, "At least I have the consolation of knowing that Harry didn't really turn into a cad, and Walter wasn't foolish enough to get drunk and kill himself on the country lanes of Hampshire. And to know that I still have friends I can trust."

"You mean Hazel? You'll be seeing her?"

"I will, but I meant you and young Ferguson, Ms. MacPhee. I wish he were here with us now."

Conversation stopped when Guy Prendergast's housekeeper bustled through the open door with a plate of bruschetta for us. For the first time since I'd arrived in Italy, I planned to taste the food and savour the wine. It would be worth waiting for.

The phone call from Canada came first.

I held my ear away from the phone. Alvin shrieked, "I got

my passport! 'Three-day expedited', and it was worth every penny. I'm on my way. And I got a way better price on a ticket than you did, Camilla. Everything's under control here now."

"What do you mean, everything's under control *now?*" I said.

"What? Nothing. I mean Hazel's getting out of the hospital. She sends her love to everyone, and she's really hoping to see Violet."

"And she will."

"Don't tell Violet I'm coming. I want it to be a surprise. I hope you'll give me some time alone with her to catch up."

"That can be arranged," I said, glancing across the table and watching Ray's sandy hair ruffling in the light evening breeze.

"Your sisters said they'll walk Gussie and feed the cat, and even look after those evil lovebirds."

"They did? I'm amazed."

"And news flash! You know what I heard from the Super? Your nasty neighbour in 1604 got evicted. Arrested, too. Guess there was a smell of marijuana coming from his apartment, when the cops came around to check Violet's place, after Ray called with all the news. Lord thundering Jesus, what a lot of fuss about a little weed. But what goes around comes around, right?"

"For sure," I said, not wanting to know who might have made that happen.

"I have a surprise for you when you get back. I think you'll be overwhelmed."

Overwhelmed is one of my least favourite things.

"Alvin? Wait. Don't tell me, it will give me something to look forward to." Maybe my house was now a replica of a pharaoh's tomb, or possibly a space station. Perhaps Gussie was sporting a m3ohawk, or the little calico cat now had a stylish touch of sky blue fur. With Alvin, the possibilities are endless.

I had an entire week left in Italy with Ray. I didn't want anything in the world to take my mind off that.

Photo by Giulio Maffini

Mary Jane Maffini is a lapsed librarian, former co-owner of the Prime Crime Mystery Bookstore in Ottawa, author of two mystery series and a double Arthur Ellis winner for short crime fiction.

The books in the Camilla MacPhee series are: *Speak Ill of the Dead*, which was shortlisted for an Arthur for Best First Novel, *The Icing on the Corpse, Little Boy Blues, The Devil's in the Details* and *The Dead Don't Get Out Much*. In 2003, she launched a new series, the Fiona Silk mysteries, the first of which, *Lament for a Lounge Lizard*, was shortlisted at the 2004 Arthurs for Best Novel.

Mary Jane Maffini resides in Ottawa, Ontario.

Also by Mary Jane Maffini

LAMENT FOR A LOUNGE LIZARD
A Fiona Silk Mystery

As if it weren't bad enough being a failed romance writer with no sex life, poor Fiona Silk has to cope with the spectacularly embarrassing demise of her old lover, the poet, Benedict Kelly. It's exactly the sort of thing people notice in St. Aubaine, Quebec, a picturesque bilingual tourist town of two thousand. Now the police start getting nasty, the media vans stay parked on her lawn and the neighbours' tongues keep wagging in both of Canada's official languages. Worse, someone's bumping off the other suspects. Can Fiona outwit a murderer in the mood for some serious mischief?

"stylish and amusing..." -Maclean's Magazine

"..as adept at comedy as she is at laying out a tangled crime trail...Maffini surrounds Fiona with memorable—but often annoying—friends... Surviving their needs and obsessions is almost as daunting as solving the murder."
-Foreword Magazine

$13.95 CDN, $11.95 U.S. ISBN 1-894917-02-2 280 pages

The Camilla MacPhee Mysteries

"With its sassy heroine and eccentric but lovable cast of supporting characters, Mary Jane Maffini Camilla MacPhee mystery series is a bright new addition to the Canadian crime writing scene."
-Lyn Hamilton, author of the Lara McClintoch archaeological mysteries

Speak Ill of the Dead

ISBN 0-929141-65-2
$12.95 in Canada, $10.95 U.S.

The Icing on the Corpse

ISBN 0-929141-81-4
$12.95 in Canada, $10.95 U.S.

Little Boy Blues

ISBN 0-929141-94-6
$12.95 in Canada, $10.95 U.S.

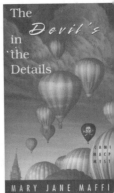

The Devil's in the Details

ISBN 1-894917-12-X
$13.95 in Canada, $11.95 U.S.

www.maryjanemaffini.ca
www.rendezvouspress.com